UNDER THE YOKE

UNDER THE YOKE

BY
IVAN VAZOV

TRANSLATED BY
MARGUERITE ALEXIEVA
AND
THEODORA ATANASSOVA
EDITED BY
LILLA LYON ZABRISKIE

Twayne Publishers, Inc. New York

Library of Congress Catalog Card Number: 70-146052
PRINTED IN THE UNITED STATES OF AMERICA

This edition of *Under the Yoke* was prepared from a translation by Marguerite Alexieva and Theodora Atanassova, edited by Marco Mincoff, which was published by the Foreign Languages Press, Sofia, in 1960. After being edited in the United States, the manuscript was read in Sofia by Professor M. Mincoff, who responded most fully and helpfully to all questions which arose.

CONTENTS

PART TWO

PART THREE

introduction

Ivan Vazov (1850-1921) is one of the foremost authors of Bulgaria, and *Under the Yoke* is certainly his finest and best-known work. Indeed Vazov is considered one of the fathers of Bulgarian literature, which has had a relatively brief existence, and this book, known and loved by all Bulgarians, is one of the classics of that literature.

Vazov wrote the book between 1887 and 1889, when he was in self-imposed exile in Odessa because he was against the political leaders then in power. *Under the Yoke* is the story of the April Uprising of 1876 as the residents of one of the rebellious towns, "Byala Cherkva," experienced it. This uprising, which ended so badly for those who took part in it, focused world attention on Bulgaria and ultimately led to its liberation from the Turks who had taken such massive and cruel reprisals against the Bulgarians.

For five centuries Bulgarians had suffered under the yoke of Turkish rule, and their unrest increased in the nineteenth century as other Balkan portions of the Ottoman Empire, such as Rumania and Herzegovina, began to break away, providing both an example and a refuge for Bulgarian revolutionaries. Bulgaria's development of political consciousness and her struggle for liberation went hand in hand with the birth and growth of a truly national literature. One of the more oppressive aspects of Turkish rule had been the suppression of the Bulgarian language. Books in Bulgarian had been prohibited; the Slavic liturgy of the church was replaced by Greek, and the only schools were Greek schools. Not until 1835 was the first Bulgarian school founded, and only in the nineteenth century was the first Bulgarian grammar published. In 1838 a Bulgarian printing press was established in Salonika; in 1846 came the first Bulgarian newspaper; and in the 1860's a Bulgarian literature blossomed.

Not surprisingly, the leaders in Bulgaria's cultural renaissance were also the leaders of her revolution. Foremost among them was Ivan Vazov. Born in Sopot—the Byala Cherkva of *Under the Yoke*—in 1850, Vazov studied at the Greek school in Plovdiv, and then embarked on the wandering life typical of the Bulgarian revolutionary intellectual, spending time in Rumania and Constantinople, centers of revolutionary activity. He returned to Sopot in the midst of the town's preparations for the April Uprising, and, like the hero of his book, was a member of the local revolutionary committee. After the failure of the uprising, he fled to Rumania, where he published his first collection of poetry. When he returned to Sopot in 1878 after the establishment of Bulgarian independence, he found that the town had been destroyed and his father killed by the Turkish *bashi-bazouks* (irregulars) who had crushed the revolt.

During the years which followed, Vazov not only took an active part in the political life of his country, but also experimented with nearly every literary form. With *Under the Yoke,* he introduced the novel to Bulgarian literature. The hero of the novel, like Vazov, is a wandering revolutionary, escaped from a Turkish prison, who arrives in a Bulgarian town on the eve of the April Uprising. Vazov must have drawn very much on his own experience, for his account of events is both realistic and lively. An American audience will surely find most engaging and appealing this portrait of a small Bulgarian town as a time of intense excitement and change is lived through by a real cross-section of folk heroes and villains.

It is fascinating to learn how rich and varied the life in Byala Cherkva, and in the country villages and mountain huts around it, could be. Vazov brings the people to life in a very human and sympathetic way, with humor and perceptiveness. He has a sharp ear and eye for details of speech and manner, for the small pomposities and verbal flourishes with which the townspeople launch their desperate rebellion, and for the large and painful courage with which they carry it through. We see how hatred of the Turk brought people together across age-old divisions of class and wealth, so that even the *chorbadjis* who had been getting along comfortably under Turkish rule became gradually drawn into revolutionary activity. When Vazov celebrates the pride and independence and courage of the peasants, when he shows us those who risked death to shelter or feed the revolutionaries and those who died rather than yield to the Turks, he shows us real heroes, and we are moved.

The scene of the April Uprising was the region known as the Valley of the Roses, where in the nineteenth century Bulgarians began to cultivate fields of roses whose petals yield the attar essential as a base for perfume, a profitable cultivation which continues today. As Vazov describes it, it is a beautiful land, worth fighting for and worthy to be free. Writing from abroad, he spoke of Bulgaria with deep feeling. It is impossible to resist his enthusiasm for his land and his people, and his obvious sincerity. It is clear why this is his best-known and best-loved book and why Bulgarians have taken it to heart.

LILLA LYON ZABRISKIE

UNDER THE YOKE

chapter 1

a visitor

On that cool May evening, Chorbadji Marko,* bareheaded and in his dressing-gown, was having supper with his household in the garden. The master's table had been set as usual under the arbor, between the clear cold brook that ran through the garden and twittered like a swallow, day in and day out, and the tall spreading box trees, always green, winter and summer, whose dark shapes stood out against the wall. The lantern was lit and hung from the branch of a friendly lilac bush which bent its scented sprays over the heads of the family.

It was a numerous one. Besides Bai Marko,** his mother and his wife, a swarm of children sat around the table, big ones and little ones, armed with knives and forks, who polished off the bread and meat in a flash, and fully deserved the Turkish epithet "enemies of the loaf."

From time to time, their father beamed at these panting workers with their sharp teeth and indomitable appetites, encouraging them with a cheerful smile: "Eat away, my children, eat and grow strong! Pena, fill the bowl again."

The maid went to the spring where the wine was cooling, poured it into a deep china bowl and brought it back. Bai Marko passed it around to the children, saying benevolently, "Drink, you rascals!"

The wine went around the table. Eyes grew brighter, cheeks pinker, and lips were smacked with pleasure. Marko then turned to his wife, who was frowning with disapproval, and said sternly: "Let them drink in front of me; don't let them thirst for wine. I don't want them to be drunkards when they grow up."

Marko had his own practical views on bringing up children. Although he was an old-fashioned, uneducated man, he had a thorough understanding of human nature, and knew that forbidden fruit is sweetest. Because of this, to counter any inclination to pilfer, he used to give the key of his money chest to the children. "Gocho, go and

* *chorbadji:* one of the wealthy class of Bulgarians.

** *bai:* from *brat,* brother, a form of address to an older man.

open the sandalwood chest and bring me the bag with the coins!" Or he would tell another one, "There, my boy, go and count out twenty liras from the little basket and have them ready for me when I come back." Then he would go out.

Although it was the custom of most fathers in those days to keep their children standing while they themselves had their meals, supposedly to teach them respect for their elders, Marko always sat his down at table. When he had visitors he also wanted his sons to be present. "Let them get the habits of gentlemen," he would explain," and not be like wild animals and hide from people, like Anko Razpopche." For Anko Razpopche writhed with embarrassment whenever he met a man dressed in the European fashion.

As he was always occupied by his business, Marko only saw all his children together at table, when he completed their upbringing in a somewhat original manner: "Dimiter, don't reach across your grandmother at table; you're becoming a regular freemason! . . . Iliya, don't hold your knife like a butcher; don't slaughter the bread, cut it properly! . . . Gocho, why have you unbuttoned your jacket like a Turkish kitchen-boy? And take your fez off when you come to table. Your hair's too long again, like a wild man of the woods; go to Ganko and have him cut it, Cossack-style. . . . Vassil, pull in your long legs and give other people some room. You can stretch them when we're out in the fields. . . . Abraham, what do you mean by leaving the table without crossing yourself, you Protestant!" It was only when he was in a good humor that Marko's remarks were made in this tone; when he was displeased or angry, dead silence reigned at table.

Profoundly religious and pious himself, Marko took great pains to inculcate religious feelings in his sons. At night, the older children had to be present when he read evening prayers before the icons. Every Sunday or saint's day they all had to go to church. This was an unbreakable rule. Any attempt to evade it aroused a perfect storm in the house.

One Lent he told Kiro to go to confession since he was to take communion the next morning. Kiro came back from church very soon. He hadn't even had a glimpse of the priest.

"Did you go to confession?" his father asked him suspiciously.

"I did," the son answered.

"Who heard your confession?"

Kiro was confused, but answered confidently, "Father Enyu." That was a lie, for Father Enyu was a young priest who did not hear confessions.

Marko sensed the lie at once, jumped up angrily, seized his son by the ear, took him out into the street and from there to the church in the same posture, where he handed him over to the confessor, Father Stavri, with the words, "Father priest, confess this donkey," and sat himself down in a pew until the confession was over.

He was still more severe with those who played truant from school. As he himself had had no education, Marko loved learning and the learned. He was one of those public-spirited and zealous promoters of the new movement for education, thanks to whom Bulgaria had been covered with a network of schools within a short time. He had a somewhat vague idea as to the practical benefit which knowledge might confer on this people of farmers, craftsmen and merchants. Marko observed with anxiety that life did not make a gift of work or bread to those who finished school. But he instinctively felt that a mysterious force lay hidden in knowledge which would change the world. He believed in science as he believed in God, unreasoningly. That was why he did his best to serve it. He had one ambition, to be elected a trustee of the school in his native town, Byala Cherkva. And he always was elected, because he was universally respected and trusted. Marko spared neither time nor labor in this modest public office, but he avoided all others, although they were often accompanied by power and advantages, and most of all he avoided the konak.*

When the table was cleared Marko rose. He was a man of about fifty, of giant stature, slightly stooping, and still slender. His face, ruddy and tanned by wind and sun because of his frequent journeys to fairs all over the country, had a cold and serious look even when he smiled. His bushy eyebrows, jutting out over the blue eyes, stressed the stern expression of his face. But there was a good nature, honesty and sincerity in it which made it attractive and invariably aroused respect.

Marko sat down on the little bench by the tall box trees, over which a red blanket had been thrown, and began to smoke his chibouk.** His family settled themselves comfortably on a rug near the brook while the maid brought coffee.

That evening Marko was in a good mood. With absorption he watched the well-fed, rosy-cheeked children tumbling about and rending the air with their ringing laughter. At every moment they formed a picturesque group from which came loud shrieks, merry laughter or cross words. They were like a flock of birds sporting in

---

* *konak:* the governor's residence, seat of the local Turkish government.

** *chibouk:* a long pipe.

the branches of a tree. But suddenly this joyful, innocent game became aggressive. Arms waved around more wildly, fists dealt blows, threatening cries were heard, and the bird concert turned into a free-for-all. . . . Victors and vanquished made a dash for their father, to complain or to justify themselves. One called on his grandmother to defend him, another took his mother as prosecutor.

From being an impartial onlooker Marko now became a judge. By right and by duty he should have examined the facts. But in defiance of legal precedent the judge refused to hear either accusation or defence and gave judgment at once: some he caressed, others he pulled by the ears, and the smallest—the injured parties—he kissed on both cheeks. The children quieted down.

Just then the youngest, asleep in Granny Ivanitsa's arms, awoke crying at the noise. "Sleep, my darling, go to sleep or the Turks will get you," said Granny Ivanitsa, rocking the baby on her knee.

Marko frowned. "Mother," he said, "you've frightened the children long anough with the Turks! The fear will stick in their hearts."

"Well, that's how I know it," answered Granny Ivanitsa. "They used to frighten us with the Turks, too—and aren't they enough to frighten anybody, God's curse on them! I'm a woman of seventy, and I'll go to the grave, as the saying goes, with my eyes open. The good days haven't come yet."

"Granny, when I grow up and brother Vassil and brother Georgi, we'll take our swords and kill all the Turks," cried little Peter.

"Well, leave just one alive, granny's boy."

"How is Assen?" Marko asked his wife as she came out of the house.

"The fever's down; he's asleep now," she answered.

"What did he have to see those things for?" Granny Ivanitsa said uneasily. "Now he's ill."

Marko frowned but answered nothing. It should be mentioned that Assen had run a temperature that day because, through the window at school, he had seen the headless body of Gencho the Dyer's boy which had been brought in from the fields to the churchyard. Marko quickly changed the subject and said, turning to the children, "Now, let's keep quiet; let's hear what your brother has to tell us. Afterwards you'll all sing a song. Vassil, tell us what your teacher taught you today."

"A lesson in general history."

"Very well, tell us about the history; what was it?"

"About the War of the Spanish Succession."

"About the Spaniards, was it? Leave them out; they're no concern of ours. Tell us something about Russia."

"What shall I tell you?" asked Vassil.

"Well, about Ivan the Terrible, for instance, or Bonaparte, when he set Moscow on fire or. . . ." But Marko never finished his sentence. Something crashed at the dark end of the yard; tiles came tumbling down from the top of the wall. The chickens and hens set up a frightened cackle and came flying out with ruffled feathers. The maid who was bringing in the washing near there, screamed and cried out, "Haidouks! Haidouks!"*

Terrible confusion arose in the yard. The women took refuge in the house, the children were neither to be seen nor heard, and Marko, who was a brave man, after peering into the darkness where the noise had come from, disappeared through a door. A moment later he came out at another one near the stable. He held two pistols in his hands. This action, as resolute as it was unwise, was accomplished so rapidly that Markovitsa had no time even to think of holding her husband back. When he dashed out, only her faint voice could be heard, merging with the hideous barking of the dog who stood bristling near the spring.

There was indeed a stranger in the shadows between the henhouse and the stable, but it was so dark that nothing could be distinguished. The blackness was still more intense for Marko, who had just passed from the light of the lantern into the darkness of the night. Marko tiptoed into the stable, patted the horse's buttocks to quiet it, and looked out through the bars of the little window. Whether his eyes had gotten used to the dark or whether it was his imagination, he saw something standing outside in the corner right next to the window that looked like a man who was absolutely motionless.

Marko crouched down, took aim, shouted in a terrible voice, "Hands up!" He waited a moment with his finger on the trigger.

"Bai Marko," answered a voice.

"Who's there?" asked Marko in Bulgarian.

"Bai Marko, don't be afraid; I'm one of your own people!" And the unknown stood up by the window. Marko clearly saw his shadow.

"Who are you?" Marko asked sharply and suspiciously, withdrawing the pistol.

"Ivan, the son of Dyado Kralich** of Vidin."

"I haven't seen you around here—what are you doing here?"

"I'll tell you, Bai Marko," answered the visitor, lowering his voice.

"I can't see you. Where did you come from?"

---

* *haidouk:* outlaw, brigand, famed in folksongs as the Robin Hood type.

** *dyado:* grandfather, used of old men.

"I'll tell you, Bai Marko. From far away."

"From how far away?"

"From a very great distance, Bai Marko," the visitor whispered.

"From where?"

"From Diarbekir."* The word brought a flash of memory to Marko. He remembered that Dyado Manol had a son exiled in Diarbekir. Manol was an old friend of his with whom he had business dealings, who had done him many a service. He came out of the stable, approached his night visitor in the dark, took him by the hand and led him through the stable to the hay loft.

"Ivancho, is it you? I remember you as a little boy. . . . You'll spend the night here. Tomorrow we'll see," said Marko softly.

"Thank you, Bai Marko. I know nobody here but you," whispered Kralich.

"Why, of course, your father has no better friend than I. You are at home here. Did anybody see you?"

"No, I don't think there was anybody in the street when I came in."

"When you came in! Is that the way to come in, my son? Dashing over the wall like that! But there's no harm done; Dyado Manol's son is always a welcome guest for me, most of all when he comes from such a distance. Are you hungry, Ivancho?"

"Thank you, Bai Marko, I'm not."

"No,, you really must eat something. I'll go and calm down the household, then I'll come back and have a talk with you, to fix things up. God help you, what I was about to do!" said Marko, carefully uncocking his pistol.

"Forgive me, Bai Marko, it was terribly stupid of me."

"Wait till I come back." And Marko went out, shuting the door of the stable behind him.

He found his wife and mother almost fainting with terror, but when they saw him safe and sound they cried out and clutched at his hands as if they feared his going out again. Marko pretended to be calm and lied to them; he assured them that he had found nothing in the yard, that probably a cat or a dog had pushed down the tiles and foolish Pena had raised an outcry. "All we've done is rouse the neighborhood," he said, putting his pistols back in their holsters which hung on the wall.

The household quieted down. Granny Ivanitsa called to the maid, "May your eyes wither, Pena, you gave us such a fright. Take the

---

* *Diarbekir:* town in Asia Minor whose fortress was used as a prison for political offenders.

chidren out quickly and have them pee on blue stone!"*

Just then a thundering knock was heard at the gate. Marko went out into the yard and called out, "Who's there?"

"Open, chorbadji," came the answer in Turkish.

"The onbashi,"** whispered Marko anxiously to himself. "We must hide him somewhere else." And without paying further attention to the knocking at the gate he ran to the stable.

"Ivancho," he called into the loft. No answer.

"He's gone to sleep. Ivancho!" he called louder. No one answered.

"Oh, poor lad, he must have run away," said Marko, who only then realized that he had found the stable door wide open. Then he added anxiously, "What will become of the poor boy now?"

He called again once or twice just in case and getting no answer, turned towards the gate, on which the blows were thundering as if to smash it down.

---

* A sovereign remedy for shock, according to folk medicine.

** *onbashi:* police sergeant.

chapter 2

the storm

Indeed, at the very first knock, and without later remembering or knowing how, Ivan Kralich leaped back over the wall and dropped into the street. For several moments he stood there dazed. Then he looked cautiously around, but all he saw was impenetrable darkness. Black storm clouds now covered the sky; the evening breeze had turned into a cold wind which wailed drearily through the deserted streets. Kralich took the first turning he came across and set forth quickly, feeling his way along the walls and stumbling across gutters. All the gates, all the shutters, all windows were closed and silent—not a ray of light through the slats, not a sign of life. The little town was dead, dead as all provincial towns are long before midnight.

For quite a long time he wandered about haphazardly, hoping to reach the end of the town. Suddenly he started and paused under the wide eaves of a house on the street. He had made out a group of dark figures ahead. Kralich stood still and carefully shrank back against the gate where he had stopped. A growl, followed by an angry bark, made him jump. He had disturbed a watchdog, sleeping just inside the gate. The bark and his movement gave him away. The night patrol moved forward, rattling their weapons. There was a cry of "Stop!" in Turkish.

In moments of unavoidable danger common sense treacherously leaves one in the lurch, and a blind instinct of self-preservation alone takes over. At such times he has, in effect, no head, but only hands to protect himself with and legs to carry him away. Kralich had but to turn back—the darkness would have formed an impenetrable barrier between him and the patrol. Instead he dashed forward, broke through the watchmen like a whirlwind, and fled straight ahead. The men rushed after him; the street rang to their steps and shouts. Among the rest he could hear the shrill cry of the Bulgarian constable: "Stop, man! Or we'll shoot!" Kralich raced onward without turning back. Several shots were fired but missed him; he was saved by the darkness. Yet he did not seem to be making headway, for he soon felt someone seize his sleeve. He pressed forward, slipped out of his coat and left it in the hands of the pursuer. Two more shots were fired after him.

Kralich went on running ahead, not knowing where. Stumbling with fatigue, he could hardly draw breath. At every step he felt like dropping. Unexpectedly a blinding flash of lightning illuminated the darkness, and Kralich saw that he was out in the country, no longer pursued by anyone. Then he threw himself down exhausted under a walnut tree to catch his breath. The wind from the mountain was blowing strong and fresh. The rustle of leaves blended with the roaring wind and the distant rumble of thunder which came ever more close and threatening, until it broke in a deafening clap over the fugitive's head and vanished somewhere in boundless space.

The short rest and fresh air restored Kralich's strength. He saw that it was going to rain, and set out once more to find shelter somewhere. The trees around him soughed plaintively; the tall elms bent before the wind; the grasses and weeds hissed—all nature seemed to be on the alert and roaring mightily. Large drops of rain began to fall, hitting the earth like bullets. Lightning flashed over the mountains again, and immediately the thunder followed with a tremendous clap, as if to bring the heavens down with it. The rain came pouring down, lashed by the gale; flashes of lightning split the clouds and the darkness, their bluish light giving the trees and the mountains a fantastic appearance. These weird glimpses followed immediately by total darkness seemed like some strange and terrible vision. There was a savage beauty about this battle of the elements, this conflict of the horizons, this infernal illumination of the abysses. It was a majestic spectacle in which the collision of limitless and mysterious forces blended into one unearthly and demonic harmony. In a storm nature reaches the heights of poetry.

Soaked to the skin, blinded by lightning, deafened by thunder, Kralich stumbled on at random among bushes, trees, and planted fields that gave him no shelter. At last the noise of water falling from a height broke through the other sounds and reached his ears. It was a mill race. At the same time, a new flash of lightning showed him the roof of the mill itself, sheltered among willows. Kralich ran to it and stopped under the eaves. He tried the door; it opened, and he went in. The mill was dark and silent. Outside the storm died away. The rain stopped suddenly, the wind died, and the moon gilded the ragged clouds. The night became clear. Such swift changes of weather are peculiar to the month of May.

Steps soon approached from outside. Kralich hastily edged into a narrow space between the grain bin and the wall.

"Look, the wind has opened the door," said a rough voice in the dark; a moment later a kerosene lamp was lighted. Kralich, hidden in his hole, peered out and saw the miller, a big, lean peasant. He was with a girl, barefoot and in a short red dress, who was probably his daughter. She was closing the door and trying to padlock it. She was about thirteen or fourteen years old, but still had the movements of a child; her black eyes with long lashes had a friendly look. Under her careless dress the slender form of a future beauty was discernible. Apparently the two had come from another mill, for they were dry.

"It's a good thing we stopped the wheel," the miller went on, "or this flood would have broken it. Old Stancho's gossip is endless; it's lucky nobody slipped in and robbed us." He looked around. "You go to bed, Mariika. Whatever did your mother mean by sending you here? Just to add to my worries," the miller went on, as he began to hammer down one of the boards of the funnel which had been torn loose, humming a song as he worked.

Mariika without more ado went to the end of the mill, spread out rugs on the floor for her father and herself, performed several obeisances by way of prayer, threw herself down on the goat hair rug and immediately fell asleep, as all carefree souls will do.

Kralich watched this simple scene with tense curiosity. The rough but good-natured face of the miller inspired him with confidence. It was impossible for that honest face to hide a treacherous soul. He had decided to come out and ask for advice and help, but just then the miller stopped his humming, straightened up and listened to the sound of voices outside. There was a loud knock at the door.

"Open up, miller!" came a command in Turkish. He went to the door, leaned up against the latch and turned around with an ashen face. The door was kicked again. A new shout was heard, followed by the yelping of a dog.

"Hunters!" said the miller, who recognized the bark of a hound. "What are the devils up to now? It's Emeksiz-Pehlivan." Emeksiz-Pehlivan, the worst of evil-doers by day or night, filled the whole countryside with terror. A fortnight before he had cut down the entire family of Gancho Daaliya in the village of Ivanovo. It was also said, and not without reason, that it was he who had cut off the head of the child that had been brought into town the day before in a cart.

The door shook under a rain of blows. The miller stood there perplexed, his head in his hands, as if wondering what to do. Then he bent down, drew an axe out from under a dusty shelf, and took his stand with it by the door, which was creaking loudly under the pressure. But this momentary resolution left him as soon as he looked at his daughter. A terrible hopelessness, pain and suffering showed on his face. At last the feelings of a father won out over his indignant spirit. He remembered the Bulgarian proverb, "No sword cuts a bowed head," and decided, instead of resisting, to beg for mercy from the merciless. He quickly put the axe behind the bin where Kralich was hiding, covered Mariika up well and opened the door.

Two armed Turks, with guns on their shoulders, stood on the threshold. One of them had a hound on a leash. The first, who was indeed the bloodthirsty Emeksiz-Pehlivan, looked searchingly inside and then entered. He was tall, stooped, cadaverously thin, and beardless. His face was not terrible like his name and his deeds. Only the small colorless gray eyes danced slyly and spitefully, like those of a monkey. His companion, stumpy, muscular, lame, with the face of an animal on which cruelty and the most bestial instincts could be read, came in after him with the hound and closed the door.

As both men threw off their soaking cloaks, Ekmesiz-Pehlivan glared at the miller. "Why didn't you open the door, miller?" he asked.

The miller muttered a confused excuse, bowing submissively to the ground and throwing an agitated glance at the back of the mill where Marika was sleeping.

"Are you alone here?" And Emeksiz looked around.

"Alone," assented the miller quickly. Then, realizing that a lie was useless, he added, "The child is asleep over there." Just then Mariika threw back the cover and turned her face towards them. The pale light of the lamp played upon her white neck. The Turks turned greedy eyes on the sleeping girl.

Emeksiz turned to him with feigned good nature: "Chorbadji, bestir yourself. Go and buy us a bottle of rakiya."*

"Pehlivan-Aga,** it's the middle of the night and all the taverns in town are closed," the miller answered, trembling at the thought of leaving Mariika alone with these people.

"Go along," the cripple retorted, "there's sure to be a shop open in our honor somewhere. We want you to treat us here; that's the way to make friends. . . ." He spoke these words with a sneer, sure of his victory. Nor did he even try to hide his intentions from the unfortunate father.

---

* *rakiya:* the local brandy, usually distilled from plums.

** *aga:* master.

Emeksiz's eyes were intently fixed on the girl, who lay there in a carefree, sensuous posture. When he noticed the miller still standing there he scowled, but with pretended gentleness he said good-naturedly: "Chorbadji, you have a lovely daughter, mashallah.* How lucky she's there to serve your guests! Come now, go for the rakiya and we'll look after the mill." Then he added threateningly, "You know who Emeksiz-Pehlivan is!"

The miller had at once grasped their vile intention. His simple, honest soul was outraged. But he was caught in a trap, alone against two armed ruffians. It was madness to fight, and useless too: his death, which seemed nothing to him just then, would not save his daughter.

He tried to soften the hearts of his enemies by pleading. "Agalar,** have pity on a sick man and on my old bones . . . I am dead tired from work today . . . let me go to bed . . . do not dishonor me."

But he spoke to deaf ears. The cripple growled, "Come, come, chelebi,† we're thirsty. You chatter too much because you live in a mill, don't you! Go fetch that brandy!" And he pushed him toward the door.

"I never leave my mill at this time of night; let me be!" said the miller dully.

Then the two Turks threw off the mask of gentleness and their savage looks shot through the miller like arrows. "Why, the swine! He's showing his teeth! D'ye see?" said Emeksiz drawing his yataghan. His eyes grew bloodshot.

"Kill me if you like, but I will not leave my child alone!" said the miller submissively yet resolutely.

Emeksiz stood up. "Topal-Hassan, throw this dog out, or I'll soil my knife!" The cripple leaped at the miller and knocked him down in front of the door. Then he began to push him out with kicks.

The miller got to his feet and rushed back crying, "Mercy, mercy!" Mariika awoke at the noise and started up in fright. When she saw Emeksiz with a bare knife in his hand she shrieked and ran to her father. "Aman,‡ have mercy, agalar!" cried the unfortunate father, hugging his daughter's head to his breast.

At a sign from Emeksiz the powerful Topal-Hassan sprang behind the miller like a tiger, seized his arms and twisted them. "That's

* *mashallah:* bravo.

** *agalar:* plural of *aga,* master.

† *chelebi:* gentleman.

‡ *aman:* mercy, have mercy.

right, Topal-Hassan, let's tie the old mill-rat up; he can stand here and watch the show since that's what he wants. It's all such a fool deserves. . . . He can stay tied up when we set fire to the mill, so there'll be a show for us too."

Deaf to his cries, the two bandits thrust the miller against one of the posts and began tying him to it. Maddened by the thought of what he was about to see, the miller howled like a beast for help although he never expected it in this deserted spot. Mariika opened the door and shouted through her tears. But only the echoes answered.

"You stay here, miller's daughter! We'll be needing you," cried Emekzis, and he pulled her back to keep her from running away, then turned to Topal-Hassan.

"Aman!" the miller kept shrieking in despair, "help me, people! Is there no one to help? Mariika, come here!" he cried desperately, unconsciously turning for help to the weak child.

Till that moment Kralich had remained motionless, watching the scene taking place before him, his legs trembling unnaturally, his hair standing on end, and shivers running all through his body. All that he had lived through and seen that night from Marko's house to this place was so unexpected and terrible that it seemed like a nightmare to him. The whistling bullets first, the peals of thunder afterwards still echoed in his ears.

At first he had thought that the Turks had come for him and that his fate was sealed. The conviction of his utter helplessness drained all his energy, so that he had only just enough left to give himself up to the Turks to save the miller from responsibility. But when he saw that he was about to witness something far more terrible and when he heard the miller calling on Mariika for help, a fury of madness and despair set his blood on fire. So far he had never looked on blood, but now the Turks seemed to him no more than flies. Exhaustion, weakness, hesitation—all left him. His hands reached out mechanically for the axe; mechanically he left his hiding-place; mechanically he slipped past the sacks of wheat, crouching for cover behind them. Then he straightened up, as white as a corpse, hurled himself at Emeksiz who was standing with his back to him, and drove the axe into his head. All this he did as one in a trance.

The Turk fell to the floor without a sound.

Faced by this unexpected and dangerous enemy, Topal-Hassan dropped the rope with which he was tying up the miller, drew his pistol and emptied it at Kralich. Smoke filled the mill; the lamp went out at the blast, and all found themselves in total darkness.

Then in this darkness a terrible struggle began with tooth and nail, hand and foot. The fighters, two at first, then three, reeled and stumbled in the dark with savage cries, panting and groaning, and all these sounds were mixed with the wild barking of the dog. Topal-Hassan, who was as strong as an ox, desperately resisted his two opponents who had to get the better of him somehow, or they were doomed. . . .

When the lamp was lighted again Topal-Hassan was writhing in the throes of death. Kralich had managed to get hold of the other's knife in the struggle and had stuck it into his throat. The two bodies lay in pools of blood.

Then the miller straightened up and looked in amazement at the stranger who had so unexpectedly come to his aid. Before him stood a tall young man, pale as death, olive-skinned, with sunken, piercing black eyes, his long, tousled hair thick with dust. His jacket was ragged, mud-stained and wet; his vest had no buttons and was open, showing that he had no shirt under it; his trousers were frayed and his shoes broken—in short, a man who had escaped from prison or was on his way there.

Just such a man the miller thought him. But he looked at him with pity and said, much moved, "I don't know who you are, sir, or how you came here. But I shall never be able to repay you as long as I live. You've saved me from death, and from something still worse, from having my child shamed and my old age. . . . God bless you and reward you. All the people will thank you. Do you know who that is?" He pointed at Emeksiz. "It's he who made children weep in their mother's wombs. The world is rid of the brute at last. Thank you, my son!"

Kralich listened to these simple and sincere words with tears in his eyes, then said, still pausing for breath, "I didn't do much, dyado; we've killed two of them, but there are thousands and thousands of such brutes. The Bulgarian people will never be free until they all take up their clubs and crush these oppressors. But tell me, dyado, where we can bury these two bodies; we must leave no trace."

"I have a grave ready for the heathens; only help me to drag them out," said the old man. Then the two men, whom that bloodstained night had bound to each other forever, dragged the corpses out to an old pit in the thicket behind the mill, crammed them in, and covered them well with earth to efface all traces.

When they returned to the door with the pickaxe and shovel, something white came bounding up to them. "Ah, the hound!" cried Kralich. "It'll come poking around here and give us away." He lay in wait for it and aimed a blow at its head. The dog crawled off along the river, yelping piteously. Kralich pushed it into the water with his pickaxe and it sank from sight.

"We should have buried it with the other two dogs," remarked the miller.

They washed the blood off their clothes and scattered earth over the ground. "Why, what's this," said the miller, "you're bleeding?" looking at Kralich's hand.

"It's nothing. The brute bit me when I had him by the throat."

"Let me bind it up for you quickly," said the miller, and bandaged him with a piece of rag. Then, dropping his hand, he looked Kralich straight in the eye, and asked, "Excuse me, my son, but where do you come from?" And again he cast a wondering look at the stranger.

"I'll tell you later, dyado. Just now I'll only say that I'm a Bulgarian and a good Bulgarian. Don't doubt me."

"Lord save us! Didn't I see that? You're a man of the people, sir, and I'd give my soul for such brothers."

"Where can I find clothes to change into, dyado, and a place to sleep?"

"Come, we'll go to the monastery to Deacon Vikenti. He's a relative of mine. Many's the good turn he's done for the likes of you. He's a good Bulgarian too, sir. Come, we'll all spend the night there. It's a good think nobody saw us."

But Dyado Stoyan was wrong. Against the trunk of the walnut tree a little way off, the moon shone down on a motionless witness of the burial of the two Turks. But our men noticed nothing.

A little later the miller, Kralich and Mariika, who had run away and hidden under an elm during the fight and was whimpering with fear, were on their way to the monastery, whose white walls showed between the dark branches of the walnut trees and the poplars. The unknown figure set off after them towards the monastery.

chapter 3

the monastery

They crossed a meadow over which large boulders were scattered under the boughs of ancient walnut trees whose trunks were hollow with age; then they saw clearly the high walls of the monastery before them. In the mysterious moonlight it looked like a Gothic castle with fantastically outlined turrets.

Some years earlier a giant pine tree had been the pride of those old walls. With its shaggy crown, in which innumerable birds sang in their nests, it had sheltered the old-fashioned church. But a storm had brought down the pine tree, and the abbot had built a new church. With its tall cupola built in the new fashion, it stood there today in odd contrast to the other shabby old buildings, monuments of the past; it was even ugly, like a piece of new paper stuck onto an old parchment. The old church and the old pine had fallen under the blows of fate, and since then the monastery seemed to have grown darker. It no longer gladdened the eye with the gigantic tree which rose to the clouds, and the painted figures of the saints, archangels, holy fathers and martyrs which, although their eyes had been scratched out by brigands and robbers, had once lifted people's souls up in piety, were no longer there.

Our three friends went around the monastery and stopped at the back wall, as it was easier to scale and nearer Deacon Vikenti's cell. On this side the dogs would not be aroused, nor would the servants hear them. The mountain waterfalls thundered nearby, filling the whole neighborhood with their wild echo.

Someone had to scale the wall to fetch a ladder and hand it down to the others. Naturally it was Kralich who did so—he had started the night by storming a wall. Soon the three were over the wall, at the risk of being shot at by the fierce abbot, should he happen to catch sight of them from his window. They found themselves in a small back yard which communicated with the main courtyard through a door that was locked on the inside. The deacon's cell was on the ground floor and looked out on this very yard. They went up to the window through which a light was still shining.

"Vikenti is still at his books," said the miller, standing on tiptoe and looking in. He tapped on the window.

It was opened and some one asked, "Uncle Stoyan, is that you? What are you doing here?"

"Give me the key of the door, deacon, and I'll tell you. Are you alone?"

"Yes, I am. They're all asleep. Here it is."

The miller vanished in the shadows, returning in a few minutes to lead Kralich and his daughter into the inner courtyard, locking the door behind him.

The big courtyard which they now entered was quiet. The fountain murmured dreamily and monotonously in the silence. The sound it made was like a chant for the dead. Gloomy rows of open galleries, silent and lifeless, surrounded the court on all sides. The black cypresses bent their heads mysteriously like gigantic ghosts. The door of the deacon's cell opened, and the nocturnal visitors entered.

The deacon, a young man with a lively face, intelligent dark eyes and a smooth chin, gave Kralich a friendly welcome, knowing of him already from his uncle's terse explanation. He gazed with respect and admiration at the hero who had slaughtered two ruffians as easily as a couple of chickens and saved the old man and his daughter. In his guest the deacon's honest heart divined a man as noble as he was brave.

Dyado Stoyan gave a rapid account of all that had happened at the mill in a voice that trembled with emotion and blessed his savior. Vikenti noticed his extreme exhaustion and pallor, and offered to lead him to the cell in which he was to spend the night. They set out for it. The deacon, with a bundle of clothing and some food under his arm, went ahead across the sleeping courtyard. They reached the staircase of the three-storied gallery opposite and went up it. They passed through corridors and up further flights of stairs to the upper floor. Although they stepped softly the whole floor creaked under their footsteps, as in every deserted wooden building.

Vikenti lit a small candle in the cell they entered. It was bare and cheerless—a straw mattress with a cover and a jug of water were the only furnishings it could boast of. This shelter looked more like a prison-cell than anything else, but Kralich could have wished for nothing better at that moment.

After discussing the adventure at the mill for a while, Vikenti started to say good-night. "You're exhausted and you must get some rest. So I won't bother you with questions. And it isn't necessary anyhow. The courage you showed tonight has told me all I need to know. Tomorrow I'll see you again, and let me assure you, don't worry about anything. Deacon Vikenti is entirely at your service. Good night." And he put out his hand.

Kralich took it, but did not let it go. "No," he said, "you have given me hospitality on trust and you're exposing yourself to danger on my behalf. You must at least know who I am. My name is Ivan Kralich."

"Ivan Kralich, the exile? When did they free you?" the deacon asked in surprise.

"They didn't. I escaped from the fortress of Diarbekir. I'm a fugitive.

Vikenti shook his hand warmly. "You are welcome, Bai Kralichev; you are my still more honored guest and brother. Bulgaria needs her good sons. There is much to be done, very much. The tyranny of the Turks is unendurable, and popular indignation will reach its height. We must prepare. . . . Stay with us, Mr. Kralichev. Nobody will know you're here. Will you work with us?" The enthusiastic young deacon spoke with animation.

"That's what I intend to do, Father Vikenti."

"We'll have a long talk tomorrow. You're perfectly safe with us. I have even hidden Levski* here. Nobody comes here—there's more fear of ghosts than of men. Good night!" the deacon concluded jokingly as he went out.

"Good night, deacon," said Kralich, closing the door behind him. He quickly changed his clothes and ate his supper. Then he blew out the candle, but he tossed and turned for a long time before sleep closed his eyes. Agitating memories troubled him. All the terrible scenes of the night passed through his mind with loathsome and cruel clarity. This painful state lasted for a long time. Finally nature won out; thoroughly exhausted, mentally and physically, he gave in to his crying need for sleep.

But suddenly he started and opened his eyes in the dark. He heard some one walking along the gallery, heavily, slowly. Then came a sound of singing, or rather howling. The steps approached and the strange chanting grew louder. Sometimes it sounded like a funeral dirge, and sometimes again like a sad wailing. It seemed to Kralich that the sounds came from somewhere else, but that the silence of the spot brought them nearer, distorted. But no, the footsteps sounded very clearly on the gallery.

* Levski was a young deacon who became a leading revolutionary and was executed by the Turks in 1873.

Suddenly a dark figure appeared at the window and peered in. In horror Kralich fixed his eyes on the apparition and realized it was making awkward, loathsome gestures with its hands, as if beckoning to him. This was quite clear in the faint light of the night. Kralich's eyes never left the window. He began to think that the mysterious figure looked like Emeksiz-Pehlivan, the murdered man. Then he thought he must be dreaming, and rubbed his eyes. He looked again; the shadow was still there looking in.

Kralich was not superstitious, but this deserted building with its deathly stillness and its silence as of the grave made him tremble in spite of himself. He remembered the deacon's joke about ghosts, and the place seemed to him all the more eerie. But he felt ashamed of himself at once. He groped for his pistol, found it, got up, opened the door quietly and went out barefooted onto the gallery.

The tall mysterious figure was walking about again, continuing its weird chant. Kralich went up to it fearlessly. Instead of vanishing as in stories, the singing ghost roared out in fright, for Kralich looked even more ghost-like in the white underclothes the deacon had given him.

"Who are you?" the new ghost asked the old one, seizing him by the coat.

But fear had rendered the latter speechless. He could only cross himself, gape and shake his head like an idiot. Kralich realized that that was just what he was and let him alone. Vikenti had forgotten to warn his guest of the nightly wanderings of Mooncho, the harmless idiot who had lived in the monastery for years. He was the unknown who had watched the burial of the Turks.

chapter 4

at Marko's again

When Marko opened the gate that night after Kralich's flight, he met the onbashi and his zaptiehs,* who advanced cautiously into the yard. "What's up here, Marko chorbadji?" the onbashi asked.

Marko explained calmly that nothing was up; the frightened maid had only thought there was. The onbashi was only too glad to accept such a simple explanation and withdrew, thankful to have avoided any unpleasantness. Marko had just shut the gate when his neighbor appeared on the scene.

"Greetings, Bai Marko!"

"Ah, Ivancho, come in and let's have some coffee."

"Good evening, Bai Marko. Is Assencho better?" called a tall young man from the street as he came running along.

"Come in, doctor, come in." And Marko led them into a room which was at once brightly lit by two paraffin candles in shining brass candlesticks. This room, which was for guests, was small, cheerful and quiet. It was carpeted and furnished in the naive, odd taste of that day, which still holds undisputed sway in certain provincial towns. The floor was covered with gaily colored rugs and the two window seats with red ones, all home-made. There was an iron stove against one wall which was used in winter, and never removed in summer because it served as an ornament.

Opposite the stove, on the icon-stand where a float-light was burning, stood some icons, behind which one saw prints from Mount Athos, the pious gifts of pilgrims. The icons were painted and very old, and therefore had still greater value in Granny Ivanitsa's eyes, as old weapons have for connoisseurs. One of them, of very great antiquity, enjoyed her particular respect and veneration. She proudly told people that this wonderful painting had been done by her great-grandfather, Father Hadji Arseni,** with his feet—a statement which no one dreamt of contradicting as it was so convincing. A

---

* *zaptieh:* a Turkish policeman.

** *Hadji:* title given to Moslems and Christians alike who have made the pilgrimage to Mecca or Jerusalem.

bunch of basil had been stuck over the iconostasis,* and a bunch of willow sprigs, both blessed on Palm Sunday. They were in the house to bring health and prosperity.

All around the walls ran a shelf on which stood porcelain dishes, the inevitable decoration of every self-respecting house, and in the corners were triangular shelves with vases on them. Time had long since done away with the fashion for chibouks, which now decorated the walls with their amber mouthpieces and silver-inlaid bowls. Out of respect for tradition Marko kept only one chibouk for his personal use.

The wall opposite the windows played the important part of a picture gallery. It was the "Hermitage" of Marko's house. It contained six gold-framed lithographs from Wallachia. This strange assortment bore witness to the easily satisfied artistic taste of that day. Some were scenes of the domestic life of the Germans; one depicted Sultan Abdul Medjid on horseback with his suite. The rest showed episodes of the Crimean War: the Battle of Alma, the Battle of Eupatoria, the Raising of the Siege of Silistra in 1852. This last bore an erroneous Rumanian inscription, "The Battle of Silistra," which a knowing hand had translated into Bulgarian below as "The Batter of Silistra." The final picture included portraits of all the Russian commanders in the war, all shown only from the knees up. And since Father Stavri assured people that their legs had been blown off by the cannon balls of the English, Granny Ivanitsa called them "the martyrs." "Who has been touching the martyrs again?" she would ask the children crossly.

Over the martyrs hung a big clock with a pendulum, whose weights and chains hung down to the very cushions of the window seat. This ancient timepiece had long since completed its allotted span—its works were worn out, its springs had lost their resilience, the white enamel of its face was chipped and cracked, and its hands were crooked and loose. It was a living ruin. But Marko prolonged its life with great efforts and skill. He himself mended it, took it apart, wound it, cleaned it with a feather dipped in oil; he protected the axles of the wheels with bits of paper, and thus breathed life into it for a little longer, until it stopped again. Marko jokingly called it "my old consumptive," but his family was so used to this patient that when his pulse, that is, his pendulum, stopped, the house seemed dull and still. When Marko pulled the chains to wind it up, his "martyr" emitted such angry hollow rattlings that the cat would

* *iconostasis:* where the icons are placed against the wall.

flee in alarm. Two family photographs on the same wall completed the treasures of this picture gallery, which the antique clock turned into a museum.

Doctor Sokolov was a young man of twenty-eight, well-built, with shining fair hair, blue eyes and a frank, open face; he was by nature hot-headed, flighty and frivolous. He had served as a medical assistant in a Turkish camp at the Montenegrin frontier, had learned the language and customs of the Turks well, drank rakiya with the onbashi and kept him company of an evening, sent gunshots up his chimney at night to frighten him, and was training a bear. Looked upon askance by the chorbadjis, who entrusted themselves to the Yanina-trained healer,* he was very popular with the young men because of his cheerful, open nature and his fiery patriotism. He was always first in any merrymaking or revolutionary plots that were afoot, and devoted all his time to these two activities. He had not graduated from any medical school, but, to put him higher than the Greek healer, the young people had given him the title of doctor, and he did not think it necessary to protest. As to the treatment of his patients, he left it to his two able assistants, the healthy climate of this mountainous region, and nature. That was why he seldom needed to consult his pharmacopoeia, whose Latin he did not understand, and his dispensary occupied one small shelf. No wonder that by these means he was soon able to take the wind out of his rival's sails.

Sokolov was Marko's family doctor and had come to see Assencho. The other visitor was Ivancho Yota. Like a good neighbor, he had come to chat and to reassure Marko. For some minutes the conversation turned around the evening's adventure, and Ivancho described his impressions and anxieties most eloquently.

"So, as I was telling you," Yota went on, "just as our Lalka was clearing the table, and so forth, I heard a turbulent propaganda at your place, Bai Marko. And the dog was barking most admirably, too. I was frightened—that is to say, I wasn't frightened, but I said to Lala, 'Gracious, Lala, what's happening at Bai Marko's? Go and have a look at their yard from the balcony!' But then I thought, 'That's not a woman's job,' and temeritously I went up on the balcony and looked out. It was dark in your yard. 'What's all this propaganda about?' said I to myself in my thoughts—that is to say, the whole neighborhood was aroused. And Lalka stood behind me

* Those trained in Yanina, in northern Greece, received only very rudimentary ideas of medicine.

holding onto my coattails. 'Where are you off to?' says she. 'You're not going to jump into Bai Marko's yard?' 'There's nothing up,' says I. 'Lock the gate into Bai Marko's!' "

"There was no need, Ivancho; it was nothing, really."

"Then," Ivancho went on, "I said to myself in my mind, 'We must send word to the konak. Mr. Bai Marko is a neighbor, and we cannot leave him in this imprecarious condition. . . .' So I instaneously retreated from the stairs and Lala was still shouting turbulently at me. 'Hold your tongue!' says I masterfully. I went out to the gate and looked out on the street—universal quiet."

"Is Assencho asleep now, Bai Marko?" asked the doctor, to stem Ivancho's flow of eloquence.

But Ivancho hastened on with his tale. "When I saw the universal quiet of the street I said to myself, "That's what you have to fear, Ivancho.' Then I came back and slipped through the back gate, that is to say, into the blind alley, from the blind alley through Bai Nedko's fence, then through Mahmoud's place, then over Uncle Gencho's dung heap and straight to the konak. I went in, looked around, and instanteously told the onbashi temeritously that there were robbers at your house and the hens were flying about the yard."

"As I told you, there was nobody; you took all that trouble for nothing, Ivancho." Outside the storm was at its height.

"Ah, Bai Marko, I forgot to ask you," said the doctor suddenly. "Did a young man come to see you this evening?"

"What young man?"

"A strange young man, rather badly dressed. . . . But he looked intelligent, as far as I could see. He was asking for your house."

"Where did you see him? Nobody came here!" answered Bai Marko in obvious confusion, though his guest had no chance to notice this.

"A young man caught up with me at dusk near Hadji Pavel's rose-field," the doctor went on calmly. "He asked me politely, 'Can you please tell me, sir, if Marko Ivanov lives far from here? I want to see him,' he said. 'It's my first visit here.' I happened to be coming this way so I asked him to come with me. On our way I took a good look at him. He was almost naked, poor devil; his coat was thin and torn, as far as I could see in the dark. He himself was thin and pale and barely managed to stay on his feet. The weather had grown cool too. . . . I didn't dare ask him where he came from or why he was in that state, but I felt sorry for the poor fellow and unhappy about him. I looked at my Garibaldi coat. It was worn, giving up the ghost, you might say. 'Will you be offended, sir, if I offer you my coat?

You'll catch cold like that!' He thanked me and took it. So we came to your house and there I left him. I wanted to ask you who the man was."

"I told you, no one came here."

"That's odd," said the doctor.

"Might that be the robber who climbed your wall, Bai Marko?" asked Ivancho. "The propaganda wasn't for nothing."

"That young man couldn't possibly be a robber," remarked the doctor. "You had only to look at him."

The conversation had taken an unpleasant turn and to change it Marko turned to Sokolov. "Have you read the paper, doctor? How's the Herzegovina uprising going?"

"It's dying out, Bai Marko. They're a heroic people and they've done wonders, but what can one do against such odds?"

"Just a handful of people and how long they've held out!" said Marko. "We could never do anything like that!"

"Have we ever tried?" asked the doctor. We are five times as many as they, but we don't yet know our own strength."

"Don't say such things, doctor," said Marko. "The Herzegovinians are one thing and we're another; we're in the very bowels of hell. If we so much as stir we'll be slaughtered like sheep. There's nowhere we can turn for help."

"I ask you, have we ever tried?" the doctor repeated with heat. "They slaughter us and massacre us anyway, even when we don't do anything. The more sheep-like we are the more they abuse us. What had Gancho's innocent little child done to them, to be brought here yesterday without his head? They threaten us with the gallows the moment we want to protest against tyranny, but the Emeksiz-Pehlivans can run riot unpunished. What kind of justice is that? Can even the most faint-hearted stand such oppression? 'Even a sieve has a heart,' as our people say."

Granny Ivanitsa came in. "Do you know," she said, "a little while ago, before the rain, Pena heard shots. What could it have been? Holy Virgin, another poor Christian soul sent to his grave. . . ."

Marko started and his face changed. He had a premonition that something had happened to Kralich, and his heart sank with a grief he could not hide.

"Why, what's the matter, Bai Marko?" asked the doctor, seeing the pain in his face. The rain had stopped, and the guests rose to leave. The news had upset them.

“It must have been shutters banging; the maid is mistaken again. Don’t be afraid—temeritously!” Ivancho Yota strutted about. “Granny Ivanitsa, is your gate unlocked?” And while Marko saw the doctor out at the front, Ivancho fled through the little side gate which his wife opened for him.

chapter 5

the night wears on

Doctor Sokolov knocked at his own gate. It was opened by an old woman, and he went in asking quickly, "What's Cleopatra doing?"

"She's asking for you," answered the old woman with a smile.

The doctor crossed the long yard and went into his room. Spacious, and bare, with cupboards built into the walls and a deep fireplace, it served him as living room, office, and bedroom. All his drugs and medicines were arranged on a little shelf; on the table there was a small mortar and pestle, several medical books scattered about and a pistol. Over his bed hung a double-barrelled musket with a pouch. Only one picture decorated the room, a portrait of the Montenegrin Prince Nicholas, and beneath it hung the photograph of an actress. Obviously the room of an absent-minded bachelor, it was untidy, quiet and carefree. In a corner the little door of a closet stood ajar. Three years before, the executed Levski had spent several nights here.

The doctor carelessly threw down his fez and coat, went up to the small door, clapped his hands and cried out, "Cleopatra! Cleopatra!" No one answered.

"Cleopatra, come out, my dove." A sound came from the closet.

The doctor sat down on a chair in the middle of the room and cried out, "Here, Cleopatra!"

A bear walked out. Or rather a bear-cub. She approached, dragging her big paws along the floor and rumbling joyfully. Then she rose up and put her front paws on the doctor's knees and opened her large mouth with the sharp white teeth. She fawned on him like a puppy. The doctor stroked the fluffy fur of her head and gave her his hand to lick. She licked the whole hand, then seized it in her mouth.

This wild animal, caught as a small cub in the mountains of Sredna Gora, was the gift of a peasant hunter whose son Sokolov had cured of a dangerous illness. The doctor had grown attached to the beast and devoted much care to her training. Cleopatra throve under this tender care, easily grasped her lessons in gymnastics, and her devotion to her master increased daily.

Cleopatra could already dance a bear-polka, hand the doctor his hat, wait on him and guard his room like a dog. This was indeed a dubious service, because her presence in the doctor's house drove patients away. Little the doctor cared about that. As the polka reached its wildest point Cleopatra always roared most terribly, and the whole neighborhood knew that she was dancing. At such times the light-hearted Sokolov danced with her.

That evening he was particularly well-disposed towards the dainty Cleopatra. He took out a piece of meat and let her take it from his hand. "Eat, my dove, for hungry bears won't dance, the old folk say, and I want you to dance for me like a princess tonight."

The bear understood and roared. That meant 'I'm ready.' The doctor picked up a copper tray and began to thump it energetically as he sang:

> "Dimitra, my fair-haired lass,
> Tell your mother, Dimitra,
> Not to bear another child like you. . . ."

Cleopatra rose up on her hind paws and began to dance spiritedly, roaring the whole time. But suddenly she ran to the window and let out a terrifying bellow. The doctor, startled, saw that there were people in the yard. He seized his pistol. "Who's there?" he called, giving Cleopatra a push to keep her quiet.

"Doctor, will you please come to the konak?"

"Is that you, Sherif-Aga? What the devil do you want me for at this time of night? Is somebody ill?"

"Shut the bear up first." The doctor gestured to Cleopatra, and she ambled off to her closet, growling sulkily. He pushed the door shut.

"We have orders to take you to the konak. You're under arrest," said the onbashi sternly.

"Why under arrest? Who accuses me?"

"You'll hear about it there. Come on, get moving." And they took the doctor off, bewildered and uneasy, for he sensed trouble. As he was going through the gate he heard Cleopatra's heart-rending roars which sounded exactly like somebody crying.

The konak was buzzing. They took the doctor into the bey.* He was sitting in his usual place in the corner. Next to him Kiriak Stefchov was reading some papers with Necho Pironkov, the coun-

---

* *bey:* Turkish governor.

cilor, peering over his shoulder. The bey, an old man of sixty, greeted the doctor with a frown but nevertheless asked him to sit down. The Turks adopted these tactics with suspects to predispose them to confess. Sokolov, moreover, was the bey's family doctor and a favorite of his.

The doctor looked around him carefully and was surprised to see on the window seat the coat he had that night given Kralich. This discovery gave him a hint of what lay ahead.

"Is this coat yours, doctor?" asked the bey. The doctor saw no use in denying an obvious fact. He answered that it was.

"Why isn't it in your possession?"

"I gave it to a poor devil tonight."

"Where was this?"

"In Hadji Shado's street."

"When was this?"

"Just about two o'clock."*

"Did you know the man?"

"No, but I was sorry for him, because he was ragged and almost naked."

"How the rascal lies," remarked Necho contemptuously.

"Well, Necho, a drowning man will clutch at a straw, you know," whispered his neighbor. And the bey smiled slyly at what he thought was an obvious lie. He was firmly convinced that the coat had been pulled off the doctor himself, as the watchman asserted.

"Kiriak Effendi,** let's have the papers. . . . These papers, do you know them?" The doctor saw a newspaper, the *Independence,* and a printed revolutionary proclamation. He denied all knowledge of them.

"Who put them in your pocket then?"

"I told you, I gave the coat to a man; they may be his." The bey grinned again. The doctor felt that matters were taking a bad turn for him: they were making out that at the very least he had had dealings with a rebel. So that's what the stranger had been. If he had only known, he could have saved both himself and the other man from terrible trouble.

"Call in the wounded Osman!" ordered the bey. A zaptieh came in with his arm bandaged from the elbow up. It was the same man who had pulled Kralich's coat off, and who had been accidentally wounded by his companion's bullet. He was firmly convinced, or

* Turkish time, i.e. after sunset.

** *effendi, effendim:* title of government officials and members of learned professions.

pretended to be, that the commitadji* they had chased had wounded him.

Osman went up to the doctor. "It was he, effendim."

"Did you tear the coat off him? Are you sure you recognize him?"

"That's the man who wounded me in Petkan's street."

The doctor looked at him astounded. "The zaptieh is lying unconscionably!" he cried.

"You may go, Osman-Aga. . . . Chelebi," the bey went on with a serious look, "do you deny all this?"

"It's a lie and a slander. I don't even carry a pistol, and I never went through Petkan's street tonight."

The onbashi went up to the candle, examined the doctor's pistol, taken from his table, and said suggestively, "There are four bullets here; the fifth chamber is empty." The bey nodded portentously.

"You're mistaken there too; I wasn't carrying the pistol this evening. . . ."

"Chelebi, where were you tonight, about three o'clock, when all this was happening?"

This unexpected question left the doctor aghast. He grew red with embarrassment, but answered confidently. "About three o'clock I was at Marko Ivanov's; his child is ill."

"When you went into Marko's it was almost four; we were just coming out," objected the onbashi, who had met the doctor on his way there. The doctor was silent. Circumstances were very much against him. He saw that he was getting involved.

"Or tell us, rather, where you were from the time you gave away your coat in Hadji Shado's street to the time you went to Marko Chorbadji; where were you?" the bey craftily changed his question.

Such a clear question inevitably demanded a clear answer. But Doctor Sokolov did not give it. A severe struggle accompanied by moral suffering was apparent on his face. His embarrassment and silence were clearer than a confession. They completed the case. The bey saw the guilty one before him, but asked for the last time, "Tell me where you were at that time, chelebi?"

"I can't tell you," the doctor answered quietly and resolutely. This answer astounded them all. Necho the councilor winked ironically at Stefchov, as if to say 'He's fallen into the trap, poor devil.'

"Speak up, chelebi! Where were you at that time?"

"That I cannot possibly tell you—it's a secret which my honor as a doctor and a man does not allow me to disclose. But I was not in

---

* *comita, comitadji:* a revolutionary, member of a revolutionary committee.

Petkan's street." The bey pressed his question, pointing out the dangerous consequences of such a silence. But the doctor was now calm, like a man who has said all that he has to say.

"Have you nothing to say?"

"I have told you everything."

"Then, chelebi, you will be our guest tonight. . . . Take the chelebi to the cells!" said the bey sternly.

The bewildered doctor went out dazed by this heap of accusations which he was unable to disprove. For, as he had said himself, he could not possibly reveal where he had been that night at three o'clock.

chapter 6

the letter

Marko had a bad night. The events of the evening had robbed him of his calm, and he went out earlier than usual to have his coffee at Ganko's café. The owner had just opened his shop and lit the fire. Marko was the first customer.

Café-keepers are great gossips, and after several of the usual jokes, of which he delivered himself while serving Marko his coffee, Ganko hastened to tell him about the doctor's adventure in Petkan's street, with all its consequences, adorning his tale with a heap of wild and senseless fabrications and telling it with great animation.

In general, the misfortunes of others inevitably arouse three feelings in the minds of little people: first, amazement; second, satisfaction that they themselves have been spared; and third, a secret, spiteful joy. Such are the dark instincts hidden in the depths of human nature. As for Ganko, he had a more important reason for enjoying the doctor's misfortune, the latter having struck twelve coffees off his bill as the price of a visit. Ganko could not forigve him for such an unheard-of thing.

Marko could not get over his amazement. He had talked to the doctor the night before, but neither his face nor his conversation had betrayed anything extraordinary. Moreover the doctor would not have concealed such an affair from him. The appearance of the onbashi, who came into the café, gave Marko a chance to learn the facts for himself. He realized that the doctor was the victim of a terrible mistake on the part of the police, and also that Kralich had slipped through their fingers. Secret joy lit up his face. He turned to the onbashi, "I'll stake my head that the doctor is innocent!"

"Please God," said the onbashi, "but I don't see how he's going to clear himself."

"He'd manage it, but they may do him in first. When is the bey coming to the konak?"

"In an hour. He comes early."

"You must let the doctor out. I'll go bail for him—I'll stake my house and my children. He is innocent."

The onbashi looked at him in amazement. "There's no need to go bail for him; they've already taken him away."

"When? Where?" cried Marko.

"This very night, we sent him to K. on foot with zaptiehs." Marko's indignation flared up and he was unable to hide it.

The onbashi, who respected him, said to him in friendly though significant tones, "Marko Chorbadji, you would do better not to meddle in this business. What's the use? In these times nobody knows anybody well."

The onbashi drank up his coffee and went on, "I'll be setting out myself in half an hour with the bey's letter in which the doctor's rebel papers are enclosed. If you ask me they're all that matters, and they will cook his goose. Osman's wound doesn't seem to have been caused by the doctor—one of our men shot him, as can be seen by the wound. Well, that's for the bigwigs to see to. Ganko, give me a piece of paper you don't need, to wrap up the letter; I don't want to crush it." And he took a big envelope with a red seal out of his breast pocket and wrapped it up in the sheet of paper which the café-keeper gave him. After smoking another cigarette, the onbashi shook hands with Marko and left.

Marko stayed where he was, deep in thought. With his back turned to him, the cafe-keeper, who was also the barber, was already washing Petko Buzounyak's head. Marko got up and went out.

"Good-bye, Bai Marko! Why are you off so soon?" cried the barber, energetically rubbing his customer's head in its white waves of lather. "Or are you taking the doctor's troubles to heart? Everybody has to lie on the bed he's made for himself. Why don't they come to get Bai Petko Buzounyak? What d'you say, Buzounyak?"

The head burbled something through the lather, but nobody understood a word. The barber soon washed Buzounyak, dried his hair and face on a towel of doubtful cleanness, handed him the cracked mirror and wished him good health.

As he was going out to empty the slops in the street, he met Bai Marko on the threshold. "I've forgotten my tobacco box," he said and quickly went over to the bench where he had been sitting and had left it. Buzounyak left a coin on the mirror and went out. Ganko came back.

"Look here, Ganko, while we're about it, you might as well give me my bill and let me pay it. I pay at the end of the month," said Marko.

Ganko pointed to the ceiling on which there were rows of chalk marks. "There's your account, count up and pay me."

"But I don't see my name anywhere?"

"That's how I do things, à la Franca. . . ."

"With accounts like these you'll soon be down and out, Ganko," said Bai Marko jokingly, taking out his purse. "Why, just look, that fellow's forgotten his letter," he added pointing at the little shelf.

"Ah, the onbashi's letter!" cried Ganko and he threw a questioning glance at Marko, as if asking for his opinion.

"Send it to him, send it to him as quick as you can," said Marko frowning; "there you are, twenty-eight groats and a piastre, you've fleeced me properly, haven't you!"

Ganko looked at him in amazement, and whispered to himself: "What a strange man Bai Marko is. Ready to stake his house for that bear-dancer, and yet he doesn't throw this letter in the fire. It could have been done in the twinking of an eye. . . ." Just then new customers came in, and the café was soon filled with clouds of smoke and conversation about the doctor's misfortune.

chapter 7

heroism

The sun stood high in the heavens, sending its rays through the green vines that shaded the court of the monastery. This court was as calm, cheerful, quiet and bright by day as it had been gloomy and ugly by night, when every object took on a ghostly appearance. The birds filled it with their joyful chirping. The crystal jets of the fountain plashed pleasantly and merrily; the tall cypresses and poplars rustled gently in the morning breeze that came from the mountains. Everything was bright and festive here. Even the galleries with their gloomy cells all around seemed more attractive and rang to the twittering of the swallows which were flitting round their nests.

An imposing old man, bareheaded, with a white beard which reached down to his waist, and dressed in a long purple quilted coat moved out to the middle of the court under the vines. This was eighty-five-year-old Father Yerotei, an imposing relic of the last century, almost a ruin, but a mighty ruin, worthy of respect. He was living out the last days of his long life quietly and simply. Every morning he took his walk here, breathing the fresh mountain air and taking an almost child-like pleasure in the sun and the heavens towards which he was journeying.

Beside the trunk of the vine, close by, and in contrast to this monument of the past, stood Deacon Vikenti, book in hand—he was preparing to enter a Russian school of theology. Youth and hope were reflected in the young deacon's face; strength and life shone in his dreamy eyes. This young man was the future, and he faced it with the same confidence with which the old man faced eternity. Only the calm of monastery walls can dispose the soul to such meditation.

On the stone steps of the church sat tubby Father Gideon, profoundly occupied: he was carefully observing the turkeys which strutted about the yard, their tails spread out like fans. He compared them to the proud Pharisee in the Gospel, and their gobbling reminded him of wise King Solomon, who understood the language of the birds. Deep in these pious reflections, Father Gideon calmly awaited the blessed call to lunch, the sweetness of which he anticipated by taking in the pleasant aroma that emanated from the kitchen.

On its threshold the cross-eyed monastery idiot, Mooncho's companion, sat sunning himself. He observed the family life of the turkeys with no less philosophical profoundity than Father Gideon. However, observing the turkeys is scarcely the right expression here, since the idiot's view took in not only the turkeys' progeny, but the entire horizon as well, for one of his eyes looked east and the other west.

Next to him stood Mooncho himself, wringing his hands, turning his head and looking up timidly at the upper gallery. He knew why. With the addition of the abbot, who was absent, and a few laborers, we have the entire population of the monastery.

Unexpectedly the abbot came clattering up on his horse, dismounted and, handing the reins to the squint-eyed idiot, spoke gloomily to Vikenti. "I've been in town, and I have bad news." And he related all the details of Sokolov's misfortune. "Poor Sokolov," he ended, sighing.

Abbot Nathaniel was a big, strong, black, shaggy person with a manly face and energetic movements. Beyond his monk's habit, there was little of the monk about him. The walls of his cell were hung with guns; he was an excellent marksman, swore like a trooper, and was as skillful in healing as he was in inflicting bullet wounds. It was an accident that had made him abbot of a monastery rather than a voivoda* in the mountains.

"Where's Father Gideon?" asked the abbot looking around.

"Here I am," called Father Gideon in a squeaky voice, emerging from the kitchen. He had gone to see if lunch would be ready soon.

"You've been sneaking into the kitchen again, Father Gideon; don't you know that gluttony is a mortal sin?" And he told him to put the saddle-bags on the donkey and set out for the village of Voinyagovo, to make the rounds of the men who were mowing the monastery meadows.

Father Gideon was as tubby, round and greasy as a bladder of oil. The small exertion had brought the sweat of suffering out on his face. "Father abbot," spoke Father Gideon in a supplicating, breathless voice, his hands on his belly, for he had no desire for such a journey into the sinful world, "Father abbot, would it not be better to remove this bitter cup from your submissive brother?" And he bowed low to the abbot.

"What bitter cup? Am I asking you to go on foot? You'll ride the donkey and all you have to do in the villages is to hold the reins

---

* *voivoda:* commander, haidouk chieftain.

in one hand and bless people with the other." The abbot looked at him and grinned.

"Father Nathaniel, it's not the work; we are in this holy spot for work and active life, but the weather is bad."

"Why, what's wrong with the weather? An outing in May will be good for your health."

"Times, Father, I should have said the times," countered Father Gideon with animation. "Look, they have caught the doctor and the Christian may go to his doom. The children of Hagar are a merciless breed. God help us, should they accuse me of rousing the people, the monastery would suffer also! No small peril!"

The abbot guffawed. "Ha, ha, ha . . .," he went on laughing unrestrainedly, with arms akimbo, looking at Father Gideon's rotund body. "D'you think the Turks would suspect you? Father Gideon a political apostle! Ha, ha, ha! They say, set a sluggard to work and he'll teach you wisdom, don't they! The sin be on your soul, for you have made me laugh when I felt least like it. Deacon Vikenti! Deacon Vikenti! Come and hear what Gideon says. Mooncho, go and call Vikenti, or I'll choke with laughter." The abbot's wild laughter had indeed awakened the echoes of all the galleries around them.

When he heard this order, Mooncho twisted his head still more fearfully, his eyes wide with a dull terror. "Rouss-i-yan!" he cried out trembling, and pointed to the gallery to which the deacon had gone. Then so he would not be forced to go he strode off quickly in the opposite direction.

"Roussiyan! What does he mean by roussiyan?"

"A goblin, your reverence," explained Father Gideon.

"Since when has Mooncho grown so timid? He used to live on the moors like an owl."

"Truly, Father Nathaniel, an unclean spirit walks in the gallery. Last night Mooncho came to my cell. He was stiff with terror. He had seen a ghost in white garments come out of the cell with the glass windows. He told me other things too, but God only knows what. We must sprinkle holy water on the upper gallery."

Mooncho had stopped at a distance and was casting frightened glances at the gallery. "What can he have seen? Come, Father, let's make the rounds," said the abbot, who was suddenly struck by the thought that thieves might have broken in.

"The Lord preserve us!" said Gideon crossing himself. The abbot set out for the gallery alone.

When the abbot called him Deacon Vikenti had in fact gone in to

Kralich. "What's the news, Father?" the latter asked seeing the troubled expression on Vikenti's face.

"Nothing dangerous," the deacon answered quickly, "but the abbot has brought very bad news. Sokolov was arrested last night and taken to K."

"Who is this Sokolov?"

"A doctor in town, a nice boy. They found rebel papers in his coat. Who can tell? I knew he was an ardent patriot," said the deacon anxiously, then went on a moment later, "When the night watch chased him last night he shot at them with his pistol and wounded the zaptieh who pulled off his overcoat. He's lost, poor doctor. Thank heaven, you got off—and nothing has been heard about you in town."

When the deacon finished speaking he saw to his amazement that Kralich was holding his head in both hands, pacing back and forth like a madman and groaning dreadfully. At these signs of boundless despair he stood there quite startled and at a loss. "What are you doing? There's nothing wrong, thank heaven!" cried Vikenti.

Kralich stopped before him, his face distorted with anguish, and cried almost fiercely, "Nothing wrong, nothing wrong. That's easily said!" and he struck his brow. "What are you staring at me for, Vikenti? Don't you understand? Oh, my God, I forgot to tell you this morning that I was wearing that overcoat. Last night, near the town, a kind young fellow who showed me Bai Marko's house, probably this Sokolov, gave it to me, for my clothes were in rags, and afterwards I left it in the zaptieh's hands. I shifted the *Independence* and a proclamation I had been given at a hut near Troyan, where I spent the night, to the pocket of this coat. And as if that weren't enough, they have accused him of shooting the zaptieh when I never even touched my pistol. Oh, the devils! Do you see now? This man is my victim. I'm cursed by fate to bring misfortune to those who help me!"

"A great misfortune," whispered Vikenti bitterly. "It's a still greater pity that it's impossible to help him—as things are."

Kralich looked at him with a flaming face. "Why should it be impossible? Can I let such a noble man and good patriot, as you say, be destroyed because of me? That would be dastardly!" The deacon looked at him in amazement. "No, I'll save him from his misfortune, even if it cost me my life!"

"What can be done? Tell me! I'm ready for anything," cried Vikenti.

"I'll save him myself!"

"You!"

"Yes, I'll save him—I'm the one who must save him and can do so," cried Kralich with fervor, as he paced from end to end of the cell, his face set with terrible resolution and courage.

Vikenti stared at him astounded and frightened! Was the man out of his mind? he asked himself. He cried, "Mr. Kralich, how do you intend to save the doctor? Are we to attack the prison?"

"I shall give myself up."

"What! You'll give yourself up? Alone?"

"Do you want me to ask anybody else to do it? Listen, Father Vikenti, I'm an honest man and I don't want to buy my life at the cost of another man's suffering. I haven't traveled 600 hours to do something so base. If I can't give up my life gloriously, I can at least do it honorably. Do you see? If I don't present myself this very day before the Turkish authorities and tell them, this man is innocent and I have had no dealings with him, the coat was torn off my back, the papers were mine, I am the dangerous man, I am the guilty one, even—I shot the zaptieh, do what you will with me—then Doctor Sokolov is lost, particularly as he either cannot, or will not clear himself. Is there any other way, tell me?"

The deacon was silent. At the bottom of his honest heart he realized that Kralich was right. His sense of justice and humanity imposed this sacrifice on him, and he did not wait for others to remind him of his duty. The man now appeared to him more noble than ever and attracted him still more strongly. Vikenti saw him now lit by that radiance with which nobility illumines the human face. These words of Kralich's, energetic, direct and deeply felt, found a sweet and solemn echo in his heart. He would have liked to be in his place, to have spoken and carried out those words himself. Tears of emotion blurred his eyes.

"Show me the road to K.," said Kralich.

Suddenly the abbot's big shaggy head appeared at the window; they had not heard his footsteps on the gallery in their heated discussion. Kralich started, and cast a questioning glance at the deacon.

Vikenti ran out, drew the abbot to the balustrade and spoke to him long and earnestly, gesturing energetically and frequently glancing at the cell in which Kralich waited, impatient and deeply moved. When the door opened again, and Vikenti returned with Nathaniel, he greeted the abbot and asked for his hand to kiss.

"I am unworthy to have you kiss my hand," cried the abbot with tears in his eyes, and putting both arms round Kralich's neck he kissed him warmly on the lips, as a father kisses a long-lost son.

chapter 8

at Chorbadji Yordan's

There was a party at old Chorbadji Yordan's that day to celebrate a recent marriage in the family. All his friends and relations and associates had been invited.

Yordan Diamandiev, who was already an old man, and sickly, morose and irritable, was one of those Bulgarian chorbadjis who had made that term odious. His wealth grew apace, his numerous family flourished, his word was respected, but nobody loved him. Old injustices, his robbing of the poor, his intimacy with the Turks, had made him hated even when he no longer did any harm or was able to do any. He belonged entirely to the past.

In spite of Yordan's moodiness, the meal was a cheerful one. Aunt Ghinka, his married daughter, still good-looking, sociable, a chatterbox and a madcap who beat her mild husband when necessary, amused the guests with the jokes and banter which her indefatigable tongue rained right and left. The three nuns giggled the most. One of them, Gospozha Hadji Rovoahma,* Yordan's sister, a lame and spiteful scandal-monger, entered into Aunt Ghinka's mood and from time to time made cutting remarks on the absent. Hadji Smion, the host's brother-in-law, laughed heartily with his mouth full. Hadji Pavli, his son-in-law's father, also laughing heartily, was absent-minedly eating with Mihalaki Alafranga's fork; the latter, somewhat annoyed at this inattention, gazed around with a frown on his face.

Mihalaki well deserved the nickname of Alafranga.** Thirty years before he had been the first in town to wear trousers and to learn some French. But that was as far as he got. Even now his coat was still cut in the style prevalent during the Crimean War and his slender French vocabulary had grown no richer.

But his reputation as a learned man persisted, along with his flattering nickname. Mihalaki was well aware of this and was rather conceited; he always looked solemn, spoke pompously and allowed

* *gospozha:* Mrs.; an honorary title.

** In the French fashion.

no one to call him "Bai Mihal" because of Mihal the constable with whom he did not wish to be confused. Indeed, Mihalaki was very particular about his title. For years he had harbored a hatred of his neighbor Ivancho Yota because at a meeting the latter had called him Mihalaki Malafranga, thinking it was all the same.

Across from Alafranga sat Damyancho Grigor, a man of fifty, long-faced, thin, dark, who had a sly and waggish look and supple ironical lips, but an importantly solemn expression on his face. He was a voluble raconteur, with an inexhaustible fund of stories and an imagination as rich as Halim's treasury: he made an ocean out of a drop of water, a mountain out of a molehill, and when there was no molehill he just did nicely without it. The main thing was that he believed himself, which is the only way to make others believe one. In addition, Damyancho was one of the leading merchants, loved his country, and was a man of good counsel.

Aunt Ghinka's husband sat eating and looking straight ahead of him meekly. He did not dare to let himself go in her presence because whenever he happened to say anything or to laugh heartily, she threw him a withering look. Cowardly and weak, he had been quite effaced, and instead of her being called Ghinka Ghenkova, after him, he was known as Ghinka's Ghenko.

Next to him Necho Pironkov the councilor whispered in Kiriak Stefchov's ear from time to time; the latter, in his dandified clothes, nodded at him without listening and threw smiles at Lalka, Yordan's daughter. However this lack of attention brought its own punishment, for it entered Necho's head to clink glasses with him and the glass of wine spilled over Stefchov's white trousers.

This young man whom we have already met at the bey's, and who will play a further role in our tale, was a chorbadji both in spirit and background, being the son of a man just like Yordan Diamandiev. He was a young man with rusty notions who remained inaccessible to the new noble influence of liberal ideas. Perhaps that was why the Turks looked upon him with favor. Other young people kept him at arm's length, for they considered him a Turkish spy. His haughty nature, his spiteful and envious soul and his corrupt heart added to his general unpopularity. In spite of this, or because of it, Chorbadji Yordan had a weakness for Stefchov and never hid his good opinion of him or how well he was disposed to him. That was why, rightly or wrongly, rumor had singled out Stefchov as Yordan's future son-in-law.

The table was cleared and coffee was served by a tall, rosy-cheeked girl dressed in black to whom nobody paid the least attention. The conversation begun at the table was continued afterwards, thanks to Aunt Ghinka's active skill in sustaining it with her tireless loquacity. They soon came to the topic of the day, Sokolov's misadventure. This subject immediately focused all attention and gave a new and pleasant animation to their after-dinner ease.

"What is the doctoritsa* doing now?" laughed Gospozha Seraphima.

"Which doctoritsa?" asked the mother-in-law.

"Why, Cleopatra, mother-in-law."

"We ought to go and talk to her and remind her to write him a letter, for he'll be longing for his lady now," said Aunt Ghinka.

"Mihalaki," said the old lady turning to Alafranga, "what kind of a word is Cleopatra? Granny Kouna can't say it, but calls her Kalevra."

Mihalaki frowned, was thoughtfully silent for a while and then announced ponderously, "Cleopatra is a Hellenic, that is to say, a Grecian word; Cleopatra means weeps for, weeping. . . ."

"Weeping for the doctor, to put it simply," said Hadji Smion and then began a needless search through his coat pockets.

"Eh, well, that's her name," said Gospozha Hadji Rovoahma, "but somebody else is going to weep more for the doctor." And bending over Hadji Smion's wife and another matron she whispered in their ears. All three smiled slyly. These smiles infected the other guests.

"You don't say so, Ghina! The bey's wife herself?" asked Micho's wife amazed.

"Don't you doubt it. The wolf will take the sheep from the shepherd too," said Aunt Ghinka. More laughter.

"Kiriak! What were the papers they found on Sokolov?" asked Yordan who could not understand what his guests were laughing about.

"Rebel papers from the first line to the last. The bey sent for me in the middle of the night to translate them for him. They were the sort of sloppy nonsense, Bai Yordan, that only nitwits can think up. As for the proclamation of the Bucharest Committee it tells us to make a bonfire of everything, but to set ourselves free."

"All of you die, so we can be free," remarked Necho Pironkov ironically.

"These rascals, they burn and destroy right and left, but what do they burn? Other people's property. They have nothing to lose here.

* *doctoritsa:* feminine of doctor, the doctor's wife.

Bonfires indeed! That's easily done! Zanies and mountebanks!" said Chorbadji Yordan angrily.

"Scoundrels, the lot of them," said Hadji Smion.

Damyancho Grigor, who had so far been impatiently waiting for a subject for a long tale, seized on Hadji Smion's last words and said, "Scoundrels ye say, Hadji; that calls to mind there are scoundrels and scoundrels. . . . It happened once upon a time that I had to go to Shtip—that was in 1863—in May too, but on the 22nd, at three o'clock in the morning, on a Saturday, and cloudy weather. . . ."

Bai Damyancho then told an interminable tale of brigands, in which, furthermore, a part was played by the inn-keeper of Shtip, two pashas, a Greek captain and the sister of the Wallachian Prince Kouza. Everyone listened with great attention, if not with complete belief, to Damyancho's exciting tale as they savored their coffee.

"Lawks, if they want to burn, will they set fire to the convent too?" asked Gospozha Seraphima.

"May the fire of Heaven consume them," Gospozha Hadji Rovoahma broke out.

"Just think," Stefchov went on, "how corrupting the dissemination of such appalling stuff is. And it destroys the proper spirit of the young and makes them loafers, or leads them to the gallows. Just look at Sokolov—what a pity."

"A great pity, yes," assented Hadji Smion.

Mihalaki Alafranga spoke up. "Only yesterday, in a talk with the doctor, I discovered what gods he serves. He was lamenting that there are no Lyubobratiches here!"

"And what did you say to that?"

"I told him there were gallows, even if there were no Lyubobratiches."

"That was well put," commented Yordan.

"Well, what are these Lyubobratiches?" asked the curious old lady.

Ghinka's Ghenko, who read the *Pravo* regularly and knew all about politics, opened his mouth to answer, but Aunt Ghinka shot him a telling look and answered herself. "The voivoda of the Herzegovinians, Granny Dona. Eh, if we had a Lyubobratich, I'd be his standard-bearer, and we'd be off to cut cabbages."*

"Eh, if we had a Lyubobratich, things would be different then. Even I'd go over to his camp," said Hadji Smion.

* The green turbans worn by the Turks were contemptuously called cabbages.

Yordan looked at them sternly. You shouldn't even joke about such things, Ghina. Hadji, you're talking nonsense. . . ." Then turning to Alafranga he asked, "What'll happen to the doctor now?"

"According to the law," answered Stefchov, "it's death, or Diarbekir for life, for attacking an official. And he looked around triumphantly.

"Serves him right," twittered Hadji Rovoahma, "What's the convent done to him that he should burn it?"

"He was looking for trouble," said Necho the councilor. "Last night's shooting had something behind it."

"Shooting, you said, Necho, and that reminds me . . . ah, God save us, in the Crimean War, Ivan Boshnakov and I were on our way to Bosnia. I remember as if it were yesterday; it was a day or two before St. Nicholas' Day; night overtook us beyond Pirot when a terrible storm broke out, but what a storm!" And Grigor told how lightning had flashed over their heads, setting light to a walnut tree, killing fifty sheep and tearing off the tail of his bay horse, which he afterwards had to sell for next to nothing.

Grigor recounted this so conscientiously and with so much eloquence that his audience listened to him with unabated attention to the end. Stefchov and Necho looked at each other, grinning. Mihalaki leaned forward pompously, while Hadji Smion listened with his mouth open, amazed at the destructive force of Damyancho's lightning in winter.

While Damyancho was still telling his tale Aunt Ghinka had looked around for Lalka. "Where has Lalka gone, Rada? Go and call her," Hadji Rovoahma turned commandingly to the young girl in black.

After Stefchov's words, spoken with such cruel callousness, Lalka had quietly withdrawn and gone into one of the rooms; there she had thrown herself down on the window seat and begun to sob aloud. A flood of tears poured from her eyes as if they had long been pent up in one place. The poor girl sobbed so hard she could scarcely draw breath. Burning pity and sorrow were reflected in her face. Those people who jeered so heartlessly at the doctor's misfortune aroused her indignation, and increased her suffering. Dear God, how pitiless they were!

Tears bring relief even to the most desperate grief. The doctor's fate was not yet known, so there was still room for hope. Lalka rose, dried her pretty flower-like face and sat down at the open window to remove the traces of her tears as quickly as she could. She looked out listlessly without seeing the passers-by in the street who were walking along, carefree and indifferent. This cruel world did not exist for her; she wanted neither to see nor hear anyone, for her heart was completely filled by one person.

Her attention was suddenly caught by the clatter of horse's hoofs. She looked out and stood staring in amazement. There was Doctor Sokolov, gaily returning on a white horse. He bowed to her politely and passed on. In her joy she never even thought of answering him, but rushed back to the guests as if driven by an irresistible force, crying with emotion, "Doctor Sokolov has returned!"

Disagreeable surprise was painted on all faces. Stefchov went white, then spoke with feigned indifference. "They must be bringing him for a new examination. He won't escape Diarbekir or the rope as easily as all that." At the same moment he met Rada's contemptuous gaze which wounded him cruelly and a sudden blaze of anger reddened his face.

"Don't say that, Kiriak! I do hope he gets off, poor devil; I do pity his youth," said Aunt Ghinka with emotion. Her former mockery of the doctor had come from her tongue, not her heart. The bright spark in the human soul is always ready to ignite under the blows of suffering, as long as it is there in the first place.

It should be said to Hadji Smion's credit that he too was sincerely glad, but he did not dare express his feelings in front of Yordan, like his wild daughter, Aunt Ghinka.

chapter 9

explanations

As soon as the doctor got home, he went out, quickly passed Ganko's café, where many saluted him with "Gechmish-ola,"* the café-keeper himself most cordially, and went towards Marko's. As he was going in he noticed Stefchov passing by, on his way from Yordan's house.

"My salutations, sir interpreter," cried the doctor with a contemptuous smile.

Marko, having already lunched, was sitting on the small bench among the box trees, drinking his coffee. He gave the doctor an enthusiastic welcome. After cheerfully answering the congratulations of his friend, Sokolov said, "Now I'm going to make you laugh, Bai Marko."

"What was it all about?"

"I can't make it out myself. It's like a fairy tale, I can't believe it. Here I am, hauled off from home as soon as I got back from your house, and taken to the konak. You know all about how they questioned me and what they accused me of. Who would ever have thought that my shabby old coat would raise such a dust! So then they locked me up. After about an hour two zaptiehs came in. 'Doctor, get ready!' 'What for?' I asked. 'You're going to K. The bey's orders.' 'Very good.' So we left the prison and set out, one before me, one behind me, with rifles. We got to K. just at the break of day. There they shut me up again, because it was still early and the court was not yet in session. So I stayed there in the lock-up for four hours, which seemed like as many years to me. Finally they brought me up before the judge. There several councilors and notables read me some kind of minutes of which I understood nothing. More questions and more nonsense about my unlucky coat. There it lay on the green table, looking at me piteously. The cadi** opened a letter, evidently from our bigwig, took out the papers and asked, 'Are these your papers?' 'I don't know them.' 'How did they happen

* *gechmish-ola:* welcome.

** *cadi:* judge.

to be in your pocket then?' 'My hand never put them there.' He went on reading the letter. Bai Tinko Baltooglou took the newspaper and unfolded it. 'Effendim,' he said to the judge in a low voice, 'there is nothing unlawful in this paper, it's printed in Constantinople.' And he looked at me with a smile. I certainly understood nothing at all about the whole business and stood there like a log. The cadi asked: 'Isn't this a comitadji newspaper from Wallachia?' 'No, effendim,' answered Baltooglou, 'this paper says nothing of politics, it only talks about religion; it's a Protestant newspaper!' Then I looked at it, Bai Marko, and simply couldn't believe my eyes. It was *Zornitsa!* Tinko Baltooglou took the proclamation, read it, looked at me and laughed again. 'There's nothing seditious here either, effendim; it's an advertisement!' And he read aloud, *'Practical Handbook of Healing* by Dr. Ivan Bogorov.' The cadi looked amazed. They all began to laugh, the cadi laughed, and so did I. I couldn't help it. Who wouldn't have laughed? But the main thing was, how did that miraculous transformation of the papers come about? Well, anyhow. . . . After a short consultation with the notables the cadi said to me, 'Doctor, there's been a mistake here; excuse the inconvenience.' He called my being dragged from prison to prison and from konak to konak, inconvenience. 'Find some one to go bail for you, and go your way, safe and sound.' I stood there dazed."

"Well, didn't they say anything about the wounded zaptieh?"

"They never even asked me about him. As far as I could make out, our bey, whether some one suggested it or whether he thought of it himself I don't know, had gone into the matter thoroughly, and added in his letter that he did not consider me guilty of wounding the zaptieh. Probably the man himself admitted he was lying."

Marko's face was radiant with pleasure. He had assumed that Dyado Manol's son had fired the shot and had been anxious about possible consequences. "Now you're free, thank God!"

"As you see. But wait a minute, there's something more wonderful still," said the doctor after looking around to see that none of the family were around. 'Bai Nikolcho gave me his horse to return; he went bail for me too. I left K. and had just reached the Jewish cemetery when I saw two men coming from the mountains, one of them Deacon Vikenti who shouted to me to stop. 'Where are you off to, Dr. Sokolov?' he asked me, astonished to see me free. 'I'm going home. It was nothing.' His eyes nearly popped out of his head. I told him all about it. He threw himself on my neck, embraced me, hugged me. 'What's all this about, Deacon Vikenti?' 'Let me introduce you to this gentleman—Boicho Ognyanov,' and he indicated his companion. It was only then I looked at him. Well! I recognized him! It was the same man I gave my coat to last night!"

"What? Dyado Manol's son?" cried Marko involuntarily.

"Why? Do you know him?" asked the doctor astounded.

Marko pulled himself together. "Go on and we'll see," he said, deeply moved.

"We shook hands. He thanked me for the coat and begged my forgiveness in a despairing voice. 'Never mind, Mr. Ognyanov; I never regret it when I manage to do some one a good turn. And where are you going?' I asked. 'Mr. Ognyanov was coming to look for you here,' answered Vikenti. 'For me?' 'Yes, he wanted to save you.' 'To save me?' 'Yes, by giving himself up to the authorities and admitting he was guilty of everything.' 'Is that why you were coming here? Oh, Mr. Ognyanov, what were you going to do?' I cried in horror. 'My duty,' he answered simply. I couldn't control myself, tears came to my eyes and I hugged him in the middle of the road, as if he were my own brother. What a noble soul, eh, Bai Marko? What chivalry! Bulgaria needs people like that."

Marko said nothing. Two long tears were rolling down his cheeks. He was proud for Dyado Manol's sake. The doctor was silent for a while, then went on:

"We parted. They went off across country again, and I came straight here, but I'm still amazed at this meeting, and still more by the changed papers. I tell you that here I saw the *Independence* and the proclamation itself with my own eyes! How were they changed? Who changed them? Was it a mistake of the bey's? I keep racking my brains and can't make out a thing. Tell me what you think, Bai Marko?" and the doctor folded his arms and waited for an answer.

Marko sucked his chibouk importantly and with a barely perceptible smile on his lips said, "Don't you see that a friend must have done this? How can it be a mistake? You don't suppose the bey would have Protestant papers and Bogorov's news lying about?"

"But who is the unknown benefactor who saved me from danger and Ognyanov from sure destruction? Help me to think—I must thank him, I must kiss his hands and the hem of his coat."

Marko leaned toward the doctor and said in a low voice, "Listen, doctor. You must keep what I am going to tell you secret to your grave."

"I give my word of honor."

"It was I who changed the papers."

"You, Bai Marko!" cried the doctor jumping up.

"Sit down and keep quiet. And now listen. Very early this morning I went to Ganko's café and it was from him I first heard of your arrest. I was surprised and dazed. Just then the onbashi turned up and told me you had been sent to K. in the night, and that he was going there too with the bey's letter, in which the dangerous papers were enclosed. I didn't know what to do! The onbashi stayed a while and went out again. Then I saw he had forgotten the letter. Ganko was busy washing somebody's hair. I thought of hiding it and tearing it up, but that wouldn't have helped you much. They would still have dragged you around; suspicion would have remained. What was I to do? And I had no time to think. Then something came into my mind such as I had never thought of in all my life. You see me, doctor, my hair has grown white in trade, and I've never opened another man's letter. I always held that as most dishonorable, God forgive me, but I did it today for the first time in my life. I ran home, locked myself in my room, carefully unstuck the seal of the envelope and slipped in some other newspapers, whatever I found at hand. The Turks are pretty dense, you know. Then I put the envelope back in its place, without the café-keeper noticing. Thank God it all turned out well! My conscience doesn't bother me so much now."

The doctor listened, absorbed, then said with emotion, "Bai Marko, I am eternally grateful. You call this dishonorable—it was noble of you, a glorious act. You saved two people from ruin at the risk of your own life. A father would not have done more for his son." The doctor was so moved he could not go on.

Marko continued, "Last night Dyado Manol's son did find me, indeed, but he came over the wall and made such a racket that the police came."

"Boicho Ognyanov?"

"Is that what you call him? Yes, he. His father is a great friend of mine, and as he knew no one else, poor devil, he wanted to hide in my house. You brought him here. I didn't want to tell you in front of Ivancho, but he fled within the hour."

"Where did he come from?" asked the doctor, fascinated by the man.

"Didn't he tell you? He escaped from Diarbekir."

"From Diarbekir?"

"Softly. Where are you off to?"

"I'm going to the monastery, where the deacon is hiding him. I must talk to him. Will you let me tell him, only him, what you just confided to me? He should know to whom he owes his life, because he would have given himself up if they hadn't let me go."

"No, I beg you to keep silent about it as long as you live, and try to forget it. I only told you as a confession to unburden myself. Just give my greetings to Dyado Manol's son. Tell him to come and see me, but to come by the gate. . . ."

The doctor went out.

chapter 10

the convent

The convent in Byala Cherkva was a complete contrast to the monastery, hidden in the mountains and always silent and deserted. Here, on the contrary, sixty or seventy nuns, old and young, came and went the live-long day across the court and the galleries, filling with their cheerful talk the cloistered space which sheltered them from the vanity of the sinful world. This coming and going went on from morning to night.

The convent enjoyed the reputation of being the most fertile hotbed of gossip in the town. It was the cradle of all the scandal that went the rounds of the homes of the sinful laity, disturbing their peaceful hearths. Here engagements were foretold and arranged, and matches broken off. From here all the innocent little tales set out to make the rounds of the town and return again lively and well, having assumed colossal proportions on the way. Or, on the contrary, they would enter here as straws to emerge again as mountains. Such a bustling center drew flocks of visitors from the outside world, particularly on holidays, and these the pious women treated to town gossip and morello jam.

Gospozha Hadji Rovoahma, whose acquaintance we made at her brother Yordan's, was famed as the most skilful in nosing out every secret of the town and as the most adept at scandal. Once an abbess, she had been deposed by a revolt in this republic, but she still retained her moral leadership in it. Hadji Rovoahma was consulted about everything. It was she who checked the accuracy of true rumors, or sanctioned the false ones, she whose caprice dealt out the news which supplied the republic with mental nourishment for days on end before passing beyond its walls.

Gospozha Hadji Rovoahma was feeling cross these days at the liberation of Dr. Sokolov, a dangerous enemy of the convent. Secretly she was furious and wondered who had helped him. Who had deprived her of the pleasure of hearing new tales of his fate every day and of inventing others herself? What a shocking thing! For the last four or five days she had been a martyr to insomnia, sleep had fled her eyes. She racked her brains to discover why the doctor had refused to say where he had been at three o'clock on that memorable night when they arrested him. And then who had changed the papers? A brilliant idea finally flashed into her mind when she was reading her evening prayers. She clapped her hands joyfully, like Archimedes when he discovered his great law of physics. Then she went out and crossed the court to see Gospozha Seraphima, who was already undressed, and said to her in a trembling voice, "Sister, do you know where the doctor was that night when he wouldn't tell the bey?" Gospozha Seraphima pricked up her ears.

"With the bey's wife, I tell you!"

"Is it possible, hadjiika?"*

"That's it, Seraphima; that's why he won't tell. He's not crazy. Holy Virgin, and I didn't think of it before," said Hadji Rovoahma, standing before the icon-stand and crossing herself. "And do you know who set the doctor free?"

"Who, sister hadjiika?" asked Gospozha Seraphima.

"Why that one, I tell you!—The bey's wife again!"

"Good Lord, you don't say, hadjiika?"

"Oh, Blessed Virgin! Why didn't I realize it before!" Having thus unburdened her soul, Gospozha Hadji Rovoahma went back to finish her prayers and got into bed much relieved.

The next morning the whole convent was busy with the same conversation. The story of the doctor and the bey's wife was growing, and assuming ominous proportions. Every one who heard it asked, "Who found out?"

"Why, Gospozha Hadji Rovoahma." That name disarmed all the doubting Thomases. And all rushed to Hadji Rovoahma, greedy for particulars. Within two hours the rumor was all over town.

But every piece of news, no matter how interesting, grows stale in three days. Fresh fare was needed for the community, which was beginning to yawn. The appearance in town of Kralich, whom almost nobody seemed to know, again stirred up the convent, and it hummed anew. Who was he? Where had he come from? and why? Nobody knew. The most inquisitive went out into the town. But with the exception of the name they brought back contradictory data.

Gospozha Sophia said he had come to improve his health. Gospozha Ripsimiya averred that he was a merchant of attar of roses. Gospozha Nymphidora declared that he had come to seek a job as a teacher. Gospozha Solomona and Gospozha Paraskeva hinted that

---

* *hadjiika:* feminine of *hadji.*

it was neither the one nor the other, but that he had come as a suitor, they even knew the girl. . . .

Gospozha Apraxia swore that he was a Russian prince in disguise who had come to see the old fort and to give a present of vestments to their church. But few believed Gospozha Apraxia, because she had no connections with the best houses, but drew her news from Petko Buzounyak's wife and from Fachko Dobiche's in-laws; moreover, she was growing deaf.

Gospozha Hadji Rovoahma listened to all this chatter, and smiled slyly beneath her moustaches. She knew how matters stood, but wanted to torment the sisters a little. It was only late in the evening that the oracle spoke. By next morning all the convent knew that this unknown Ognyanov was a Turkish spy! One of the chief reasons, perhaps even the only one, why Hadji Rovoahma set such an ugly rumor afoot about Ognyanov, was that he had not yet paid his respects to her. This was a mortal affront to her vanity, and Ognyanov made himself a dangerous enemy thereby.

It was a Sunday. The service in the convent church was coming to an end; the place was packed with women. They had overflowed into the court and crowded around the church windows, under the huge pear tree with its many branches.

Some of them belonged to the laity, young brides and married women decked out and dressed up like dolls in many colors. They chattered gaily and kept glancing towards the convent gate to examine the clothes of the other representatives of the fair sex who continued to stream in. The others were nuns, mostly young ones who looked around no less noisily than their lay sisters, whispered to each other and often giggled aloud. From time to time they would descend in a swarm to pick a ripe, golden pear which was about to drop from the tree, even pushing each other in the struggle for the prize, then they would go back with flushed cheeks to join the congregation, crossing themselves.

The service ended. A stream of layfolk left the church, scattered in the yard and vanished into the cells.

Hadji Rovoahma's small cell, quiet and fairly richly furnished, was hardly big enough to hold her visitors. The nun received them and saw them off with smiling face, while Rada, in a clean black dress and kerchief, served jam and coffee on a red tray. An hour later the rush had subsided. Hadji Rovoahma often glanced out of the windows as if she expected some special guests. Several new ones came in, among them Alafranga, Stefchov, Father Stavri, Necho Pironkov and a young teacher. The nun's face brightened. She had evidently been waiting for them, and she shook hands amiably with the newcomers, who also shook hands with Rada. Stefchov even squeezed her hand and winked at her. This made the young girl blush hotly with shame, and she grew as red as a peony.

"Kiriak, I wanted to ask you again—what was going on with the doctor?" the nun asked after the usual greetings had been exchanged. "You know, a lot of nonsense is being talked about it."

"What are they saying?" asked Stefchov.

"They say that you made up on purpose in front of the bey that the papers were rebel ones, to slander Sokolov."

Stefchov flared up. "Whoever says that is an ass and a scoundrel. The *Independence* No. 30 and an appeal were taken out of his pocket. Bai Necho can tell you that too." Necho confirmed this with pleasure.

"There's no need to ask Necho. What does Necho know?" said Father Stavri. "We always knew what the doctor was like. Give him enough rope and he'll hang himself. I said so to Selyamsuz only the other day. I had gone to see him, to taste his new rakiya. He really knows the right amount of aniseed to put in. And you, hadjiika, are you well, are you in good health?"

"Just as you see me, father priest, I'm young with the young," the nun answered, then turned again to Stefchov: "But you don't know who changed the letters for him, eh?" Hadji Rovoahma's tongue itched to tell him of her discovery.

"The police will find out."

"Your police aren't worth a brass farthing. I'll tell you who it was." She grinned at him, then leaned over and whispered a name in his ear. But the secret was confided in such a loud whisper that everybody heard it.

Necho the councilor threw his beads* up in the air, laughing at the ceiling, the little teacher looked knowingly at some one else, while Father Stavri muttered, "Preserve us, O Lord, from the temptations of the Evil One."

Rada, embarrassed, took refuge next door.

"Look at him, look at him," cried Stefchov pointing at Sokolov, who was crossing the courtyard with two other men. One of them was Vikenti, the other, Kralich, dressed in new French clothes of gray homespun. They all crowded around the window.

This gave the nun the opportunity to announce her second discovery. "D'you know who that one is?"

"The stranger? He's a certain Boicho Ognyanov," answered

* A sort of rosary, but used for fidgeting with, not for prayers.

Stefchov, "but it seems to me he too will soon hang himself. . . ."

Hadji Rovoahma shook her head.

"You don't think so?" asked Stefchov.

"No, let's bet on it."

"He's a rebel."

"No, a spy!" said the nun emphatically. Stefchov looked at her bewildered.

"Even the deaf king has heard it; you're the only one who hasn't."

"Anathema!" muttered Father Stavri.

Hadji Rovoahma looked on spitefully to see where they would go. "They've gone in to Gospozha Christina!" she cried. Gospozha Christina had a bad reputation. She was known to be a patriot and to deal with the committees. Levski had once spent a night in her cell.

"Well, the deacons are fond of that pesky Christina," added Hadji Rovoahma with a malicious smile. "Do you know that Vikenti wants to shed his monk's cowl? And quite right of the lad, too. Who was it cooped him up so young?"

"He did well; either marry young or take your vows young," objected Father Stavri.

"It seems to me he'll be doing the former, father priest."

"God save us!"

"He'll be sending someone to ask for Orlyanko's girl. As soon as they accept his ring, he'll throw off his monk's habit and get married in Wallachia.—But I have an idea he won't have any luck." And the nun threw a knowing patronizing look at the little teacher for whom she herself intended the girl. The little teacher grew red with embarrassment.

Just then new visitors appeared. "Ah, brother's coming!" cried Hadji Rovoahma, running to meet Yordan Diamandiev. The visitors rose and followed her.

Stefchov lagged behind a little, caught Rada's hand to say good-bye and kissed her boldly on her flaming cheek. She struck him across the face and jumped back. "Aren't you ashamed of yourself?" she cried in a strangled voice and ran off to hide in tears.

Stefchov, as brutal with women as he was haughty with men, straightened his fez, which was awry from the blow, uttered fierce threats against Rada and went out, somewhat dazed by the blow.

chapter 11

Rada's emotions

Rada Gospozhina—as she was called to show that she belonged to Gospozha Hadji Rovoahma—was a tall, slender, beautiful girl with artless, bright eyes and a sweet, pure, delicate face which was further enhanced by the black kerchief she wore.

An orphan from childhood, Rada had long lived in the care of Hadji Rovoahma, who had taken her in as a foster-daughter. Her protectress had later made her a novice at the convent and dressed her in the black clothes they were obliged to wear. Rada now worked as a teacher of the girls in the first class for a salary of a thousand groats a year.

The life of all orphaned girls is a hard one. Deprived at an early age of a father's love and protection and of a mother's tender care, thrown at the mercy of people's charity or hard-heartedness, they grow up and live among indifferent strangers without feeling the warmth of a kind, life-giving smile. They are like flowers grown indoors, joyless and scentless. But if a ray of generous sunlight falls upon them, their hidden perfume scents the air.

Rada had grown up in the stifling and deadly atmosphere of the convent, under the stern, unfeeling supervision of the old mischief-maker. It had never occurred to Hadji Rovoahma that she might have treated the poor orphan more kindly, nor did she realize how irksome and unbearable her despotism had become as Rada's consciousness and human pride awoke in her. So it was that not long ago we saw Rada, already a schoolteacher, waiting on table like a servant at the house of Hadji Rovoahma's chorbadji brother.

Rada was particularly busy at school these days, as the annual examination was approaching. The day of the examination soon came. From early morning on the school filled up with schoolgirls, dressed up in their best, with neatly combed hair and decked out like butterflies by their mothers. Their books open in front of them, they hummed like a swarm of bees, reviewing their lessons for the last time.

The church service was over and people began crowding into the school, as was the custom, to see how the pupils had done that year.

Beautiful garlands decorated the doors, the windows and the teacher's desk; while the pictures of Saints Cyril and Methodius* looked down from the middle of a wonderful wreath of roses and fresh flowers, with sprigs of pine and box. The front benches were soon filled by the schoolgirls, while all the remaining room was taken up by the audience. The more prominent people stood near the front, and some were even given chairs. A number of our acquaintances were among them. A few chairs remained, however, for the distinguished visitors that were expected.

Rada was shyly seating the girls and giving some instructions in a low voice. Her sweet face, animated by the emotion of the solemn occasion and brightened by her big luminous eyes, grew enchantingly beautiful. The flush of color on her cheeks, like a transparent cloud, did not hide the trepidation in her sensitive soul. Rada felt a hundred curious glances falling on her and was ill at ease, losing her self-possession. However, as soon as the headmistress began her speech and attracted the attention of the crowd, Rada felt a sense of relief and looked about her with more self-assurance than before. She noted with pleasure that Kiriak Stefchov was not there. Her courage revived. The speech came to an end amid solemn silence—the custom of applauding had not yet been introduced at that time.

According to the program the examination was to begin with the first class. The calm and goodnatured face of the headmaster Kliment and his kind manner gave the little girls confidence. Rada followed their answers with rapt attention and their occasional slips were painfully reflected in her face. These clear ringing little voices, these small rosy mouths which asked for kisses, were to seal her fate. She poured the radiance of her look upon them, she encouraged them with a heavenly smile, her soul hung on their tremulous words.

At that moment the crowd around the door was pushed aside to make room for two belated visitors who quietly occupied the empty chairs. Rada looked up and saw them. One of them, the older man, was a member of the School Board, Chorbadji Micho, the other—Kiriak Stefchov. An involuntary pallor spread over her face. But she tried not to see this unpleasant person who so troubled and frightened her.

Kiriak Stefchov exchanged a few greetings with a nod of his head, without however shaking hands with Sokolov, his neighbor, who never even glanced at him; he crossed his legs and began to look around moodily and haughtily. He listened absent-mindedly, often

---

* Inventors of the Cyrillic alphabet and patron saints of schools and learning.

looking in the direction of the group where Lalka Yordanova sat. Only once or twice did he eye Rada from head to foot, sternly and disdainfully. His arid soul and his cruelty were clearly marked on his face. He often raised a carnation to his nose and then looked around again, conceited and indifferent. Kliment, the teacher, turned to Mihalaki Alafranga with the book. Mihalaki refused and said he would examine in French. The teacher turned to the right and repeated the invitation to Stefchov. He accepted and moved his chair slightly forward.

A murmur ran through the crowd. All eyes were bent on Kiriak. The subject he was examining in was Bulgarian history, the abridged version. Stefchov left the book on the table, rubbed his temples as if to stir his brain and loudly asked a question. The little girl was silent. The cold, unpleasant look penetrated into her childish soul like an icy blast. She was frightened and could not even remember the question. She looked at Rada piteously as if begging for help. Stefchov repeated the question. Again she was silent.

"Let her go," he said drily to the teacher, "call another one." Another little girl came up. She was asked a question. She heard it, but did not understand it, and stood there speechless. The whole audience was silent and stirred uneasily. The little girl stood as if nailed to the spot, but her eyes filled with tears of grief which dared not fall. Again she forced herself to say something by way of an answer, stammered painfully and was silent. Stefchov gave Rada an icy look and murmured, "Rather careless teaching. Call another girl." Rada called out another name in a toneless voice. The third schoolgirl answered at random; she hadn't understood the question. When she saw disapproval on Stefchov's face, she grew bewildered, then looked despairingly about her. Stefchov asked her another question. This time the girl didn't answer at all. Her eyes became blurred with confusion, her bloodless lips started to tremble and she suddenly burst out crying and made a dash for her mother. Everyone felt pained and heavy at heart. The mothers whose daughters had not yet been examined looked straight before them in bewilderment and fright. Every mother trembled with fear that her child's name would be called.

Rada stood there dumbfounded. Not a drop of blood was left in her face; her pale cheeks quivered; several large drops of perspiration stood out on her forehead and her temples, nor was there a trace of the delicate feelings reflected there before. She was afraid to raise her eyes. She felt the earth sinking beneath her. Something was stifling her, she felt like crying aloud, and could hardly restrain herself.

The audience, unable to bear the strain any longer, broke into restless murmurings. People looked at each other in amazement, as if to ask what was wrong. Everyone longed to find a way out of this impossible situation. The noise, the protests grew louder. Suddenly dead silence fell and all eyes were drawn to the front. Boicho Ognyanov, who had been standing there half-hidden till then, stepped out from the audience and, turning to Stefchov, said firmly, "I don't have the honor of knowing you, sir, so you will excuse me. Your questions are not clear and too abstract. Even pupils of the fifth class would find them difficult. Have pity on these inexperienced children. . . ."

Then, turning to Rada, he asked, "May I have your permission, ma'am?" And as he stood there he asked for one of the little girls who had already been examined to be called.

There was general relief. Ognyanov's action was greeted with exclamations of sympathy and approval. In a moment he had everyone looking at him and had won everyone's sympathy. The slander spread by Hadji Rovoahma fell flat. His noble face, pale with suffering and lit up by a strong and manly look, won all hearts irresistibly. People's faces cleared, they began to breathe freely. It was evident to all that Ognyanov was master of the situation. And everyone was pleased.

Ognyanov asked the girl quite simply the same questions she had been asked by Stefchov. This time she answered. The mothers heaved a sigh of relief and sent looks full of gratitude to the stranger. His name, new and strange, went from mouth to mouth and was engraved in all hearts.

The other little girl was called. She too gave a satisfactory answer, for her age. Then all these children, frightened out of their wits a moment ago, gave Ognyanov friendly glances. Their spirits rose; they squabbled about who should be the first to talk with this good man, whom they had already grown to love.

Rada felt an increasing sense of wonder. Astonished, moved to tears, surprised, she cast a grateful look at this great-hearted man who had come to her aid at so difficult a moment. This was the first time she had come across a warm expression of brotherhood, and from a stranger at that. Could this be the spy? There he was standing before her like a guardian angel! He had crushed Stefchov like a worm. She was jubilant, her spirits soared, she looked all around her with pride and joy, and from all quarters met looks of sympathy. Gratitude welled up in her, tears rose to her eyes. . . .

Ognyanov asked the third little girl the following question: "Raina, now tell us: under which Bulgarian king did the Bulgarians become Christians and were baptized?" And he looked in that calm and friendly way of his into those innocent little eyes, now turned towards him and still bearing traces of tears.

The little girl spent some time in thought, moving her lips, then in a clear, ringing, high voice like that of a lark singing in the morning air said: "The Bulgarian Tsar Boris baptized the Bulgarians."

"Very good, bravo, Raina. . . . Now tell me: who invented the Bulgarian alphabet?"

The little girl found this question rather difficult. After blinking a few times to help her thoughts, she was about to say something, but checked herself, hesitated, about to lose her head. Ognyanov came to her aid. "Who wrote our ABC, Raina?"

She brightened. She stretched out her little arm, bare to the elbow, without saying a word. She pointed to Saints Cyril and Methodius, who looked down upon her benevolently. "That's right, that's right, it was Saints Cyril and Methodius," a few voices chimed in from the front seats.

"God bless you, Raina! Saints Cyril and Methodius, may they help you to become a queen too," said Stavri the priest, deeply moved.

"Well done, Raina, go to your seat," said Ognyanov pleasantly. The triumphant Raina, beaming all over, ran off to her mother, who embraced her and pressed her to her heart, covering her with ecstatic kisses and tears. Ognyanov turned to the headmaster Kliment and handed him the book.

"Do examine our Subka, won't you, sir?" said Chorbadji Micho to Ognyanov.

A lively, fair haired little girl stood before him, looking at him meekly. After some thought Ognyanov asked her: "Subka, now tell me: which Bulgarian king liberated the Bulgarians from Greek oppression?"

"The Bulgarians were freed from the Turkish yoke . . ." the little girl began mistakenly.

"Subka, stop!" Chorbadji Micho cried out. "You just name the king that liberated them from the Greek yoke, dear, there's a king all right to free them from the Turks. . . ."

"God's will be done," said Stavri the priest. Chorbadji Micho's naive hint called forth many sympathizing smiles. Whispering and suppressed laughter swept the hall.

Subka spoke out in ringing tones, "It was Tsar Assen who liberated the Bulgarians from the Greeks, and Tsar Alexander of Russia will save them from the Turkish yoke!" She had misunderstood her father's words.

A hush fell upon the audience after the little girl's words. Many faces expressed bewilderment and disquiet. Mechanically all eyes turned on Rada who blushed scarlet and bowed her head in confusion. Her bosom heaved with emotion. Some of these looks were reproachful, others approving. But all felt ill at ease. Stefchov, who had till this moment felt crushed, now raised his head again with a look of triumph. Everyone knew of his intimacy with the bey and of his fondness for the Turks, and searched his face for some sign. The general sympathy, which only a moment ago had gone out so warmly to Rada and Ognyanov, now cooled down and was mingled with some resentment. Stefchov's followers voiced their protest with glee; those who favored the teacher kept silent. The old priest Stavri was very upset. He was now frightened at his own words and repeated the litany to himself.

The two camps stood out more clearly in the women's section. Hadji Rovoahma, who was particularly enraged because Stefchov had been put to shame, glared fiercely at Rada and Ognyanov and was most vociferous. She even called the latter "a revolutionary," forgetting that only a few days ago she had called him a spy. There were others who no less boldly championed them. Aunt Ghinka was shouting so loudly as to be heard all around, "Why are you all so dumbfounded! You'd think the poor girl had crucified the Lord! She's right, too! I for one also say that Tsar Alexander and no one else will deliver us!"

"You crazy creature, hold your tongue, can't you!" her mother said in a whisper. Subka herself stood there the picture of dejection. She kept hearing these things every day from her father and his guests, and couldn't make out what all the commotion was about.

Stefchov stood up and turned to the front seats: "Gentlemen, revolutionary ideas against the State of His Majesty the Sultan are being voiced. I cannot remain here. . . ." Necho Pironkov and three or four others went out after him. But Stefchov's example was not followed by others.

After a moment's dismay people realized that the matter should not be given undue attention. A child in her innocence had spoken a few misplaced, but nevertheless true words. Well, what of it? Quiet reigned again, and along with it the original feeling of sympathy for Ognyanov, on whom friendly looks were showered from all sides. He was the hero of the day; all honest hearts and all mothers were on his side.

The examination continued and came to an end without further disturbance. The schoolgirls sang a song and the people went their way well pleased. When Ognyanov approached Rada to say good-bye to her, she said to him with emotion, "Mr. Ognyanov, I thank you with all my heart, for myself and my little girls. I shall never forget this kindness." And her eyes were radiant.

"I have been a teacher myself, ma'am. I congratulate you on the success of your pupils." And he shook her hand warmly and left. After he had gone Rada saw none of the guests who were bidding her good-bye.

chapter 12

Boicho Ognyanov

The appearance in public of Boicho Ognyanov (for Kralich took the name under which Vikenti had spontaneously introduced him to Sokolov at their meeting near the cemetery of K.), an appearance which immediately aroused comment, had been decided on after consultation with his new friends—Vikenti, Dr. Sokolov and the abbot. At first they would not agree to it, but Ognyanov easily allayed their fears. He assured them that from distant Vidin, where almost none of the inhabitants of Byala Cherkva ever went, except Marko Ivanov, hardly anyone knew him and was even less likely to recognize him. His eight years of exile in Asia, the hardships and the climate, had aged him and changed him completely.

Instead of cooling his ardor for the cause for which he had suffered, his exile with all its attendant hardships had brought him back more enthusiastic than ever, more of an idealist, fearless to the bounds of recklessness, fanatically in love with Bulgaria, and honorable to the point of self-sacrifice. Stirring events have shown him to us in action. Yes, he had returned to Bulgaria to work for her liberation. For a man like him, who had escaped from forced exile and was living here under an assumed name, a man without any family or social ties, exposed at every hour to discovery or betrayal, without any future, without any hope in life—only a great cause such as this could have served to bring him back to Bulgaria and to keep him there after the double murder. . . . How was he to work and be useful? How did the land lie here? What could he do? Was his purpose attainable? He did not know. He only knew that he would meet with great obstacles and perils, which were not slow to bear down on him from the very first hour.

But for such chivalrous natures, obstacles and perils are the element in which their strength is tempered. Opposition invigorates them, persecution attracts them, danger whets their appetites, for they mean a struggle, and every struggle rouses a man's spirit and ennobles him. It is fine in a worm, that it raises its head to bite the foot that has trodden on it; it is heroic that a man will fight for self-preservation; it is god-like when such a contest is undertaken for mankind.

In the first days the rumor Hadji Rovoahma had spread kept away the people his friends wanted him to know. But his generous behavior at the examination immediately closed the month of slander and opened all doors and all hearts to him. Ognyanov became a welcome guest to the whole town. He gladly accepted the invitation of Marko Ivanov and Micho Beizadé and became a schoolmaster to make his stay in the town more plausible.

His colleagues were Kliment Belchev, the headmaster, Frangov, Popov, the usher, and Stefan Merdevendjiev, the cantor, who also taught Turkish. The first was a Russian seminarian, and as such, goodnatured, impractical and enthusiastic; whenever the trustees went to see him, he recited verses by Homyakov and Derzhavin's *God* to them. But Bai Marko preferred to hear him tell about the greatness of Russia, and about Bonaparte. . . . The third was a hotheaded, enthusiastic boy, formerly a friend of Levski's, who dreamed and thought of nothing but committees, revolutions and detachments. He gave his new colleague an enthusiastic welcome and became passionately attached to him. Only Merdevendjiev was a repulsive creature, with his devotion to the psalter and his love of the Turkish language. The first indicated a mildewed mind, the second, a votary of the scourge, because for a Bulgarian to love the Turkish language meant love of the Turks themselves, or expectation of Turkish favor. Quite naturally this similarity of tastes bound him closely to Stefchov.

In line with his duties, Ognyanov taught in the girl's school too, so he saw Rada daily. Every day he discovered new delightful traits of character in this girl, and one morning he awoke to find himself in love with her. Needless, to say, she already loved him in secret. From the very day on which he had so generously defended her, she fell captive to that strong feeling of warm gratitude, which is gratitude at one moment and love the next. This poor heart, so thirsty for tenderness and sympathy, fell in love with Ognyanov ardently, purely and without limit. She saw in him the once vague ideal of her dreams and hopes, and under the charm of this life-giving feeling Rada began to bloom and to grow as lovely as a May rose.

Neither much time nor much beating about the bush was needed for these two open and honest hearts to come to an understanding. Every day Ognyanov parted from her more fascinated and happy. This love blossomed and spread its perfume through his heart by the side of his other love. The one—a gigantic pine which awaited stormy blizzards; the other—a tender flower, thirsty for sunlight and for dew—both sprung from the same soil, but lit by two different suns. . . .

Yet sad thoughts often fell like lead upon his heart. What would become of this innocent creature whom he was involving in his unknown fate? Where was he leading her? What lay ahead of them? He, the fighter, the man of danger and hardship, was dragging this pure, loving child who had just begun to live, warmed by the beneficent rays of love, along his terrible road. She wanted, she expected of him a clear and happy future, calm and joyful days under the new sky she had created for herself. Why should this girl be compelled to feel the blows which fate had in store for Ognyanov alone?

No, he would have to reveal everything to her, to remove the veil of her blindness, to tell her with what kind of a man she was binding her fate. These thoughts weighed heavily upon his honest soul, and he decided to find relief in an open declaration and confession.

He set out to speak to Rada. She had moved from the convent to a room in the school, modestly and poorly furnished. Its only pleasant ornament was the occupant herself.

Ognyanov opened the door and went in. Rada greeted him with a smile through her tears. "Rada, you've been crying! Why these tears, my darling?" and he tenderly took her head in his arms, stroking her blushing cheek. She drew back, drying her eyes.

"Why this?" asked Ognyanov, amazed.

"Gospozha Hadji Rovoahma was here a while ago," answered Rada through her sobs.

"And she hurt you? Did she try to tyrannize over you again? Why, my songs . . . just see, some one has trampled on them. Radka, please explain to me!"

"That was it, Boicho, Gospozha Hadji Rovoahma trampled on them; she found them on the table. 'Rebel songs!' she cried and said such ugly things about you, so how could I help crying?"

Ognyanov grew serious. "What ugly things could she say about me?"

"What didn't she say? She called you a rebel, a haidouk, a bloodthirsty villian! . . . Good heavens, how could she have the heart?"

Ognyanov looked at Radka thoughtfully, then said, "Listen, Radka, we've become closer, you and I, but we don't really know each other, or rather, you don't know me. . . . That's my fault. Would you love me if I was what they make me out to be?"

"No, Boicho, I do know you well; you are the noblest of men and that's why I love you." And like a child she put her arms around his neck and looked at him lovingly. He smiled bitterly, touched by this simple trust.

"And you know me, too, don't you? Otherwise we wouldn't love each other," whispered Rada, looking at him with her big ardent eyes.

Ognyanov kissed them lovingly and said, "Radka, my own, my child, if I am to be the noble man you think me I must tell you things which you don't know. My love wouldn't let me hurt you, but my conscience dictates otherwise. You must know what kind of man you are joining your fate to. . . . I have no right to be silent any longer. . . ."

"Tell me everything; you'll still be the same to me," she said, troubled.

Ognyanov made her sit down, then sat himself down beside her. "Radka, Hadji Rovoahma said that I was a rebel. She doesn't know. She calls every honest young man a rebel."

"That's it, Boicho; she's a very spiteful woman," said Radka quickly.

"But I really am one, Radka." Radka looked at him in surprise. "Yes, Radka, a rebel and not only in words, one who thinks of preparing an uprising." He was silent a while. She answered nothing. "We are thinking of raising a rebellion in the spring; that's why I'm in this town." Rada was silent. "That's my future, an uncertain future, full of dangers. . . ." Rada looked at him in amazement but never said a word.

In this cold silence Ognyanov read his doom. At every word of his the girl's devotion was vanishing into thin air. He made an effort and went on with his confession. "That's my future. Now let me tell you my past." Rada fixed her troubled eyes on him.

"It's still darker, if not stormier. You must know that I was exiled to Asia for eight years for political reasons . . . and I escaped from Diarbekir, Radka!" Rada sat as though thunderstruck. "Tell me, Radka, did the nun mention that?"

"I don't know," answered Rada drily.

Ognyanov remained in gloomy thought for a moment and then went on. "She calls me a bloodthirsty villian and a murderer. . . . She doesn't know that either, Radka. A short while ago she called me a spy. But listen. . . ." This time Rada felt there was something terrible coming and went white.

"Listen, I killed two men, and not so long ago at that!" Rada drew back involuntarily. Ognyanov did not dare look at her; he talked on to the wall. His heart was breaking as if iron pincers were tearing it apart.

"Yes, I killed two Turks; I who wouldn't hurt a fly. . . . I had to kill them, because they were going to rape a girl before my very eyes—in front of me and in front of her father, whom they had tied up. Yes, I'm a bloodthirsty villian and Diarbekir threatens me again, or—the gallows."

"Go on, go on . . ." she whispered faintly.

"I've told you everything; you know all about me," Ognyanov answered in a trembling voice. He expected to hear the terrible sentence he read in her face.

Rada threw her arms around his neck. "You are mine, you are the noblest of men," she cried. "You are my hero, my handsome knight." And the two young people embraced passionately, sobbing with love and happiness.

chapter 13

the pamphlet

Heavy steps resounded on the stairs outside. Whoever was coming up walked so heavily and at such a mad pace that the whole wooden building shook. This put an end to the rapturous embrace of the young couple.

Boicho raised his head to listen and said, "That whirlwind must be the doctor." Rada went over to the window and put her hot face against the pane to hide her emotion.

The doctor came into the room in his usual rush. "Read this," he said, thrusting a pamphlet into Ognyanov's hand. "It's strong language, by God . . . enough to set you off! . . . Oh, if I could kiss the golden hand that wrote it!"

Ognyanov opened the pamphlet. It had been published by the emigrants in Rumania. Like most of these outpourings, this one too was a somewhat mediocre compilation, crammed with patriotic phrases worn threadbare by constant use, commonplace rhetorics, desperate exclamations and curses against the Turks. But that was just why it aroused the enthusiasm of the people in Bulgaria who hungered for each new message. The sad state of its leaves, soiled and dog-eared, almost falling apart from much handling, showed that it had passed through hundreds of hands and fed thousands of persons with its fiery fare.

Sokolov was almost intoxicated from reading it. Ognyanov himself, though his taste in literature was more developed, was delighted with it and could not tear his eyes from the booklet. The doctor watched him greedily and impatiently snatched it from his hands.

"Give it to me; let me read it to you!" he cried, and began to read aloud, growing more and more enthusiastic, sawing the air with his right hand, stamping his foot at every strong phrase and darting flashing looks at Boicho and Rada, in whose souls the sweet emotions of a short while ago were replaced by Sokolov's fierce enthusiasm. The room and even the whole school rang to the thunder of his voice, which ran up a whole octave.

When he had read most of the pamphlet and reached the long

poem with which it ended, he stopped, trembling and covered with sweat, and turning to Ognyanov cried:

"Hot words, brother, very hot words! . . . There, you read this. I'm tired. . . . No, give it to me; you read songs like Father Stavri reading prayers. You'll spoil my impression. You read it, Radka!"

"Yes, you read it, Radka, you recite well!" said Ognyanov.

The young girl began to read. Like the prose of the pamphlet, the poem was distinguished by much lachrymose pathos, digressions and lack of talent, but Rada read with understanding and skill. Her ringing, tremulous voice gave every verse a semblance of life and power.

The doctor drank in every word and kept stamping on the floor. At the most interesting place the door was opened without warning and the caretaker's old wife came in. "Did you call me?" she asked.

The doctor looked at her fiercely, gave her a push without speaking a word and kicked the door hard, locking it behind her. The unfortunate old woman, who lived below, went down abashed, and told her grandchildren to keep quiet because schoolmistress was giving schoolmaster and the doctor a lesson.

"Who the devil is that now?" roared the doctor in despair. "I'll throw him out of the window," and he opened the door. A little girl came in with a letter in her hand.

"Who's that for?" he asked roughly. The little girl went up to Radka and handed her the letter. Rada looked at the address, which was written in a hand she did not know, in surprise, and opening the letter, she began to read it.

Boicho stood there, no less surprised, and watched her. He saw her flush and at last smile. "What is it?" asked Boicho.

"A letter. There, read it!" Boicho took it. It was a love letter from Merdevendjiev.

Boicho laughed loudly. "Oh, that Merdevendjiev! So he's my rival now, Rada, and a terrible one too. It's a wonder that empty skull ever managed to hammer such a letter out! We must have a look at the letter-book and find out from how many different places he's taken sentences to patch it together." Rada laughingly tore up the letter.

"Why did you tear it up? You should answer it!" Sokolov told her.

"How can I answer it?"

"Write: 'O-o-o-oh, most sweet-voiced nightingale! O-o-o-oh, musicological gander! O-o-o-oh tender-hearted popinjay!' I had the honor today, at the hour of six," Sokolov went on, looking at his watch, then he added to Boicho: "You see, that ninny's an awful little sneak. . . . D'you see the loathsome intriguer? A spy, eh? My compliments! When you go to school today spit at him. If I were you I'd box his ears."

"Just a fool—let him be!"

"No, no, it's not enough to despise sneaks, you must punish them. . . . You leave that to me!" said the doctor threateningly.

"Better let well enough alone. Never throw a stone in a muddy pool; it's sure to splash you. . . ."

"Ah, wait!" cried the doctor putting a hand to his brow as if to retain a thought that had just come into his head.

"What?"

"Just something! You wait!" and he laughed out loud. Ognyanov gave him a questioning look.

"Nothing, nothing. . . . Goodbye. . . . And don't forget tomorrow, at Silistra-Yolou!"

"What, again? Why, what a Sardanapalus you are, eh?"

"I'll see you later, good-bye!"

He went home and wrote the following note to Merdevendjiev, imitating a woman's writing:

"Thank you. I find it inconvenient to correspond. I await you tonight at Granny Yakimcha's garden. The gate will be open. Oh! Oh!

September 28, 1875.

You know who."

The cantor was punctual at the rendezvous. Instead of Rada it was Cleopatra who greeted him with a terrible roar, for Sokolov had taken her there and kept her tied up in a dark corner of the garden, which was next to his house.

chapter 14

Silistra-Yolou

Silistra-Yolou, or the road to Silistra, was the name of a lovely green meadow by the side of the Monastery River in the valley of the monastery, which was surrounded by branching willows, tall elms and walnuts. Although it was already autumn, this lovely spot, because it was sheltered, still kept its green freshness, like Calypso's isle where eternal spring reigned. Through the leafy branches two peaks of Stara Planina were visible to the north of this happy meadow —the Crook and Needle Peak. Between them the mountain gorges closed in with their steep gullies and overhanging rocks and at their foot the river flowed noisily. The cool mountain breeze gently shook the leaves and brought mountain scents and the dull thunder of the waterfalls. Beyond, across the river, white cliffs rose steeply, terribly slashed and furrowed by torrents.

The sun was moving towards noon and its rays, passing through the leaves, showered down a rain of quivering gold flakes on the meadow. A wonderful freshness and joy reigned in this poetic spot which bore such a prosaic and inaccurate name, for no road, either to Silistra or anywhere else, passed through this lonely meadow which nestled so agreeably among the almost inaccessible foothills of Stara Planina.

Its name came not from its geographical situation but from another circumstance, a historical one so to speak. Its seclusion, beauty and coolness had for many years made this a favorite spot for all excursions, parties and picnics. In this Byala Cherkva Capua many frivolous merchants had ruined themselves and many heirs to rich estates had run through their inheritance. Afterwards they had gone to seek new profits in Silistra where, thanks to the undeveloped and abundant resources of that region, they easily made a living and even grew rich again.

The success of these first Jasons from Byala Cherkva had attracted other ruined brothers to that promised land, the plain of Silistra. Thus by this time Silistra and its villages contained numerous settlers from Byala Cherkva who played a role as pioneers of civilization there. Among other things they gave the region some ten priests and twenty-two teachers. All that aside, for the inhabitants of Byala Cherkva, here was the quickest road to Silistra.

In spite of its fatal significance the fame of Silistra-Yolou still flourished and attracted those who enjoyed making merry and feasting. And they were many. For along with its evils, oppression has one advantage—it makes people merry. Where the arena of political and intellectual activity is closed with lock and key, where the appetite for rapidly acquiring wealth has nothing to arouse it, where great ambitions find no scope, society spends its energies on petty local and personal intrigues and looks for the consolation and distraction offered by the small, ordinary and easy joys of life. A flask of wine drunk in the cool shade of willows by a babbling, crystal-clear river makes one forget slavery; a stew baked with red tomatoes, fragrant parsley and hot peppers, eaten on the grass under the hanging branches through which you see the blue sky high above is a kingdom in itself, and if there are fiddlers, it is the height of earthly bliss.

Oppressed peoples have their own philosophy which reconciles them to life. An irremediably ruined man often ends with a bullet in his brain or in a noose. People enslaved, no matter how hopelessly, never commit suicide; they eat, drink and beget children. They amuse themselves. Look at the folk-songs in which the people's soul, life and outlook are so strikingly reflected. There, intertwined with black sorrow, long chains, dark dungeons and festering wounds are paeans to roast lambs, ruby-red wines, burning brandy, joyful weddings, boisterous dances, green forests and shady bowers, from which whole oceans of songs have sprung.

When Sokolov and Ognyanov arrived, Silistra-Yolou already rang to the noise of the gay company. Among others, Nikola Nedkovich, an educated and intelligent young man, was there, as were Kandov, a student at a Russian university who had come home to recover his health, a well-read man and an extreme ideologist, who was carried away by the utopias of socialism; Fratyu Frangov, a school teacher and a hot-head; Popov, an exalted patriot, Father Dimcho, also a patriot and a drunkard, and Blind Kolcho. The latter, who was entirely blind, was a small young man with a haggard, suffering, and intelligent face. He was gifted at playing the flute, with which he traveled all over Bulgaria, a great story-teller and wit, and therefore indispensable at any festive occasion.

The meal had already been set out on a bright cloth on the grass. Two demijohns of wine, one white, one red, were cooling in the mill-stream, which ran past the meadow itself. The Gipsies were drawing their bows over their rebecs and throatily singing Turkish songs. A clarinet and two tambourines with rattling metal discs completed this noisy orchestra. The meal was a very cheerful one. Toasts followed each other in rapid succession, and were proposed seated as was the custom then.

The first toast was offered by Iliicho the Inquisitive. "Your health, friends! Whatever each one wishes, may God make it his! Whoever wishes us ill, may God settle his bill! Whoever bears us hate, may he crack his pate!" The glasses were noisily drained.

"Long live all of us!" cried Frangov.

"I drink to Silistra-Yolou and its pilgrims," cried Father Dimcho.

Popov raised his glass and cried, "Brothers, I drink to the Balkan lion."

The band which had stopped playing, struck up again and cut the toasts short, but Mr. Fratyu, who had not proposed his, waved at the fiddlers to stop, rose to his feet, looked around and cried enthusiastically, glass in hand, "Gentlemen, I propose my toast for Bulgarian *Liberté! Vivat!"* and he drank up his wine.

The company, who had not quite understood his toast, kept their glasses full, thinking he was going to make a speech. Fratyu was surprised at finding no response, grew confused and sat down.

"What do you mean, sir?" Kandov, who was sitting opposite, asked him coldly.

Fratyu frowned. "I think I spoke clearly enough, sir; I drank to Bulgarian freedom." Fratyu spoke the word low, casting suspicious glances at the Gipsies.

"What do you mean by freedom?" asked the student again. Sokolov turned round. "I think you should drink to Bulgarian slavery; no Bulgarian freedom exists."

"It doesn't exist, but we will obtain it, my friend."

"How are we to obtain it?"

"By drinking," answered some one ironically.

"No, by fighting!" answered Fratyu warmly.

"Fratyu, just try it: you tie an ox by his horns and a man by his words," said Iliicho the Inquisitive mockingly.

"Yes, the sword, gentlemen!" cried Fratyu excitedly shaking his fist.

"If that's how the wind blows, I drink to the sword, the God of slaves!" said Ognyanov, raising his glass.

This electrified the company. "Agoush," cried some one, "play 'Proud Nikifor Demanded.' " That was the Bulgarian Marseillaise in those days. The band struck up and the whole company took up the song. When they came to the verse "Slay and slaughter our country to free," enthusiasm waxed high, and knives and forks were brandished aloft.

Mr. Fratyu seized a big knife and fearsomely cleft the air with it. In one of his fiery gestures he hit a big glass of red wine which the boy was bringing up. The wine spilled all over Fratyu and dyed his summer coat and trousers. "You donkey!" roared Fratyu.

"Mr. Fratyu don't be cross," said Father Dimcho to him. "If there's slaughter, blood is sure to be shed, we all know that."

All this time everybody was talking noisily without hearing anybody else, because the band had started on a Turkish march of sorts, and the tambourine was being thumped deafeningly. Ognyanov and Kandov had withdrawn from the others and were arguing heatedly about something. Nikolai Nedkovich had joined them.

"You tell me that it is necessary to undertake this struggle," Kandov went on with the conversation they had begun, "because its aim is freedom. Freedom? What kind of freedom is it to reinstate a prince, in effect, a little sultan, civil servants to rob us, monks and priests to grow fat on our backs, and an army to drain the very life of the people? Is that your freedom? I wouldn't give a drop of blood from my little finger for it!"

"But listen, Mr. Kandov," Nedkovich answered, "I too respect your principles, but they have no place here. What we need above all is political freedom, that is, to be ourselves the masters of our land and our fate."

Kandov shook his head in dissent. "But just now you explained things differently to me. You appoint new masters for yourselves who are to replace the old ones. Because you don't want the Sheikh-ul-Islam, you embrace another who bears the name of exarch,* that is, you change tyrants for despots. You impose chiefs upon the people and destroy every idea of equality; you consecrate the right of the strong to exploit the weak, the exploitation of labor by capital. Give your struggle a more contemporary and more human aim; make it a struggle not only against Turkish oppression, but for the triumph of contemporary principles as well, that is for the destruction of the stupid customs hallowed by age-old prejudices, such as a throne, religion, the right to property, and the right of the fist, which human folly has raised to the level of inviolable principles. Read Herzen, gentlemen, Bakunin, Lassalle. . . . Free yourselves

---

* Head of the Bulgarian Church, which had attained independence from Greek control in 1870.

of this narrow-minded patriotism and raise the banner of modern rational humanity and sober science. Then I'm with you."

"The ideas you express," replied Ognyanov with animation, "merely prove how widely read you are, but they are a damningly eloquent sign of your ignorance of the Bulgarian situation. Under such a banner, you'd find yourself alone; the people wouldn't understand it. Observe, Mr. Kandov, that there's only one reasonable and possible aim we can present to them: the breaking of the Turkish yoke. For the moment we see only one enemy—the Turks—and it's against them we're rebelling. As for the principles of socialism to which you've treated us, they are not for our stomachs. Bulgarian common sense rejects them, nor will they now or ever find favorable soil in Bulgaria. Your noisy principles and banners, 'contemporary thinking humanity and the sober science of reason,' only veil the subject in mist. Here it's a matter of preserving our hearths, our honor, our lives from the first mangy zaptieh. . . . Before exploring the question of common humanity, or rather of vague theories, we must rid ourselves of our chains. . . . Those whose doctrines you read neither think nor know of our sufferings. We can depend on none but the people, and among the people we find both the chorbadjis and the clergy: they are a power, and we shall make use of them. Destroy the zaptieh, and the people achieve their ideal! If you have another ideal, it's not theirs."

Just then the band stopped and the noise quieted down. The blind man began to play his flute, and tones of a wonderful sweetness floated over the meadow. "Come here, you three, what are you philosophizing about?" people called to those who were arguing. But they never even turned. The conversation was too heated.

The blind man played on for a while amid a solemn silence, for all of them, even though their heads were more or less heated by wine, were enchanted by the melody which came from the blind man's black flute. Suddenly he stopped and said, "Do you know what I see just now?"

They all smiled. "Guess then," said Kolcho.

"What'll you give if we guess?" asked a few.

"My astronomical telescope."

"Where is it now?"

"In the moon."

"Wait a minute, you see the red cheeks of Todorichka's Milka," said Father Dimcho.

"That's not it. I'd much rather bite them than see them!"

"You see Mr. Fratyu," said Popov, because Mr. Fratyu was standing before the blind man and waving his arms in front of his eyes.

"That's not it: you can't see the wind, can you?"

"The sun?"

"No, you know I have a quarrel with it and have sworn my eyes won't see it as long as I live."

"You see the night," said the doctor.

"That's not it either; I see a glass of wine you'll be handing me; you've gone and forgotten me, that you have!" Several people quickly poured out glasses and offered them to him with a smile.

"Your health, good company!" said he and emptied his glass. "What do I win as you weren't able to guess?"

"The other glasses we handed you."

"How many were there?"

"The seven saints!"

"I've more respect for the Forty Holy Martyrs," remarked Father Dimcho.

"Your health!"

"Long life to you!"

"Vive la Bulgarie, vive la république des Balkans!" cried Mr. Fratyu. Kolcho began to sing the nun's litany.

The fun went on until nightfall, when the company got up to return to town. "Brothers, there's a rehearsal at school tomorrow," Ognyanov called to them.

"What play are you playing?" the student asked Ognyanov.

"Genevieve."

"Where did you dig up that old chestnut?"

"We decided on *Genevieve* for two reasons: first, it isn't likely to excite people — the chorbadjis insisted on that; second, everybody has read it and wants to see it. We had to please people's taste. Our aim is profit, isn't it? We've got to buy books and papers for the reading-room, and . . . *other things."*

Noisy and happy, the company set out for town. They were soon lost among the hedges of the market gardens, over which dusk was already falling. A quarter of an hour later they were triumphantly entering the dark streets of the town, singing rebel songs at the top of their lungs. This seditious procession brought groups of women and children to the gates.

Ognyanov alone was missing. A boy had whispered something in his ear at the meadow, and he had left his friends unnoticed.

chapter 15

an unexpected meeting

Ognyanov set off for the north. He was going towards the mountain gorge. Dusk was falling.

The sun had set calmly and magnificently. Its last rays, which gilded the high summits of Stara Planina, gradually vanished. Only several small clouds, their edges gilded to the west, still smiled at the sun from their diaphanous heights. The valley lay entirely in shadow. The white cliffs to the west were sinking into the evening dusk which enveloped the monastery meadows, the crags, the elms, and the pear trees more and more closely, their outlines growing blurred and dim. Not a bird's voice, not a chirp was to be heard. The winged creatures who brought gaiety to the valley by day now huddled silently in their nests, in the branches or under the eaves of the monastery wall.

Darkness and silence reigned, the wonderful melancholy silence of night. Only the thunder of the mountain waterfalls filled the solitude. From time to time the wind brought the distant tinkle of the bells of belated flocks returning to town. Soon the moon came out and added to the magic of this idyllic hour. Silvery freshness poured over meadow and trees, throwing strange shadows on the ground. The cliff stood out more clearly, looking like the wall of an ancient ruin; the new cupola shone forth white above the poplars and the overhanging roofs of the monastery while behind it the peaks of Stara Planina rose high, high up into the sky and melted into its dark blue depths.

Ognyanov passed behind the monastery, entered the dark, deserted valley, and after picking his way for some minutes among the stones that covered it, approached a mill. Dyado Stoyan welcomed him outside the door. "What is it?" asked Ognyanov quickly.

"A friend has come."

"What friend?"

"Why, one of us. . . ."

"One of us?"

"Well, a man of the people."

"Who is he?"

"I don't know him. He came down from the mountain this evening and came straight to me. I was frightened at first. He's a haidouk, I said to myself. . . . You should see the state he's in. . . . Legs like sticks. . . . And then he turned out to be one of our people. So I gave him some bread."

"Take me to your visitor!"

"I've put him in a safe place; follow me." And Dyado Stoyan took Ognyanov into the mill. It was dark.

He lighted an oil lamp, led Boicho between the wall and the millstones and between two bins, then stopped before a small door, on which torn and hanging cobwebs witnessed that it had long stood closed.

"What, is he shut up here?"

"Why not? The cats won't lap up your milk when it's covered—isn't that so, schoolmaster?"

And Dyado Stoyan knocked on the door and called, "Your worship, come out, sir!"

The door opened and a man stooped down to step out. He was a young man, not very tall and rather thin, fairhaired, with a very small face that had long been unshaven, lively eyes and nimble movements. But Ognyanov was horrified at his terrible gauntness and weakness. He was dressed in the white clothes of a revolutionary which fitted close to his lean body and were decorated with the traditional tassels, ornaments and braidings on the back, the chest and the knees; they were terribly torn too, so that the wanderer's bare flesh showed through.

At the very first sight of each other, he and Ognyanov let out a cry of amazement. "Mouratliiski!"

"Kralich!" And they shook hands and embraced.

"Is it really you? Where did you come from?" asked Ognyanov, who recognized in Mouratliiski a friend from his detachment.

"I? . . . Well, where were you, and where do I see you?! Is it really you, Kralich?"

Kralich, astonished, looked around, peered into the mill, then at Dyado Stoyan, who stood there, motionless, staring, and still holding the light for them. "Dyado Stoyan, put out the light and close the door. . . . Or no, we'd better go outside. We can't hear each other for the noise."

Dyado Stoyan went ahead with the light and closed the door after them, saying, "Well, tell each other what you have to say, and I'll go to bed. When you get sleepy, come in and lie down where you please!"

The valley lay in total darkness, but the ravine opposite was well lighted by the moon. Ognyanov and his friend went to a still darker spot and settled themselves on a big boulder around which the river curved and softly murmured.

"Now let's embrace again, brother," said Ognyanov with emotion.

"Well, Kralich, what the devil, eh? I thought you were in the paradise of Diarbekir?"

"What about you, Dobri, haven't the gallows claimed you yet?" laughed Boicho. Their old intimacy was re-established. A similar fate and sufferings will draw even the greatest strangers close to each other. And Boicho and Mouratliiski had been comrades-in-arms and shared the same ideals.

"Now let's hear it all," Mouratliiski went on. "You've come from further away, so you speak first. When did you get back from Diarbekir?"

"You mean, when did I escape?"

"What? Did you escape?"

"In May."

"And you managed to get here without being caught? How did you come?"

"I went on foot from Diarbekir to Russian Armenia, then through the Caucasus to Russia and to Odessa, always with Russian aid. From Odessa by boat to Varna. From there through the mountains to the hamlets above Troyan. Then across Stara Planina to Byala Cherkva."

"But why did you choose Byala Cherkva?"

"I was afraid to go where I knew no one. And where I had friends, I didn't know how they felt about things now, and I wasn't sure of them. I remembered that my father's best friend was in Byala Cherkva, a very fine fellow. And apart from him I was sure that no one knew me there; he wouldn't have known me either, if I hadn't told him who I was."

"Well, I knew you at once, didn't I? And so you stayed on here?"

"Yes. That man, my father's friend, helped me again, so I became a schoolteacher, and so far, thank God, all's well."

"So you've taken to teaching, eh?"

"Officially I teach. Secretly I'm at my old trade."

"Apostleship?"*

"Yes, revolution. . . ."

---

* The revolutionaries who organized revolutionary committees and preached the idea of liberty and revolution became known as "apostles of liberty."

"Well, and how are things going in your region? We've made a mess of 'em."

"For the time being, well enough. Spirits are very high, the atmosphere's positively explosive; Byala Cherkva was one of Levski's nests."

"Well, what's your plan?"

"We haven't got one yet. We're only preparing theoretically for an uprising, so to speak, and just waiting for time to teach us what to do. And unrest grows every day, both here and all around; sooner or later the uprising will come. . . ."

"Bravo, Kralich! That's a splendid fellow!"

"Now, tell me your adventures."

"You know all about them anyhow. We got into it up to our necks in Stara Zagora, and we're ashamed to look people in the face."

"No, no, begin at the beginning: from the time our detachment was defeated and our parting. For eight years in Diarbekir I've heard nothing about you or so many other comrades."

Mouratliiski stretched out on the rock, clasped his hands under his head and in that relaxed position told his story at length. He had taken part in the Sofia conspiracy under Dimiter Obshti, and in the mail-robbery in Orhaniye.* Flung into prison after the betrayal, he had escaped Diarbekir and the gallows by a miracle. Then he had gone to Wallachia, where he had wandered about and struggled with hunger and misery for a year and a half, then returned to Bulgaria again on a mission, to struggle alone with the dangers and hardships which beset an agitator. That spring he had gone to Stara Zagora and worked enthusiastically to prepare the rebellion.

After the unfortunate conclusion of the movement, when he had been slightly wounded by the Turks in the skirmish at Elhovo, he had taken to the Stara Planina, hounded by Turkish posses and by the Bulgarian peasants themselves, whom he had asked for bread, or for peasant clothes to replace his rebel's uniform. For ten days he had wandered about the mountains thus, exposed to thousands of dangers and sufferings. Terrible hunger had forced him to come down from the mountains to beg for bread from the first living soul he met and to put his pistol to the man's chest. Fortunately he had come across Dyado Stoyan. Deeply touched, he told of the kind reception the miller had given him, the first man to treat him as a brother since his wanderings in Stara Planina had begun.

* It was this robbery that cost Levski his life.

Ognyanov listened to Mouratliiski's story of his perils and adventures with deep emotion. He lived through all the alarms, sufferings, bitter disappointments and shame at the people's dastardly behavior, which accompany the defeat of every revolution. With brotherly compassion he considered Mouratliiski's fate.

Mouratliiski fell silent. The river murmured at their feet. All around them it was quiet and deserted. The crags opposite rose mute in the moonlight; along their crest the night breeze rocked the wild lilac and other shrubs.

chapter 16

the grave talks

In the morning Ognyanov set out for town. He went through the gorge which led him out to the monastery. Under the great walnut trees in the meadow in front of the monastery the abbot was walking bareheaded to and fro. He was enjoying the beauty of this romantic spot and drinking in the fresh, invigorating air of the mountain. The autumn landscape had a new charm with the golden leaves of the trees, the yellowed velvety hills of the Balkan range, and the bitter-sweet atmosphere of decay and melancholy.

Ognyanov and the abbot greeted each other. "Lovely places, Father," said Ognyanov. "You're a lucky man to live so close to nature and enjoy its divine beauties in peace. If I ever feel drawn to your calling, it will only be for love of the eternal beauties of nature."

"Beware of becoming a monk, Ognyanov, after having been an apostle: it would be a descent of several steps. Stay as you are. Besides, I wouldn't take you into my monastery. You're such a godless fellow, you'd corrupt Father Yerotei himself," said the abbot jokingly.

"What is that old bird really like?" asked Boicho suddenly.

"A very pious and reverend brother, very like the Lord God, but he has one fault: he buries his money until it grows moldy; whenever we hint at his giving something for the common cause, he always turns a deaf ear. . . . So we've made it a proverb 'You turn a deaf ear, like Father Yerotei,' we say to some people. Where do you come from so early?"

"I slept at Dyado Stoyan's mill."

The abbot looked at him in surprise. "Are you afraid of anything?"

"Not at all, but a brother has arrived there." And Ognyanov briefly recounted his meeting with Mouratliiski.

"Why didn't you come to the monastery?" asked the abbot reproachfully. "You must have slept on the wheatsacks there."

"We revolutionaries make do with what we find."

"Well, God bless you. . . . And what name did you give him?"

"Yaroslav Burzobegounek, an Austrian Czech, and photographer in Byala Cherkva."

Father Nathaniel laughed outright!

"You apostles seem to be very bold lads! See you don't break the pitcher at the third try. . . ."

"Never you fear, there's a God for comitadjis too, just as there is for haidouks," said Boicho, and smiled knowingly. "So you've brought out the carbine?" he cried looking at Father Nathaniel's gun that was propped up against the trunk of a willow.

"I thought I'd try it out this morning. I haven't touched it for ages. You've driven the whole world mad, and I have music every day . . . in front of the monastery. This new craze would stir the dead, let alone an old sinner like me. . . ."

"It's not a bad thing to try your hand, Father abbot." And walking together the two came to the mill of that terrible night. The very sight of the spot brought deep furrows to Ognyanov's forehead. The mill was closed now. Stoyan, the miller had left it immediately afterwards and rented another, as we know, on the Monastery river. Deserted as it was, and overgrown with hemlock, it looked like a grave in this lovely spot.

Just then Mooncho approached stealthily, stopped and fixed his gaze on Ognyanov. A strange smile played about the lips of his senseless, idiot's face. Both friendliness and fear and the admiration which Ognyanov aroused in Mooncho's soul were to be read in that look, deprived of reason. Years ago he had cursed Mohammed in front of an onbashi, who had nearly beaten him to death. Since then only one feeling, only one thought, only one ray of understanding, had remained in his dim consciousness: a terrible, fiendish hatred of the Turks. As an accidental witness of the killing of the two at the mill and of their burial in the pit, he had acquired an inexpressible admiration for Ognyanov and stood in awe of him. This feeling almost amounted to idolatry. He called him "Roussiyan," nobody well knew why.

At first he had been frightened by him in the gallery that night, but later he grew used to Ognyanov who often came to the monastery. He goggled at him and never took his eyes off him; he considered him his protector. When the monastery servants offended him, he threatened them with Roussiyan. "Ah'll t-t-tell Roussiyan t-t-to cut your throat t-t-too" and sawed his throat with his finger. But nobody understood the sense of his words, fortunately, for he used to repeat them in town when he went there. The abbot and

Boicho paid no heed to Mooncho, who went on shaking his head and grinning in friendly fashion.

"Look there, the onbashi is coming this way!" said the abbot. And indeed the onbashi appeared, his rifle over his shoulder, his knapsack on his back. He was going out shooting.

He was a man of thirty-five with a puffy, sallow face, a big protruding forehead, small gray eyes and an insolent and lazy look. Evidently he was an opium-eater. After exchanging greetings and a few words about the game that year, the onbashi took up the carbine and examined it carefully with a sportsman's eye, then said, "Despot-Effendi, a good carbine. Where are you going to shoot?"

"That's what I was wondering, Sherif-Aga. . . . I haven't handled it for a year, so I thought I'd empty it at least."

"What's your target?" asked the onbashi, unshouldering his rifle with the obvious wish to show his skill.

"The cliff," said the abbot simply. "That bush over there that looks like a hat, near where clay has been dug."

The onbashi looked at him in surprise. "That's very far, isn't it?" And he squatted down by a rock, propped his rifle on it and took aim for about ten seconds. The shot exploded; the bullet struck several paces away from the mark.

Slight annoyance clouded Sherif-Aga's suddenly scarlet forehead. "Another try," he said, again crouching down by the stone, and he took aim for nearly a minute. When the rifle spoke again he stood up and gazed at the bush. But he saw that the dust was rising on the cliff far above the bush.

"Confound the thing!" he said angrily. "Despot-Effendi, one should never choose such a distant target. You shoot now! But I tell you, you'll only waste your bullet. . . . Try and hit the cliff at least," he added ironically.

The abbot picked up his gun, aimed at the target standing, and fired at once. The bush swayed. "So it still obeys me!" said the abbot.

"Here," cried the onbashi, "do that again. . . ." The abbot took aim once more and fired. The bullet hit the bush again.

The onbashi went white. He said angrily, "Kishish-Effendi, you have a true eye, but I don't believe the story that you haven't done any shooting for a year. . . . It wouldn't be a bad thing if you gave your young men a lesson; they come shooting here every day. . . ." Then he added spitefully, "They've grown very fierce. . . . Something's biting them. But the devil will wear out his sandals one of these days. . . ." The onbashi's look grew more brutal and full of hate as he turned to Ognyanov.

All that time Mooncho had stood at a respectable distance from him. But how he changed now! Unreasoning fear and animal hatred distorted his features terribly. He had fixed a threatening look on the onbashi, his mouth gaping, his arms widespread like a man who was preparing to hurl himself at him. The onbashi mechanically turned towards him and gave him a contemptuous look. Then the madman's expression grew still more ferocious and he cried, foaming with rage; "Rouss-i-yan'll cut your throat too!" and added the worst of oaths.

The onbashi knew a little Bulgarian but could make neither head nor tail of Mooncho's words. "What's that cur roaring about?" he asked the abbot.

"Nothing bad, effendim. Don't you see what he is?"

"What's got into Mooncho here? When he comes to town he's always so meek," remarked Boicho.

"Don't you know? Every cock crows on his own dung heap."

Just then a beautiful hound with black spots on its haunches and a leather collar round its neck, from which the leash still dangled, came running down the meadow. They all turned to the dog. "That hound must have run away," remarked the abbot. "Somebody must be out shooting there."

Ognyanov started involuntarily. The hound came up to the mill, stopped, sniffed at the door and began to circle the grass, howling pitifully. Cold shivers went over Ognyanov.

"Ah, that's the hound of Emeksiz-Pehlivan, who's disappeared!" cried the onbashi.

The hound, which Ognyanov had recognized at once, was going around the mill, scratching the threshold, digging up the weeds with its paws and howling. Then it raised its long moist muzzle as if to draw attention and began to bark angrily. That bark echoed terribly in Ognyanov's soul! The abbot and he looked at each other, dumbfounded. The onbashi watched amazed, an expression of bewilderment on his face.

The hound kept on barking and howling, looking in their direction. Suddenly it dashed at Ognyanov. He went white and drew back, for the dog hurled itself at him like a wolf, barking desperately. Mechanically he drew his dagger and began to defend himself from the angry animal, which the abbot unsuccessfully tried to drive off with gestures, as he could not find a stone.

The onbashi looked on in silence at this strange scene. He shot suspicious and sinister looks at Ognyanov and the dagger which flashed in the light. But when he saw that in self-defence Ognyanov might stab the dog, which avoided the knife only to attack on the other side, he intervened and separated them. Then he turned to Ognyanov, who was all flushed and breathless, "Chorbadji, why is the dog so angry with you?"

"One day, I don't remember where, I hit him with a stone," answered Ognyanov with forced composure. The onbashi looked at him distrustfully and searchingly. Obviously he was not satisfied with this reply. Dim suspicions were forming in his mind. But he decided to think them out later. Pretending to find Ognyanov's answer satisfactory, he said: "This breed of dogs does bear grudges." He saluted the abbot, set out towards the gorge and was soon lost from sight. Tail in air the hound crossed the meadow to catch up with its new master.

"I thought you'd killed the beast," said the amazed abbot.

"I threw it half dead into the mill-race, to drown there, but here it is alive again, unfortunately," muttered Ognyanov worriedly. "Dyado Stoyan was right; we should have buried it with the other curs. And why did that fool of a Sherif-Aga have to be here just at this moment! Trouble comes when it's least expected."

"Did you kill them all right too? Won't one of them come to life again like the dog?" said the monk reproachfully. "When a man sets his hand to a job like that he has to go through with it to the end, and then leave it. You're a novice at this job, Boicho; but let's hope it'll turn out all right. The rumor we set afoot about those two has lulled the Turks. . . . But I'll keep my ears open."

In the meantime Ognyanov had turned his eyes on the spot where the Turks were buried. To his amazement he noticed a considerable cairn of stones collected there. Neither he nor Stoyan the miller had placed those stones there. He expressed his amazement to the abbot. The latter calmed him, telling him that they must have been piled up there for some quite simple reason. They did not know that Mooncho went there every day to throw stones on the graves of the Turks with curses, and that by now he had collected every stone from all around.

Ognyanov put out his hand.

"Where are you going?"

"Good-bye; I'm in a hurry. I have lots to do about the performance. That cursed dog has put my whole part out of my mind."

"Who are you going to be?"

"The Count."

"A count, eh? And where's your county?" joked the abbot.

"The fortress of Diarbekir. . . . I'll bequeath it to whoever wants it. . . ." And Ognyanov went off.

chapter 17

the performance

Few of my young readers will be familiar with the play *The Long-suffering Genevieve* which was to be performed that evening at the boy's school. Yet thirty years ago, along with *Alexandria, Berthold the Cunning* and *Michael* it had influenced the taste and excited the admiration of an entire generation. The plot is briefly as follows. A certain German Count Siegfried sets off to war against the Moors in Spain, leaving his inconsolable wife, the young Countess Genevieve to grieve for him. No sooner has he departed than his steward Golos appears before the Countess and makes offensive proposals which she indignantly rejects. The vindictive Golos kills her devoted servant Drako, throws her into prison, and denounces her to the Count, saying that she had been surprised with Drako. The infuriated Count sends orders to behead his faithless wife. But the executioners to whom Golos entrusts this task take pity on the Countess and leave her to the mercy of fate, in a forest cave with her child, telling Golos that they have beheaded her. Seven years later the Count returns from the wars, wretchedly unhappy, and learning of her innocence from a letter left by Genevieve, laments her untimely death. Golos is put in chains and goes mad from remorse.

The Count then goes hunting in the forest to distract himself, and accidentally comes upon the Countess and her child in their cave, with a doe which had fed them with her milk. They recognize each other and joyfully return to the castle. This naive and touching plot had drawn tears from all the old ladies and young matrons of the town. Even to that day everyone remembered the legend of Genevieve, while many ladies knew the play by heart.

That was why the evening's performance had provoked general excitement for many days past. Everyone looked forward to it impatiently as a great event which would add pleasant variety to the monotony of life in Byala Cherkva. One and all made ready for the theater. The rich ladies were getting their dresses ready, and the poor women sold their yarn at the market and got themselves tickets with the money at once before it was spent on salt or soap. The performance was a topic of general discussion and had ousted all social or family scandal. At church old women asked each other, "Ghena, are you going to *Genevieve* tonight?" And they prepared to shed tears over the long-suffering countess. At home the cast was eagerly discussed and the knowledge that Ognyanov would be the count gave great satisfaction.

The role of the treacherous Golos, who afterwards goes mad, was taken by Mr. Fratyu, who relished strong emotions. (In order to create more of a sensation in the part Mr. Fratyu had purposely not had his hair cut for a month.) Iliya the Inquisitive was the servant Drako and for the twentieth time that day he practiced how to die by the sword of Golos. He had also been requested to bark later on as the count's hound. This part too he practiced very assiduously. For the part of Genevieve some people had proposed Deacon Vikenti because of his beautiful long hair, but when they learned that none of his cloth were allowed to appear on the stage, the part was given to someone else, together with a pot of white pomade with which to cover his moustache. The remaining parts had also been distributed.

The setting was not so easy to manage, as the whole had to be done at very little expense. All available funds went for the curtain, made up of some red cloth, and for decoration they had asked an icon-painter from Debr to paint a lyre on it. It turned out to look more like a pitch-fork than anything else. To decorate the Count's palace most of the better furniture in town had been pressed into service. Hadji Gyuro's window-curtains with the poplar design had been taken, and also a pair of Anatolian rugs of Karagiozolu's, Micho Beizadé's magnificent glass vases, Micho Saranov's large carpet, Nikolai Nedkovich's Franco-Prussian battle scenes, Benchoolu's old broken-down sofa, the only one in town, Marko Ivanov's big mirror from Bucharest, and the picture of the "martyrs," some down cushions from the convent, the map of Australia and the celestial globe from the school, and the smaller chandelier from the church, to illuminate this universal exhibition. Even the konak contributed its shackles—for Golos.

As for the costumes, they were the same ones used three years before when *Princess Raina* was performed. Thus, the Count garbed himself in Svetoslav's royal purple, and Genevieve in Raina's. Golos added something resembling epaulettes to his costume, and a pair of very shiny Wellingtons. Gancho Popov, who played Huns, one of the executioners, wore his long dagger, which he had readied for the insurrection. Drako was resplendent in the shabby top-hat of Mihalaki Alafranga. In vain did Boicho protest against this medley. Most of the actors stubbornly insisted on making the scene more effective, and at last he gave up in despair.

As soon as the sun had set, the theater began to fill up. The front benches were occupied by the notables and the bey, who had been specially invited. Next to him sat Damyancho Grigor in order to keep him amused, as he well knew how. All the remaining space was filled with a motley crowd, buzzing with excitement, which could scarcely wait for the curtain to rise. Among the ladies the noisiest of all was Aunt Ghinka, who knew the play by heart and was telling everyone right and left what the Count's first words would be. Hadji Smion, on another bench, was telling people how much larger the Bucharest theater was, and explaining the meaning of the pitch-fork on the curtain. The orchestra consisted of the local Gipsy fiddlers who mostly played the Austrian anthem in honor, no doubt, of the German Countess.

At last the solemn moment came. The Austrian anthem ceased, and the curtain went up amid abominable creakings. The first to appear was the Count. Silence descended. One might have heard a pin drop. The Count began to speak, Aunt Ghinka prompting him from the benches. Whenever the Count missed or changed a word, she would cry out, "That's wrong."

The sound of a horn is heard and the messengers of Charlemagne enter; they have come to call the Count to war against the Moors. He bids the fainting Genevieve farewell and departs. When the Countess comes to and finds the Count gone, she bursts into tears. Her sobs make everyone laugh. Again Aunt Ghinka speaks up: "Come on! Don't you know how to cry?" The Countess sets up a howl to which the audience responds with thunderous laughter. Aunt Ghinka, whose laughter is the loudest of all, cries out, "Just let me get up there—I'd show you what crying is!" Hadji Smion explains to the audience at large that weeping is an art, and that in Wallachia women weepers are specially hired to cry over the dead. Somebody hisses at him to keep quiet and he hisses back at those who are listening to him. . . . Golos's appearance changes the situation. He puts the virtue of the Countess to the test; she replies with disdain and calls Drako to send him to the Count with a letter. Drako enters, provoking general mirth with his top-hat; this confuses him. Aunt Ghinka calls out to him, "Drako, what are you doing with Alafranga's saucepan? Off with it!" Whereupon he takes it off. Renewed giggling from the audience. But the scene takes a tragic turn. Golos, enraged, draws his sword to pierce Drako through. But before he can touch him, Drako drops down like a sheaf of corn, lying there dead and motionless. The audience is dissatisfied with such a false death scene, and some shout to Drako to twitch. He is dragged off the stage by the feet, his head bumping over the floor. Drako bears the pain heroically and sticks to his part as a dead man. The Countess is thrown into prison.

The act was finished and the Austrian national anthem began again. The hall buzzed with criticism and laughter. The old ladies were displeased with Genevieve, whose acting lacked pathos; while Golos on the contrary, acted his thankless part quite well and deservedly won the hatred of some of the old women. One of them approached his mother to say, "Why, Tana, that's not at all nice, the way your Fratyu's going on; what harm has the poor girl done him?"

On the first bench Damyancho Grigor was telling the bey in detail exactly what had happened in the first act. Carried away by his own eloquence he related the story of a certain French consul who had left his wife because of a love affair. The bey listened to him with great attention and at last grasped the fact that the Count was a French consul, and held him as such to the end. "That consul is a great fool," he said severely. "How could he order his wife to be killed without investigating the matter thoroughly? I don't detain even a street-drunkard without making Mihal the Constable smell his breath."

"Bey-Effendi," said Damyancho, "It is written like this to make the history more curious."

"The writer's a fool, and the consul's a bigger fool still."

Not far off Stefchov was also criticizing the Count. "Ognyanov," he was saying conceitedly and authoritatively, "has never been near a theater."

"Why? He acts well enough," rejoined Hadji Smion.

"Acts well indeed! . . . like a monkey. He has no respect for the audience!"

"Yes, I noticed that too; he lacks respect. . . . Did you see how he sat on Benchoolu's sofa? As if he were the very brother of Prince Kouza. . . ." said Hadji Smion.

"He could do with some hissing," said Stefchov angrily.

"He could, indeed," Hadji Smion affirmed.

"Who's going to hiss?" somebody shouted from the same bench. They both turned round. It was Kableshkov.* Kableshkov had not

* A leader of the April Uprising.

yet become a revolutionary leader. He was in Byala Cherkva quite by chance, visiting a relative. Hadji Smion was abashed by the fiery glance of the future apostle; he leaned back to let him see the culprit—Stefchov.

"I am!" was Kiriak's straightforward answer.

"You are free to do so, sir, but you'll have to go out into the street for that."

"Who asked for your opinion?"

"This is a charity performance, and the actors are amateurs. If you can do any better, get onto the stage yourself!" said Kableshkov with spirit.

"I've paid for my seat and no one can tell me what to do!" returned Stefchov.

Kableshkov flushed. The quarrel was about to flare up. Micho Beizadé hastened to put an end to it. "Kiriak, you're a reasonable person. . . . Todorcho, keep quiet!" At that moment the Austrian anthem ceased. The curtain went up.

This time the stage represented a prison, lit by a small night light. Genevieve, holding the child she had borne there, was lamenting and sobbing. Her acting was more natural now. The midnight hour, the gloomy prison, the sighs of an unhappy, helpless mother—all this moved the audience. Tears rolled down the faces of many a woman. Like laughter, tears are contagious. The number of weepers increased, even some of the men shed tears as she wrote her letter to the Count. Even Kableshkov was moved and burst into applause at a pathetic moment. His clapping expanded, a lonely thing, into the complete silence and died out without an echo. Many angry looks were turned on the self-willed person who chose the finest passage to make a noise. Ivan Selyamsuz, who was sniffing loudly, looked at him ferociously. Genevieve was dragged away to the forest —to be put to death. The curtain dropped. Kableshkov clapped again, but once more no one followed his example. The custom of applauding had not yet been introduced in Byala Cherkva.

"There be wicked people in that land," the bey whispered to Damyancho, "where did this take place?"

"In German parts."

"In German parts? I've never seen any of those giaours."*

"How so, Bey-Effendi, we have a German in the town!"

"Would he be that beardless, whiskered fellow with the blue spectacles?"

---

* *giaour:* unbeliever, infidel.

"That's it, the photographer."

"That one, is it? A good little giaour. . . . Always raises his hat à la Franca when he meets me. . . . I thought he was a Frenchman."

"No, he's a German, from Drandabour* at that."

Then came the third act. The stage again represented the castle. The Count has already returned from the war, moody and full of grief at not finding Genevieve. The maid gives him Genevieve's letter, written in prison in her last hour. She tells him that she is a victim of Golos's baseness, that she dies innocent and forgives him. . . . The Count reads all this aloud amid sobs. He weeps, he is in the depths of despair. The spectators also share his suffering; they too weep, some sobbing aloud. The bey, who no longer needs Grigor, is crying too. The emotional strain grows still more painful when the Count orders the treacherous Golos, the cause of his misfortunes, to be brought before him. Golos appears, dishevelled, ugly, tortured by remorse and wearing the fetters of the konak prison. He is greeted by a hostile murmur from the audience. Angry looks pierce him. The Count reads him the letter in which the Countess includes him in her forgiveness, and breaks down again, tearing his hair, beating his breast. The audience sobs again unrestrainedly.

Aunt Ghinka is also shedding tears, but wants to reassure the others. "There's nothing to cry about, Genevieve is alive in the forest!"

Some of the old women, who don't know the play, speak up in surprise. "Heavens, Ghinka, is she really? Why don't somebody tell him, poor man, and stop him crying?" said Granny Petkovitsa; while Granny Hadji Pavlyuvitsa, unable to restrain herself, called out through her tears: "There, my boy, don't cry; your bride's alive!"

Meanwhile Golos is raving. He casts terrible looks around him, with staring eyes, his dishevelled hair is standing on end, he waves his arms about, writhing with his whole body, and gnashes his teeth most desperately. His conscience is tormenting him terribly; but his sufferings give relief to the audience. Their faces express a grim satisfaction. "Serves him right," say the women. They are even annoyed at Genevieve for having forgiven him in her letter.

His mother, seeing the sad state of Mr. Fratyu, borne down by the weight of his fetters and of the general indignation, is wondering what to do. "They've done for my boy; they've made a zany of him!" says she and is about to drag him off the stage, but she is

---

* Damyancho's version of *Brandenburg*.

held back. This act was a brilliant success. Shakespeare's Ophelia has never wrung so many tears in one evening. . . .

The last act takes place in the forest. A cave. From its entrance appears Genevieve, dressed in skins, with her child. A goat, which had been given juicy leaves to nibble to keep it on the stage, represents the doe who fed them with her milk in the cave. Genevieve speaks sadly to her child of his father, but, hearing the baying of hounds, crawls into the cave with her child, and drags the reluctant goat in after her by the horns. The baying grows louder and the audience finds Iliicho the Inquisitive more successful in this part. He increases his zeal to such an extent that he sets several dogs outside to barking. There comes the Count, dressed in hunting clothes, together with his retinue. The spectators hold their breath, everyone straining his eyes to see the meeting with Genevieve. Granny Ivanitsa is afraid he may pass by the cave and suggests they should tell him his wife is there. But the Count has seen her. He bends forward and calls into the cave, "Thou, whosoever thou art, be thou man or beast, come forth!"

But instead of issuing from the cave the answer came from the hall. A loud hiss was heard. Everyone turned in amazement towards Stefchov. He had flushed scarlet.

"Who's that hissing?" Selyamsuz cried out angrily. The audience buzzed with displeasure.

Ognyanov's eyes sought out the interrupter. Catching sight of Stefchov, who was staring at him insolently, he said in a low whisper, "I'll rip your long ears off!"

A new hiss, louder still. The audience was horrified. In a trice a storm of protest broke out.

"Catch hold of that Protestant, throw him out the window!" fiercely roared Anghel Yovkov, a giant eight feet tall.

Other cries were heard: "Out with the man! Stefchov out!"

"We haven't come here to listen to hissing and clapping!" was shouting Selyamsuz, who had misunderstood Kableshkov's applause before.

"Kiriak, I don't agree!" Aunt Ghinka also cried out angrily from her place beside Rada, who was bathed in tears.

Hadji Smion was whispering to Stefchov, "For heaven's sake, Kiriak, I told you before: You mustn't hiss. . . . These are simple people here, don't you see?"

"Why is the gentleman hissing?" the bey asked Damyancho. Damyancho shrugged his shoulders.

The bey whispered something to a zaptieh who went up to Stefchov. "Kiriak," he said quietly, "the bey said you were to go and smoke a cigarette outside if you feel restless." Stefchov went out with a haughty smile, pleased at having spoiled the effect of Ognyanov's acting.

With his exit the disturbance subsided. The play continued, the Count found the lost Countess. Embraces, exclamations, renewed tears. Again the audience was moved. The triumph of good over evil was complete. The Count and Countess told each other all their sorrow and their joy. Granny Petkovitsa said to them, "Now, granny's children, go home and see that you get on well together, and don't believe any wicked Goloses again."

"Wicked yourself!" burst out Mr. Fratyu's mother behind her.

The bey gave much the same advice as Granny Petkovitsa, only less loudly. There was a general feeling of satisfaction and joy. The Count was greeted on all sides with looks of sympathy. The play ended with a song which the Count and the Countess, and their retinue took up, "Count Siegfried now rejoice!"

But after the first two verses of this virtuously joyful song, the strains of a revolutionary march rang out on the stage:

> Blaze up in us, oh love, so bright,
> Against the Turks we'll go and fight. . . .

It was as if a thunderbolt had struck the hall. At first only one sang it, then the song was taken up by a few of the actors on the stage, then by all of them, and at last the audience itself took up the refrain. A wave of patriotic fervor swept over everyone. The brave tune of this song grew like an invisible wave, filled the hall, flowed over into the yard and burst out into the night. . . . The song rent the air, stirred up and exhilarated people's hearts. These martial notes struck a new chord in the audience. Everyone who knew the song began to sing it, both men and women; it united all souls, it made the stage merge with the hall, and rose heavenward like a prayer. . . .

"Sing on, boys, long life to you!" shouted Micho ecstatically. But others among the older people protested under their breath, considering this mad rapture ill-placed.

The bey also listened with satisfaction to the song, of which he understood not one word. He asked Damyancho Grigor to explain every verse to him. Anyone else would have muddled things, but Damyancho was never at a loss to answer difficult questions. This was a chance if ever for him to prove his worth. He fooled the bey in the most natural and entrancing manner. The song, according to Damyancho, expressed the great love of the Count for the Countess. The Count says to her, "I love you a hundred times more now," and she says to him, "I love you a thousand times more now." He says that he will build a church where the cave had stood in memory of it, and she says that she will sell all her diamonds to give alms to the poor, and she will build a hundred marble fountains.

"That's a lot of fountains; she'd better make a few bridges for the good of all," the bey interrupted.

"Fountains, because there isn't much water in German parts, so the people drink beer mostly," answered Grigor. The bey nodded approvingly at this decision.

"And where is Golos?" asked the bey looking for Mr. Fratyu among the actors.

"It is not fitting that he appear here."

"That truly spoken. . . . They should have hanged the rascal. If the play should be acted a second time, tell the Consul not to let him live. It is more proper thus!" And indeed Mr. Fratyu was not among his comrades. He had prudently slipped away as soon as the dangerous song began, preferring not to wait for any laurels from the audience.

The song came to an end and the curtain fell amid cries of "Bravo!" The Austrian anthem thundered out once more and played the audience out of the hall, which was soon empty.

The actors were changing behind the curtain and gaily talking with their friends, who had come to congratulate them. "The devil take you, Kableshkov, what possessed you? You suddenly pop up behind my back and start roaring like a tempest. You Gipsy. . . ." said Ognyanov dragging off Svetoslav's boots.

"I just couldn't help it, brother. I got sick of all those tears and that chicken-hearted lamentation over your long-suffering lady. We had to bring all those people to their senses somehow. And then it came into my head to get onto the stage. . . . You saw what a brilliant effect it had."

"I kept looking round, expecting to see a zaptieh at my elbow," laughed Ognyanov.

"Don't worry. Stefchov took himself off before that," Sokolov said.

"The bey sent him out. . . ." said Frangov the teacher.

"But the bey stayed behind," another said. "I watched him and saw how carefully he was listening . . . there'll be trouble tomorrow. . . ."

"Oh, don't you worry about him. Bai Damyancho Grigor was next to him, wasn't he? He must have told him some tall tales to take his breath away. If he didn't, we'll take his diploma back."

"I invited him on purpose and put him next to the bey who likes a good tale. Don't worry, nothing will come of it," remarked Nikolai Nedkovich, taking off Father Dimcho's summer cassock, in which he had played the part of Genevieve's father.

But he had not counted on treachery. Next morning Ognyanov was summoned to the konak. He appeared before the bey, who was in a bad temper. "Consulos-Effendi," he said to him, "it seems you sang comitadji songs last night. Is that so?"

Ognyanov protested.

"But the onbashi tells me the contrary."

"He has been misinformed. You were there yourself."

The bey sent for the onbashi. "Sherif-Aga, when did they sing such songs, in my presence or after I had left?"

"They sang a revolutionary song in front of you, Bey-Effendim. Kiriak-Effendi wouldn't tell a lie. . . ."

The bey looked at him severely. His vanity was offended. "What are you talking about, Sherif-Aga? Was Kiriak there or was I? Didn't I listen with my own ears? Didn't Damyancho-Chorbadji translate the song to me word for word? I talked last night with Marko-Chorbadji, and he too liked the tune very much. . . . I'll have no more dirty tricks like these!" fumed the bey, then turned to Ognyanov. "Consulos-Effendi, apologies for troubling you; it was a mistake. Just a minute, what did they call that fellow, the one in chains?"

"Golos."

"Yes, Golos. . . . You should have had him hanged. That's what I would have done. You shouldn't be led by a woman's advice. But it was very good, and the song was better still," said the bey, getting up with difficulty.

Ognyanov bowed and went out. "You'll be hearing another song soon, and one you'll understand without Bai Damyancho's help," he muttered to himself as he passed the gates. He did not see the sinister look with which the onbashi was regarding him.

chapter 18

in Ganko's café

Some days after this event Ganko's café was full, as usual, with customers, noise and smoke. It was the meeting place for young and old alike, where public matters were discussed, and the Eastern Question too, as well as all the domestic and foreign policy of Europe. A miniature parliament, one might say. But for the time being, the performance of *Genevieve* held the floor and was the main topic of the day. It would in fact occupy minds for many a day to come, and leave a profound impression. Many also turned their attention to the revolutionary song, which gave rise to the liveliest discussions. At the moment, after cool reflection, many condemned Ognyanov, to whom the name of "Count" had stuck, as generally happens with amateur actors who have made a deep impression on the spectators.

Mr. Fratyu also remained "Golos." That very morning he had been surprised to ecounter the cross frowns of certain respectable old people who were unable to forgive him for his conduct with Genevieve. One old granny stopped him in the street and said to him, "Eh, granny's boy, why did you do it? Wasn't it a sin before God?"

However, the appearance of Chorbadji Micho Beizadé in the café again turned conversation today into the boundless realm of politics. Chorbadji Micho Beizadé was an old, short and dark little man, dressed in baggy Turkish trousers and a short cloth jacket. Like his contemporaries, he was uneducated and rather limited, but life and its many trials had made him wise and of good counsel. His lively black eyes gleamed wisely in his withered face which was furrowed by deep wrinkles. An oddity which made him proverbial among his fellow-citizens was his unbounded partiality for politics and his unshakeable faith in Turkey's approaching downfall. Naturally he loved the Russians in the extreme, to the verge of fanaticism, to the verge of the ridiculous. Everyone remembered how angry he got at an examination when a pupil said that Russia had been defeated at Sebastopol.

"You're wrong, my son, Russia can't be defeated; you must ask the school master who taught you that for your money back," Chorbadji Micho told him irritably. But because the teacher proved then and there, with history book in hand, that Russia had been beaten in the Crimean War, Micho began to shout that his book lied, and as he was on the school board he would not let that teacher be hired again.

Nervous and irritable by nature, he would flare up all of a sudden when anyone dared to contradict his cherished convictions. He grew scarlet with rage, shouted and swore. Today he was cheerful and as he sat down he said with a triumphant air, "Our people have taken a drubbing again!"

"How's that?" cried several voices in surprise.

"Lyubobratich and Bozhko Petrovich have cut down several thousand Turks," said Bai Micho, who was letting his news seep out to prolong the pleasure.

"Bravo, long life to them!" shouted several voices.

"And Podgoritsa has been taken," Bai Micho went on. Wonder rose to the utmost, as if it were Vienna instead of Podgoritsa that had fallen.

"Arms and as many volunteers as you like; they come from Austria."

"Really?"

"And Bosnia's on fire again. Serbia's stirring and preparing troops. And if Serbia moves, it will set us off too. It's all up with our man. . . ."

"The devil take him!"

"And Austria will keep still because Gorchakov in Petersburg will tell her: 'Stop! Whether they cut each other's throats or fight, it's their own business there.' It's all up with him, I say." All pricked up their ears and listened with satisfaction to the encouraging news which Chorbadji Micho had brought.

"How many men have been killed?" asked Nikodim.

"Turks? I tell you thousands of them, say two, say five, say ten, you won't be wrong. Those characters in Herzegovina don't mess around."

"That's good if it's true!"

"I tell you it's true!"

"Where did you hear all this?" asked Chorbadji Marko.

"From a reliable source, I tell you. Kir Georgi Izmirliya heard it day before yesterday from Yanaki Daphnis, the grocer in K., that *Clio,* the Trieste newspaper, had written about it."

"I don't believe the Herzegovinians can do such a big job. . . . They'll fight and fight; then they'll get tired. How many are they?

A handful of people," said Pavlaki, looking round at the others for support.

"That's what I say, Pavlaki, what are the Herzegovinians? A handful of people. Turkey's not afraid of 'em," Hadji Smion spoke up, pulling his socks straight.

Chorbadji Micho answered heatedly, "You, Pavlaki, you'll forgive me, and you too, Hadji, you're a greenhorn. In politics something may come of nothing. Gorchakov himself has said that from Herzegovina will fly the spark which will set fire to the whole Turkish kingdom."

"I think it was Derby who said that," interrupted Mr. Fratyu pompously.

Chorbadji Micho frowned. "Derby, as an Englishman, cannot say such uncomplimentary things about the Sultan. I know English policy: 'Everything is fine in Turkey; everything is flourishing in Turkey.' I tell you, Derby couldn't say such a thing."

"Fratyu, that's so; that's so, he didn't say it," Hadji Smion asserted.

"If only a fire would break out and burn up Constantinople so that we could free ourselves once and for all from these heathen," said Ivancho Doudo the cobbler, who was to tell the truth, a complete novice at politics.

"It's another fire we're speaking of here, Ivancho," Pavlaki remarked seriously.

"The real blaze will come when Bulgaria is set on fire," remarked Mr. Fratyu.

"Why should Bulgaria be set on fire? There's no need to have Bulgaria in flames. We have to lie low for all we're worth. Didn't we see the other day what a mess they made of it at Zagora?" Chorbadji Dimo answered sullenly.

"You say so, Fratyu," remarked Dancho the baker, "because when it happens you'll scamper off to Podoumogoushoy in Wallachia, and shout at them from there, but it's our heads they'll be breaking here! Don't tell me — brother Dancho knows all about people."

"On the contrary, I'll be here too, and I'll make sacrifices."

"Well, if anything is going to happen, let it happen soon. What sort of a kingdom is this? It's burning even now, but there's no smoke. They've taken the very shirts off our backs. You don't dare show your nose outside the town. Is that a kingdom? Rubbish!"

"Don't you worry about that; it won't be long," said Bai Micho. "It's written that Turkey will fall soon."

"Turkey's an absolutely rotten state, a skeleton, nothing more. Give it a push and over it goes!" remarked somebody.

"And if we don't give it a push we're fools," said Father Dimcho fierily.

"That's so, that's so," Father Stavri put in, "things are stirring. You have only to look, old and young talk of nothing else. And the womenfolk and the very children, day and night, that's all they talk of. Listen to their songs even, no more 'oh's' and 'ah's,' nothing but rifles and rattling swords; 'When the drum beats, my heart does leap. Up and fight the Turks!' and other such new-fangled madness. As for the boys, if you look for them they're always at the monastery meadow—bang! bang! all day long with the muskets—you can't go that way to Bozalan. My Ganko's got together all the pistols and guns he could find, and as soon as school's over he does nothing but play with them. 'What do you want all that old stuff for, my son?' I ask him. 'They'll be needed soon, dad,' says he. 'The time will come when an old pistol will be worth its weight in gold. . . .' Between ourselves, I'm afraid these stormy times will hatch something. The Lord preserve us!"

Father Stavri's simple and sincere words were true. For some months past, say since Ognyanov's appearance, as Stefchov had noticed, a restlessness had been observed which grew from day to day, particularly after the September movement in Stara Zagora.

Patriotic toasts were proposed at parties, and an uprising was openly talked of; the country around the monastery rang to gun fire from the young men's target-practice. Rebellious songs became the fashion and were heard everywhere, in the houses, at spinning parties, and from there out into the street; everywhere patriotic subjects had displaced the sentimental love songs of the song books. One was surprised to hear the girls at their gatherings singing:

Ah mother, sorrowful mother
Do not weep, mother, nor sorrow
That I have become a haidouk,
A haidouk, mother, a rebel.

Or to hear respectable mothers of large families singing ardently:

Courage, brave comrades, united and free,
No longer submissive rayah* will we be.

---

* *rayah:* the non-Moslem subjects of the Sultan.

But these were cries which the Turks ignored because they did not fear them. But after the failure of the unfortunate Stara Zagora movement in September, the Turkish population was alarmed, and its fury broke out in bloodthirsty reprisals against the Bulgarians. To the rifle fire at the bare screes it responded with bullets shot into Bulgarian flesh; to the rebellious songs of the Bulgarian women it responded by violating their sisters, or cutting the throats of their brothers. The Turks killed unarmed travellers, set fire to houses, took prisoners and shared their spoils with the zaptiehs. All Thrace was groaning under violence and atrocities.

Though he agreed with Bai Micho on many questions, Chorbadji Marko thought entirely differently about an insurrection. He called such an idea madness and severely scolded Ognyanov, whom he loved and protected, for every dangerous word spoken before him.

"I'm not surprised at the fools who go to fight the monastery cliff and spout balderdash; but I can't understand white-haired people, how they can have such bees in their bonnets! We're playing with fire! An empire of five-centuries' standing, that has put fear into all the world—how's it going to be overthrown by a few whipper-snappers with their flint-locks? Yesterday I met our Vassil, dragging my old musket to the monastery—he's going to overthrow Turkey too! I tell him to kill a chicken, and he goes and begs somebody else to cut its head off for him—he's afraid to see a drop of blood. 'Back you go,' I said to him, 'you nitwit; whoever you want to kill, better let God do the job! We're in hell here.' An insurrection? The Lord preserve us from any such thing; it'll mean ruin! Not a stone will be left standing here. . . ."

Ganko, the café-keeper, spoke up, "Bai Marko's right. An insurrection means ruin for us all . . ." and he looked up at the ceiling on which his unpaid accounts were lined up in the shape of regiments of chalk strokes.

Marko's reproach angered Micho. "Marko," he said, "you speak wisely, but there are wiser men than we who have foreseen that all this will really happen. Somehow or other Turkey will have to fall."

"I don't believe in your prophets," said Marko alluding to Martin Zadek, in whom Micho had a religious faith. "If King Solomon himself were to come here instead of your Zadek, and tell me that we could do anything, I wouldn't believe him. . . . I'll have no childishness."

"Look here, Marko, if God has willed it?" remarked Father Stavri.

"God has willed that we lie low, father priest. If he has decided to destroy Turkey, he won't trust us simpletons with such a job."

"We all know who's going to do it," said Pavlaki.

"Dyado Ivan,* Dyado Ivan!" exclaimed several.

Satisfaction was to be read on Chorbadji Micho's face; he went on eagerly: "You're telling me? And when I say that, I mean we'll march ahead and he'll come after us with the big guns, right as far as St. Sophia! Can we do anything without asking him? Would Lyubobratich be slaughtering them by the thousands, those curs, if he hadn't a strong back to lean on? But what I mean to say is that the days of the Turkish empire are numbered, just like a consumptive's. It's down in black and white; I haven't made it up. Listen here, whoever doesn't believe: 'Constantinople shall fall, the high city of the Turkish Sultan, and no drop of blood shall be shed. The land of the Turks shall be destroyed, hunger and sickness shall be the end of all misfortunes, and they themselves shall perish miserably!' And in another place it says again: 'Your dreams shall be shattered, and your idols and Alkoran shall be utterly destroyed! Mohammed! Thou Eastern Antichrist! Thy time is past, thy sepulchre is built, and thy bones shall be turned to ashes. . . .' " In his enthusiasm Bai Micho had risen to his feet and was sawing the air with his hand.

"But when is this to be?" asked Father Stavri.

"Soon I tell you; the hour has come!"

Just then the door was opened and Nikolai Nedkovich came in. He held the latest number of *The Century* in his hand; it had just arrived.

"Is that the new one, Nikolcho?" cried several voices, "read it to us, read it!"

"Let's see how many cabbages Lyubobratich has chopped down," said others impatiently.

"Thousands, I tell you. Sit here, Nikolcho!" and Bai Micho made room for him beside himself. Nikolai Nedkovich opened the paper.

"Read about the insurrection in Herzegovina first," ordered Bai Micho. Nedkovich began to read amid solemn silence. All pricked up their ears, but the glad news of the victory published by *Clio* was not confirmed. On the contrary, the news from the battlefield was bad: not only had Podogoritsa not been taken, but even Lyubobratich's last detachment had been beaten to a pulp, and he himself had fled to Austria.

Nothing but long faces could be seen now. Deepest disappointment and sorrow were evident on all of them. Nedkovich himself was upset and his voice broke and grew weak.

---

* A reference to Russia.

Micho Beizadé, suddenly bathed in sweat, pale and trembling with anger, cried out, "Lies, lies and lies! They can tell all that nonsense to my old fez! Lyubobratich has beaten them and done for them! Don't you believe a word of this paper!"

"But Bai Micho," remarked Nedkovich, "those telegrams are taken from various European newspapers. There must be some truth in them."

"Lies, lies, Turkish lies, forged in Constantinople! You find *Clio* and read it."

"I don't believe it either," said Hadji Smion, "newspaper men lie like Gipsies. In Moldavia, I remember, there was a newspaper; all it ever said was a lie."

"Put-up jobs."

"Well, isn't that just what I'm telling you? You have to take Turkish news the other way round: if they write that one hundred Herzegovinians have fallen, you may know for certain that it means one hundred of the Turks; if you put it at a thousand you won't be wrong."

Bai Micho's words calmed people's spirits. They were convincing, because they corresponded to the secret wishes of all. The news had to be false because it was bad, so the newspaper was not to be believed. But when that same newspaper published Lyubobratich's success, it entered no one's mind to doubt its veracity. Nevertheless that day's news disturbed the spirits of the customers of Ganko's cafe. Further conversation languished; there was a weight on everybody's mind.

Bai Micho himself felt embarrassed. He was cross with himself, cross with the newspaper and the whole world, because he had found no confirmation of the news in *Clio*. So he exploded when Petraki Shiikov said ironically amid the general silence, "It seems, Bai Micho, your Herzegovinian spark will just remain a spark and nothing more. You listen to me—Turkey will remain alive and well this year, and next year, and in a hundred years; we'll just be hoodwinked by your prophecies until we die."

"Shiika," cried Micho enraged. "Your noodle isn't big enough for this; you hold your tongue! Cattle of your sort can't understand anything even if it's rammed down their throats." A quarrel broke out, but the appearance of Stefchov put an end both to it and to the dangerous talk of Turkey's downfall.

chapter 19

criticisms

Calm reigned once more. Stefchov's presence restrained the customers. He sat down, bowed to several men and began to listen with a triumphant air, for he thought that the interrupted conversation had been about the lampoons of Ognyanov and Sokolov which had been scattered all over the town in large numbers the night before. But nobody said a word about them, either because they knew nothing, or because they despised them.

Bai Micho went out furious. Several men left the café after him. At the same time two newcomers entered. They were Ognyanov and Sokolov. They had just sat down when Hadji Smion turned to the former, "Won't you give us another comedy at Christmas time, Count?"

"*Genevieve* wasn't a comedy; it was a tragedy," remarked Mr. Fratyu. "It's called a comedy when the performance is funny, and a tragedy when there are tragic scenes and it's sad. What we acted was a tragedy. My part was a tragic one," explained Mr. Fratyu with the air of a man who knows it all.

"I know, I know, the number of them I've seen in Bucharest. But the way you did the madman—grand! I don't want to jinx you, Fratyu, but I said to myself, a real madman. The hair helped a lot," said Hadji Smion, praising him.

Ivancho Yota, who had just come in, joined in the conversation. "What, are you talking of the acting?" he broke in. "The year before last I saw a play in K., when they acted—what was it? I can't remember, eh, *Ivan the Haidouk*."

"*Ivanko the Assassin*," Mr. Fratyu corrected him.

"That's right, *The Assassin*, but ours turned out more magnanimous. . . . Our Lala had nightmares all night long. She kept screaming 'Golos! Golos!' most turbulently, and quaked in fear." Mr. Fratyu looked important, flattered by this praise.

"Yes, yes, and that's why I tell the Count to give us another comedy. Believe me, it's the thing to do. . . . Only have a different song," said Hadji Smion and he began a thorough search of all his pockets, because he had indirectly expressed disapproval.

"*Genevieve* is not a comedy but a tragedy," remarked Mr. Fratyu sternly once more.

"Yes, yes, a tragedy, in a word, play-acting."

"Bah, it was a comedy all right; it aroused laughter," Stefchov spoke up from his corner with an evil smile.

Ognyanov interrupted his conversation with Sokolov and said, "I'm afraid, Bai Hadji, that I might be made ashamed again. . . ."

Stefchov did not raise his eyes from the newspaper he had taken up.

"Who's the man who can shame you? Nobody can shame you!" chattered Dyado Nistor. "You give us *Genevieve* again—the children talk of nothing else. Our Penka was feverish then, she couldn't go. And now it's nothing but 'Daddy, I want *Genevieve,* that I do.' "

"All very well, Dyado Nistor, but I simply tremble at the thought of a hiss," said Ognyanov, shooting a look at Stefchov.

"Particularly when it comes from the dung heap," added Sokolov insultingly. Stefchov reddened with suppressed rage, but went on looking at the newspaper. He felt embarrassed under Ognyanov's contemptuous look, for he feared him. And Ognyanov's eyes were indeed burning with fury.

"I'll add my word to yours, Dyado Nistor," said Chono Doichinov, "I'm all for *Genevieve.* Only Kiriak had better take the part of Golos —it suits him down to the ground. Fratyu's a windbag, but there's no harm in him; people were wrong to curse him."

Stefchov turned red to his ears at this simple compliment, so full of poison. At the same time Mr. Fratyu took offence at the praise. Ognyanov and Sokolov smiled involuntarily. So did Hadji Smion without exactly knowing why.

Stefchov raised his eyes and looked at Ognyanov and Sokolov irritably. He said with feigned compusure, but in a voice that trembled with rage, "Yes, I hope Bai Ognyanov of *Lozengrad* will soon give us a tragedy too. He may rest assured that no one will laugh at it, least of all himself."

Stefchov emphasized the word Lozengrad (the town in which Ognyanov claimed he was born). Ognyanov noticed this and his face changed. But he answered firmly, "As long as there are such skilled movers behind the scene, I mean to say spies, as Stefchov, it wouldn't be surprising if there were to be a tragedy." And he gave him a contemptuous look.

Sokolov now gave his sleeve a tug.

"Leave him alone, or he'll be raising a worse stink," he whispered.

"I can't stand snakes in the grass!" Ognyanov said aloud, loud enough for Stefchov to hear.

Just then Boicho noticed Mooncho standing at the open door of the café. He saw that Mooncho had fixed his eyes on him and was shaking his head and smiling amicably. The idiot's expression was so kind, so gentle, so happy! Boicho had noticed at other times too, that Mooncho looked at him so attentively and affectionately, but he couldn't imagine the reason for this devotion.

When their eyes met a still more radiant smile spread over Mooncho's face and his eyes shone with an incomprehensible and senseless enthusiasm. He peered in, his eyes still fixed on Ognyanov, and grinning with all his might, called out slowly, "Rouss-i-yan! . . ." And putting his finger on his throat he began to draw it backward and forward to imitate the cutting of a throat.

Everybody stared at him in amazement. Ognyanov was no less puzzled than the rest. It wasn't the first time Mooncho had made such signs. "What's Mooncho telling you, Count?" several people asked him.

"I don't know," answered Ognyanov, smiling, "he's very fond of me!"

Mooncho probably sensed their amazement and, to explain his admiration of Ognyanov better, he looked at them all with stupid triumph, pointed at Ognyanov and cried still louder, "Rouss-i-yan! . . ." And waving his hand towards the north be began to cut his throat with his forefinger ever more energetically.

This repetition disturbed Ognyanov in spite of himself. It crossed his mind that by some ill chance Mooncho must have seen or sensed the event at Dyado Stoyan's mill. He looked at Stefchov uneasily, but grew calmer when he noticed that the latter had turned round and was whispering to somebody, without paying any attention to Mooncho.

At the same time Stefchov got up, pushed Mooncho aside from the door and went out, throwing a spiteful and vindictive look at Ognyanov.

Stefchov was boiling with rage. He had suffered so many blows to his self-esteem at the hands of Ognyanov, and had not yet had a single opportunity of revenging himself. He wanted revenge, but hidden, because he was afraid of an open fight with Ognyanov. The rebel song that had been sung at the theater had given him a weapon against the man, but, as we have seen, he missed his aim. The bey had not considered it possible for Ognyanov to have sung a rebel song in his presence and did not believe Stefchov.

The latter had thought it imprudent to insist in that case, but on the other hand he had discovered something else. Three days earlier in K., he had found out by chance from a man from Lozengrad that in his town there was no Boicho, and no Ognyanovs either. This was a clue which was to lead Stefchov to further discoveries. Probably another person was hiding behind the mask of Boicho Ognyanov, and for some very good reason. He was always with Dr. Sokolov, who had long been known for his rebellious spirit. Something probably bound the two men to each other, but exactly what? Probably something shady.

From one circumstance and another Stefchov instinctively felt that Ognyanov had something to do with the mysterious affair in Petkan's street, which still remained a mystery to him. It was at just that time that Ognyanov had appeared in town, and a stirring of spirits had begun to which he himself remained alien. Kiriak decided to pierce the obscurity of all this business and he set about it with all the persistence and passion which hatred can give to an evil and envious soul. New and sinister circumstances came to Stefchov's aid in his underhanded struggle with Ognyanov.

chapter 20

trouble

And so storm clouds gathered over Ognyanov's head. But he hardly suspected this. His six-months stay in Byala Cherkva, without any mishap, had increased his self-confidence to the point of recklessness. Fully absorbed by cares of a totally different nature, he had little time to think of his personal safety. Of all feelings, fear was the least developed in him. Furthermore, his feelings for Rada were like a brilliantly-hued prism through which he viewed the world.

At the moment, however, he was not entirely calm and on leaving the café, he said to the doctor, "What do you think? Was there anything serious in Stefchov's threat?"

"Stefchov has it in for you, and if he could have done you a bad turn, he'd have done it by now. He wouldn't have been satisfied with undercover plots."

"That Mooncho, what do those antics of his mean? It's beginning to bother me."

The doctor laughed. "Don't be childish!"

"Yes, they don't deserve attention, but Stefchov—could Stefchov know anything?"

"What can he know? Probably Hadji Rovoahma has started some hare again about us. You know that rumormonger can't spend an hour without inventing some nonsense or other."

"No, she's a dangerous old hag, and she might sniff out what anyone else would have to see or hear. She's Stefchov's mentor, too, as well as Rada's tormentor."

"It was she who started the rumor—you remember—that you were a spy. I tell you, she only jabbers away."

"But she said something else about you that was true. Of course she's better at women's scandal. Do you know, Stefchov is getting engaged tomorrow."

The doctor's face changed. "To Lalka?"

"Yes."

"How do you know?"

"Rada heard. Hadji Rovoahma is the go-between, naturally. The official suitors are Hadji Smion, that ubiquitous chameleon, and Alafranga."

The doctor was unable to hide his emotion. He quickened his pace. Ognyanov looked at him in surprise. "You never told me that your heart wasn't free, doctor."

"I love Lala," answered the doctor gloomily.

"Does she know?"

"She loves me too, or at least she likes me better than Stefchov. I don't believe there's any deeper feeling in her than that." Involuntarily the doctor's face grew red.

"Well, luckily or unluckily for you, it goes deeper than you think, brother; I know that for sure," said Ognyanov looking at his friend with sympathy.

"How do you know?" asked the doctor, redder still.

"Rada told me; you know they're friends. Lalka tells her everything. You don't know what tears she shed when they drove you off to K. And how overjoyed she was when you were set free. Rada saw it all."

"She's an innocent child," said the doctor in a hollow voice, "they'll kill her if they give her to that man."

"Why didn't you ask for her hand before, then?" asked Ognyanov with sympathy.

"What, don't you know that her father won't even see me?"

"Then steal her away."

"Now? When we're planning an uprising? It may break out in two years' time, and it may break out tomorrow, who knows? I don't even want to think of marrying in such uncertain times—and then, it would be a sin to drag that girl into misfortune. . . ."

"That's true," said Ognyanov thoughtfully: "the same idea has stopped me from marrying Rada. I could save her, the lovely darling, from so much bitter pain that way, and make her happy. A wonderful heart, brother mine! But she's killing herself now; she has linked her fate to mine. Poor girl." Ognyanov's face darkened.

The doctor was not quite clear in his mind about his feelings for Lalka. He was right in saying that he could not make up his mind to take her in these dark days. True love knows no obstacles or barriers. He did indeed feel something like love for Yordan's daughter, but this feeling was still quite weak; it was not a passion but an accidental liking, without deep roots. His temperament and his frivolous, merry life made him incapable of strong devotion to one object alone. His heart was divided between the bey's wife, if the rumor about them was true, and Cleopatra, as well as Lalka, as well as the revolution, and who knows what besides. . . . But now, after Ogynanov's news of Lalka's devotion—which sweetly and deeply flattered his self-esteem—and of the misfortunes which threatened her, his heart was heavy within him with unexpected grief and sorrow. It seemed to him that he had always been in love with Lalka and that he could not live without her. Perhaps it was the egoism so profoundly rooted in human nature that awoke in him; perhaps a sincere and ardent passion had flamed up; but he was terribly crushed at the thought that Lalka would be forever lost to him. How could he postpone this engagement? How could he destroy his rival? How could he save Lalka? These questions passing through his mind were very clearly reflected in Sokolov's gloomy and sorrowful face.

Ognyanov understood him. The doctor's grief and Lalka's fate aroused deep sympathy in him. "I'll challenge that mangy cur! I must kill him! Or he'll kill others!" Ognyanov blazed up suddenly. The two friends walked gloomily on.

Ognyanov stopped resolutely.

"Do you want me to go and tell him to keep his fingers out of the pie and box his ears in the middle of the cafe?"

"He'll swallow it as he did the rest. He's an impudent fellow. That won't help."

"At least I'll disgrace him."

"A box on the ears won't disgrace him in Yordan Diamandiev's eyes."

"It will in the girl's. She'll hear of it!"

"They don't ask Lalka what she thinks, and she bows to her father's will," answered the doctor and held out his hand.

"Are you off? Well, are you going to Father Stavri's tonight?"

"I don't feel like it; go alone."

"No, we must go. We promised. Father Stavri is a rough diamond, but an honest heart. And we might think of something. . . ."

"Very well, I'll wait for you at home." And the friends parted.

Ognyanov went to the school. In the faculty room he found no one but Merdevendjiev, deep in a Turkish book. Ognyanov gave him no greeting. From the very first he had had an aversion to this young man with the psalter under one arm and the "inshah"* under the other, two testimonials of an underdeveloped brain. The letter to Rada, on the other hand, had turned this aversion into loathing of the cantor, which increased when he saw the man's servile attitude towards Stefchov.

* A Moslem theological book.

Ognyanov strode up and down the room, blowing out clouds of smoke, still engrossed by his conversation with the doctor and paying no attention to the cantor's sleepy and apathetic face, bent over his book. Suddenly he caught sight of the new number of *The Danube,* the only newspaper to be received in the town, and that by Merdevendjiev, for its columns in Turkish. He cast an absent-minded glance at the Bulgarian columns, and when he was about to throw it down, his attention was drawn to a heading in big letters. Appalled, he read as follows:

"Escape of an exile from the Diarbekir fortress: Ivan Kralich, of the town of Vidin, Danubian District; age 28, tall, black-eyed, curly haired, olive-skinned, condemned to exile for life in the fortress of Diarbekir for participation in the riots of 1868, has escaped from there in March of this year and re-entered His Imperial Majesty's realm. He is being sought by the authorities, who have received the necessary instructions. Loyal subjects of the Sultan are bound, furthermore, on pain of severe punishment for disobedience, to inform on or give up the above-mentioned escaped criminal as soon as they recognize him to the lawful authorities, to suffer his well-deserved penalty, in accordance with the just imperial laws."

In spite of all the strength of his will Ognyanov was unable to remain calm in front of the other man; his face changed, his lips went white. The blow was so unexpected. He cast a quick glance at Merdevendjiev. The cantor, still in the same attitude, was bent over his book. He had probably noticed nothing of Ognyanov's emotions. Nor was it likely that he had paid any attention to the little paragraph, which was in itself uninteresting. Under the influence of these reassuring reflections, Ognyanov got back some of his self-possession.

His first idea was to destroy this dangerous evidence. He overcame his loathing of the cantor and humiliated himself to speak to him. "Bai Merdevendjiev," he said calmly, "have you read the paper? Would you let me take it home to read there? Its chronicle is very interesting."

"I haven't, but take it just the same," answered the cantor indolently and went on with his reading.

Ognyanov went out with the only copy of the ill-omened *Danube* which was received in Byala Cherkva.

chapter 21

intrigues

That day Kiriak Stefchov again left the field of battle at the café, with the intention, however, of returning to hurl himself more fiercely on his enemy.

His terrible hatred of this man, nurtured by various occasions, deadened the few honest feelings in his soul, which was overgrown with the weeds of mean instincts. For the first time that day, in the café, the cruel thought of destroying his enemy by treachery had flashed upon him. He had both the necessary information and the means. The paltry intrigues and calumnies which he had spread were no use; on the contrary, Ognyanov shattered them triumphantly and grew all the more in the eyes of the world. The attitude of the audience at the performance of *Genevieve* had finally convinced him of that. Had he been Mihalaki Alafranga, he would have performed his act of treachery with a clear conscience, believing that he was doing something good. Kiriak, corrupt though he was, still felt the vileness of such an action, but he did not have the strength to refrain. A raging thirst for revenge consumed him. He decided to go about it without coming into the open.

"Yes, first, this rascal's name is not Ognyanov; neither does he come from Lozengrad; second, it was he they were chasing in Petkancho's street, and no one else, and the subversive papers were his. . . . Doctor Sokolov really was with the bey's wife at that hour. . . . Hadji Rovoahma is right. . . . Our Filyo, the constable, also hinted as much. . . . It was she who hid the papers too. . . . How? I don't know. Third . . . we'll learn of that a little later. And that is the most terrible of all. That'll send him not merely to Diarbekir, but to the gallows. . . . I'll fix him, the blackguard!"

He was on his way to the convent where he had arranged to meet Merdevendjiev. "You were right, Madam," he said to Hadji Rovoahma upon entering her room.

"May the Lord bless you, Kiriak, and here I've been thinking I was off the track," said she jokingly, understanding perfectly well what he was referring to. "Who's been chasing you? You're puffing like a pair of bellows."

"I had a quarrel with Ognyanov a little while ago. . . ."

"That confounded whipper-snapper! He's turned the head of our fool of a Rada. . . ." the nun burst out. "He gives her a pack of rebel songs to learn. . . . Why, it's a positive epidemic! Even the old grannies are all singing rebel songs. . . . They've come here to set the world right by plunder and the sword! Here are some people gathering goods all their life, like ants, begging and piling up supplies and filling granaries, while others are out to make a bonfire of it all. If they were decent people at least! Young louts, the lot of them. . . . And our Rada! Holy Virgin, the first thing you know she'll be a second Christina, taking in revolutionaries, and have the very Gipsies mocking her. . . . Why, look at the muck they sang at the theater the other day; whatever are the Turks about?"

"I had a serious quarrel with Ognyanov and now I'm determined to crush him," said Stefchov angrily. But then he considered that it would be unwise to confide in the talkative nun and added; "That is, the police will do their work. . . . Only, silence, Madam."

"Why, you know me, don't you?"

"I do, that is why I say, silence."

Just then footsteps were heard on the gallery. Stefchov looked through the window and said with satisfaction; "There's Merdevendjiev!"

"Well?" he asked of the cantor, who entered hurriedly.

"The mouse is in the trap!" said Merdevendjiev, taking off his muffler.

"Really? Did he give himself away?"

"He grew pale, then green, and went all atremble. . . . It's he!"

"And what did he say?"

"He asked me to let him take it home with him to read. . . . It's the first time anything of the sort has happened. He used to despise the paper, just as he despises me. . . ." Stefchov stood up and clapped his hands.

"What is it?" Hadji Rovoahma asked in bewilderment.

"And he didn't guess it was a trap?" Stefchov asked.

"Not in the least. . . . I pretended I was reading and didn't see anything, but actually nothing escaped me; the bear sleeps, but his ears keep moving. . . ." Merdevendjiev added with pride.

"Bravo, Merdeven! The lampoons were a master-stroke too. You were meant to be an editor."

"But don't let me remain plain Merdeven forever. . . . Keep on working for that vacancy."

"Don't worry, I shall." The cantor gave thanks with his hands in Turkish fashion.

"I think I'll send that Popov packing too. . . . He looks at you like a bull, and he's as devoted to Kralich as a dog."

"Who is this Kralich?" asked Hadji Rovoahma again, surprised at not knowing something for once. Stefchov looked through the window absent-mindedly, without answering her, deep in his own thoughts.

"Ha, do you know? The churchwardens came to the school yesterday," Merdevendjiev said.

"Which ones?"

"All of them. Mihalaki proposed they should tell him he was expelled. But the others defended him. Especially Marko Ivanov. . . . They only reprimanded him about the song. In short, nothing came of it. You'd think Bai Marko was married to that Kralich, but one day he'll pay dearly for it. Why does the fool poke his nose in such matters?"

"And Micho?"

"Bai Micho? He's for Ognyanov too."

"Of course. Honor among thieves. . . ."

"Micho curses the government all over the place, just as Marko curses the Faith."

"Birds of a feather flock together," mumbled Hadji Rovoahma.

"What about Grigor? And Pinkov?"

"They're swimming in the same waters."

"I'll be damned if I don't close down that school! Then only owls will nest in it!" cried Stefchov, beside himself with rage, pacing the room with quick steps.

"That's it, that's it. Bind the priest and have peace in the village!"*

"All the subversive rebel songs come from those schools," remarked the nun. "But who is this Kralich, Kiriak?"

"Kralich? A kinglet, the future kinglet of Bulgaria!" he answered ironically.**

Merdevendjiev took his fez and opened the door. "And you won't forget my business, Kiriak?" he said pleadingly as he went out. The poor cantor thought it was simply a matter of getting rid of Ognyanov, whose place he coveted.

"Caesar shall have his due!" Stefchov remained alone with the

* The priest in those days was likely to be the most educated man in the village and a leader in any protest or action against the authorities.

** Kral in Bulgarian means "king."

nun to discuss another important matter: his engagement to Lalka.

By nightfall he was on his way to the konak. He met Mihalaki Alafranga in Piperkov's street.

"Where are you off to?" the latter asked him.

"Have you heard? *The Danube* has completely unmasked Ognyanov; it gives a full picture of him! It seems he's escaped from Diarbekir and is being hunted everywhere. . . . I swear it's he. . . . And his name isn't his own either."

"You don't say so, Kiriak! That fellow's dangerous. He'll be the ruin of innocent people. I was right yesterday when I suggested we should give him the sack—he's not the man for us. . . . Where are you going? Tell the bey to take steps."

"It's none of my business, I haven't even got the paper; Merdevendjiev has it; he knows. . . ." Stefchov answered cunningly, not wanting to expose himself and be suspected of treachery. He purposely mentioned the cantor's name to focus all suspicion on him.

"Inform on him, do; you'll be doing the population a great service," Mihalaki repeated quite simply and naturally, just as he would have told Stefchov that there was good fresh fish at the market and to go and get himself some. "Well, tomorrow the Hadji and I are going to old Yordan's. I congratulate you ahead of time. It's a dead certainty," and Mihalaki shook his hand.

"Thank you, thank you." It was quite dark. Stefchov and Mihalaki spoke to each other in whispers for some time more in the darkness, then parted. Stefchov went on his way, humming a Turkish love song. He was going to the konak.

chapter 22

a party at Father Stavri's

It was quite dark when Sokolov and Ognyanov set out for Father Stavri's house. It was nearly at the very end of the town. The two friends walked along several dark streets in silence. They were both deep in thought. Ognyanov had destroyed the only existing copy of *The Danube* in town, and that had calmed him somewhat. Nor had he noticed anything to worry about in Merdevendjiev later. After that, he had become incredibly bold, to the verge of recklessness. Such is the way of all those whose natural element is danger and risk. Yet a shadow of doubt still troubled him. The doctor was, of course, more seriously troubled. The further away they got from the center of town, the fewer people they met. The narrow, crooked streets grew still and deserted. They heard only dogs barking.

"Gracious, who's that there?" asked the doctor, pointing to what looked like the shadow of a man, standing upright by the wall. At the same moment the stranger darted away.

"The gentleman's taken fright! Let's go after him and ask him what he has against our wishing him good evening" said Ognyanov, dashing after him. The doctor was not in the least inclined to such exercise at the moment, preoccupied as he was with his troubles, but he too ran after him.

The stranger ran for dear life. Either he was a doubtful character himself or had taken them for such. He soon outstripped his pursuers, for if boldness gives wings to the shoulders, fear sticks them onto the heels. The friends soon realized they were chasing the wind. The stranger had hidden behind some gate and not a sound was to be heard. Then they laughed.

"Why did we chase that little fellow?" asked the doctor.

"I suspected he might be some agent of Stefchov's. The lampoons are spread by night. I'm itching to lay my hands on one of those rascals."

Sokolov walked on deep in thought. "Doctor, where are you off to? This is the priest's gate," Ognyanov called out to him, giving it a good knock. The absent-minded doctor turned back.

The gate was opened and the black figure of the old priest appeared. "Knock, and it shall be opened unto you! Come in! Doctor! Count!" Father Stavri chattered away jovially.

As has already been mentioned, the nickname "Count" had stuck to Ognyanov; only the bey called him Consul. The sympathy which Genevieve's husband had aroused in the theater passed over to Ognyanov in the streets as well. Children ran after him crying: "The Count, the Count!" and went up to him to be patted on the cheek. In the beginning, the old priest had rather grumbled against him, but since the performance Stefchov had lost another ally.

The sound of a flute could be heard from a room which opened onto the verandah. When the priest led the guests into the large room they saw quite a company there, among them Kandov, Nikolai Nedkovich and the blind man. They exchanged greetings. Gancho, the priest's son and a friend of Boicho's, brought some rakiya and some green pickles, diced, dressed with olive oil and abundantly strewn with red pepper. The sound of the flute had stopped.

"Kolcho," Nikolai Nedkovich said, "go on!" Kolcho began again and played several European airs with great success.

"Well, how about some brandy and a bite of pickles to set the flute's voice right; you've forgotten me altogether," he said, ending his song.

"That's right, Kolcho. Who begs has something to carry home," said the priest.

Ognyanov poured out a glass and handed it to him silently. He felt his hand, recognized him and said: "That's Bai Ognyanov, isn't it? Thank you. . . . The rest of them call you Count, but owing to a minor detail I wasn't able to see you as a count in the theater."

The guests exchanged smiling glances.

"Bai Kolcho, do sing us the nun's litany!" Ognyanov asked him with a smile.

Kolcho put on a solemn air, cleared his throat and began in imitation of the old church cantor, Hadji Athanasius: "Bless, oh Lord, thy righteous servant, Gospozha Seraphima and mild Cheruvima, the dark-eyed Sophia and the fair Ripsimia, the plump Magdalena and the skinny Irina, the beautiful Enocha—the convent's shining light—and Gospozha Parashkeva, the guileless virgin; and Hadji Rovoahma—the sinless madam. . . ."

Kolcho enumerated all the nuns in turn, appending to each an epithet the very reverse of their true characteristics. The whole company went into peals of laughter.

"Come, come now, sit down at table. Why poke fun at all the holy women?" the priest's wife rebuked them jokingly. The priest said grace, and all the guests did full justice to the meal, with the exception of Sokolov, who felt something gnawing at him inside.

A gigantic flask of amber wine stood in front of the priest to spread cheer right and left. "Wine gladdens the heart of man and fortifies his flesh!" he said, filling the glasses. "Drink, Count! Nikolcho, take a big swig! Kandov, down it; you're Russian bred! Come on, Doctor, don't be so abstemious; this isn't medicine, this is a gift of the Lord! Kolcho, gulp it down, my child, then you'll sing us the Wallachian song; 'Lina, Lina, may it pass.' " With such jovial encouragements did the old priest, now in the highest spirits, arouse and quench the thirst of his guests, and the glasses crossed, met and touched as in a veritable quadrille.

The conversation after dinner was both spirited and varied. Naturally, *Genevieve* was discussed as well as Stefchov's hissing, about which the old priest didn't mince his words. Ognyanov skilfully diverted the conversation into less dangerous channels, such as that year's vintage. The old priest was in his element like a fish in the sea, and expatiated in detail on the qualities of the wines from all the vineyards.

That of the Piklindol vineyards he considered the champagne of champagnes. "It shines like the sun, sparkles like gold; it's as yellow as amber, and as sharp as a razor. It was by such wine that the prophet David was rejuvenated. . . . Ten drops of it make a man a philosopher, fifty—a king, a hundred drams—a saint!" Father Stavri exclaimed in an ecstasy that would have made even a Syrian hermit thirsty.

He puffed with satisfaction and the candle went out. "Ho, some light, light the candle!" he said.

"Father, you have three things," said Kolcho, "the clergyman, the candlestick and the candle, but, to tell you the truth, I can't see any of them."

"And what have you, my child?" asked the priest, who had not grasped the delicate irony.

"I have three things too: my person, my poverty and my poor sight." They all laughed at Kolcho's witticism.

Soon the conversation became general. Suddenly the following gay song sounded in the street. Probably it was some young wag, proud of his vocal powers, who was singing it.

Who bought you your necklace,
Lovely Milka Todorkina,
Your necklace, the silver one?"

'Twas Kiriak who got it for me,
For my white neck,
For me to wear and him to admire.

Who bought you the little skirt,
Lovely Milka Todorkina,
The little skirt—the taffeta one?

'Twas Kiriak who got it for me,
For my slender waist,
For me to wear and him to admire.

The song passed and died away in the streets beyond. But it brought the conversation round to Milka Todorkina, a close neighbor of the priest's. Milka was a pretty but wanton girl, who was much talked about in the small town; and her bad reputation grew daily to the great comfort of all gossip-mongers. A song about Milka had soon been composed. Her neighbors frowned in displeasure. They didn't like having such temptation in the neighborhood; bad examples are contagious. Her father and mother were advised to marry her to Rachko Lilov the coppersmith, who was mad about her. But his parents wouldn't hear of it. Give their son to such a girl?

"And who's Lilo the coppersmith, that he won't even hear of the match?" the priest's wife was saying. "Whom does he want to marry his pock-marked Racho to? To a chorbadji's daughter, perhaps, or a nobleman's? Milka is a pretty young girl. . . . Well, she made a slip or two, out of foolishness; it doesn't mean she'll always be of that mind, does it? Reason comes with age. . . . And if they love each other, let them marry. Let them live in love and peace, as the Lord has ordained. Is it any better this way?"

"Well, the girl's a fool all right; on the other hand it's true they give her no peace with temptations of the evil one," the old priest added. "There isn't a rake who isn't after her, nor a song that doesn't mention her. What is one to do? People make a mountain out of a molehill and a lion out of an ant! So now Milka Todorkina is the talk of the town. I've been telling her father to catch that son of a bear, Rachko, when he visits her, to marry them without a fuss—and there's an end to it; marriage veils everything."

"Wasn't there talk some time ago of Chorbadji Stefchov's son marrying Milka?" asked one of the lady-guests. "The girl hadn't lost her reputation then."

"There's been talk of so many people by now! . . . The poor girl has nothing but a bad name," another woman said.

"By the way, do you know the news? Kiriak Stefchov is getting engaged to Lalka Yordanova!" a third lady put in. These words pierced the doctor like a lance.

"Yes, of course; Stefchov would have nothing less than the best . . ." remarked the priest.

"And does Milka take to Rachko?" asked Ognyanov to change the subject.

"Haven't I been telling you? He visits the girl in secret, so people say . . . they love each other. . . . There's nothing to ponder about: just a wedding veil over the pair, and tongues will stop wagging. Oh, Lord, Jesus Christ, forgive me—we have sinned in worldly temptation. And tomorrow is St. Andrew's Day! Gancho, pour out a glass of the Dolna Reka wine, will you, for our throats are fairly parched. . . . Anka, Mihalcho, it's bedtime, my dears. You're small children." The children got up and retired reluctantly; they were keenly interested in the talk about their Auntie Milka Todorkina.

"It's my feeling, they should leave this Milka alone; why should they force her to marry at all costs?" said Kandov.

The old priest stared at Kandov in surprise. "How could she not marry?" he asked quite bewildered.

"She should have her freedom; she has human rights too," said the student forcefully.

"What do you mean, free? Free to hang up her shift on a pole? Let's get this straight."

"What strange ideas of human rights!" Nikolai Nedkovich remarked.

"As long as she doesn't encroach upon the liberty of others, she should be able to live as she pleases; it doesn't matter," Kandov explained.

"And if she becomes most luxurious, it doesn't matter again?" asked the priest.

"What do you mean by luxurious?"

"A *res publica,* you know!" the priest explained impatiently. Kandov looked mystified. Nedkovich explained to him in a low voice the meaning the priest quite arbitrarily gave to those words.

"It is a matter of principle," Kandov answered importantly. "The advanced ideas of our liberal century endeavor to emancipate woman from the state of slave-like submission to man which is a heritage of the barbarian epochs."

"Well, what's the long and the short of it?" asked the priest, who hadn't understood a thing.

Kandov continued, turning to Ognyanov and Nedkovich, "Contemporary science admits that woman has abilities equal to those of man, and adjudicates equal rights to her. Till now she has been the victim of a whole series of silly prejudices, which bind her will in iron chains. She has groaned under the burden of degrading obligations, imposed upon her by the tyranny of men's animal instincts. A whole series of forms, customs and laws have been created for her, to trip her up at every step of her life! . . ."

Kandov spoke with conviction. He had an honest heart, the indiscriminate swallowing of the utopias of various socialist doctrinaires had confused the ideas of truth and falsehood in him; the high-sounding phrases and rounded fashionable catchwords meant more to him than the real truth of life; he was struck by their novelty and wanted to show off with them. Kandov suffered from the sickly idealism of the circles he had moved in. Living in Bulgaria for a short time would be enough to bring him to his senses.

"And pray, tell me the meaning of such high-sounding words," the student continued, "as chastity, marital fidelity, the sacred obligations of motherhood and other such nonsense? Simply, exploiting woman's weakness!"

"He reels it off as if he were reading it!" the priest muttered to himself.

"Mr. Kandov," Nedkovich remonstrated, "every reasonable person sympathizes with the ideas you expressed at the beginning. But from there you take a breakneck jump and fall into the wildest extremes. You reject the laws—not of man, but of nature; you undermine the eternal foundations on which human society is built. What will happen to the world if we destroy matrimony, the family, the mother, and deprive woman of her great mission?" At this point the old priest understood and frowned.

"I want her emancipation."

"Pardon me, you want her degradation," remarked Ognyanov.

"Mr. Ognyanov, have you read the philosophers who have written on the question of woman? I advise you to read them. . . ."

"Kandov, my lad, Kandov, my lad!" the priest turned to him. "And have you read the Gospels?"

"Yes, I have . . . sometime or other."

"Do you remember the place where it says, 'Wives, submit yourselves unto your own husbands!' And further, 'For this cause shall a man leave father and mother, and shall cleave to his wife?'

"I found my judgment only on solid science, Father."

"And what science is more solid than that of the Lord?" the priest continued angrily. "You'd better clear your head of such protestant thoughts, my boy. Marriage is a holy sacrament. How can you do without marriage, son? What use then are the church, and faith, and clergymen if people are going to breed like pigs, without wedlock, without the Lord's blessing?"

The door opened and Gancho entered. "There's a terrible racket outside, at Milka's house," he said.

"What's up?"

"I don't know for certain," Gancho answered with a stutter, "but I think the coppersmith's locked in there. The whole neighborhood has gathered."

"If it's Racho, I have an idea of whats going to happen," said the old priest. "Come on, boys, let's go and see; they may need your old priest there. . . . Nothing can be done without a priest's blessing. . . . Let Kandov prattle all he likes. I knew all about these things when he was still a babe." They all went out.

chapter 23

another is caught in the trap

Milka Todorkina's gate was a few doors away from that of the priest. A babel of voices could be heard in the narrow little yard in front of the steps. The noise increased every minute. The crowd grew as curious neighbors joined it; two or three lanterns flickered here and there. Many people tried to catch a glimpse of the locked-in lovers through the window. Milka's father was shouting; her mother was scolding and running about like a frightened hen. Racho's father appeared in a little while, pushed the crowd aside and started pounding on the door to drag his son out of the room. But several strong hands pulled him back.

"Who's lording it here, I declare!" he cried and again dashed at the door.

"Bai Lilo, keep quiet," a neighbor called out to him; "don't you see how matters stand?"

"My boy!" Lilovitsa was shrieking, "I won't have my son marry such a wanton slut!" and she fell upon the people who were in her way like a kite.

"Dame Lilovitsa!" cried a coarse voice. "Wanton slut indeed! What business has Racho with her then? We'll have it done here, as is the custom."

"What'll you do to him? You won't hang him, will you? He hasn't killed anyone, has he?" And she again hurled herself towards the door, her hair dishevelled, like a mad woman.

"We'll marry them, as is proper."

"I won't have that witch!"

"Your son seems to want her—he's the one we'll marry."

The desperate mother didn't know what to do. She felt that this tribunal of public opinion was stronger than herself. She fell to lamenting her fate. "My child is done for! My life's not worth living! A plague on that bitch for seducing my son!"

The clamor increased with the crowd. A few voices could be heard more distinctly through the uproar, but all in the same vein. "Wedlock! Wedlock! And then it'll be just a nine days' wonder," a fellow shouted.

"Bind the priest and have peace in the village," another neighbor added.

"It's what he was asking for," a third was saying.

"Now, wait a bit, she may have called him, for all you know!"

"Come, come, the boy doted on her."

"If that's so, what's all the fuss about?"

"They're waiting for someone to come from the konak; then they'll open the door."

"There, the onbashi has just come!" people cried.

Sherif-Aga and the two Christian constables pushed their way through the crowd.

"Let's marry them here and now," someone yelled.

"No, first we take them to the baths, with the big drums," called Gancho the Spider.

"Why all this fuss? Let's have a quick wedding here and drink a glass to their health."

"Have they called the priest?" Ghencho Stoyanov was asking.

"Here he is!" said old Father Stavri, pushing his way forward with his guests. "Don't worry, your old priest knows the Christian law. . . . Gancho, go and fetch me my chasuble and the prayer book!"

At that moment the door was unlocked. "Come out!" cried the onbashi.

"Milka, Rachko! Come out!" some others cried too. The crowd pressed round the onbashi. They all rushed forward to have a look at the boy and the girl, as if they had never seen them before. Lanterns were raised above the people's heads, throwing abundant light on the open door. Milka was the first to appear. She cast down her eyes in shame. She was dazed and didn't even answer her mother who was mumbling something indistinctly. Only once did she raise her eyes with a look of surprise and fright. Milka was prettier than ever now and won over the sympathy of the angered neighbors. Youth and beauty immediately disarmed the crowd's indignation. Many faces expressed forgiveness.

"She'll make a bonny bride!" some said.

"All's well that ends well. . . . May happiness be theirs!" said Nistor Frakaltsé.

Father Stavri stood in front with his guests, some of whom did not know the boy. "Rachko, you come out too!" cried the old priest, peering into the dark room through the open door.

"Come out; don't be ashamed; there's a fine lad!" someone else was saying, "everything will be forgiven and father priest will bless you for ever after."

Kandov turned to his friends. "A difficult situation!" he said in a low voice. "Such moments add ten years to one's age."

"A very original national custom," said Nedkovich. "The week before last another pair of lovers were married like this."

"It's a custom that smacks rather of violence," remarked Ognyanov.

The young man did not come out of the room.

"He's inside, isn't he? Why doesn't he come out?" the priest asked of Milka. She nodded affirmatively and looked at the room in surprise.

The onbashi grew impatient. "Come out, will you!"

Other voices joined in, calling Rachko. The crowd was surging forward. Curiosity was as lively as in the theater when the audience is waiting for the curtain to go up. Here the curtain had already gone up—they were only waiting for the hero. But he did not appear.

Finally the onbashi entered the room, the crowd rushing in after him. The young man stood in a corner, motionless. But it was not Rachko the coppersmith. It was Stefchov.

They all stood dumbfounded and motionless. The onbashi withdrew a few steps. He couldn't believe his eyes. Neither could the others. Father Stavri dropped his chasuble; his friends looked at each other in consternation. Sokolov fixed a look of triumph and hatred on his enemy; his face lit up with a smile of malicious joy. He took in the sight of this crushing disgrace with infinite delight. Stefchov, weighed down with so many eyes upon him, humiliated, lost, crushed, was unrecognizable. He cast furtive glances here and there. "Stefchov! Stefchov!"—his name swept the crowd in whispers. He looked about him again as if to find a place to hide in, or for the earth to swallow him up. How did he come to be here? Through a fatal series of events.

That evening, after parting with Mihalaki, he had continued on his way to the konak. When he reached the gate he stopped, troubled by something. However black and embittered his soul was, he was after all a Bulgarian and something within him stirred in protest. He was frightened by his action and put it off for the next day, in order to perform it in a bolder frame of mind. He then passed by the konak and set out towards the house of a relative of his at the end of the town, but not finding him at home, walked back along the street. It was just then that he met Ognyanov and the doctor in the darkness, recognizing them by instinct and—the guilty flee though none pursue—he dashed off in a fit of blind fear. Passing by Milka's gate he unconsciously pushed it to seek shelter, and hid in the thick weeds of the yard. He stayed there quite a while; not a sound was to be heard from the street. The figure of a woman crossed the yard and went up the steps. By her gait Stefchov recognized Milka. He had been the first to seduce her, deserting her after some time. One fall led to the next, and Milka gradually slipped down the path which inevitably leads to the abyss. But today, on the eve of his engagement, he remembered, not without anxiety, that Milka had a few letters in her possession which she might use to harm him once his engagement was known. Some enemy of his might easily incite the angry girl. So he decided to get the dangerous letters back from her, that very evening if possible. He walked stealthily up to the door and entered the room of his former mistress.

All these movements of Stefchov's had been observed by Milka's father, or rather stepfather. He was on the lookout for Rachko, intending to follow his neighbors' advice. In the darkness, however, he took Stefchov for the coppersmith and locked him in with Milka. Whereupon he ran off to call the next-door neighbors who were followed by the whole neighborhood.

It didn't take the onbashi long to come to a decision. "Go away, gentlemen; I shall question him at the konak!" he called out harshly to the crowd and took Stefchov by the arm.

"You won't go to the konak! Everything shall be done here!" somebody cried at the back, not having understood that it was Stefchov who was caught and not Rachko.

"It's Stefchov, don't you see?" some others said.

"Stefchov! How's that?" The confusion increased.

"Well, what if he is the son of a chorbadji," someone shouted. "It'll be the same with him as with Rachko—he hasn't horns by any chance?"

"It's all one; let's marry them!" another was crying.

"But that's not the sort of girl for him," a voice spoke in his defense.

"Then what's he up to in her room at midnight? Or can the chorbadjis make light of people's honor, and the law's only for the poor?"

A few more voices were heard in favor of Stefchov.

"Off to the baths, off to the baths!" from Ghencho the Spider.

Ognyanov said in a low voice to the onbashi, "Sherif-Aga, get the gentleman away as soon as possible; such a crowd looking on . . .

it is hard." He forgot his enemy and only saw a victim crushed by disgrace. The sight of the man's humiliation was more than he could bear.

The onbashi looked at Ognyanov suspiciously.

"Leave him alone. What business is it of yours! Let him blush with shame!" said the revengeful Sokolov, pulling him by the sleeve.

It was only now that Stefchov saw his two pursuers. It struck him that they were the originators of his disgrace; he noted the smile. Fiendish rage sprang up in his soul and the look he cast would have frightened them, had they noticed it. . . .

The onbashi led Stefchov away. "Stand aside," he cried, "This is none of your business. You were looking for Rachko here. . . . Go ahead, sir." The crowd moved slowly behind them.

"How did this happen?" asked Sherif-Aga in a low voice with much concern.

"Ognyanov and Sokolov betrayed me," Stefchov whispered.

The crowd moved slowly behind them.

"Bring him here, effendi, the girl is left in the lurch; all she can do now is die!" shouted Ivan Selyamsuz, who had just come.

Everyone present objected strongly but their protest went no further than that. "Why are you silent? Speak up all of you, come on!" Selyamsuz was shouting in his booming voice. "Or has Chorbadji Stefchov's son put plums in your mouths?" Selyamsuz had long hated Stefchov. But his voice called forth no response.

Meanwhile others had gathered around the steps. They were pouring water over Milka who had fainted. The unfortunate girl could no longer bear the strain of these nerve-racking events which had crushed her for good. The people went their way discontented.

chapter 24

providence intervenes twice

The next morning was a holiday. Abbot Nathaniel was officiating in the monastery church by the lectern and had nearly finished his chant. Somebody tugged at his sleeve. Mooncho was standing in front of him.

The abbot looked at him sternly. "What do you want, Mooncho? Get along, be off with you," he scolded, and turned again to his singing.

But Mooncho's hand once more gripped him firmly by the elbow and would not let go. He again turned round, angrily, and then saw that Mooncho was quite out of breath; his eyes shone with a strange fear and his whole body was trembling. "What's the matter, Mooncho?" asked the priest severely.

Mooncho turned his head to one side, his eyes popping out still further, then he made a great effort and said loudly, "R-ou-ss-i-y-a-n . . . at the m-m-mill . . . Turks!" but instead of continuing he made a motion of digging with his hands.

At first the abbot looked at him in amazement. Then suddenly a terrible thought struck him. Mooncho must know what was buried at the mill; and since he mentioned Roussiyan too he evidently knew the whole secret. How? It passed his comprehension. One thing only he did understand: the secret was already known to the authorities!

"Boicho's lost!" Nathaniel whispered to himself, the picture of despair, oblivious both of the chant and of the singing and without noticing Father Gideon who was making desperate signs at him and winking from the opposite lectern, to remind him that it was his turn. Nathaniel glanced towards the altar where Vikenti was busy with the service, left Father Gideon to manage the chant as best he could and went out of the church. It took him a minute to get to the stable, another to get onto the horse, and off he dashed towards town, swift as an arrow.

It was intensely cold that morning and there was a blizzard. It had snowed during the night and the grass and the branches of the trees were all white. The abbot mercilessly spurred his little black horse, from whose nostrils clouds of steam issued. He knew that the rumor they had spread which explained the disappearance of the two ruffians had been accepted and had removed the last shred of suspicion. Who had stirred it now in the mind of the sluggish police-chief? There was treachery here without a doubt. On whose part, he couldn't yet guess. He didn't believe it of Mooncho—supposing Mooncho really had found out the whole business—for he knew how the idiot worshipped Ognyanov. Could he have given him away unconsciously? But there was treachery all right. And it was bound to have terrible consequences for Ognyanov.

He covered the distance to the town in four minutes instead of the usual fifteen. The horse was all in a lather. He left it at his brother's on the way and went to Ognyanov's rooms on foot.

"Is Boicho here?" he asked anxiously.

"He's out. Just before you some zaptiehs came and searched for him in every nook and cranny. What do they want him for, those wretches? One would think he'd killed someone!" the landlord answered angrily.

"Where did he go?"

"I don't know."

"That's bad, but there's still hope," the abbot said to himself and ran off to Doctor Sokolov's. He knew that Ognyanov was not much of a churchgoer, so he didn't even think of looking for him in the church. Passing by Ganko's café, he looked in, but didn't see him there. "I may find out from Sokolov where he is, if he isn't in prison already," said Nathaniel to himself, dashing into Sokolov's yard.

"Any one at home, granny?"

"There's no one, your Reverence," answered the old woman of the house, throwing aside the broom to come and make her obeisance and kiss the cleric's hand.

"Where's the doctor?" he asked angrily.

"I don't know, reverend Father!" answered the woman, stammering and looking off in confusion.

"Dear me!" the abbot groaned and started towards the gate.

"Wait a minute, wait a minute, Father!" The old woman ran after him.

"What is it?" he asked impatiently.

With a mysterious air she said in a low voice, "He's here, but he's hiding, for the Turks, may the devil take them, were after him a little while ago. . . . Forgive me, Father!"

"You don't suppose he's hiding from me? Why didn't you tell me at once?" and he crossed the yard hurriedly and knocked on the door, which was immediately opened by the doctor.

"Where's Boicho?" were his first words.

"At Rada's. What's up?" Sokolov felt he was about to learn of a great calamity. He grew pale.

"This very minute they're digging at the mill. There's been treachery."

"Oh, Ognyanov's done for!" cried the doctor in despair. "He must be told at once."

"They searched for him at his place but didn't find him," the abbot continued with emotion. "I raced here like the wind on my horse to warn him. . . . Oh Lord, what will become of the boy? Protect him! . . . Where are you off to?" he asked in surprise.

"I'll get hold of Boicho. We must save him if it isn't too late," said the doctor, opening the door.

The abbot looked at him in still greater surprise. "They're after you too, aren't they! I'd better go. . . ."

The doctor made a gesture with his hand. "It's out of the question. Your appearing at Rada's at this time, in her room, will be noticed; it will cause a scandal."

"But you'll be caught!"

"It doesn't matter. I must warn him somehow. The real danger is for Boicho. I'll go by the back streets. . . ." And Sokolov was off. The abbot blessed him with tears in his eyes.

The doctor knew that Ognyanov was going to be at the Girls' School that morning as it was empty today and he had agreed to meet there with a courier from the committee in P. In a few bounds he had reached the churchyard without being seen by a policeman and rushed up the stairs to the Girls' School where Rada lived. He burst into the room like a hurricane. The sudden appearance of Sokolov, and in such a manner, amazed Rada.

"Has Boicho been here?" he asked breathlessly, without even greeting her.

"He went out just now," answered Rada. "Why are you so pale?"

"Where did he go?"

"To church. . . . What's the matter?"

"To church!" cried Sokolov without further explanation and opened the door to leave. But he drew back dumbfounded, for he saw that the onbashi was placing guards at the exits to the church.

"What's the matter with you, doctor?" cried the poor school teacher, sensing trouble.

Sokolov pointed to the zaptiehs through the window. "Look, they're watching out for Boicho. He's been betrayed, Rada! They're after me, too. . . . Oh, what a calamity, what a calamity!" he cried, gripping his head with his hands.

Rada dropped down on the window seat. Her round face, pale with fear, grew still paler. It seemed to be made of marble.

Sokolov stared out of the window. He could no longer show himself with the zaptiehs there and was on the lookout for a trustworthy person whom he could tell to warn Ognyanov of the danger. At the same time he visualized it in all its horror.

Unexpectedly he saw Mr. Fratyu passing under the window on his way to church. "Fratyu, Fratyu," he called to him softly, "come closer!" Mr. Fratyu stopped.

"Fratyu, you're going to the men's church, aren't you?"

"Just so, as always," Mr. Fratyu answered.

"Please tell Boicho—he's there—that there are zaptiehs stationed at the doors to catch him. Tell him to be on his guard." Mr. Fratyu looked at the church anxiously and saw indeed that its three entrances were guarded by zaptiehs. Fear spread across his small face.

"Will you tell him?" the doctor asked impatiently.

"Who, I? All right, I'll tell him," the prudent Fratyu answered with obvious hesitation. He then added not without suspicion, "But why don't you go yourself, doctor?"

"They're after me too," the doctor whispered. Fratyu's face changed again. He was in a hurry to get away from such a dangerous interlocutor and went on straight ahead.

"Fratyu, hurry, do you hear?" Sokolov repeated for the last time. Mr. Fratyu nodded his consent, walked on a little distance, then turned and went into the convent.

The doctor saw it and tore his hair in despair. He wasn't thinking of himself; he was suffering torment for his friend; he realized that even if he were told now, it would be late and only by some miracle would he be able to escape from the clutches of the authorities. Only this little ray of hope remained—and it was only hope.

There had indeed been treachery. That very night Stefchov, on being taken to the konak, had told the bey about all his discoveries and suspicions regarding Ognyanov's identity. And in the same moment a terrible idea flashed upon him. He remembered the business with Emeksiz's hound, of which the onbashi had told him earlier. Neither he nor the onbashi had thought then of investigating the cause of the hound's fierce hatred of Ognyanov, or why it scratched the ground at the mill. What was the animal digging for? Why had it attacked Ognyanov? Wasn't that the clue to the mysterious disappearance of the two Turks? And that had coincided with Ognyanov's appearance in the town. Ognyanov had most certainly had something to do with it. Stefchov's malignant mind thought all this out with lightning speed and the ugly suspicion was hatched with irresistible force and clarity.

Stefchov advised them to start digging at Stoyan's mill immediately. The bey bit his lips and gave his orders without delay. He decided to have Ognyanov arrested early in the morning so that he would not escape somehow in the dark or cause bloodshed. . . . That morning the two corpses were dug up, moreover, and Ognyanov's fate was sealed. He was now cornered like a beast. The onbashi preferred to watch for him at the entrance rather than seize him in the church. That might provoke an unpleasant panic among the people and challenge Ognyanov to desperate self-defense. It was better to take him by surprise.

While Sokolov was in the depths of despair on one side, and Rada on the verge of fainting on the other, heavy footsteps sounded unexpectedly on the stairs outside. The doctor started and pricked up his ears. The footsteps approached slowly, accompanied by the tap of a stick, and stopped before the door. And Kolcho's well-known chant was sung in a priestly voice. "Bless, oh Lord, thy righteous servants: the holy Seraphima and the meek Cheruvima, the black-eyed Sophia and the fair Ripsimia; the plump Irina and the lean Magdalena; and Gospozha Rovoahma, may something harm her. . . ."

"Kolcho!" said the doctor opening the door. Whereupon the blind man entered freely; he was at home everywhere.

"Were you in the church just now, Kolcho?"

"Yes, I was."

"Did you see Ognyanov there?" the doctor asked impatiently.

"My glasses haven't come from America yet, so I didn't see him. But I know he's there, in the pew next to Frangov."

The doctor spoke to him earnestly, "This is no time for joking, Kolcho. The police are after Ognyanov and the zaptiehs are watching for him at the church doors. He doesn't know a thing. He's done for unless we can warn him."

"I'm going!"

"Please do, Bai Kolcho!" added Rada, whom hope had somewhat revived.

"I'd go myself, but the police are after me too. They won't pay any attention to you—go!" said the doctor.

"I would give my miserable life for Ognyanov, if they asked for it. . . . What am I to tell him?" the blind man asked with much concern.

"Only tell him this: everything's discovered; zaptiehs are guarding the doors of the church; save yourself as best you can!" He then added gloomily, "If they haven't tricked him into coming out already."

Kolcho realized the importance of every second and left quickly.

chapter 25

no easy task

Kolcho set off down the stairs, feeling his way, and tapping with his stick on every step. But once in the yard he quickened his pace with great assurance and entered the porch. There he stopped and started searching in all his pockets for his handkerchief, as a pretext to hang around long enough to hear the instructions Sherif-Aga was giving.

"Hassan-Aga," he was saying in a low voice, "go and tell the others to keep their eyes open. If he gets difficult, they're to shoot without asking me. . . ."

"Nenko, my lad, just go in and call the Count, the schoolmaster Ognyanov. Tell him somebody wants to see him," Filcho the constable was saying to a boy, as Kolcho made out by the voices.

Then he was afraid that they would reach Ognyanov before him; he pulled aside the heavy curtains of the door and went in. The church was packed with people. Hadji Athanasius was singing the last psalm and the service was coming to an end. The crowd was very thick, as there were many people taking holy communion and several requiems, and the crush was terrific. In fact the path through the church was quite blocked. The blind man seemed to plunge deeper and deeper into an impenetrable forest, dark as the night which was eternal for Kolcho. His instinct was a perfect guide; but how was he to break through that dense wall of arms, thighs, chests, shoulders and legs? Small and weak as he was, it was unthinkable that he could succeed in making his way to Ognyanov's pew in front of the very altar. That was a task hard enough even for a Goliath! He wedged his way in to a certain point, then stopped, tired out. He tried pushing to one side, then to another—in the darkness—all in vain: the wall did not give an inch. Many people even scolded him and told him not to push ahead like that, or he would get suffocated or crushed. Several iron elbows dug into his weak ribs, nearly breaking them. He was out of breath. In two minutes the priest would say: "Draw ye nigh in the fear of the Lord and the Faith!" and the stream would flow back and carry Kolcho with it. And then Ognyanov would be lost! And who could tell, maybe at this very moment the boy was coming up to Boicho by another way, and he was starting off without suspecting the trap. The boy might be passing by Kolcho, might be touching his elbow, and Kolcho would not notice him. His hand instinctively groped about in search of a boy. He actually got hold of a body which he could tell was not that of a grown person, and in his fright he imagined this was the fateful boy on his way to call Ognyanov. Almost demented he gripped him firmly by the arm, pulling him back, and cried without realizing what he was doing, speaking very fast, "Is that you, boy? What's your name, boy? Stand back there, boy!"

But the pressure of the crowd behind immediately separated them. Kolcho was in despair. His poor, noble soul suffered anguish. He realized with horror that Ognyanov's life hung by a thread, and that thread was he, Kolcho, feeble, insignificant, lost, nearly invisible in that sea of people. And the psalm was already nearing its end. . . . That Hadji Athanasius, whose singing was usually so slow and drawn out, seemed to him terribly fast now. What was he to do? Critical moments give rise to extreme decisions. Kolcho started crying in a desperate voice, "Make way, good people! I'm dying. I'm passing out, oh Lord!"

And he began bumping the backs in front of him. At these cries the people who felt his blows made room with great efforts to let the unfortunate dying beggar through; no one was anxious to have him expire against his back. Thus Kolcho, more dead than alive, managed to crawl up to the pew where Ognyanov was sitting. He found him without asking anyone, so extraordinary is the instinct of those deprived of sight. Without the least hesitation he got hold of a coat and inquired in a low voice, "Is that you, Bai Boicho?"

"What is it?" answered Ognyanov. Ognyanov put his ear to Kolcho's mouth. When he raised his head he was very pale. He thought hard for a minute. The protruding veins of his temples showed the intense working of his mind.

Again he bent down and whispered something to Kolcho. Then he descended from the pew, moved forward and was lost in the crowd of communicants who were waiting in front of the altar. At the same moment the central doors of the altar enclosure were opened. Father Nikodim, chalice in hand, proclaimed: "In the fear of the Lord!" and the service was over. The crowd, like a pent-up stream, surged back towards the door.

In half an hour even the last old woman taking communion had left the church. Only the officiating priest remained within to take off his vestments. Then the zaptiehs and constables entered. The onbashi was furious because Ognyanov had not come out. So he was hiding in the church! The doors were locked on the inside, and the search began. Some went up to the latticed women's section, others remained below, to search under the pews and in the corners, while still others entered the area of the altar by the small side doors. They turned everything upside down, examined every nook that might serve as a hiding place, got up onto the pulpit, moved the lecterns, looked under the high altar, in the cupboards for the vessels and vestments, in the chest with the old icons, in the recesses of the windows, but nowhere did they find anything. Ognyanov couldn't possibly be hiding there.

Suddenly Father Nikodim also started rummaging about, shambling hither and thither with a perplexed expression on his face. He even began searching among the vestments and among the objects and books on the high altar. The onbashi himself was rather surprised at the priest's assiduity. Mihal the constable, however, remarked to him that not even a chicken could be hidden among those things, let alone a man.

"What's that? Why, I'm looking for something else," the priest answered bewildered.

"What is it?"

"My fur coat is missing, and my hat, and the blue glasses in it." The poor priest was by now shivering with cold.

"Ah, it's all clear now, Sherif-Aga!" said Bai Mihal. Sherif came up, sweating profusely and quite out of breath.

"What a rogue!" added the Bulgarian constable with secret satisfaction. "He's stolen the old priest's clothes."

Sherif-Aga stood aghast. "How's that, priest?"

"I can't find my fur coat, nor my hat, nor my glasses, I can't find them anywhere!" said the priest, mystified.

"That fellow must have stolen them!" said Sherif-Aga with the air of a man who has just made a great discovery.

"Of course, the Count must have put on the gown and the hat, and gone out disguised like that without our recognizing him," the constable explained.

"That must be it," the priest affirmed. "While I was busy administering the sacrament someone must have taken them."

"That's right, I saw a priest with blue glasses at the door," said a zaptieh in confirmation.

"And you didn't catch him, you fool!" his chief shouted at him.

"How was I to know? We were watching for a man, not for a priest," said the zaptieh in justification.

"So that was he; I'll be damned!" said Bai Mihal in surprise. "That's why he was all wrapped up; all I saw was his spectacles. His own father wouldn't have recognized him."

There was a loud knocking at the door. Sherif-Aga gave orders to open it. Filcho the constable and the tax-collector entered. "Sherif-Aga, the Count is in the trap!" cried Filcho.

"He's hiding in the convent, he was seen there," added the tax-collector.

"Off to the convent!" And they all hurried out.

chapter 26

an unpleasant visit

In a trice the policemen were at the convent gates. Sherif-Aga left two men there with drawn swords and cocked pistols. "Don't let anyone in or out!" were his orders while he and the rest of his men went into the court.

Their sudden invasion caused a great commotion in the convent and spread fear and confusion in all the cells. The nuns all popped out and started running along the galleries; their guests followed suit, and clamor, hubbub and confusion arose. In vain did the onbashi wave to them not to be afraid and shouted something in Turkish which they could not understand, and heard even less. Meanwhile the zaptiehs laid hands on all the priests they saw, seized anyone wearing spectacles—blue or not—and even two persons bearing the name of Bocho, and shut them up in a room.

Among them were Kandov and Burzobegounek. The latter was, however, immediately released with due apologies by the onbashi as being no rayah, but a subject of the Austrian Emperor. . . . Kandov, fuming with rage, protested vehemently from the windows against such a bare-faced violation of his liberty; his companions were calmer, for they knew what Turkish rule meant.

"Why, Kandov, one would think you'd never seen a Turk," a priest said.

"But this is violence, tyranny, lawlessness!" the student shouted.

"Shouting's no answer to such tyranny and lawlessness—do you think Sherif-Aga's noodle can grasp a word of it? Here's the answer," said Bocho the butcher, taking out his knife.

In his hurry Sherif had not thought of making sure who had seen Ognyanov enter the convent or how he was dressed, but immediately set about searching the gallery where the fugitive had gone up. The door of Hadji Rovoahma's cell opened onto this gallery too. The nuns were calming down after their first fright and protested vociferously, declaring it was most offensive that they should be suspected of concealing an enemy of the Empire in the convent. Hadji Rovoahma was the most indignant of all at such an insulting suspicion; she scolded the onbashi for all she was worth, for she knew Turkish, and finally drove him out most ignominiously. But the hectic search continued in the other cells; no stone was left unturned in the search for Ognyanov, and sooner or later they were bound to get him. Sherif-Aga had staked his all on the success of this mad rummaging of cupboards, chests, closets and secret nooks. Most people expected with dread to see the unfortunate Count dragged out of some cell.

Suddenly someone called out ominously, "They've got him!" but it turned out to be only Mr. Fratyu, whom they had dragged out from under Gospozha Nymphidora's window seat, and they let him go.

Rada, leaning on the gallery railing, followed the search with strained attention. She was faint with dread; tears streamed down her cheeks. This rash burst of feeling convinced every one that she loved Ognyanov. They cast hostile looks upon her, but she cared little for the good opinion of those garrulous old women, so indifferent to the misfortune which was threatening her lover. She wept freely.

Not far off two nuns were speaking in low whispers, pointing to the cell of Hadji Dariya, an aunt of Doctor Sokolov's and Boicho's supporter. Boicho must be there now and the search was approaching Hadji Dariya's cell. Rada's heart was breaking. . . . Terror gripped her. . . . O God, what was to be done!

Kolcho came up to her—he recognized her by her sobs—and said softly, "Radka, are you alone here?"

"Yes, Bai Kolcho," she answered between her sobs in a quivering voice.

"Don't worry, Radka," he whispered to her.

"How so, Bai Kolcho? And when they find him? He is here. . . . You said yourself that he was seen in the convent."

"I don't think he's here, Radka."

"Everyone says he is."

"I was the one who spread that rumor. Boicho told me to in the church. Let the police keep themselves busy here. Ognyanov is as free as a wolf in the forest now."

It was all the poor young girl could do not to embrace the blind man. Her face shone with the radiance of the sky after a storm. She calmly and triumphantly entered Hadji Rovoahma's room, and the old woman did not fail to notice her strange change of mood immediately.

"Can the trollop have found out that the fellow is not in the convent?" she thought to herself with bitterness.

And with a searching look she said: "Well, Rada, have you had a good cry? A fine thing indeed, making a laughingstock of yourself in front of everyone; go on, cry for that haidouk, do, that cut-throat!"

Rada's heart was bubbling over with happiness. "I shall cry," she answered boldly, "there should be someone to cry while others rejoice. . . ."

This audacious reply seemed to the nun unbecoming beyond words. She was not used to being talked back to. She hissed between her clenched teeth, "You brazen hussy, you!"

"I'm not brazen."

"You are brazen, and you're mad! Your accursed cutthroat will hang on the gallows this very day!"

"If they catch him," Rada retorted bitingly.

Hadji Rovoahma lost her temper. She seemed to choke with wild rage. "Out with you, you vile creature! Never cross my threshold again!" screamed Hadji Rovoahma, pushing her out of her door.

Rada went out on the gallery again, as if nothing had happened. What did it matter that Hadji Rovoahma despised her or had thrown her out of her cell so roughly? She was calm and light-hearted. She was thankful to have broken every tie with this cruel patroness.

Tomorrow, or even today, they might drive her out of the school, and she might find herself without a roof over her head, without a morsel of bread, and quite alone. What was that to her? She knew that Boicho was safe. He was now as free as a wolf in the forest, as Kolcho had said. Really, what a good fellow that Kolcho was! What a merciful soul, what a loving heart, sympathizing with other people's misfortune—he doesn't see his own, he forgets it, poor fellow! How many people with sound eyes become blind on purpose, blind and cruel towards the sufferings of men! And that Stefchov—the brute, how impatiently he must be awaiting Boicho's tragic end! But Boicho was far away from danger now. . . . His enemies would not be able to rejoice, and how happy all honest people would be! But no one, no one, would be as happy as she.

Absorbed by these innocent and radiant feelings she suddenly noticed Kolcho slowly going down the steps. "Kolcho!" she called, without knowing why.

"Radka, is that you?" and Kolcho turned back.

"Goodness, why did I call the poor man just to tire him?" she asked herself. Then she ran down to stop him and said, "Bai Kolcho, it's nothing . . . let me shake your hand." And she pressed it in deep gratitude.

The search continued. Sherif-Aga left the work to his men, while he, tired out, went to the arrested priests and spectacle-wearers. It was only now that it occurred to him to set them free.

Kandov again protested against the violence done to his person in defiance of elementary justice. The onbashi, quite surprised, asked someone to translate the words of this irate gentleman.

"Say it again, Kandov, so I can tell the effendi," said Bencho Derman, who was better versed in the Turkish tongue.

"Please, tell him," began Kandov, "that my personal inviolability, my most cherished human right, in defiance of all legality and every principle of justice. . . ."

Bencho Derman waved his hand in despair. "Why, such words don't even exist in Turkish! Come on, drop it, Kandov!"

The convent was finally freed of its unwelcome guests, who went off to search the little town and its surroundings.

chapter 27

a fugitive

Ognyanov's presence of mind had saved him once again. Having left the town behind him, his first concern was to hide the priest's hat and fur coat in some bushes.

The blizzard which helped him to pass unseen through the deserted streets was still blowing strong here. The mountain gales roared; the crest of Stara Planina looked as if it had been sprinkled with salt. The plain, dead and deserted, appeared infinitely sad under its grey, icy shroud. By good fortune, the sun unexpectedly pierced through the clouds and sent forth warm rays over the frozen scene.

Ognyanov was making for the west, keeping away from the paths, through the vineyards cut up by small dells and gullies. He stopped to rest in a secluded spot and to consider his situation. It was serious. A fatality that must surely be in league with Stefchov was dogging him relentlessly. In less than an hour he saw the edifice, built with so much love and enthusiasm, undermined. He saw the deacon, the doctor, Dyado Stoyan, possibly some other close and devoted friends, in prison, Rada crushed with grief, his enemies jubiliant. He could not make out what circumstances had played into their hands. The news item in *The Danube* and the cantor's vile espionage had given his enemies powerful weapons. All the terrible consequences now loomed up before his eyes. Was the cause irretrievably lost? Would this misfortune lead to other disclosures elsewhere? His flight seemed to him now a very cowardly act. He wanted to return and see for himself the extent of the harm done; he was not thinking of himself now; his boldness was capable of such an act. . . . But he thought things over; he should at least be unrecognizable. That made him continue on his way. He decided to make for Ovcheri, the most loyal of the neighboring villages, and the one he stopped at most frequently on his rounds. He had ways and means of disguising himself at Uncle Dyalko's. But the road to Ovcheri, nestling in one of the folds of the nearer slopes of Sredna Gora, was fraught with danger for Ognyanov, for it passed through the closely scattered Turkish villages around there. The news that the bodies of the two cutthroats had been dug up was bound to pass through these brigands' nests like wildfire that very day. If they didn't seize him as a suspicious character, they would kill him as a giaour; scarcely a day passed that some Christian was not cut down in this district. His town clothes still further increased that possibility. It was insane to expose himself to certain death. He decided to wait for nightfall. With this in view he withdrew still closer to the slopes of Stara Planina, where he would be under cover of the dense hornbeam forests.

After threading his way painfully through steep ravines and wild places for two hours he reached the first wood. There, hidden among the dry brushwood, he lay on his back to rest, or rather to let his mind work. The sky had cleared completely. The autumn sun shone cheerful and warm, turning the snow on the blades of grass into sparkling dewdrops. An occasional sparrow flitted over his head or alighted on the paths in search of food. A mountain eagle circled high above. Either it saw carrion not far off or took Ognyanov himself for such. The thought crossed his mind and only intensified his gloom. This eagle now seemd to him very ominous indeed. It was like the living image of his merciless fate, as if this bird of prey were waiting for its bloody meal to be prepared in order to dive down from its blue heights. And anything was possible. This wild deserted spot, frequently crossed by Turkish hunters who were brigands incarnate, was not without its dangers. Ognyanov impatiently waited for the sun to set and several times sought a safer hiding place. Time was heavy on his hands, and the sun crawled along at a wearisome pace. And the eagle kept on circling overhead. It would flap its wings a few times, then spread them motionless and black in the air. Ognyanov's eyes were turned to that floating form, but his mind pierced other depths. Memories of the past chased each other in his excited brain: youthful years, years of struggle and suffering and of faith in high ideals. And Bulgaria, for whose sake they were borne, was so beautiful, so worthy of sacrifice. She was a goddess kept alive by the blood of those who believed in her. Her blood-stained halo was formed of sheaves of radiant names; Ognyanov sought his own there, and it seemed to him that he saw it. . . . What pride he felt and what readiness to die, and even more, to fight for her! Death was a glorious sacrifice, the struggle a holy sacrament.

A gun-shot made Ognyanov start. He looked about him. The mountain echoes repeated the shot and fell silent. "It must be hunters shooting game," he said to himself.

Ognyanov was reassured, but not for long. A quarter of an hour later a dog's bark resounded, and near at hand too. The bark was closely followed by a man's voice. The thought of Emeksiz's hound, who came from a near-by village, involuntarily flashed through Ognyanov's mind. The bark was familiar or so it seemed to him. It was repeated quite close and still more distinct, the undergrowth rustled as if shaken by the wind, and two hounds appeared with their muzzles lowered, following a scent along the ground.

Ognyanov heaved a sigh of relief. The hound of Emeksiz Pehlivan, who had trained it to attack people as though they were game, was not here. That cursed animal, though hounds are in general dull and innocent enough by nature, bore malice, as we saw at the monastery. It had appeared as Stefchov's ally and prepared Ognyanov's undoing. . . . Noticing him huddled up in the brushwood the hounds came up, sniffed at him, and were soon out of sight.

Suddenly Ognyanov heard men's footsteps approaching. He made a dash through the brushwood without turning around. Three shots rang out; he felt something sting his thigh, and ran on three times as hard. Was he being pursued? What was happening behind him? He hadn't the slightest idea. He was brought up short by a gully, and slipping in between the low hazelnut bushes which filled it, he pushed his way into the thicket. The hunters probably lost him.

Ognyanov was on the lookout for some time, but heard nothing. It was only then that he felt something warm and wet against his legs. "I've been hit," he thought in a fright as he saw that his shoe was full of blood. He took it off and found his left leg covered with blood. It was spouting from both sides; the bullet had only pierced the thigh and passed through it. He tore off a piece of his shirt and stuffed it into the holes. The pain grew more intense, and he still had a long and difficult trip ahead of him. The loss of blood weakened him greatly; moreover today he had not had a bite of food to sustain him.

It soon grew quite dark, and he left the spot, which would be scoured by Turkish posses the next day. As the darkness increased the cold grew more intense. Not a soul was stirring in the first Turkish village he passed through. As soon as dusk falls Turkish villages become deserted and seem like graveyards. Only in a grocer's shop did he hear the sound of voices. But Ognyanov did not dare knock at the door, although he was dying with hunger. He walked on for two more hours, passed several villages and finally something white appeared before him. . . .

It was the Strema. He waded across with some difficulty and sat down on the opposite bank, as the water had chilled his leg and the wound was very painful. He realized that his thigh was swollen and was afraid of the inflammation spreading, which might force him to stop on the road. Then he got up, cut some dry rushes along the bank and pulled down his trousers in order to wash the wound in the way he had learned when he was in Hadji Dimiter's band. He sucked water into the long reed and blew it into the first bullet hole; it poured out through the second. He did this several times. Having thus dressed his wound by himself, Ognyanov again set out towards Sredna Gora, in whose foothills he now was. . . .

The darkness of the night grew more intense. Ognyanov was on his way to Ovcheri, but he could not see it. He soon discovered that he had lost his way; he found himself in unfamiliar scrub. In a daze he stopped and listened. He was already in Sredna Gora. The sound of men's voices reached his ears indistinctly. He figured out that at this midnight hour there could be no one here but charcoal-burners. Now he remembered a little red flame he had noticed in the distance. Yet what would they be—Bulgarians or Turks? He had lost his way; he was frozen and exhausted. If they were Christians there was a chance of their taking pity on him. He climbed a little further and then again saw the fire close at hand. He started walking towards it. The shadows of men sitting around the fire could be clearly distinguished through the branches, and he managed to hear some Bulgarian words. Now how was he to make himself known? He was spattered with blood. His appearance might drive these Bulgarians away or else have bad consequences for himself. . . . There were three of them, one lying covered up, the other two talking beside the dying fire. On one side a horse covered with a blanket was munching hay. Ognyanov pricked up his ears.

"Put a log or two on the fire, that's enough talk . . . and I'll give the mare some more hay," said the older man getting up.

"Why, I know this fellow; he's from Verigovo! That's Nenko, Dyado Ivan's son!" Ognyanov said to himself joyfully. Verigovo was a village on the other side of Sredna Gora, which was also well-known to Ognyanov.

Nenko approached the horse and bent down to pull out some hay from a home-spun goat hair sack. At the same moment Ognyanov crept up to him through the bushes and said, "Good evening to you, Bai Nencho"

Nencho stood up startled. "Who are you?"

"Don't you recognize me, Bai Nencho?" The dim glare from the fire lit up Ognyanov's face.

"Is that you, schoolmaster? Why, come along; we're all friends here. . . . That's our Tsvetan, and Bai Doichin. Good Lord, you're icy cold, you're simply frozen. . . ." the peasant said moving towards the fire with Ognyanov.

"Tsvetancho, stack up the fire, make a good blaze. We've a Christian here to dry and warm up. Do you know him?"

"Schoolmaster!" cried the young man joyfully. "What are you doing in these parts?" and he put down some dry branches for Ognyanov to sit on.

"May you live to sound old age, Tsvetancho!"

"Those brutes have winged him, they have!" said Nencho angrily, "but thank goodness, it's not bad."

"Pooh!"

"Dyado Doichin, up with you, we have a guest!" said Nencho waking up the sleeper, or rather giving him a kick.

Soon a great fire was blazing in front of them. The charcoal-burners looked sympathetically at Ognyanov's pale face while he gave them a brief account of his adventure. He soon felt the invigorating effect of the fire. His frozen limbs grew warm, and his wound was no longer so painful. Dyado Doichin took out a hunk of bread and an onion from his torn sack and handed them to Boicho. "That's all we have to offer you. As for warmth, the Lord has provided; we're better off than the king. Help yourself, schoolmaster."

Ognyanov felt still better. A feeling of comfort, new and vast, spread through his being. The lovely golden, great-hearted flame, the deep forest about him, the blackened faces, rough and simple, lit up by an expression of warm friendliness, and the black, chapped, toil-worn hands which held out to him the poor man's modest morsel in true Bulgarian hospitality—all this seemed to him inexpressibly touching. If it hadn't been for his bodily pain Ognyanov would have started singing in delight, "O forest, you green forest. . . ."

It was already near dawn when Nenko, who was leading the horse with Ognyanov on it, knocked at a door in Verigovo. The dogs in the yard started barking and Dyado Marin himself appeared. By the unusual hour of the knocking, he rightly guessed that an unusual visitor had come.

The first words of greeting were followed by explanations. "Ay, God blast them, infidels that they are! Ay, may curs devour them! Ay, may devils take their souls!" Dyado Marin said as they carefully lifted down Ognyanov, whose pain had increased from the jolting.

He was led into a room that was off by itself, where he had spent the night more than once before. Dyado Marin examined his wound carefully and bound it up. "It'll heal as easily as a dog's," he remarked. It was almost broad daylight.

chapter 28

in Verigovo

Ognyanov's wound was healing well, though not as fast as Dyado Marin had foretold. His hospitable family showed the utmost solicitude towards the sick man in order to relieve his suffering. Dyado Marin himself doctored him—he knew something of medicine—while Granny Marinitsa did herself proud in showing her skill as a cook. The barrels of white Sredna-Gora wine were broached one after the other; every morning a headless chicken lay twitching in the yard—to appear later on the table of Ognyanov, who used to eat alone as this was the time of the Christmas fast.

Ognyanov spent three weeks, surrounded by much attention and care, in this Bulgarian household and gained strength daily. But he was burning with impatience to find out what was going on in Byala Cherkva, how Rada and his friends were faring, and how things stood with their organization, from which he was so unfortunately cut off. He begged Dyado Marin to send someone to find out, but the old man would not consent.

"No, I'm not sending anyone, I shall go myself next week to get a thing or two for the feast. Have patience till then, my son. You just keep quiet, so as to get well soon. The Lord is merciful."

"But by next week I can go there myself."

"Do you think I'll let you? That's my affair. I'm your doctor and you must ask my permission. I'm the one to give orders," remarked the peasant with fatherly severity.

"If Rada could at least be told that I'm alive!"

"Schoolmistress knows you're alive as long as you're not in the hands of the Turks." And Ognyanov submitted.

A few trusted peasants visited him; after much entreaty they had received permission from Marin to visit the sick man. They were burning with desire to hear the inspired words of the schoolmaster and always left his room with faces full of hope and eyes shining. Father Joseph, who was president of the committee, was Ognyanov's most frequent visitor. He had already been chosen as leader and kept the standard hidden among the sacred vestments in the church. The old schoolmaster, Dyado Minà, also came to see him.

Ognyanov was sure that besides these men and Uncle Marin's family no one in the village knew his secret. His host assured him of this. Meanwhile he noted with surprise that the food he was served grew richer from day to day: fried chickens, buttered eggs, rice pudding, cheese pie, and often even wild duck and hares. Various wines appeared on his table. This luxury troubled him; the expense incurred on his behalf made him somehow feel ashamed. Sometimes when he went out into the yard, he saw that the henhouse was bare. He said to Dyado Marin, "Uncle Marin, you'll ruin yourself. If you don't come to your senses, I'll stop eating your food and buy myself bread and cheese from the grocer. That's all I need."

"Now don't you worry about whether I'm ruining myself or not. I'm your doctor and I'm treating you as I know best."

Ognyanov, deeply moved, no longer raised the question. He didn't know that all the villagers were vying with each other to provide for their beloved teacher. His secret was common knowledge. But betrayal was out of the question. His popularity now was immense. The rumor that he had killed the two cutthroats raised him high in the eyes of even the most indifferent. Bravery of all the virtues enthralls the common folk the most!

Ognyanov's wound however was slow in healing, and curbed his lively and impatient nature. He was a prey to anxieties. Of all his visitors, good Dyado Minà relieved his feverish impatience most. Ognyanov spent several hours with him every day; he got used to him and could no longer get on without him. Old man Minà was a relic, a last survivor of that bygone generation of schoolmasters of the breviary and the psalter who first opened the famous cellschools in Bulgaria. He was now fully seventy, white-haired, burly, broad-faced, and dressed in old-fashioned baggy trousers. After a long and active life he had cast anchor in this quiet, remote village where he was peacefully spending his old age. Behind the times, no longer of any use with his outdated book learning, he still sang without remuneration in church; innovations had no right of entry there. On feast days the villagers surrounded him and listened open-mouthed to his tales of old times which resembled sermons, interspersed with texts from the Holy Bible. That was all he read, and all his mind had to feed on.

Ognyanov took a real pleasure in this ancient relic and listened with gratitude to the wise musings of the white-haired pioneer, a living echo of a forgotten age. When a man is under the stress of suffering, be it moral or physical, he is inclined to religious thoughts; he finds unexpected comfort in the words of the great book. It soothes his pain like a magic balm. It was the first time that Ognyanov fell under the charm of the inspired sentences which made old Minà's own words glow.

When he visited him for the first time, old Minà said sternly: "Another Christian victim! Once more innocent blood has been shed! O God, how long shall the adversary reproach? Why withdrawest thou thy hand, even thy right hand? Arise O Lord! And judge! Lift up thy hands against their pride at last!" He then greeted him and questioned him with concern.

In trying to turn around Ognyanov groaned with the sharp pain the movement had caused. "Be of good cheer, my son! Blessed are they that mourn, for they shall be comforted," the old man said sadly.

"Well, Dyado Minà, it seems there was a spot of suffering chalked up for us. After all, we call ourselves apostles, and the path is thorny!" said Ognyanov, half-smiling.

"Your work on this earth is hard, schoolmaster, hard indeed; but it is glorious and praiseworthy, for God himself has inspired you to serve the people. Ye are the light of the world: a city that is set on a hill cannot be hid. Did not Jesus say unto his disciple, 'The harvest truly is great, but the laborers are few. . . . Go your ways: behold, I send you forth as lambs among wolves!' "

These simple words brought sweet comfort and cheer to Ognyanov's soul. He asked the old man to give him some sacred book to read, and he brought him the Book of Psalms. With deep fervor Ognyanov began to read that inspired work, from which wells forth such great poetry. Those songs of struggle, of desperate grief and impassioned prayer, found an echo in his troubled soul. The psalms of David were never out of his hands.

At last the time came, and Uncle Marin went to Byala Cherkva. Ognyanov anxiously awaited his return. The gloomiest thoughts kept running through his mind. For over a month he had had no news of those dearest to his heart. What was Rada doing? What insults and persecution she must have suffered after his escape! She had faced the whole storm of society, possibly the cruelties of the authorities as well, and alone. Poor girl, she was not fated to be happy with him. There she was, unhappy, again exposed to the blows of fate, her fondest hopes dashed, and herself disgraced in the eyes of the world. People in their cruelty would look on her devotion to him as a crime, and make her atone for the few joys that feeling had given her by cruel disillusionment and bitter suffering. And he wasn't there to comfort and give support to that weak child. . . .

Deep in these sad thoughts, he welcomed the arrival of old Minà with real joy. At least he had someone to open his heart to. Dyado Minà listened to him with concern. "Hope, teacher, hope in the Lord; be not downcast; the Almighty does not leave the sufferers who trust in his mercy. They that trust in the Lord shall be as Mount Zion. . . . For the rod of the wicked shall not rest upon the lot of the righteous. They that sow in tears shall reap in joy!"

As if partly to justify these gentle words, the door opened and Dyado Marin entered. Ognyanov, agog with excitement, tried to read his news in his face. "Good evening! Steady, steady on, schoolmaster! Let me tell you. . . . You haven't been moving too much, have you?" he said, taking off his heavy cape.

"Those townsfolk of yours are strange people," continued Dyado Marin. "You can't catch them to have a chat with them."

"But didn't you go straight to the doctor?"

"He's been arrested."

"And to the deacon at the monastery?"

"He's in hiding."

"Did you find Dyado Stoyan?"

"God rest his soul! He died the same night he was taken to prison of the beating they gave him; they say he told them everything, poor fellow, under torture."

"Oh, poor Dyado Stoyan! But Radka, what about Radka?"

"I wasn't able to see her."

"How's that? What's happened to Rada?" He went pale.

"She's all right, don't worry; but she was turned out of the school."

"If you had only looked for her at the convent, at Gospozha Hadji Rovoahma's!" cried Ognyanov anxiously.

"The nun threw her out most heartlessly."

"Oh God, she has nowhere to go! They've killed her!"

"Chorbadji Marko arranged for her to stay with a relative of his, but I wasn't able to find the house, and my friends were in a hurry. But I asked about her; the girl's all right."

"I'll never be able to repay Bai Marko. And what are they saying about me?"

"About you? They all call you by another name there—it took me ages to catch on to it."

"Was it Count?"

"That's it, Count. Everyone is saying of the Count that he was shot in the Ahievo forest by hunters."

"That's true."

"Not quite true. You're alive, and they believe you're dead—and all the better, say I."

Ognyanov jumped up as if he had been bitten by a snake. "What? And she? Does she think I'm killed? That's the last straw for her, poor girl." He started pacing the room, as if testing his foot.

"Don't walk, or you'll harm the wound."

"I can already travel," said Ognyanov resolutely.

"Where to?" asked Dyado Marin in surprise.

"To Byala Cherkva."

"Are you mad?"

"No, I'm not, but I will be if I stay here a day longer. Get some clothes ready for me. And will you give me your horse?"

Dyado Marin knew how stubborn Boicho was, so he didn't even try to stop him. "Take both the clothes and the horse. I'm only sorry for your youth," he said quite downcast. "The roads are full of Turkish rabble; there's no end of robbers and the harm they do. . . . Don't you have any concern for yourself?"

"Don't you worry about me. I'll come back to you safe and sound, like a falcon. Unless you close your door to me," added Ognyanov half-jokingly.

The old man looked at him glumly. "No, you shall not start!" said he firmly. "I'll gather the whole village and they'll shut you in here by force. You're as necessary to us as the sacred water—and you're going straight to your death. I don't want the world to say later that Uncle Marin let schoolmaster Boicho, our apostle, throw his life away!" old Marin shouted angrily.

"Don't shout so, Dyado Marin, you don't know how your voice carries," remarked Ognyanov. Old Minà smiled softly to himself. Marin's face also expressed mischievous mirth.

Ognyanov looked at them in surprise. His last words seemed to have amused them. "What's the joke?" he asked.

"Come, God bless you, schoolmaster! Who do you think you're hiding from? The whole village, down to the very children, know you're staying at my house. Every man jack of them has been working to deck your table. . . . We're simple people, but we don't denounce Christians, and as for such as you—we'd give our lives for you!" Now it was Ognyanov's turn to smile as he realized that his hiding place was a public secret.

After much arguing Ognyanov overcame the apprehensions of his host and his departure was settled.

chapter 29

a troubled halt

An hour later a Turk was riding out of Verigovo.

We said a Turk; we should have said, a very common Turk. A ragged green turban, faded beyond recognition, covered his forehead down to his eyebrows; the nape of his neck was shaved clean; a short cotton waistcoat with torn frogs, unbuttoned at the neck; a ragged jacket on his shoulders with frayed sleeves; a greasy belt around his waist into which were tucked a flintlock pistol, a short dagger and a yataghan, and a pipe; tight-legged threadbare breeches, unbuttoned at the ankles; and strapped sandals. On top of all this was thrown a coarse woolen coat in tatters. Thus clad, Ognyanov was unrecognizable.

The winter, now entered into all its prerogatives, had covered the ground with its white mantle through which the black rocky sides of Stara Planina jutted out. Nature was silent and sad. Only large flocks of crows flew here and there and filled the drowsy air with noise.

The direct road to Byala Cherkva lay northeast, but Ognyanov did not follow it; he would have had to pass through the village of Emeksiz Pehlivan, which filled him with fear in spite of himself. There came to his mind the dead man's dog in which the detested spirit of the Turk seemed to be embodied, to threaten and pursue Ognyanov even from the grave. He therefore decided to set out due north to the Karnari inn, and from there to turn east along the slopes of Stara Planina towards Byala Cherkva. This was a more roundabout way, but one which presented fewer dangers, although it also passed through Turkish villages.

When Ognyanov approached the first village the snow was falling in large flakes, veiling everything before the traveler's eyes. The cold grew more intense and stiffened his limbs; his hands hardly felt the reins of the horse who was guided by instinct alone, for the snow had covered the whole plain and no trace of the road could be seen. Noiselessly he entered the deserted village streets where not a soul was stirring, and soon stopped at the single inn, opposite the mosque. He wanted to rest his horse, which was tired out by the snowy road, and also to warm himself a little. A boy led the horse away; he pushed the door of the café, which seemed to be empty, as no noise from within could be heard. When he entered he was quite taken aback, for it was full to overflowing with agas! To leave immediately was awkward. He decided to sit down, and made his salaam, which they politely returned. As he had long lived among the Turks he knew their customs and their language very well. They were squatting on straw-mats, their shoes off, pipes in hand. A dense fog of tobacco smoke filled the room. "A coffee!" he said sternly to the host. And he started filling his pipe, bending low over it to hide his features as much as possible. In that posture he lent an ear to the conversation while he sipped his coffee noisily. For a time he listened with indifference, but all at once he pricked up his ears: the talk had turned to the murder of the two ruffians. It was a long time since such an event had been heard of in the district, and it still provoked and infuriated the Turks. A sudden animation seized the company in the café, hitherto so silent and phlegmatic. Vile oaths and bloody threats were showered on the Bulgarians like rain. Ognyanov continued to sip his coffee noisily, with a scowl on his face, to show that he too shared the common indignation. Next they began to talk about the murderer of the Turks, and he saw with amazement how familiar his name and his person were here too. There already existed legends about him.

"This infidel of a consul can neither be caught nor recognized," said one of the men.

"He's got a devil who helps him; sometimes you see him as a teacher, and then he's a priest, or a peasant, or a Turk maybe. He changes his appearance all at once: from a boy he turns into an old man; now he's beardless and dark-eyed, a moment later and he's got a great beard and fair hair. Catch him if you can! Ahmet-Aga was telling me that at one time they were on his tracks and a posse chased him towards the Tekia forest reserve. He was dressed as a peasant; suddenly they saw a crow in front of them—no peasant or anyone. They all fired, but the bird vanished and all they heard was a cawing overhead."

"Nonsense!" a few men put in incredulously.

"Sooner or later we'll lay our hands on the giaour—if we could only find the nest where he lies hidden," remarked another.

"And I tell you that he can't be caught, the scoundrel," the first speaker continued. "He doesn't even hide, but can you see him? He may be here now, with us, in the café, and we not knowing a thing." At these words all the company automatically raised their eyes and looked at each other. Several curious glances fell on Ognyanov.

He was now furiously sipping his third cup of coffee, while at every other moment he blew out a cloud of smoke, which wreathed itself around him, but he felt the stares turned on him and drops of perspiration ran down his cheekbones. He could no longer stand this state of tension and watched for an appropriate moment to leave the cafe and breathe freely in the fresh air.

"If it has been appointed, where are you bound for?" a man asked him.

"For Klissoura, with God's will!" answered Ognyanov, calmly untying a long dirty purse to pay for the coffee.

"In this snow and such a blizzard? You'd better spend the night here; you'll still get there in time for market."

"The traveler has his road, the frog its pond," said Ognyanov smiling.

"Those are old wives' tales, Rahman-Aga, your giaour is neither a devil, nor a crow, but simply a comita just like any other comita."

"Why don't you catch him then?"

"We shall catch him all right. We've traced him to his nest."

"Just let us lay our hands on him," a few of them cried with fierce looks.

"I wager my head that today or tomorrow Boicho-comita will be in the trap."

"And where are they looking for the cur?"

"It seems he was hiding in a village in Sredna Gora, a giaour village; he found a warm nest. Yesterday several zaptiehs went through Bankya, others through the Abrashlar meadows; we'll get him."

"Are you after him too?"

"I am! We're to meet in Verigovo and we'll start from there."

It was only now that Ognyanov noticed that the speaker was a zaptieh whom he had not yet observed in the corner. He was still more alarmed to hear of the danger that threatened him in Verigovo. The suspicious glances moved away from him, but this café stifled him. He made his salaam to all present and went out.

On finding himself alone outside, in the pure air, fully free under the snowy sky, he drew a breath of relief and jumped onto his horse. Three hours later he and his horse, covered with snow, stopped at the Karnari inn.

chapter 30

a civil acquaintance

The Karnari inn is the stopping place for the high Troyan pass. It is here that travelers rest, eat, warm themselves and then, their strength restored, begin the ascent of Stara Planina. For one or two weeks during the winter, however, the inn has no travelers to welcome, as the blizzards cover the old Roman road over the mountain with great snowdrifts and it becomes impassable. All communications between Thrace and Danubian Bulgaria are cut off until the Troyan carriers cut a narrow path through the snow with Sisyphean toil.

Just now the road was shut and the inn deserted. The Bulgarian innkeeper, a small grinning little fellow with a stupid face, welcomed his guest very politely and led him into the large guest-room which also served all other purposes. A fire was burning in the hearth, and Ognyanov lit his pipe. "Have you any other guests?" he asked the innkeeper.

"No, there are no guests. When the mountains shut down, they shut my inn as well. Where are you bound for, eh?" asked the innkeeper, examining his guest with curiosity.

"Can you make me a cup of coffee?" asked Ognyanov by way of reply.

"Of course I can! And where are you going?" the innkeeper insisted.

"To Troyan."

"Where from?"

"From Byala Cherkva. Is the road further on good?"

"I come from Byala Cherkva too, but you can't go to Troyan. I tell you, believe me. . . ." chattered the innkeeper, handing him the coffee and staring intently at Ognyanov as though trying to recognize him. Ognyanov bent his head and frowned to avoid that annoying stare. The innkeeper threw another sidelong glance at him and smiled slyly.

"Innkeeper, you've made the coffee too sweet!" said Ognyanov severely, pushing the cup away.

"I'm sorry, aga! I thought you liked it sweet. Shall I make you another?"

"No need!"

"No, drink a cup, do. I'm telling you it's good."

"What's the news in your parts?"

"Horrors, murders, robberies every day. . . . There are no travelers, the mountain's blocked, I'm losing. And especially since they dug up Emeksiz Pehlivan—you know him of course—the Turks have been doing a lot of mischief. They say they're looking for comitas, but it's the innocent people they kill. I'm telling you the truth, you just listen to me. . . ."

Ognyanov was amazed at the innkeeper's boldness: one could only speak in that fashion to a Bulgarian. And so, to sustain his role as a Turk, he scowled. "If you babble too much, you'll get into trouble yourself, you pimp."

"I know who I'm babbling to, yes I do," said the innkeeper familiarly.

Ognyanov eyed him in still greater surprise. He decided to give him a scolding. "Giaour, you must be drunk!"

"Come on, Count, don't be angry. Why, I cried over *Genevieve* myself!" the innkeeper now answered in Bulgarian and took his hand to shake it.

Ognyanov saw that he was recognized, and it annoyed him very much. Moreover he found both the face and the impudent manners of the innkeeper repulsive. He eyed him from top to toe and asked coldly: "And where may you be from?"

"From Byala Cherkva, Rachko the Stinkard!" the innkeeper introduced himself and once more held out his hand, which was left hanging in the air.

But Rachko was not offended. "Why are you afraid of me, Count? Or are you ashamed of my name? I inherited it from my father and I'm proud of it. For what can a name do to you? A name's nothing, but if a man's honest, then the name's fine too. You ask in Byala Cherkva whom they call the Stinkard and anyone'll tell you. You just listen to me. . . . When a man is an honorable man, then the name, let me tell you for instance. . . . I support a household and have three children—may you have as many yourself. I'm respected by all. And what does a man live for? For his honor and good name.

"You're right, Bai Rachko, wisely spoken."

"Of course I'm right; don't judge by my looks. I'm no fool. Many's the time I've put up the people's men. . . . As soon as I laid eyes on you just now, I said to myself, let's see if the Count will recognize me."

Ognyanov didn't recall having ever seen this remarkable man. "Have you kept this inn long?"

"About a year and a half, but I happened to be in Byala Cherkva for *Genevieve* . . . You were the Count."

"And won't you give me something to eat?"

"What the Lord has provided; that's all I've got," and Rachko set out a dish of haricot beans with red pepper, some pickled cabbage and a hunk of bread on a greasy Gabrovo table.

"I'll keep you company," Rachko added ingratiatingly and also sat down to lunch with Ognyanov.

The latter set to silently. This Rachko made a very unfavorable impression on him with his shameless manners and his still more shameless name, especially when he sat down to lunch unasked. "What an uncouth innkeeper! And a bit of an idiot too," he thought to himself.

As if to confirm his words Rachko poured out two glasses and said, "Let's clink glasses! Up and march! Long live" and he gulped down his glass of sour wine. "But I recognized you at once, eh? Many's the time I've put up the deacon Levski and clinked glasses with him! He was a friend of mine—I'm one of the people's men too; don't you mind my looks. . . ." Ognyanov noticed a contradiction here, or a downright lie, as Deacon Levski had been hanged three years ago. This increased his mistrust.

"Drink your wine, won't you? What's that? You don't drink? Then let me drink it." And Rachko downed Ognyanov's glass as well, making a terrible grimace over the vinegar he had drunk.

The lunch was soon over, despite the wishes of Rachko, who was becoming decidedly cheerful. "Wait a while, why are you in such a hurry? Won't you spend the night here? I'll just leave you for a while to go down to Karnari. . . . You wait for me. Stay here this evening. We'll have a nice chat. . . . I'm one of the people's men."

"Thank you, Bai Rachko. Get my horse out; I'll go on ahead."

"But the road's bad. . . . I'm telling you the truth, you listen to me. . . . I'd cut my head off. . . ."

"That's quite unnecessary," answered Ognyanov drily and added impatiently, "My horse!" The innkeeper went out.

Ognyanov examined the room and the adjoining small rooms carefully. He involuntarily thought of the Kakrin inn where Levski had been betrayed. The innkeepers of the Turkish villages, all of them Bulgarians, were by force and habit used to fraternizing with the Turks, so they were not to be trusted. And that chatterbox Rachko was capable of doing harm even in all innocence.

"Your horse is ready outside, but the road to Troyan's bad," said Rachko on returning.

"How much do you want for me and my horse?"

"Come on, Count, excuse me, but that was on me."

"No, say how much, so I can settle the bill; I'm most grateful for your hospitality, and above all for your wine." said Ognyanov ironically.

"Come on, the wine's good enough. . . . But I won't charge you a penny, neither for it, nor for the food, nor the bit of hay. To such friends. . . ."

"If that's how it is, I thank you, Bai Rachko," said Ognyanov, looking around him. "Is there anyone else here?"

"Only myself and the boy, Count, but I sent him to Byala Cherkva. He'll be back this evening. Now I want to pop down to the village, and have no one to leave here. . . . Come on, do stay!"

Ognyanov's eyes fell on a post. Then he caught the innkeeper by the arm and said pleasantly, "Now please oblige me, Bai Rachko, by letting me tie you up."

And with one hand Ognyanov snatched a coil of rope hanging on a nail, pressing the innkeeper to the post with the other. The innkeeper took it for a joke. "So now you're going to tie me up? Go ahead!" he said jovially.

Ognyanov calmly bound the rope about the post and when the innkeeper saw that things were growing serious, he first expressed surprise, then anger. "Now stop joking! Am I a haidouk, that you should tie me up?" And Rachko started wriggling.

Ognyanov said to him curtly, "If you start yelling, I'll rip your belly open."

The innkeeper, dumbfounded, looked at the belt with its load. He knew that the Count meant business. And he was as obedient as a child.

"I should like to tie up your mouth, but since I can't, I'm tying you," Ognyanov said with a grin, as he bound him firmly to the post. Then he asked, "When is your boy coming back?"

"This evening." Rachko was trembling.

"Well, then he'll untie you. Good-bye, Bai Rachko, I'm off to Troyan. And remember the Count—only to yourself." And throwing him a few coins, Ognyanov jumped onto his horse and continued on his way.

chapter 31

a sewing party in Altunovo

Instead of heading for Byala Cherkva, Ognyanov turned back towards the village of Altunovo, hidden in the western corner of the valley. Ordinarily it was a two-hour ride, but his horse was worn out and the going was hard, so it was nightfall before he reached the village, accompanied by the howling of wolves which had followed him all the way.

He entered the village by the Bulgarian quarter—its inhabitants were mixed, Turks and Bulgarians—and soon stopped before the gate of Bai Tsanko. A native of Klissoura, Bai Tsanko had long ago settled in this village. He was a simple-minded, jolly little fellow, and a patriot. The apostles were frequent visitors in his home.

He gave Ognyanov a joyful welcome. "It's lucky you came to me. We're having a sewing party this evening, so you can have a look at our girls. You won't feel bored," said Tsanko smiling, as he led him into the room.

Ognyanov hastened to tell him they were after him and for what reason. "We heard about it too," said Bai Tsanko. "We're still part of the world, you know, even if we are tucked away at the back of beyond."

"Won't you get into trouble because of me?"

"Don't worry, I tell you; just see that you settle on one of the girls this evening, one to carry the flag," said Tsanko jokingly. "There, you'll have a good look at them all through that window, like a king. . . ."

Ognyanov found himself in a small dark room. Its little wooden window opened onto the large room in which the party was being held. The more notable girls and young brides had gathered there to spin and sew the trousseau of Tsanko's daughter, Donka. The fire flickered merrily and illuminated all the walls, whose sole decoration was a print of St. Ivan of Rila and some gaily-colored pottery on the shelves. As in every well-to-do peasant house the furniture consisted of a row of pegs for the water-jugs, a chest, a dresser, and the large cupboard which held all Tsanko's household goods. The guests, both the men and the young women, sat on the floor, which was covered with handwoven goat hair rugs. Besides the light from the fire, two kerosene lamps were lighted, a luxury for the occasion.

It was a long time since Ognyanov had been present at such an interesting gathering, a custom inherited from the past. Huddled in the dark closet, he observed the simple scenes of the still primitive peasant life. The door opened and Dame Tsankovitsa, a prattling somewhat ribald goody, also from Klissoura, entered. She squatted down beside Ognyanov and started pointing out to him the more outstanding girls, with appropriate explanations.

"Look at that one, the fat one with the red cheeks. She's Chono's Staika. Do you see the woebegone way Ivan Borimechka* keeps looking at her? He barks like a sheep-dog when he wants to make her laugh. She's a grand worker, very neat, and as clean as they make them. Only, she does put on fat so easily, poor thing; but she'll get thin once she marries. Your town girls pile it on afterwards. . . . That one to her left is Tsveta Prodanova; she's sweet on that fellow with the moustaches, that look as if they were singed. She's a flirt all right; her eyes, are all over the place! But otherwise she's a good girl. Next to Tsveta, that's Dragan's Tsveta, and next to her, the priest's Raika. . . . I wouldn't exchange them for twenty Turkish beauties from Philippopolis: do you see what white necks they've got, like geese? Our Tsanko once said if one of them would let him bite her neck, he'd give her the pamid** vineyard on Mal-tepé; I hit him one with the poker for that, the bastard. And that one to the right, you see, next to fat Staika? She's been asked for by five of the best matches going, but her father wouldn't give her. He's keeping her for seed, old hamster that he is. You know he looks just like a hamster. I'll cut my tongue out if Nedyalko's Ivan doesn't run off with her. And over there is Milko's Rada; she's got a voice like the nightingale on our plum tree, but she's no good, between you and me. I think much more of Dinka Todorova, there, sitting by the dresser; see what a trim piece of goods she is. If I were a young bachelor I'd be after her myself. Come, I'll let you have her. . . . Next to our Dona is Peyev's daughter. She's good at work and good to look at, as the saying is, she's of a piece with our Dona. Moreover she sings as well as Milko's Rada, and laughs as prettily as a swallow, just listen to her!"

Bent over Boicho in the darkness like that, Dame Tsankovitsa reminded one of the scene in the *Divine Comedy* where Beatrice, in

---

* Borimechka—the bear-hugger.

** *pamid:* a kind of grape.

hell, points out to Dante its inhabitants one by one, telling him their story.

Ognyanov heard only part of the good woman's endless babble. He was entirely absorbed in the scene and not in its interpretation. The more forward girls joked with the boys slyly, pulled their legs and burst into peals of laughter. The male company retorted with boisterous giggles, sending a volley of arrows against the fair sex. The teasing, the gibes and jokes fell like rain; the double-entendres, which brought blushes to the most tanned of maidenly cheeks, were greeted with roars of laughter. Tsanko himself took part in the merriment; Dame Tsankovitsa was busy with the food she had prepared to treat the guests; Donka kept getting up and sitting down.

"You've been laughing your heads off long enough! What about some more songs!" gaily cried the hostess, who had left Boicho to go and have a look at the pot on the fire where the food for the guests was cooking. "Rada, Stanka, pipe up, and put the boys to shame. Our young men aren't worth beans; they can't sing for nuts."

Rada and Stanka did not have to be asked twice. They launched into a song and all the girls who could sing followed them, divided in two choirs; the first sang one verse and was then silent, while the second choir repeated it. The first choir consisted of the best singers with soprano voices, the second sang on a lower note.

Here is the song:

> Dobro-le, two young people, Dobro-le, fell in love.
> Dobro-le, were in love, Dobro-le, since their childhood.
> Dobro-le, they did meet, Dobro-le, last evening,
> Dobro-le, in the street, Dobro-le, in the darkness,
> Dobro-le, and they stood, Dobro-le, stood and talked . . . .
> Dobro-le and the moon, Dobro-le, showed her horns,
> Dobro-le, and the stars, Dobro-le, dotted the heavens,
> Dobro-le, and the young ones, Dobro-le, still are standing,
> Dobro-le still are standing, Dobro-le, still are talking,
> Dobro-le, her pails of water, Dobro-le, with frost were coated,
> Dobro-le, and her pole, dear Dobro-le, became an ash tree,
> Dobro-le, yet the young ones, Dobro-le, still they tarry.

When the song came to an end it called forth praise from the boys, who thought it a good song among other reasons because each took the reference to love-making personally. Ivan Borimechka fairly devoured Staika Chonina with his eyes, for he was courting her assiduously. "This song is sung in repeated couplets, and is danced with a forward and a backward step!" he cried in a loud voice.

All the girls laughed, looking at Borimechka with a twinkle in their eyes. He was a mountain of a man, a Goliath in size, a Hercules for strength, and with a bony, rough and rather foolish face. Moreover, he was a fine singer himself, that is his voice was as big as his body. Borimechka was somewhat annoyed. He withdrew silently, and in a little while let out a bark over their heads like an old sheep dog, which made the girls shriek with fright, then burst out laughing. Then they started to tease him. One of them sang to him:

Ivan, you colored pigeon,
Ivan, you slender poplar.

Laughter followed. Another continued:

Ivan, you scraggy bear, you,
Ivan, you long clothes-prop!

More giggling and laughter. Ivan blushed furiously. He gaped with dumb amazement at the full-cheeked Staika Chonina, who had so rudely ridiculed her fervent suitor, and then opened his mouth like a boa constrictor to bellow out:

Peika's aunt she spoke to her:
"Peika, my maiden, Peika dear,
People are constantly talking,
People, our closest neighbors,
That you are filled out and rounded,
That you are plump and big, dear,
Big by your uncle's farm-hand."

"Auntie, my very dear auntie,
Let people say what they will, dear,
People, the closest neighbors.
I'm filled out and well rounded
By my father's fine white flour.
His white flour, yes, the zagariya,*
For while I'm kneading the bread, dear,
I eat of grapes a whole basket,
And drink a flask of red wine too."

This biting taunt put Staika to shame. Her cheeks grew a deeper red, as if they had been dyed with kermes. The spiteful giggles of her

---

* *zagariya:* white wheat.

companions pierced her like arrows. Some mockingly asked with assumed simplicity, "Why, how can one eat grapes and drink wine at the same time? That's a big, fat lie."

"That's right! Either the song's lying or the girl is."

This spiteful piece of criticism still further infuriated Staika; she threw a vengeful look at the triumphant Borimechka and started singing in a voice that trembled with anger:

"Peika, you garden hollyhock,
May your knitting so fine
And my visits so frequent,
May they not be in vain,
And may we, Peika, get married!"

"Yovko, you swarthy farm-hand,
If Peika could ever love truly,
Black swineherds the likes of you,
Swineherds, yes, and such cowherds,
The Boyars' swarthy laborers,
A fence of youths I'd have woven,
And you, Yovko, I'd put
Down by the little wicket,
Its threshold, Yovko, to be,
So that when I drive out my calves,
And my slippers get muddy,
I'd wipe them, Yovko, on you."

A sharp reply to a savage insult. She had given as good as she got.

Staika looked proudly about her. Her knife had struck home. Ivan Borimechka stood there dumbfounded and motionless, his eyes popping out of his head. Suddenly a terrible, irrepressible guffawing filled the room. The whole party stared curiously at poor Ivan. Shame and hurt pride made the tears well up in his eyes. That only fanned the boisterous laughter all around.

Dame Tsankovitsa started scolding them, "What do you mean by teasing like that? Is it becoming for boys and girls to wrangle instead of cooing like doves?"

"That's right, perfect little doves," jeered a girl, "so sweet one could drink them out of a cup." The merry girls again started giggling.

"Quarreling's a sign of love," said Tsanko in a conciliatory tone. Ivan Borimechka went out in a huff, as if to protest against the remark.

"And like will to like," said Neda Lyagovichina

"Neda, do you know? God may help as a joke too," said Goran, Borimechka's cousin.

"Boys, why don't you sing some old haidouk song, to cheer us all up?" Tsanko suggested.

The young men joined in a chorus:

Poor Stoyan, poor fellow!
At two roads they watched for him,
At the third they caught him,
And they untied his black laces,*
To bind his manly hands fast;
Then Stoyan they did lead
To the garden of Erin the priest.
The priest had two fair maidens
And a third, his son's wife—Rouzha;
Rouzha was churning the butter
At the little gate to the garden,
The maidens were sweeping the yard
And they spoke to Stoyan, saying:
"Brother, oh, brother Stoyan,
On the morrow they'll hang you
In the king's own courtyard,
A sight for the queen to look on,
The queen and the king's small children."
Said Stoyan to Rouzha, said he:
"Oh, Rouzha, priest's daughter-in-law,
It's not my life that I'll grieve for,
Nor yet for the wide white world—
A hero weeps not, nor grieves,
But this I beg of you, Rouzha,
Let my shirt be washed clean,
Let my hair be well combed,
For I take pleasure, Rouzha,
When they hang a man on the gallows,
To see his shirt shining white,
To see his long hair flowing."

Ognyanov listened to the end of the song with a secret tremor. "Now, that Stoyan," he thought, "is the type of the legendary Bulgarian haidouk: looking upon death with gloomy calm. Not a word of regret, of repentance, of hope. All he wants is to die handsome. If only that heroic fatalism could be passed on to the Bulgarians of today! Oh, then I'd have no fear for the outcome of the struggle.

* Wound in a criss-cross pattern over his leggings.

That's the struggle I long for; those are the forces I seek. . . . To know how to die, there's the secret of victory."

At that moment the shepherd's flutes struck up. The tune, at first soft and melancholy, rose higher and higher; the eyes of the players shone; their faces were flushed with enthusiasm; the clear sounds vibrated and filled the night with the wild melody of the mountains. They carried the spirit of the mountain peaks and glens; they reminded one of the silence of forest vales, of the whisper of the shady places where the sheep rest at noon; of the scented wild marjoram, of mountain echoes and of love-sighs passing into the plains. The kaval* is the harp of the Bulgarian mountains and fields.

They all listened with rapt attention, taking in the native sounds of this musical poetry they understood so well. Dame Tsankovitsa, standing by the hearth, her hands on her hips, was transported. Ognyanov himself, enraptured to real enthusiasm, all but applauded.

Noisy talk and laughter broke out again. Upon hearing his own name, Ognyanov paid attention to the conversation. Peter Ovcharov, Raichin, Spiridoncho, Ivan Osten and a few others were discussing the future uprising. "I'm quite ready for the wedding now, I'm only waiting for my revolver from Philippopolis. I sent a hundred and seventy groats for it; it cost me three rams," Peter Ovcharov, the president of the local committee, was saying.

"But we don't know for certain when they'll raise the standard. Some say we'll be fleshing our knives around the Annunciation, others say St. George's Day, while Uncle Bozhil says it'll be on the first of May itself," said Spiridoncho, a handsome, stalwart youth.

"You be on the lookout, as soon as you hear the cuckoo and the forest is in leaf . . . but I'm ready even now, any time they say."

"Well, our Stara Planina has welcomed many brave fellows before now; she'll welcome us too," said Ivan Osten.

"Peter, you were speaking of the schoolmaster; so he's polished two of them off, eh? He's a brave one!"

"When will he come to visit us? I'd like to kiss the hand that dealt such blows!" said Raichin.

"He's got the lead on us, the schoolmaster, but we'll do our best to catch up with him. I think I know a thing or two about that trade myself," answered Ivan Osten. Ivan Osten was a brave young fellow and an excellent shot. The death of Deli-Ahmed last year was ascribed to him. That's why the local Turks were on the lookout for him, in vain so far.

---

* *kaval:* shepherd's flute.

At supper they all drank to Ognyanov's health. "God grant that we see him soon. . . . Follow his example, boys!" Tsanko said, lifting the bowl of wine.

"I'm willing to bet anything," spoke up the impatient Dame Tsankovitsa, "that tomorrow first thing in the morning he'll turn up here just like a falcon."

"What are you saying there, Dame Tsankovitsa? And me off to K. . . .?" said Raichin anxiously. "If he comes, see that he stays for the blood-pudding. We must have fun at Christmas time."

"What's all the to-do outside?" cried Tsanko, getting up without finishing his wine. Indeed men's and women's voices resounded from the yard. Tsanko and his wife dashed out. The guests also got up.

In a minute Tsanko's wife returned, greatly excited, exclaiming, "That's one job well done. Good luck to them."

"What's the matter, what's happened?"

"Borimechka's gone off with Staika!" There was a general cry of surprise.

"Just grabbed her, the madcap, and carried her off home on his shoulder, like a lamb on St. George's Day." Gleeful talk filled the room. "And how did it happen?"

"That's why he left early, and his cousin Goran with him."

"He waited for her behind the cart boards by the outside gate," Dame Tsankovitsa went on, "and carried her off! Alas for the boy and alack for the girl! Darned old Borimechka, whoever would have thought it?"

"To tell you the truth, they're made for each other," said a boy.

"She's a fat little Serbian pig, and he's a Hungarian shirehorse," another said with a laugh.

"Here's long life to them! Tomorrow we'll drink red brandy, said Tsanko.

"And they must give me a pair of embroidered sleeves. I want what's my due," cried Dame Tsankovitsa, "I was the matchmaker."

A little later the guests left in a gay mood.

chapter 32

God's too high, the king's too far

Tsanko hurried to Ognyanov in his dark closet. "Well, Boicho, how did you like our party?"

"It was wonderful, marvellous, Bai Tsanko!"

"And did you write down the songs?"

"How could I? There's not even a candle here, don't you see?"

Dame Tsankovitsa joined them, candle in hand. "Someone's knocking at the gate," she said.

"That's probably Staika's folks; they'll be wanting their girl from us now. . . . Well, may that be the worst of our worries." But Donka entered and said some zaptiehs were knocking at the door; old Deiko, the mayor, had brought them.

"A palsy on them and on old Deiko! Where shall I put the swine? . . . This isn't meant for you," he said to reassure Ognyanov, "but you'd better hide somewhere. Wife, show the schoolmaster where to hide." And Tsanko went out.

A little later he brought in two zaptiehs, muffled up in their hooded capes and all covered with snow. They were furious. "Why did you keep us waiting such ages, you cuckold?" grumbled the one-eyed zaptieh, shaking the snow off his cape.

"We nearly froze till you found time to open the gate!" the other zaptieh shouted in a hoarse, low voice. Tsanko muttered something by way of excuse.

"What are you muttering there? Kill a chicken and butter some eggs for us."

Tsanko tried to say something. The one-eyed zaptieh shouted at him, "Stop that chatter, giaour; hurry up and tell your wife to cook some supper! Or do you intend to treat us to some of your giaour plum-stew and nut shells?" he said, glancing contemptuously at the supper, which had not been cleared away. Tsanko went towards the door as though he had been stung, to carry out the orders.

The short zaptieh called to him, "Wait, where did you send the girls?"

"They went home; it was getting late," answered Tsanko, who was quite sober now.

"Bring them back; let them come and finish their supper, and treat us to a glass of rakiya. Why did you send them away?" Tsanko gave them a frightened look.

"Where's your girl?"

"She went to bed, aga!"

"Bring her down; let her wait on us," said the one-eyed zaptieh, drying his wet leg-bands, which gave out clouds of steam and of stench.

"Don't frighten my child, aga," said Tsanko imploringly. The mayor entered and stood there humbly.

"Ha, you swine, you took us around knocking at twenty doors like beggars! And you brought us here by force! What do you mean by hiding your . . .?" And he called the girls by an insulting name.

The Bulgarians took everything lying down. They were used to it. These times of bondage had produced the proverb, so degrading to mankind, "The sword cuts not a bowed head." Tsanko only prayed to God that they would leave his daughter alone.

"Chorbadji," the one-eyed zaptieh asked, "are you preparing a revolt?" Tsanko denied it boldly.

"And what is this dagger here?" said the short one, picking up the dagger of Peter the shepherd, who had forgotten it on the rug.

"So that's it, chorbadji; you're not making ready to revolt, eh?" asked the one-eyed one with a spiteful smile.

"No, aga, we are peaceful subjects of the Sultan," answered Tsanko, doing his best to be calm. "One of the guests must have forgotten that dagger."

"Whose is it?"

"I don't recognize it, aga."

The zaptiehs were peering at some yellow scrawls on the knife, among which they made out a few words. "And what are these words?" they asked Tsanko.

He glanced at the dagger. Near the hilt a design was worked in yellow wire and the words "Liberty or Death"; on the other side was the name of the owner. "That's a vine," lied Tsanko.

The one-eyed zaptieh hit him in the face with his muddy sandal. "Giaour, don't think I'm blind even if I have only one eye." Tsanko's answer aroused their suspicion. "Mayor, come here!" The mayor was coming in with a tin of cheese pastry to have it baked at Tsanko's. He trembled when he saw the naked dagger in the hands of the zaptieh. "Read this!"

The mayor read and stood there in confusion. "I can't make it out, aga."

The beardless fellow seized his whip and lashed out with it. It cracked and wound itself twice about the mayor's neck. A stream of blood trickled down his cheek.

"A pack of rogues!" The mayor silently wiped the blood from his cheek.

"Read it or I'll poke the knife down your throat!" shouted the zaptieh. The dazed mayor saw that there was no way out; he had to submit.

"Peter Ovcharov," he read, hesitating purposely.

"Do you know him?"

"He's from our village."

"Is it him they call Peter the shepherd?" asked the one-eyed zaptieh; it was clear he knew a smattering of Bulgarian.*

"That's right, aga," and the mayor handed him the knife, blessing the Holy Trinity that he had skipped the terrible words. But he was over-hasty.

"Look what it says on the other side!" said the zaptieh. The mayor again bent over the dagger, very frightened and hesitating. At the same moment he saw with his right eye that the short one was about to whip him.

"It says 'Liberty or Death,' aga." The one-eyed zaptieh jumped up.

"Liberty, eh?" he grinned ominously. "Who makes these daggers? Where is Peter the shepherd?"

"Where should he be, aga? At home."

"Go and fetch him. . . ." The mayor started.

"Wait, I'll come with you, you fool!" And the short zaptieh threw on his cape and went out with him.

"That's best, Yussouf-Aga, for that shepherd is a haidouk or the next thing to it."

In the meantime Tsanko went out to his wife, who was cooking and cursing at the same time: "May God blast them! May He tear their loins! May a bone choke them, so they burst. May they die of poison! That I should be cooking meat for them just before Christmas! How did those heathen devils get here to bring ruin on us and scare us out of our wits!"

"Donka, go to your uncle's tonight, dear. Slip through the fence," said Tsanko to his daughter, who appeared at the door, pale with fright.

"Why should Deiko bring them here? Only last week he brought two of them again," his wife was muttering.

---

* Ovcharov literally means shepherd's son.

"What is he to do, poor man?" said Tsanko. "He took them all over the place. They wanted to come here: they heard the songs, it seems. . . . He got five or six strokes over the back." Tsanko again went to the one-eyed zaptieh.

"Chorbadji, where've you been all this while? Give us some rakiya and pickles."

"The shepherd isn't at home," the short one, who had just returned with the mayor, said angrily.

"We'll ransack the village, but we must catch that comita at all costs," said the one-eyed one, drinking.

"Why not get it out of his father?" asked the short zaptieh and then whispered something. The one-eyed one nodded in approval.

"Kehaya, go call the old fellow! We want to ask him something more; take this too," said the short zaptieh, handing him a brandy bottle.

"For rakiya? The tavern's closed now, aga." In answer the one-eyed zaptieh hit him in the face with his sandal. Though milder by nature, he grew ferocious when drinking or when he felt like drinking.

In a quarter of an hour old Stoiko appeared. He was a man of fifty, but with a lively and energetic face, strong-willed and stubborn.

"Stoiko, tell us where your son is—you know where you've hidden him—or your own head will suffer for it!" So saying the one-eyed zaptieh raised the brandy-flask thirstily. His eye flashed. Then he handed the flask to his companion.

"I don't know where he is, aga," the old man answered.

"Yes, you do, giaour; you know all right," the zaptieh muttered viciously. The old man once more denied all knowledge.

"You shall tell us!"

"We'll knock your teeth out, and tomorrow we'll drag you on foot behind us!" the short one burst out.

"Do what you will; I've only one life to lose," answered the old man firmly.

"Go over there and think it over; then you'll repent," the one-eyed one ordered with assumed gentleness. His aim was to extract a ransom from old Stoiko, which the mayor was going to propose to him. This was sheer robbery, but they wanted to make it look like a voluntary gift. It was the usual method in such cases.

But old Stoiko stood firm. They looked at each other in amazement at such boldness, and cast furious glances at the old man. "Did you hear, old man?" the one-eyed zaptieh yelled.

"There's nothing for me to think over. Let me go," he answered sullenly. The zaptiehs began to rage.

"Mayor, throw this old fool down!" said the one-eyed one, seizing the whip. The mayor and Tsanko begged him to spare the old man. Instead of answering he gave him a kick which brought him to the ground. Then blow after blow rained down on his back. Up to a time old Stoiko cried out and groaned, and then he was silent; the torturer's forehead was covered with perspiration; he was tired out by his exertions. They dragged the old man out to bring him to. "When he recovers, tell me; I'll make him speak yet!"

"We beg of you, Hadji Aga, spare the old man; he couldn't stand any more torture, he'll die," said Tsanko imploringly.

"Long live the Sultan, you comita!" said the short zaptieh in a fit of anger. "It's you we ought to hang! You gather comitas at your house. You're probably hiding the shepherd too. We'd better search the house." Tsanko's face involuntarily expressed his dismay. Befuddled with brandy though he was, the one-eyed zaptieh nevertheless noticed his confusion. Startled, he turned to his companion.

"Yussouf-Aga, let's search the place. This giaour is hiding something," and he got up.

"You're welcome," said Tsanko in hollow voice, and led the way with a small lantern.

He showed them all over the house, leaving the closet to the last. Finally he lit it up too. There was a hole in the blackened ceiling which was quite invisible when closed. Tsanko was sure that Ognyanov had escaped through it and had replaced the concealed trap-door. So he was quite calm when he led in the Turks and lit the closet up.

The first thing he did was to look at the ceiling. The hole gaped wide. Tsanko seemed to turn to stone. The Turks examined the closet. "What is that hole?"

"It leads up to the attic," Tsanko said in a husky voice. His feet trembled and he leaned against the wall. The short zaptieh saw that it was out of fear.

"Give me more light, I want to climb up there," he said. But suddenly an unpleasant thought occurred to him and he told his companion to look instead. Hassan-Aga, when he was good and drunk, grew very brave; drinking made his heart fierce and kindled his bully's blood. He stepped on the mayor's back.

"Chorbadji, give me the lantern; don't you see I need it?" Tsanko automatically handed it to him, white as a sheet.

The one-eyed zaptieh stuck the lantern into the hole, and after it his head. One could tell by his body that he was turning in all directions with the lantern in his hand.

Then he jumped down. "Chorbadji, whom had you hidden here?"

Tsanko looked demented. He didn't know what to answer. That evening he had lived through so much fear and suffering that it all seemed a nightmare to him. His thoughts were confused. When questioned again he answered guiltily and in fear.

"The comita will give a clearer answer in Klissoura. There's a better prison there. He'll spend the night here. . . ." And the zaptieh locked him up in the dark and gloomy closet. Tsanko was so shaken that it took him several minutes to collect himself. He clasped his head in his hands, as though he were holding it lest he lose his mind. Lacking firmness as he did, the suffering soon broke him. He started moaning and groaning desperately.

There was a push against the door and he heard Deiko's voice, "What do you mean to do now, Tsanko?"

"I don't know, Bai Deiko, tell me."

"You know the weak spot of the Turks. Close your eyes and just give, to free yourself. Otherwise they'll drag you to konaks and to law courts until they finish you. Poor old Stoiko, he might have gotten off with a very small sum. . . . Come on, Tsanko—one saves money for a rainy day!"

His wife came to him in tears. "Tsanko, let's give it. Don't spare anything, Tsanko! You don't stand a chance unless you get out of the clutches of these cutthroats. . . . Old Stoiko's dead already. . . . Oh, dear, oh dear, what has come upon us!"

"What have we got to give, my dear? You know we haven't any hard cash."

"Shall we give the string?"

"What, Donka's string of gold coins?"

"Yes, Donka's; it's all we have; let's give it . . . anything to set you free. . . . Look, they've begun to ask for her again, the cursed beasts!"

"Do whatever God has taught you, wife. I'm out of my mind," Tsanko groaned from his prison. His wife and Deiko went out.

A little later the light of a candle shone through the cracks of the closet, and the door was unlocked.

"Tsanko, come out; don't worry," said Deiko. "The agas turned out to be good people. They've even left you the dagger to put you out of your fear. You're lucky to have got off so cheap."

And bending over he whispered in his ear, "The time's not far off, and then either we destroy them or they destroy us. . . . Things can't go on like this. . . . Life's not worth living as it is now."

chapter 33

the victors feast the vanquished

At that very moment Ognyanov was knocking at Peter Ovcharov's gate. Unable to bear the sight of the zaptiehs' brutality, which he had witnessed through a chink in the ceiling, incapable of restraining his hand from wreaking bloody vengeance on the scoundrels then and there, an imprudence that would have had very serious consequences, Ognyanov, nearly out of his mind, had jumped down into the street and run straight to Dyado Stoiko's house. The gate was opened.

"Where's Peter?" he asked, forgetting the boy was in hiding.

"Is that you, schoolmaster?" asked the sobbing mother.

"Where's Peter, Granny Stoikovitsa?"

"Be careful, lad; don't let those brutes hear you! Peter's over at Borimechka's."

"Where's that, Granny?"

"Next door to the priest's house, if you know it; the one with the new gates. Take care of yourself, my boy." The poor woman had no suspicion that Dyado Stoiko was already breathing his last. Ognyanov dashed away. He scarcely felt the earth beneath him. As he approached the priests house a noisy group appeared from that direction. Ognyanov recognized Peter's voice. He stopped the boys.

"The schoolmaster!" they all cried, recognizing him.

"It's me, brothers; where are you off to?"

"We were at Borimechka's," answered Peter. "He stole his bride tonight, so we went to drink his health. You should see how well they get on. You'd think they were made for each other. And when did you turn up?"

"Peter, I want a word with you." And he took him aside.

"You'll excuse me; good night!" Peter called to his friends and quickly set out with Ognyanov. They reached home.

"Is father back?" he asked his mother.

"Not yet, son." Ognyanov dragged him down to the cellar.

"Look here, Peter, I told you your father was badly beaten up because of you. Those swine may do even worse at Tsanko's. We can't stop their outrages except with arms; I could have bashed in their heads myself just now, but I was afraid of the consequences. . . . We mustn't go near Tsanko's."

"I want to revenge him, brother!" Peter cried, beside himself.

"I want vengeance too, Peter, and terrible vengeance, but without danger to ourselves."

"How shall we do it?" asked Peter, taking his gun from the wall.

"Be patient, let's think it over."

"I can't think, I must see what they're doing to father."

Himself of a violent nature, Ognyanov was now endeavoring to restrain one still more violent from a natural but fatal step. If Peter went to Tsanko's, there would be bloodshed. Ognyanov believed that the hour for a decisive struggle had not yet come, and his heart ached at the thought that such an outstanding, brave young fellow should die an untimely and useless death.

All his efforts were in vain. Peter was roaring like a lion, "I must avenge my father, come what may!" He shook off Ognyanov, who was trying to hold him back, and made for the door. Ognyanov was at his wits' end. He saw he could not influence such rebellious blood.

But before Peter had reached the gate, someone knocked on it. He cocked his gun, then opened the door. Three Bulgarians, neighbors of Tsanko's, were carrying Dyado Stoiko in a rug, or rather his dead body.

"May you live, Peterkin," one of the peasants said to him.

The yard was filled with the sobbing and wailing of the women. Granny Stoikovitsa tore her bodice and kept throwing herself on her husband's cold body. Ognyanov pulled Peter aside, for the young man was utterly crushed by this misfortune, and again he forced him down into the cellar. With tears in his eyes Ognyanov tried to restrain him, because, after a momentary fit of despair at the sight of his father, Peter was again intent on a speedy revenge.

"We'll have our revenge; we certainly will," Ognyanov kept telling him as he embraced him. "There's no holier duty for you and me now than revenge."

"Blood! Blood!" Peter shouted in a frenzy. "O father, that you should have your old bones broken by curs! O mother, what will become of you now?"

"Steady, brother, steady on; be firm, we shall inflict terrible punishment!"

In half an hour the paroxysm of grief had subsided, for even the most acute moral suffering is spent with its own force. Peter consented to stay at home after having Ognyanov, Osten and Spiridoncho take an oath before the icon that they would not leave the zaptiehs alive.

"A nice time Borimechka chose to get married!" said Osten with annoyance. "If it weren't for that we'd have had him in on this. We could do with a hurricance like him."

Their plan of revenge was this: they would stand watch on the road leading northwards towards the Lyaskovets Pass, over which the road to Klissoura runs. For the place of ambush they settled on the densely wooded valley through which the Beleshtitsa flows to join the Strema near by. There they would lie in wait for the two Turks and attack them with bare knives, after which they would drag the bodies into the bushes and hide them. But just in case the victims should escape, they took their guns along. They would only resort to them if worst came to worst. This plan was based on what Deiko knew about the zaptiehs: they were going to rise very early, before second cock-crow, and head for Klissoura, which they were in a hurry to reach; that was why he had been ordered to wake them long before dawn.

The first cocks had crowed when the little band left the silent village and came into the open country. It was snowing heavily in large flakes. A white mantle covered the whole world, making the darkness less intense. The travelers, their guns hidden under their heavy hooded capes, strode in silence through the thick snow which covered everything. Not a sound was to be heard as they marched along; they might have been ghosts of the night, vampires which wander abroad at Christmastide. The snow kept on falling, filling every hollow with drifts which slowed their progress; they did not notice it, however, for a single thought engrossed them all—revenge. The cries of Peter, their brave friend, the sobbing and grief of the mother and the rest of the family, still rang in their ears.

At the moment they feared only one thing, and that was that the zaptiehs might escape them; all other fears and interests were laid aside. They walked on for a long time without exchanging a word, till suddenly they heard a kind of bark behind them, which echoed over the deserted countryside. They turned round in surprise.

"Dogs at this hour?" asked Boicho in surprise.

"That's very odd," said Spiridoncho anxiously. The barking sounded again, still louder, and, before they could realize what it was, they saw an enormous black figure, most unlike a dog, jumping over the fallen branches and running towards them; it looked like a monster, like an enormous bear, standing upright on its hind legs.

Boicho and Spiridoncho instinctively stepped aside, against the bole of an oak tree, ready to defend themselves against the unknown aggressor. At the same moment he came running up to them.

"Borimechka!" they all cried out.

"Borimechka sure enough! You forgot all about him, I'll be damned. . . ."

It was indeed Borimechka in his great hooded cape. Hearing the commotion in the street he had gone to Peter's house, where he heard all the news. Without losing a minute, he returned home, sent his bride to her mother's, stuck his club in his waist-band, snatched up his gun, and dashed after the band to take part in the revenge.

This powerful assistance encouraged them still more. "Let's be off," said Osten.

"Forward!" added Ognyanov.

"Wait for the other one, won't you?" said Borimechka.

"Who else is there?" they all asked in surprise.

"Peter's young brother Daniel; he set out with me too."

"What did you bring him for?"

"Well, you see, Peter sent him so that his brother might see what takes place with his own eyes."

"What! Doesn't he trust us? We swore we'd do it!"

"A hundred oaths for a penny—I don't believe you either."

"And why not?"

"You start off without Borimechka! I'll be damned. . . ."

This oath was employed by Borimechka after almost every other word. It expressed his feelings and thoughts much more clearly than his words could.

"Don't be angry, Ivan," said Osten. "We thought of you, but you're a bridegroom, you know. Ah! There's Daniel!" The boy stopped before them, quite out of breath; he had only a long knife tucked into his waist-band.

The group had now increased from three to five. They went on in silence. All this time they were skirting the Sredna Gora plateau, a spur of Mount Bogdan, where the Beleshtitsa has its source. At last they reached the river. It was indeed a most suitable point of attack: on the right hand ran the Strema, which the Turks had to wade through; on the left lay a deep hollowed-out valley, overgrown by dense forest, and above it the mountain. Here the band stopped. They would thus be at more than an hour's distance from Altunovo, where the shots, if needed, would not be heard.

Dawn was already approaching when they took cover in a thicket.

The snow was falling now in finer flakes. The companions, huddling low, waited patiently, their eyes fixed in the east, where the two zaptiehs were expected to appear. But the first sound they heard was the howling of wolves. It came from above their heads and could be heard drawing nearer and nearer. The wolves were probably descending into the plain in search of food.

"They're coming towards us," said Ivan Osten.

"No shooting!"

"We'll attack with knives and the butts of our rifles, do you hear?" said Ognyanov. The companions pricked up their ears. A sound of pattering in the brushwood above them indicated that the pack was advancing en masse at a run. The howling was heard once more. It was getting light.

"Damn these wolves! What if they upset our plans!" Ognyanov groaned. At the same moment several wolves appeared on the little meadow in front of them and stopped short. They raised their sharp muzzles and started to howl. More of them appeared.

"Eight!" whispered Borimechka. "Four for you; the rest are mine."

Having made the acquaintance of their prey, the hungry beasts rushed on the thicket. It was now transformed into a fortress which the wolves attacked and the men defended. Knives and daggers flashed fiercely; guns rose and fell. Howls, roars. Several beasts rolled over in front of the thicket; others busied themselves with their fallen companions, tearing them apart while there was still life in them; the remainder were driven away from the thicket, from which Ivan Borimechka made frequent sallies, barking like a sheepdog and belaboring their heads with his club. He looked like Samson smiting the Philistines with the jawbone of an ass.

Soon the remaining wolves were driven away across the valley to the opposite slope, where they squatted down to lick their wounds. Fortunately, no one passed while the fight was on.

"The wolves won't budge from there," said Ognyanov.

"Look, there's another pack of them over there!"

"Let them wait; we'll give them a feast so they'll remember Borimechka's wedding day," said Spiridoncho.

"I'll be damned!" Borimechka mumbled, well pleased with himself. More time passed.

The Turks did not appear, yet second cock-crow was past. The group had already heard the distant crowing borne from remote villages on the silence of the night. It became lighter; the trees in the plain were more clearly discernible, and objects could already be distinguished. The boys grew restless and impatient; they felt the cold, standing as they were in one spot, and then it struck them that they might miss the zaptiehs, that they might have postponed their departure till later because of the thick snow which had covered everything during the night, or perhaps for fear of being attacked. In a short while it would be broad daylight. People would be using the road, and then nothing could be done! These thoughts were in the mind of each of them; the terrible impatience grew and grew, till it became unbearable, a veritable torture. Osten groaned in despair.

"We'll wait for them. No matter when they pass; we won't budge from here," said Ognyanov in a hollow voice.

"And if there are other people?"

"They can go their ways; all we need is those two."

"But then we'll have to attack openly!"

"If it can't be done in secret, we'll have to do it openly."

"We can fire from here, and then off to the mountains! No one'll see us in the forest," said Osten.

"Right. But if they've set out in company with other Turks?"

"Then we'll have a regular battle. We've got arms and the position's good," said Ognyanov. "Only remember this: we've taken an oath before God not to let them escape with their lives."

"I'll be damned!"

"There's just one thing I'm afraid of, boys," said Boicho.

"What?"

"That they have taken another road."

"Don't worry about that," said Osten. "There is no other road; but they may have turned back! Then God give us strength!"

Borimechka stood up and stared at something. "Somebody's coming," he said, pointing to the east. They all gazed intently in that direction. Where the road wound its way among the trees two men appeared.

"Horsemen!" cried Osten, regretfully.

"They're not our men," said Spiridoncho.

"Ours are on foot," remarked Osten.

"I'll be damned!"

Ognyanov was excited and angry; he kept his eyes fixed on the two horsemen riding side by side along the road. They were approaching and were now about a hundred paces off.

"They're our men all right!" he cried joyfully. "It's them! I can tell by their capes and their faces too. . . . The one-eyed one's on the far side." With guns cocked all of them kept their eyes fixed on the two zaptiehs who were fixed approaching them peaceably.

"And that's Tsanko's horse," said Spiridoncho.

"The other's mine," added Ognyanov.

"They've taken them by force."

Ognyanov's joy was short-lived: he now realized that the Turks might very easily escape. Since they could not fight in the open and with knives, they would have to shoot from their hiding-place, and the sound of a shot would give them away. Also the horses were a problem.

"Well, whatever happens . . ." Ognyanov said to himself in a whisper.

"We'll use our guns!"

"Look out, boys, hit them at the first go!"

"When they come to the elm we shoot," said Osten.

"The one-eyed chap's mine," said Borimechka.

"Borimechka and Spiridoncho—the one-eyed one. The schoolmaster and I—the other," commanded Osten.

The horsemen reached the elm. The muzzles were leveled from the thicket and a volley awoke the surrounding echoes. The boys looked through the smoke. One of the zaptiehs had fallen, the other hung down on one side. The horses reared a bit, then stopped.

"Which of them was it killed my father, schoolmaster?" asked Daniel, and he was the first to jump out of the ambush.

"The one-eyed fellow, the one who fell to the ground."

Daniel made a dash for the road. He immediately was at the spot and hitting away at the hapless murderer of his father with his yataghan. When his companions came up he was still hacking away like mad. He looked like a wild beast. The Turk, who was not yet dead, seemed more like a heap of hashed meat than a man. The thick snow was red with blood; there were pools of it.

Ognyanov was horrified and sickened at the sight of this butchery. Had it been done by a coward, he would have protested, but Peter's young brother was brave enough; it was only revenge that could stir him to such an orgy of savagery.

"A savage revenge," Ognyanov reflected, "but justifiable before God and one's conscience. Bloodthirstiness, but a good trait. . . . The Bulgarian has been a sheep for five centuries—it's better that he should be a beast. Men respect the goat more than the lamb, the dog more than the goat, the bloodthirsty tiger more than the wolf or the bear, and the bird of prey, the falcon, more than the hen which makes a dainty morsel for it. Why? Because they personify force, which means justice and freedom. Let philosophy flourish; nature remains what she is. Christ said, 'If they smite you on one cheek, turn unto them the other.' That is divine and I revere it. But I prefer Moses who says, 'An eye for an eye, and a tooth for a tooth!' That is natural and I follow it. That is the cruel, sacred principle on which our struggle against the tyrants must be based. . . . To have mercy for the merciless is as cowardly as to expect it from them. . . ."

Plunged in such engrossing thoughts, passionate and cruel as the moment itself, and in contrast with his humane nature, Ognyanov stood over the corpse and, as in a daze, watched the snow cover the red pools and the mass of hashed flesh and rags. Suddenly he noticed a chain of small gold coins in this ghastly heap and pointed them out to Spiridoncho. "Take them for some poor fellows to buy their Christmas dinner with." Spiridoncho raised the chain with the point of his dagger.

"The scoundrel, I wonder what Bulgarian he robbed!"

"Why, that's Donka's string! The very same!" cried Spiridoncho, bewildered and frightened. He was engaged to Donka.

"It must have been the ransom for your father-in-law," said Ognyanov.

"But this is only half the string—it must have gotten cut. The rest is probably somewhere in this garbage." And with a feeling of disgust Spiridoncho began to rummage with his dagger, but he could not find the other half. It was on the other Turk, with whom the one-eyed one in brotherly fashion had shared the spoils, as well as the punishment. At the same time, Borimechka was finishing off the other zaptieh with his club.

The two corpses were soon dragged into the brushwood. Meanwhile Tsanko's horse was trotting back to the village, while the other one, sensing that the wolves were near at hand, plunged across the Strema and tore over the plain with his tail streaming out.

"An eye for an eye! A tooth for a tooth!" Ognyanov kept whispering to himself unconsciously.

As soon as the boys had left, the wolves came down. Nature and beast joined forces to blot out all traces of this just revenge. And the snow continued to fall.

It was broad daylight now, but the surrounding country was still deserted. Nobody was stirring yet on the road or in the fields, covered with their white shroud. The early hour and the deep snow kept every traveler in his bed. No one had witnessed the murder of the Turks. But the young men did not want to be seen returning to the village. And the road by which they had come was probably no longer deserted; moreover there were mills there. They held a consultation and decided to climb up to the northern slopes of Bogdan, well covered with beech forests and underbrush, in order to descend to the village by the other ravine. This road, though a difficult one, was deserted and would give cover. Daniel was sent straight home to the village.

chapter 34

the blizzard

It was a precipitous path through the wooded ravine which the boys were climbing from the valley of the Beleshtitsa. Borimechka, who knew all these parts, led the way, his gun over his shoulder. The going became difficult as the snow piled up on the mountain path; in half an hour drops of perspiration the size of hailstones were running down their faces, as if these sturdy young men had been trudging up the ravine for hours. They reached a peak. By now it had stopped snowing, and soon the sun shone through the pale network of clouds and flooded valleys and mountains with its white rays. Their covering of snow became still more dazzlingly white, flashing in the sunshine in myriads of shimmering sparkles, as if strewn with diamond dust, like the robe of a Bagdad sultana.

Puffs of smoke rose over the villages in the valley which were already stirring. Here and there peasants moved about, breaking the first tracks through the snowbound lanes and paths. The village of Altunovo could be clearly seen at the very foot of the ridge, and a commotion was visible there; the young men noticed a black mass which was probably people moving towards the outskirts of the village where the graveyard was. They rightly guessed it to be Dyado Stoiko's funeral; now they could even hear the sound of the klepalo.*

But the ridges and mountain summits towered inaccessible, sunk in proud slumber under their virgin mantle. The majestic Ribaritsa to the west of the valley raised its giant, rounded dome into the heavens, surrounded by a ring of lower peaks; its top was shrouded in waves of moving clouds, which seemed to be smoking. Along the northern horizon extended the straight line of Stara Planina, swimming in whiteness and sunshine. Usually forbidding, it was now beautiful to behold. Only the gaping gray rocks—the beds of waterfalls which dashed down from its summit—remained bare, and gave the mountain a rather severe appearance. The ridge stretched in an

* *klepalo:* board struck with wooden mallet used instead of churchbells, which were long banned in the Turkish provinces inhabited by Christians.

unbroken wall to Ambaritsa itself, where the range of Balkan giants begins. . . .

The young men walked on, stopping from time to time to admire the fascinating beauty of the winter scene, but in silence. Peter's misfortune and the revenge which had followed had cast a pall on them. The occasional disjointed snatches of talk were solely about the road, which went up hill and down dale. In places one of them would sink into the snow and have to be pulled out by the others with great difficulty. It was then that Borimechka, Goliath that he was, proved most useful. Although they stopped often to rest, their strength was failing. They were gnawed by hunger, and in addition, an icy wind began to blow from the north; it lashed their faces and froze their noses, ears and hands.

The forest grew ever more dense and inhospitable. They trudged on to a certain point, then stopped; there was no trace of a path. An impenetrable tangle of beech thickets stretched ahead of them, blocked moreover by deep snowdrifts, while the gale blew stronger than ever. They looked at each other in consternation.

"Better drop back into the valley and take the road home?" asked Spiridoncho.

"No," retorted Osten, "we can try another direction, but don't let's turn back." The others agreed with him.

After a short consultation they decided to retrace their steps a little, then turn to the right and somehow make their way through the thickets so as to come out at the meadow on the top of the ridge; from there they could drop down into the valley beyond.

"That's where Diko's sheepfold is," said Osten. "Let's go there and get warm, and have a bite to eat. This way we won't be able to carry the rifles long."

"I agree with Osten," said Ognyanov, turning his back to the wind. "Let's stop in at the sheepfold, first to rest and have a bite; second, we may learn what's happening in Altunovo. We'd better not go down without knowing how the land lies." He could have added a third reason as well: the pain in his leg, which the walking and the cold had brought on again.

"That's true," said Spiridoncho. "Tsanko's horse must have returned, and the village will be in an uproar by now."

"Don't you worry about that," said Osten, "the wolves can't have left so much as a bone of the zaptiehs. If the Turks set out to look for them, all they'll find will be rags. And Jack Frost must have covered up all traces of the blood on the road; I noticed there wasn't a drop of blood on Tsanko's horse."

They came out onto the meadow and again consulted as to the right direction. Ivan Borimechka was observing the sky attentively. The companions waited to hear what he had to say.

"Best cut over towards the sheepfold! Ribaritsa don't look too good—I'll be damned!" said he seriously.

Whereupon they turned to the northeast and started crawling upwards. The wind was blowing furiously. It flapped about the travelers' capes, crept down their necks, up their trouser legs and played about under their shirts. The storm increased and roared more fiercely with every step. Little by little Ognyanov lagged behind. He felt his strength ebbing; there was a drumming in his ears. He felt giddy; he realized he was at the end of his tether, but would not call to the others to wait. Besides in the roaring wind his voice would not have carried. Endowed with unusual strength of will, he relied on it now to see him through, even if his muscles gave in. But man, however strong he may be spiritually, is obliged in the end to submit to the effects of physical laws. No effort of the will, no power of the spirit, can raise the muscular force beyond a certain level. The spirit may indeed spur the body to action, but its task is only to promote and apply that muscular force, not to engender it.

All the mountain valleys were ringing; the storm's icy breath numbed the limbs and chilled the blood in the veins. The air enveloped the travelers like a frozen choppy sea; the sun's rays emitted no warmth, rather seemed to prick their flesh with thorns. Soon they were caught in the blizzard, which bore down on them in stormy windswept clouds of snow. In a second it was roaring like hell, the wind scattered the snowdrifts in powdery clouds and madly whirling clumps of snow which rose in columns to the very heavens. Sun and light vanished; earth and sky were entangled and fused in a chaos of snow flying by at lightning speed. And the blizzard roared and shrieked and echoed as if the world were coming to an end.

This lasted two minutes. Then the blizzard passed on to another peak, enveloping it in its havoc-working shroud. The sun again shone with a pale icy light in a cloudless sky.

The travelers, who had prostrated themselves under a ledge of rock which offered some slight protection from the main force of the storm, were miraculously not snowed under. One by one they got up, as if waking from the sleep of death. They were completely numb; hands and feet had lost all feeling, and they were drowsy with the cold. It was now indeed that the danger was greatest. The first to collect himself was Ivan Borimechka.

"Up with you, boys," he cried out, "run for it, or we'll be frozen to death." This gave them a shock. They gripped their rifles and plodded on. Suddenly Borimechka stopped them.

"Where's schoolmaster?" They looked about them alarmed. Ognyanov was nowhere to be seen.

"The gale must have blown him away!"

"He must be snowed under!" They dispersed to look for him. The precipice yawning at their feet filled them with horror. They did not dare look down into it.

"There he is!" cried Osten.

At the very brink of the precipice, two feet, shod in sandals, stuck out from the snow. They shoveled it off and pulled Ognyanov out. He was apparently lifeless, his face leaden, his flesh rigid.

"I'll be damned! . . ." muttered Borimechka full of sympathy.

"Rub him, brothers!" cried Osten, and himself started rubbing his face, hands and chest with snow. "He's still warm; we may save him yet." They all forgot about themselves in their efforts to save their dying companion. The energetic rubbing soon brought him back to life, while it did them good too. Their blood began to tingle.

"Let's hurry to the sheepfold!" cried Osten. The three of them seized Ognyanov by the arms and legs and carried him up the snowy ravine of Mount Bogdan. In this task again Borimechka's powerful muscles were of the greatest help. After indescribable efforts they managed at last to drag themselves to the sheepfold.

chapter 35

in the hut

Diko's sheepfold was on a level meadow in a hollow; high bluffs sheltered it from the winds. Hay and boughs with dry leaves—the winter fodder for the sheep and goats—were stacked within the wide enclosure, under a low open shed that stretched along the northern wall. Smoke was rising cheerfully from the hut of the shepherd who guarded the herd in the winter months. A sheep dog flew at the travelers, but immediately recognized Osten and began to fawn on them. They carried Ognyanov into the warm hut and continued to rub him energetically. The little shepherd boy who was in charge there also helped in saving Ognyanov's life: he took off his sandals and rubbed his feet with snow. Once Ognyanov and his companions saw they were out of danger of freezing to death they crossed themselves in deep gratitude to Providence. The shepherd boy added some more logs to the fire, and the company gathered around without, however, stretching out their hands and feet to the blaze. The dog, true to its instinct, lay down by the door on guard.

"Obreiko, where's your uncle Kalcho?" asked Osten. Kalcho was Diko's brother and guarded the sheepfold.

"He went down to the village last night; he should be back any minute."

"Give us what you have in that bag of yours, my lad, and let's have a bite to eat." The boy emptied the bag with his whole food supply: a few hard crusts of rye bread, some onions, salt and savory.

"Is there no brandy, Obreiko?"

"None."

"Damnation! That's just what the schoolmaster needed to pick him up a bit," said Osten, looking at Ognyanov, who was wringing his hands and still writhing with pain.

"Never mind, schoolmaster, you got off with your life. . . . You see what a beauty our Sredna Gora is?"

"Thank goodness nothing happened to you," said Ognyanov.

"Oh, she won't play tricks on an old friend."

"If you ask me," remarked Osten, "it was Stara Planina sent us that blizzard. Borimechka was right."

"Borimechka's no fool!" Borimechka himself asserted in a booming voice.

The dog barked at him. His thundering voice irritated the animal. Ognyanov was observing Ivan with curiosity. He involuntarily drew a comparison between the man and his nickname; it suited him to perfection. A more suitable name could not have been invented for this rough, uncouth, largeheaded giant, who looked as if he had been suckled by a bear rather than a woman. He surveyed his disproportionately tall body, gaunt, lean, but strong; his angular, elongated, hairy head, with its narrow forehead, small wild eyes, its tremendous nose, broad in the nostrils, like that of a savage, and mouth large enough to swallow a hare easily (Borimechka did eat raw meat); and those abnormally long, hairy, brawny hands which might easily tear a lion to pieces like Hercules. He seemed intended rather to fight wild beasts, to which nature had made him so similar, than for such an idyllic occupation as pasturing goats. In contrast to all that, his face expressed a benevolence, a kind of bovine good nature, that gave him a comical appearance. No one could have supposed that this uncouth, rough and, to all appearances, uninhibited nature was capable of devotion and of the finer, more humane emotions. Yet it was so. His very appearance among the group in such an extremity, comical though it had been, testified to the goodness and nobility of his heart. This young man was capable of self-sacrifice. Under the impact of these thoughts Ognyanov began to find his features more pleasing and even intelligent.

"Bai Ivan, who gave you that terrible name?"

"What, don't you know, schoolmaster?" broke in Osten, "He fought with a bear."

"Really?"

"He's a terrific hunter, and he killed it too!"

"Borimechka, tell us yourself how you rolled over the cliff with the bear," said Osten.

"What, you actually wrestled with it?" asked Boicho in surprise. By way of answer Borimechka put his hand on his neck, and for the first time Ognyanov noticed a deeply pitted scar there, then he rolled up his sleeve over his hairy arm, and another scar was revealed, which seemed to have been caused by an iron hook. Ognyanov shrank with horror at the sight.

"Borimechka, tell us about your encounter with the bear. You're a champion if ever there was one!" he said.

Borimechka looked around solemnly; his doltish countenance was fired with proud remembrance as he began his tale. "I'll be damned . . ." he commenced, using his favorite expression. But the dog suddenly barked and dashed out of the hut.

"What's Murdjo barking for? Borimechka's scarcely begun," said Osten jokingly.

"Uncle Kalcho!" cried the shepherd boy. Kalcho appeared with a stick, and a sack over his shoulder.

"So I have guests, it seems? Welcome, boys!" he said hospitably, throwing down his load.

"Make room for Bai Kalcho to warm himself."

"Goodness, how cold it is; it'll be the death of all the wolves! Where did the storm catch you?"

"Down below there," Spiridoncho answered.

"Is this the time to go hunting? Are you new to the mountain not to know what it's like at this season?"

"Don't talk about it, Bai Kalcho; it was the hope of good game led us on. . . . Did you bring any rakiya?" asked Osten.

"Rakiya? Yes, I did. But I'm bringing you something better too." The brandy flask made the round of the company.

"What could be better than rakiya just now?"

"A piece of news!" They were all attention.

"This morning two zaptiehs from Klissoura were eaten up by wolves."

"You don't say!" Borimechka exclaimed cunningly. The dog again barked at him.

"Ate them up to the last hair. A band of Turks set out and found them—not them, but their rags and their bones—at Saradan Hill. By what I could make out, Hadji Yumer-Aga says they must have been set upon when they were leading their horses, and they ran for it, they in one direction, the horses in another. One of the horses got lost. The wolves sensed that the effendis' flesh was tastier, so they grabbed them. Your health, lads; may the damned lot of them die like that. They're a race of dogs and the dogs'll eat them all." And Kalcho tilted his flask. It was only then that he noticed Ognyanov, whom he did not know. "And where's this friend from?" he asked, handing him the flask.

"From Kara Saraliye, we came upon him in the mountain . . . he was after the same game," answered little Spiridoncho.

"He's a brave one. . . . Your health, schoolmaster!" boomed Borimechka. The dog growled again.

Kalcho turned to Borimechka smiling. "Well, you bear, what have you gone and done?"

"Nothing to anyone, Kalcho!"

"I'll be damned, young bachelor and all, and he goes and carries off our girl; now they're both done for. . . . Well, congratulations! And where's the game to feast your wedding guests?"

"I left it down there, Bai Kalcho," Borimechka said in his deep guttural voice. This time Murdjo was seriously roused.

"Hey, Bai Ivan, tell us how you wrestled with the bear."

"What, he?" Kalcho spoke up again with a sly look at Borimechka. "He'd better tell us how he wrestled with Staika."

They all laughed. Ivan Osten wanted to assure himself once more that the Turks had been deceived, and he began again, "So that's it! Torn to pieces by wolves! And aren't the Turks saying it was the Bulgarians that killed the zaptiehs?"

"How so? It's all over the village. Dyado Stoiko, God rest his soul . . ." said Kalcho, misunderstanding the question.

"We heard about that, but I was asking: don't the Turks suspect the Bulgarians of having killed the zaptiehs?"

Kalcho looked at him in surprise. "Who'd say such a thing? When has a Bulgarian of our village been known to kill a zaptieh? I told you it was wolves that did us a good turn, and now the Turks are getting ready to raise a posse tomorrow and drive the vermin away. Now that suits me too. Why, this winter, you can't put your nose out of doors for those pests. Your health, lads! May we welcome in Christmas in health and good spirits! And you follow in the Bear's footsteps, only not during the fasts. . . . Help yourself, friend!"

And Kalcho handed the brandy to Ognyanov, who had regained his strength from the action of the beneficent liquor. He raised the flask and said, obviously moved, "Brothers, let us cherish the memory of Dyado Stoiko, the martyr of Turkish cruelty. God rest his righteous soul, and may He give us manly courage and a strong right arm to fight the enemy of Christ, and may our revenge be a hundred for one. . . . God rest the soul of Dyado Stoiko!"

"God rest his soul!"

"God rest his soul!" said Kalcho, raising his cap, and then he turned to Ognyanov amicably. "Friend, your words were well spoken. May they find their way from your mouth to God's ears. We'll have to put up with things, but the day will come when there'll be a mighty flash, crash, bang! What do they call you? Let's be friends; I'm Kalcho Bogdanov Bookché." And Kalcho handed the flask to Ognyanov.

He gave an assumed name and drank to their better acquaintance. The company ate only a little, for they wanted to go easy on Kalcho Bookché's scanty supply of food. Then they took their leave of him.

He went out to see them off beyond the gate. Once more he turned to Ognyanov: "Goodbye, friend. I forget your name; when you happen to pass by these parts again, come and have a chat with me. You speak well. . . . Well, good luck on your journey!"

Ognyanov's few energetic words had strangely stirred the poor goatherd. Not that they were quite new to him—but the "friend" had said something about fighting, and those completely new words had touched a new chord in his soul most strongly, and it quickened to life. Later on we shall see what the impact of this meeting was for him.

The small group was soon out of sight; they came down to the village as dusk was falling. Ognyanov decided to spend the night at Bai Dochko's inn. He had just entered his room, when a few minutes later about fifteen bashi-bazouks with rifles followed him up the stairs; they were led by the zaptieh whom Boicho had seen the day before in the cafe of the Turkish village.

Alas! Kolcho was not there to warn him.

PART TWO

chapter 1

Byala Cherkva

The events of the eve of St. Andrew's shook the peaceful existence of Byala Cherkva to its very foundations. The discovery of Boicho's identity dumbfounded old and young alike and the little town was horrified at the news that the bodies of the two Turks had been dug up. It was indeed a terrible event. Not only did it awake the suspicion of the Turkish authorities, but it aroused the thirst for revenge of the surrounding Turkish population as well. While awaiting the day for a general massacre, they fed their passion on bloody reprisals. More and more Bulgarian victims fell along the roads and in the open country, and traveling from place to place became extremely perilous. Rumors of a massacre around Christmas time fed fear and anxiety in Byala Cherkva daily. The women particularly were in a state of growing panic. Everyone felt guilty. Patriotic declarations were hushed; enthusiasm evaporated. On St. Andrew's Day itself the police imprisoned Sokolov, Boicho's inseparable friend; imprisoned old Dyado Stoyan, the miller, as an accomplice; looked for Deacon Vikenti, but the latter had disappeared. The town council for its part disregarded the school board and hastened to dismiss Rada, as the dangerous man's sweetheart, from the school, while Mihalaki Alafranga suggested the boys' school should be temporarily closed down as well to get "well aired." Only Merdevendijev was retained —just for the youngest children.

All who had been on more or less friendly terms with Boicho were on tenterhooks. The committee dissolved of its own accord. Only Yaroslav Burzobegounek was secure under his golden-braided helmet. No one bothered the "Austrian." He continued conscientiously to photograph the inhabitants of Byala Cherkva, and, as he lacked some acids needed to develop the images imprinted on the glass, these remained quite dark and dim, and one was amazed to see portraits of various Negroes hanging in people's houses. At the same time Burzobegounek kept up his correspondence with foreign parts.

Finally the excitement subsided in Byala Cherkva and the young people's courage returned to them. Poor Ognyanov's fate was unanimously deplored; the rumor of his death was confirmed from all sides. The Turks coming to market said he had been hit by three bullets and had died somewhere in the Ahievo forest. The onbashi knew this had not been proved, but he too confirmed it. Some Bulgarians maintained the Count had been buried by Nikola the tailor in the gully where he had found him. Hadji Rovoahma gave a more tragic description of Boicho's end: as he was crawling wounded along the gully, he had been eaten up alive by wolves. The little town was grief-stricken by these gloomy tales. Ognyanov grew from a hero into a saint and martyr. He became a legend. The old ladies lit candles for the "holy martyr Boicho" in the church. Father Stavri held a requiem for him—in the midst of one for Hadji Boicho. All the young people were present, to the astonishment of the worthy man's relatives, who were bewildered at the priest mentioning Hadji Boicho in the prayer as Boicho "the martyr," instead of Boicho "the pilgrim."

But there were others who were pleased. They looked on haughtily, like people who had been proved right. Stefchov was particularly jubilant in spite of his shameful adventure at Milka's house. The extent of Ognyanov's misfortune, which gripped everyone's attention, diminished his own disgrace. Besides, shame itself makes a man still more impudent. And in early February Yordan's anger abated and Stefchov was married to Lalka.

We must add that Stefchov's treachery remained a secret: the entire blame and general indignation fell on the hapless idiot, from whom the abbot had extracted the confession that he had been the only witness to the burial of the bodies. That explained those mysterious signs and exclamations by means of which Mooncho had finally in all probability given Boicho away—how and to whom remained unknown. He was deprived of his liberty and locked up as a raving madman in the tower by the monastery gates.

As for Rada, she seemed quite stupefied with grief. The good people who had given her hospitality could find no means to console her. "It'll be the end of the poor girl," they said anxiously.

As time went by, kindly impulses came to the fore again. After numerous attempts Marko and Micho Beizadé succeeded in getting their bail accepted, and Doctor Sokolov was let out of prison, since he was not in any case implicated in the affair of the bodies. The two bondsmen did not know they had an ally who facilitated their task. This secret ally, who had seconded Bai Marko's efforts when the doctor was freed for the first time—it is time this was said—was none other than the person whom Hadji Rovoahma had guessed that night after vespers: the old bey's better half. Chance had brought this young Potiphar's wife and the doctor together, and he had not shown Joseph's firmness in resisting temptation. . . . Thanks to this short-lived connection, long since broken off, he got out of a tight corner this time as well: the bey's wife had made the bey intervene in K. so that Sokolov was freed as innocent in the matter.

A few days after the latter's return in February, Kableshkov appeared in Byala Cherkva as an apostle, taking up his quarters in Burzobegounek's house. There he called together the members of the committee which had been dissolved, inspired them with his fiery eloquence and led them straight to the monastery, where Abbot Nathaniel swore them in over the holy Bible, blessing the revived Revolutionary Committee. After that preparations were once more feverishly carried on and with much greater vigor. In early April Kableshkov again appeared in Byala Cherkva.

From that day we take up our detailed narrative once more.

chapter 2

Doctor Sokolov's patients

Sokolov paced his room in a troubled state of mind. He often looked through the window giving onto the yard, which was now deep in thick green foliage. The blossoming cherry trees and morellos seemed to be covered with snow. The apple trees spread out their leafy branches like garlands bowed down with white and pink blossom. Pearly bloom covered the peaches and apricots growing near the windows. The grass-grown path which crossed the little yard, now a veritable bower, was deep in shade, overhung as it was by the branches of the fruit-trees which formed a sort of pergola.

Sokolov had changed considerably. His face, still handsome and good-natured, had grown pale and lean like that of a convalescent. Long imprisonment and moral suffering had stamped their imprint of grief on that strong youth, so full of life; he had grown impatient and sarcastic. Yet another sorrow had been added to his manifold troubles in prison: he had heard of Lalka's marriage to Stefchov. That crushed him, and he moaned helplessly like a wild beast in the narrow confines of his cell. He swore to himself to kill Stefchov, who had caused so much misfortune, at the first opportunity that presented itself, for he was deeply convinced that Ognyanov's betrayal was the latter's work. Upon returning to town his first concern was to express his thanks to Marko Ivanov and Micho Beizade. He then went to see Cleopatra, whom Necho Pavlov the hunter had taken to his home and fed till then. The poor beast, grown quite large by now, had become very thin and was only able to recognize her beloved master after several minutes of hesitation. Cleopatra had already grown rather wild, and her devotion had cooled. Her wild instinct had taken over. She was easily irritated and showed her sharp teeth with intentions very far from good. In his mind's eye the doctor saw the loathsome Stefchov in the grip of her shaggy paws, and his face glowed with diabolical joy. But he soon heard that the culprit was Mooncho, and after the committee was reestablished he was wholly taken up by the great cause—the preparation of the revolt. His revenge, which had now become a personal matter, remained in the background of his thoughts. It was such a petty, miserable thing in comparison with the great task before him. He decided to set Cleopatra free for he did not know what to do with her, and he ordered Necho Pavlov to let her loose in the mountains that evening—he hadn't the heart to kill her.

Sokolov had quite given up his doctoring. He no longer had any patients; besides, no one went to see him for fear of compromising himself. The mortars, medicine bottles, the boxes of powders, along with his medical books, were thrown pell-mell into a small cupboard, where the mice soon succeeded in devouring half the pharmacopoeia. Only one patient was still seen to visit his home, and that was Yaroslav Burzobegounek. He had inadvertently hurt his hand with a revolver one day after the doctor's return. The sympathy of all the inhabitants went out to him over his misfortune, which forced the poor Austrian to give up the photography—which had given him up long ago.

Suddenly the gate banged and the doctor glanced at it. It was Burzobegounek himself. He was again dressed in the worn, shabby suit given him by Ognyanov, with a gold-braided hat on his head, and he sported a pair of enormous blond side-whiskers. His right arm, folded across his chest, hung in a white sling tied behind the neck. He advanced cautiously, probably to avoid the pain which quick movement might cause the wounded limb. He winced at every step and his face wore the expression of a man in pain. When he reached the doctor's room, he looked carefully about him and threw the sling on the bed.

"Good morning, young man!" said he, advancing his right hand. The doctor gave it a hearty shake, without the slightest sign of pain on the part of the guest. Burzobegounek's wound was a fiction; his frequent visits to the doctor had to be justified.

"What's the news?" the doctor asked him.

"Kableshkov came late last night; he's at my house," said Burzobegounek.

"We must meet!" said the doctor energetically.

"He's feverish now. He was burning with fever all night long."

"Poor fellow!"

"The worst of it is, he won't lie quiet, but insisted on dictating three long letters to me, to be sent off today. He's a wiry fellow, but he's quite exhausted. He's tormented by a cough."

"I'd better come and examine him," said the doctor seizing his fez.

"No, he's sleeping now. . . . He only ordered a committee meeting to be called for tonight and said he'd be at the meeting."

"He mustn't; he ought to stay in bed!"

"Go and make him stay in bed if you can; you know how obstinate he is. . . . Call the members for tonight."

"All right, I'll let them know."

Burzobegounek lowered his voice and said, "Well, did you get the hundred gold pieces?"

"You mean for the guns? They've been found. We'll have them today."

"Well done, Sokolov, you're a stout fellow!" the photographer shouted.

"Don't shout so!"

"Oh, how long have you had this dagger?" cried Burzobegounek, pulling out the shiny weapon from under the doctor's waistcoat and playing with it.

"Ivan Madjar made it for me. He has orders simply pouring in on him. It's a beauty, isn't it?"

Burzobegounek was trying to make out some words inscribed on the knife. " 'S. or S.' What do those letters stand for?"

"Guess!"

"Sokolov or Stefchov?" asked Burzobegounek smiling.

"Liberty or Death!"* said the doctor curtly, for the mention of Stefchov aroused an unpleasant feeling in him. Then he added: "The Stefchovs and scum of that kind are in the background now, my good friend. We've got no time to think of Stefchov, nor of personal whims and grudges. . . . If one's out to kill the tiger, one despises the worm. I want you to know that I've forgotten all about that. A man who prepares a revolution is oblivious of everything else."

Burzobegounek looked at him shrewdly. It was clear from his irritation that the doctor had neither forgotten nor could forget so easily. The blow to his heart or his self-esteem had been strong indeed. The feverish preoccupation with preparing the revolt temporarily dulled the pain of the wound which was still gaping. These all-engrossing tasks absorbed his entire being and distracted him. In this kind of exhilaration he found a way of rendering himself insensible to suffering, just as a drunkard does with wine. But in sober moments, moments of meditation, the painful thoughts awoke like hissing snakes and stung and stung mercilessly.

Kandov's appearance in the yard put an end to the awkward conversation and distracted the doctor's attention. "What kind of a fellow is he?" asked Burzobegounek.

"Kandov? A Russian student."

* Svoboda ili Smurt.

"I know, but what's he like?"

"A philosopher, a diplomat, a socialist, a nihilist . . . and goodness knows what else. In short he's not all there." And Sokolov tapped his forehead.

"And doesn't he want to take part in the national cause?"

"No, what use is it to him? He'll probably go to Russia to get himself a pretty little diploma," said the doctor angrily.

"Oh, those learned scarecrows! I can't stand them," cried Burzobegounek. "As soon as one of them gets hold of a diploma, there's no trace of humanity left in him. They don't give a damn about the people or about freedom. Give them their comfort, a pretty little wife, a pretty little house, and prudence! You don't suppose they've let their lungs go rotting away for years to come to Bulgaria to be revolutionaries and run after Diarbekir or the noose?"

"Burzobegounek, that's not true, look here—you've got a diploma yourself."

"I! God forbid!"

"It's true, Boicho had no such thing as a diploma . . ." said the doctor.

"If I had a diploma, I'd be an ass just like them. Take yourself, for instance; if you'd taken your M.D. from some medical faculty, instead of up in the Albanian hills, you'd be thinking of making money, not of revolution. . . ."

At that moment the student entered the corridor. Burzobegounek quickly put on his sling and slipped his hand into it, for the student's footsteps were already at the door. "Oh, I nearly forgot—give me some brimstone for Kableshkov."

The doctor had just handed him the powder, when there was a knock on the door. *"Entrez!"* said the doctor.

Kandov entered. Yaroslav Burzobegounek bowed to him politely and went out. Kandov was too absorbed even to notice him.

He was dressed in a close-buttoned, dark green jacket, rather shabby already, and trousers of the same color, which were too tight over the hips. The tall scarlet fez went poorly with his pale olive face, clouded over by some sorrow and preoccupation, by a melancholy which was also imprinted on his dreamy gaze. It was evident that this young man had some trouble, some grief buried in his soul, which he could neither shake off nor share with anyone. He had lately been keeping strictly to himself.

At the doctor's invitation, he seated himself on a chair. Sokolov sat down on the bed, not a little surprised by this unexpected visit.

"How are you feeling, Mr. Kandov?" asked Sokolov, thinking the student was ailing. And he carefully examined his gaunt, downy face.

"I'm all right, thanks be," Kandov answered shortly, almost mechanically. It was evident from his animated look and the frowning of his forehead that some other reason, and an important one, had brought him here.

"I'm glad to hear it. One can see you have quite recovered."

"Yes, I've recovered, I'm well."

"So you'll be returning to Russia?"

"No, I've decided not to."

"For good?"

"For good. I'm staying here," said Kandov drily.

The doctor looked at him in surprise, half ironically. This look seemed to say: "Why don't you go back to your school, young fellow, and to your philosophers? Everything here is ablaze; you have no business here." There was silence for a moment.

"Perhaps you wish to become a teacher?" the doctor asked with disdainful concern.

Kandov flushed slightly and asked harshly by way of answer, "Mr. Sokolov, when will there be a committee meeting?"

The boldness of the question astounded the doctor. "What committee?" he asked with the air of a man who is quite in the dark.

Kandov blushed a deeper red and said tensely, "Your committee. There's no use pretending. I know everything . . . who the members are and where you hold your meetings. I know everything; don't hide things from me."

"It's strange that you should know so much since you're not interested. But supposing there is a committee, what then?" asked the doctor staring at him steadily and provocatively.

"I asked you if you would be having a meeting soon?" Kandov repeated resolutely.

"Yes, this evening, sir!" the doctor answered in the same tone of voice.

"You are the president, aren't you?"

"I am!"

"I have come to ask a favor of you."

"And what is it, sir?"

"I ask you to put me up as a member." The student's voice trembled with emotion.

Sokolov was dumbfounded. He wasn't prepared for such an action on Kandov's part. "How come, Kandov?"

"Simply as a Bulgarian! I want to work too."

Sokolov jumped up. "Give me your hand, brother!" and he shook his hand and embraced him warmly. Then he added: "It will be a pleasure, a great pleasure, Mr. Kandov, for all of us to have you with us. It is a shame for capable people like you to stand aside. Our struggle will be glorious. Our country calls upon us. We must all, all of us be. . . . It does you honor, Kandov! How surprised our friends will be when I tell them! Give me your hand, brother!"

"Thank you, doctor," said the student with emotion, "and you'll see that Kandov won't be useless. . . ."

"Oh, I know! I know! Why didn't you accept before when Ognyanov asked you to join! Oh, my heart bleeds when I think of him. My poor Boicho! Why didn't I die. If only he could have lived to rouse the people with his words and his deeds! Do you know, Kandov, he was a real hero, a magnificent fellow! We shall take a terrible vengeance for his blood! A hundredfold! We'll break their mothers' hearts for them, the savages!"

"Revenge, yes!" answered Kandov. "That's the only feeling which stirs me now. One can't forgive the murder of a man like Ognyanov."

"Revenge, a terrible revenge!" cried the doctor.

"Is the committee meeting tonight?"

"Yes, at Bai Micho's; we'll go there together. . . ."

"As soon as I'm accepted I shall make a proposal."

"And that is?"

"To kill Ognyanov's murderer!"

"There isn't only one, my friend. They are many . . . and where shall we look for them? If you want to know, it's the whole Turkish empire."

"To my mind only one man is guilty."

The doctor looked at him in surprise.

"It is one man, and he is among us. . . ."

"Among us?"

"Yes, the man who is directly guilty of his death."

"Oh, Bai Kandov, is it worth while to take revenge on an idiot? Mooncho is deprived of reason. The poor wretch didn't realize he was betraying him. He was so devoted to Boicho. . . . Give the whole thing up, give it up."

Kandov flushed. It hurt him that Sokolov should believe him capable of such a suggestion.

"You are mistaken, Mr. Sokolov! You are mistaken! Who is speaking of Mooncho?"

"And whom are you speaking of?"

"Of Stefchov!"

"Stefchov!" cried the doctor, beside himself.

"Stefchov! He is the traitor! I know it for certain."

"Oh, the dirty skunk! I suspected him too at first!"

"I have it for certain that he betrayed everything to the Turks. Mooncho is quite innocent. You were all too hasty in accusing him. It was Stefchov who told the authorities that very night, the night he was disgraced, to dig around the mill; it was he who discovered Ognyanov's name through Merdevendjiev's treachery. He's the one who committed all the crimes; it's to him we owe all our misfortune. I know the whole dirty business in detail and from a most reliable source too."

"Oh, what a son of Satan!"

In the last few minutes Kandov had gained Sokolov's respect. He was even more moved when he saw the student's readiness to kill Stefchov, the enemy of the sacred cause, and to undertake such a deed of violence, such a terrible risk, in order to prove his devotion to the cause he was now embracing. Such zeal might seem suspicious in anyone else, but in Kandov it was sincere and clearly evident in the restless, fiery look of his eyes and the nervous twitching on his inspired face.

Sokolov looked Kandov in the eyes for several minutes, then jumped up and said, "Have a little patience, we'll send the dirty rogue to the devil all right. The committee will decide this evening. . . ."

"All right," Kandov said in a flat voice.

"Ah, here he comes," said Sokolov as he saw a good-looking, fair-skinned boy, quite decently dressed in European clothes, approaching. The doctor must have been expecting him for he was excited when the boy appeared.

"Is that a patient of yours?" the student asked.

"Yes, excuse me!" said the doctor and dashed out of the room. When he returned his face glowed with satisfaction.

"Who was that fellow?" asked Kandov, looking at the boy's back, as he was leaving.

"Pencho Diamandiev. He's just back from the Gabrovo Gymnasium."

"What, that coward Stefchov's brother-in-law and the son of Yordan the exploiter?" asked Kandov. "You're friends with him?"

"We're not friends, we're something more than friends and brothers, we're comrades: he is a member of the committee."

chapter 3

poles asunder

Chorbadji Yordan was aging and fast losing his strength. A gastric ailment, which had kept him in bed for a long time, had greatly affected him, making him even more irritable and impatient.

That morning the weather was fine and he had gone for a walk to a garden he owned on the outskirts of the town. The large garden, surrounded with great stone walls and filled with beautiful fruit-trees and flowers, now buried in fresh foliage, did the ailing old man a lot of good, for it was a long time since he had been out of doors. The cool, clean air and the spring sun revived him. He walked with a firmer step on his way home. But just as he got to the home of Ghinka's Ghenko, his son-in-law, he felt weak, his legs wouldn't hold him up, so he stopped at their house.

In the yard Ghenko Ghinkin, still more shrivelled up, nondescript and helpless-looking than ever, was holding a screaming infant in his arms and doing his best to soothe it, rocking it on his chest like a wet nurse.

Yordan stumped up to the little bench placed in the yard and covered with a fleecy rug, sat down heavily, and said with a disgruntled air, "So, you petticoat, you're looking after the child! Where's that woman?"

By "that woman" Yordan meant his daughter.

Ghenko grew uneasy and confused—it was his normal state—and mumbled disconnectedly, "She's busy, so I'm holding little Yordan. . . . She told me to take him and nurse him a bit. . . . She's busy."

"Doesn't she give you her distaff to hold too?" asked Yordan with a contemptuous smile. "Ghina, make me some coffee," he shouted without looking to see where she was.

"She's baking, baking all day . . . she's busy, grandpa . . . that's why I'm holding the child. . . . Coffee, coffee. . . . I'll make you some coffee, I won't be a second. I know where she keeps the coffee and the sugar," mumbled Ghenko, leaving little Yordan on his grandfather's knees and disappearing.

The baby started yelling more lustily than ever. Yordan got angry. He laid the squalling brat down on the corner of the bench, stood up and began to shout, "Hey, where have you all gone off to, hey! I might as well be a donkey for all the attention I'm getting! Ghina, Ghina!"

"Welcome, Father! How's everything? Are you all right? You're feeling all right now, aren't you? Isn't the weather just lovely; you did very well to go out for a bit!" Aunt Ghinka exclaimed from the threshold, all smiles and cheerfulness. She had tied on a blue apron, her sleeves were rolled up to her elbows, the green kerchief on her head was pushed back and her pretty face was generously powdered with flour. She looked rather picturesque in this attire and reminded one of some figure in a Flemish genre painting.

"What are you doing? What's this hen-pecked fellow's been telling me? What's all that flour on your face? You look like a miller's wife! One can't even get a cup of coffee here!" the old man muttered angrily and imperatively.

"Excuse me, Father, I've begun to get busy too. It won't take me a minute to make you some coffee. . . . Ghenko! Where's he got to? Take Yordancho and put him in the cradle, and try and get him to sleep!"

"What are you doing? What are you baking?"

"Baking I am, baking. . . . There's work to be done. . . . We're not staying out of this, no, we're not! We're true Bulgarians . . ." said Aunt Ghinka laughing boisterously.

"What Bulgarians? What are you baking?" her father asked frowning

"Rusks, Father."

"Rusks?"

"Of course! They'll be needed!"

"Why should we need rusks? Are you going to the baths? Why all this extravagance?"

Instead of an answer Aunt Ghinka started giggling. Yordan looked at her with the utmost displeasure. He could not stand his daughter's perpetual and senseless fits of laughter, for her cheerful nature was the very reverse of his choleric temperament.

She went up to him and said in a low voice, "Who would think of going to the baths now? We're making rusks for our brave fellows. They'll need them."

Yordan looked at her in amazement. "What fellows?"

"For our brave Bulgarian boys, Father, when they take to the hills."

"What nonsense is this about brave boys?" asked Yordan, more and more bewildered.

Ghinka came nearer. "For the insurrection. Those are the committee's orders, aren't they?" she said and burst out laughing again.

Yordan jumped up from his seat. He could not believe his ears. "What insurrection? What committee! Do you mean a revolt?"

"Yes, a revolt. We don't want this filthy Sultan to order us about any longer," Aunt Ghinka answered boldly, but suddenly jumped to one side, as her father raised his chibouk to hit her.

Pale with rage and trembling like a leaf, he screamed at the top of his voice, "You perfect ass of a daughter, you crazy empty-headed creature, so you're going to stir up a rebellion too, are you? Have you no distaff or needle to busy yourself with instead of dancing off after the haidouks and ne'er-do-wells, and feeding them with rusks? Have you no shame, you madcap! Look at her, she's for doing away with the Sultan too! The bitch! What's the Sultan done to to you? He hasn't taken your child, has he, or stepped on your toes? Here she drops her house and child and goes off to turn out the Sultan! . . . What are you standing there for, you popinjay, all eyes. Do you go along with her? Are you going to follow the flag, too?" said Yordan fiercely, turning upon Ghenka, who stood by the door, the picture of fright.

Ghenko Ghinkin mumbled something indistinctly and took refuge in the room again, where Ghinka was hastily changing into other clothes, for she saw that her father's shouts had attracted a crowd of curious onlookers at the gate. Upon seeing Ghenko she seized her slipper and started hitting him about the neck with it. "You fool, why did you say I was making rusks?"

Ghenko, proudly conscious of his manly dignity, did not favor his wife with an answer, but bravely dashed into the other room, bolting the door fast behind him. Having placed this barrier between his back and his wife's slipper, he protested provocatively, "Hit me now, if you can! I'm your husband and you're my wife. . . . Let's see you hit me now!"

But Aunt Ghinka could no longer hear him. She had gone out into the yard, but her father was already in the street, trembling with fury. When he got home he was well-nigh exhausted. He crossed the courtyard, breathing heavily with fatigue, and sat down on the bottom step of the staircase leading to the upper floor.

Chorbadji Yordan was beside himself with indignation. True, though he had been confined to his room for a long time, rumors had reached his ears, for the secret of the forthcoming revolt was common knowledge and even the deaf had heard of it. Preparations for it were being carried on somewhere near Panagyourishté, far away beyond forests and mountains, as Yordan had gathered, and the fire was therefore far from his own roof. Now he had learned from his crazy daughter that even Byala Cherkva was beginning to smoulder. What in the world were the Turks doing? Were they blind, were they deaf not to realize that the Empire was being undermined?

The sound of children's voices to his right aroused him. They came from a small window, a little above his head, through which light penetrated into the storeroom. Yordan got up to climb the stairs. At the third step he automatically stopped and looked through the window. There he saw his two young sons, the elder of whom had just turned thirteen, standing by the hearth which was piled with embers, busy over something. So absorbed were they in their work that they never noticed their father's head at the window.

One of the boys was holding a pan over the fire, attentively watching whatever was frying or boiling in it. The other with a knife was paring smooth a lot of shiny balls which were piled up in front of him. It was neither more nor less than cast bullets, and in the pan they were melting the lead from which the bullets were cast in the mold.

"Rascals! Jackasses!" Yordan shouted, wild with rage, as he realized what his sons were up to, and he turned back with his chibouk raised in his hand. His sons abandoned their laboratory, flew out of the room as fast as their legs could carry them and scampered off down the street.

"Haidouks! Cut-throats! Hellions! The devil take them! The limbs of Satan! Preparing for a revolt, are they?" Yordan was shouting as he hurried up the stairs, for his rage galvanized his legs.

Up on the verandah he met his wife. "Dona, you haven't joined the band by any chance, have you?" he asked throwing her a dirty look. "My whole family has gone mad! 'You'll be the ruin of me! You'll burn my soul in my old age!" And he sat there breathing heavily. His wife looked at him quite stupefied.

"Pencho! Pencho!" he cried, "where's he gone to? We'd better ask him what he's up to? If the young ones are making bullets, he must be casting cannons . . . the scoundrels. . . ."

"He's not here," his wife said, "he went to K."

"What the devil does he want in K.?"

"He may have gone to the tanner's to take him the hundred pounds."

"To Tossoun-Bey? He was to go tomorrow, the rascal! How dare he start without letting me know?" And Chorbadji Yordan went up to his desk. He quickly opened it and started hunting through the drawers and among the books and papers. But the money-bag was not there. Instead he pulled out a beautiful Lefaucheux revolver from under the papers.

"Where did this pistol come from? Whose is it? Who's been rummaging in my desk? Here I look for a money-bag and find a revolver."

"Why, nobody touches it but you and Pencho!" his wife explained.

"Oh, the son of a bitch! Oh, the vagabond! He'll come to no good! Here he is—an enemy of the Sultan too! An insurrectionist. . . . No doubt about it, it's he who set the brats to casting bullets. . . . All hands to work! They're all twisting their own rope! . . . What's this shamelessness, I ask you? My very cats will become rebels, as things are going. . . . Has Kiriak come?"

"Yes, he's here, tying the bales." Yordan hurried into the room where Stefchov was.

chapter 4

father and son-in-law

Aided by two workmen, Stefchov, who had become his father-in-law's partner, was tying some bales of woolen braid which were to be sent to the Djoumaya fair held on St. George's Day. He had taken off his jacket to have more freedom of movement; his face, flushed as it was by the exercise, still retained the repulsive expression of a sterile, colorless and unfeeling soul.

Lalka his wife, in a simple blue dress, was standing by the window sewing canvas labels onto the bales that had already been tied. It was impossible to tell by her calm, clear face, which had blossomed out and become more womanly, that she was unhappy in this forced marriage. Simple-minded, inexperienced as she was, without the slightest trace of the romantic in her make-up, for she had nowhere to take it from in the despotic environment she had been brought up in, she had gone to the altar heavy at heart and with suppressed tears. But time had come to her aid, as it mostly does in such cases; she herself grew accustomed and reconciled to her new state. She did not love Stefchov, nor could she grow to love him, but she submitted to his will and feared him. That was all he wanted of her. Instead of her heart, which he had not made any particular effort to win, he had gained a rich inheritance, by becoming the direct heir of Yordan Diamandiev. He was well satisfied.

When they saw Yordan enter the room, deathly pale and trembling, with stormy wrinkles on his forehead, he dropped the rope he was holding to tie the bale with, and Lalka, her needle.

"Well, Kiriak?" Yordan shouted, still standing on the threshold. "It seems you and I are the only people here who are true to their sovereign! Why, even the puppies have turned rebels and are buying revolvers and casting bullets. . . . The flames are ready to burst out while you and I are preparing goods for the fair. If I am ill, you at least should see and hear what's up. Here we are investing so much money in goods in such haidouk times as these!"

The two workers tiptoed out of the room. Stefchov looked at him in dismay.

"No need to stare like that, you fool!" Yordan shouted. "I tell you, my own children have caught the comitadji-fad, the children of Chorbadji Yordan, the Sultan's most loyal subject, who has entertained great men and pashas in his home. What will it be like with the rest of them, the common folk? A set of scoundrels form a committee, here under our very noses, and we sit gaping like fools!" And Chorbadji Yordan related what he had discovered that day, his rage mounting at every step.

"I had just planned to go to the bey today," said Stefchov. "They gather in Beizadé's garden; let them be caught and cross-examined. A couple of hundred blows and they'll confess their mother's milk. I should have put an end to this filthy propaganda against the state long ago. Whoever dislikes the government here is welcome to go to teacher Kliment's Muscovy and not see our houses on fire." Stefchov opened the door and gave whispered instructions to someone.

"Do you know who these donkeys are?" his father-in-law asked.

"Sokolov is the ringleader!" said Stefchov throwing a sidelong glance at Lalka, his face contorted with spite. His hatred of the doctor was also mingled with a hidden jealousy which stung like live embers. His stony heart was only open to love in its ugliest manifestation.

"Again that scoundrel?" Stefchov went to where his jacket lay and began searching in its pocket. Yordan observed him expectantly.

"Here's a letter I found in the street yesterday, right in front of your house."

"What's in this letter?"

"It's signed by Sokolov. He's sending it to Panagyourishté; no doubt to other scoundrels like him."

"And what trash does he write about? Fire and plunder, what?"

"No, quite different things, innocent enough on the face of it, but I'm willing to swear they have some other meaning," said Stefchov, unfolding the letter once more. "But Zamanov will pierce through the mystery and decipher it: he's the kind of hound who can smell out a rebel a hundred leagues away."

At that point Lalka had turned pale. She crept quickly out of the room and went downstairs to her mother. "What's the matter, Lala?" her mother asked her.

"Nothing, mother," she said in a feeble voice, holding her head in her hands. Her mother, busy as she was with her cooking, paid no attention to her daughter. She herself was irritated enough and was vigorously stirring the food in the frying pan with the spoon, cursing her sons the while.

"Blast them! May they shake with fever, the whole lot of them; they'll bring their father to his grave before his time! He's hardly up and about again, and now he all but had a fit. To the devil with their insurrection! What's taken them that they've all gone stark mad! Why that madcap Ghina and even that empty-pated husband of hers Ghenko, they're going to feed them with rusks, if you please, the scoundrels! May they choke with it!"

Aunt Ghinka came in. "Why get so worked up, mother! You should be pleased. The chorbadjis' wives should set the example. . . ."

"Ghina, hold your tongue!" her mother screamed. "I won't listen to you; you're mad."

"I'm not mad. I'm a Bulgarian woman and a patriot!" Aunt Ghina answered hotly.

"A Bulgarian woman and a patriot! Is that why you beat your husband every day!"

"So I do; he's my husband, but that's another pair of shoes: that's home politics."

"Oh, you crazy creature, do you want to be more of a Bulgarian than your father? If he knew you read Sokolov's papers, he'd give you a sound thrashing for all your forty years!"

"Mother, you lie like a Gipsy! . . . I began my thirty-second year at Christmastime. I should know how old I am." This dialogue, however, was interrupted by the maid.

"Aunt Dona, come quick. Dyado Yordan's been taken bad," she said in a fright.

"See, there you are! Lord, oh Lord Jesus Christ!" Yordanitsa cried and hurried away to her husband, leaving the frying pan on the fire.

As she climbed the stairs she could already hear the heart-rending cries of Yordan who had been seized by a fit of the colic. She found him in the upper room, writhing and rolling on the floor with the terrible pain he felt in the intestines. His distorted face had turned livid; the most piercing and desperate cries broke from his lips, but brought no relief; they struck terror in the hearts of the rest of the family and could even be heard in the street.

One of the workmen who was immediately sent to call in the Yanina healer soon returned saying he couldn't be found as he had gone to K. They then tried to see what they could do with various household remedies. Neither compresses, massage, nor spirits of camphor were any help to the sick man. He kept on wailing and curling up with pain, and threw himself about from one place to another.

Yordanitsa was at her wits' end what to do. "Should we send for Dr. Sokolov?" said she turning to the sufferer. Stefchov uttered sounds of disapproval.

"The year before last I had him in once myself and he was a great help," said Yordanitsa. Then she turned again to her husband. "Yordan, shall we send for the doctor?" Yordan made a negative sign with his finger and continued his screaming.

"Do you hear? I shall send for Dr. Sokolov!" Yordanitsa said, this time more firmly.

"I'll have none of him . . ." the old man moaned.

"You'll have none of him, but I'm not paying any attention to what you say!" Yordanitsa said decisively and turned to the workman. "Chono, go and call Dr. Sokolov, and be quick!"

Chono started for the door and had just reached the threshold when he was blasted by Yordan's terrible cry, which sounded like a sob. "Don't call him! I won't have that bastard, that haidouk!"

Yordanitsa looked about her in despair. "Would you rather die?" she cried.

"Yes, I would! Get out, you scoundrels!" the old man yelled.

Two hours later the crisis gradually subsided. Seeing that the old man felt better, Stefchov dressed hurriedly to go to the konak. It was raining.

On the stairs he met a stumpy little fellow. "Well?" he asked, "did you have a good look?"

"They're there, at Beizadé's."

"In the garden as usual?"

"No, it's raining, so they're indoors. I watched out for them. . . . I'm a sly one, I am. . . ." The man was the former innkeeper of Karnari, Rachko. He was now in Yordan's service and did some spying for his son-in-law as well.

"Bring me my umbrella!" A minute later Stefchov left the gate at a quick pace.

Lalka heard the conversation from the door. She gave her husband a strange, surprised and frightened look. Then she hurriedly went up the stairs and disappeared into one of the rooms.

chapter 5

treachery

When Stefchov entered the bey's room he found a man called Zamanov there. They were playing backgammon.

Zamanov was an official spy of the Turkish authorities who received his salary from the Plovdiv konak. He was about forty-five but looked older. His big swarthy face, with its dimly glowing, shifty dark eyes, was prematurely wrinkled and wore a most repulsive and evil expression. His shortcropped moustache was fast turning grey, as was his oily unkempt hair which stuck out at the back from under his dirty fez, while the top of his head was bald. He was dressed in a jacket of purple homespun, long since worn out, whose black broadcloth collar was shiny with grease. A tall, well-built man, he usually walked with bent head, as if bowed down by the weight of the general contempt he aroused. The whole figure of the man bore the imprint of poverty and cynicism. He generally lived in Plovdiv, but often made the rounds of the neighboring villages. He was a native of Byala Cherkva and knew everyone there, and he was equally well known to everybody.

His arrival in Byala Cherkva at that time worried all who had reasons to be anxious. He had obviously come here on an evil mission. His presence inspired dread and repugnance which he did not fail to sense, without being in the least ashamed. It was with brazen self-confidence that he met the utter contempt in people's eyes, as if saying: "What are you so surprised at? It's a job like any other; I have to make my living too!"

He had already met several notables of the town and had asked them to lend him some money. Naturally, no one refused such an honest debtor and amiable citizen. He must have known what was afoot for with a diabolical smile he asked any young man he happened to meet: "Well, how are the preparations getting on?" And in order still further to increase confusion he would add in a low voice: "Nothing will come of it," leaving the boy thunderstruck. Two or three days ago he had said something of the sort to the president of the committee. That ominous frankness and obnoxiousness of his made people avoid him and emptied every street that he passed along.

Stefchov beamed with satisfaction upon seeing such a powerful ally in the bey's room. He smiled and greeted them familiarly, shaking hands with Zamanov, then sat down to watch the game. The old bey, dressed in his black buttoned jacket, was intent on the game, nodding to Stefchov by way of greeting. When they had finished their set Stefchov immediately came to the point. He gave the bey a detailed account of everything that rumor had brought to his knowledge concerning the revolutionary unrest now gripping Byala Cherkva too.

The bey had also heard of a certain unrest among the rayah, but he didn't attach any importance to it, considering it mere childishness, and was little concerned, as were all the Turkish authorities at the time. Now, as Stefchov removed the scales from his eyes, he was astounded by the extent of the evil.

He turned to Zamanov with a severe and questioning look. "Hristaki-Effendi, here we are playing backgammon, while the place is smoldering around us!"

"I have only been here a few days, but I know all that as well, if not better than Kiriak," said Zamanov.

"You know it and haven't informed me? A fine way to serve the Sultan!" cried the bey highly incensed. "The gentleman has proved himself a more faithful pillar of the throne."

"It's my duty, Bey-Effendi."

Large drops of sweat appeared on Zamanov's forehead. He said nervously, "If this place is smoldering, it's a hundred times worse elsewhere. If a wisp of straw has caught light here, it's a whole haystack over towards Panagyourishté, and the Sublime Porte is neither deaf nor blind. They see the smoke and don't do anything about it. They have their reasons. It would be a mistake for us to make a fuss here only to compromise ourselves for nothing. What we see here in Byala Cherkva is only the shadow of the smoke which rises right up to the clouds in other places. In my opinion we should not be overhasty and should bide our time carefully." These words were most pleasing to the bey, for they suited his taste for peace and his fear of responsibility.

Stefchov noticed this and was much annoyed. He realized that with his cunning explanation Zamanov was trying to conceal his own carelessness and lack of zeal for the interests of the state. "Hristaki-Effendi has no family, no interests, not even a worn rug here, so he can afford to theorize," said he spitefully. "If anything should blaze up one of these days, what does he stand to lose?"

"I protest, sir!" cried Zamanov angrily, turning pale.

"You are right, Kiriak, I'll have the cuckolds tied up, the lot of them!" shouted the bey. Stefchov's face wore a look of triumph.

"On second thought I am of that opinion too. Let the jackasses be caught!" Zamanov said presently with a sudden spiteful expression on his face.

"In other words, we are of one mind?" said the bey sighing with relief.

"Let them be taken this very evening!" Zamanov said.

"Where have they met?" asked the bey.

"At Micho Beizadé's house."

"At Beizadé's? I see it all now. If a man's more Muscovite than the Muscovites themselves he can't be a friend of the Sultan's. Who is their leader?"

"Doctor Sokolov," Stefchov answered.

"Sokolov again? Has he taken the Consul's place?"

"The very man, Bey-Effendi, except that what the Consul did was child's play compared with what Sokolov is up to."

"Who are the others?"

"The dismissed schoolmistress and a few more ne'er-do-wells."

The bey looked at his watch. "Are they there now?" he asked.

"In the house. They usually meet in the garden when it's fine. And there they tipple their rakiya and plot away."

"Well, what do you think we should do?"

"They always leave Micho's place by night. The zaptiehs could grab them as they are leaving and bring them round to the konak, the whole lot of them."

"That won't do," said Zamanov. "You'd only get them without any proof, and they might easily deny everything. They should be rounded up at Micho's, in the very room while they're holding their meeting. They should be caught in the act, so to speak, with all their papers and minutes and various documents. Then we'll have it all down in black and white. No saying, 'I don't know, I haven't heard, I saw nothing.' I'll carry out the first cross-examination myself."

This piece of advice appealed to the bey. Stefchov himself considered it an admirable idea. The spy now stood before him in all his glory. Zamanov's ingenuity equaled his zeal.

"It ought to be done after nightfall," added Zamanov.

"So that's settled," said the bey solemnly and clapped his hands.

A zaptieh appeared.
"Is the onbashi here?"
"Sherif-Aga will be back soon."
"As soon as he gets back, he is to come to me!" the bey ordered. The zaptieh left.
"By the way, I almost forgot," said Stefchov, turning to Zamanov who sat brooding, his forehead deeply furrowed with anxiety, as if those wrinkles reflected the evil thoughts and designs which now most certainly stirred the very depths of his soul. Whereupon Stefchov produced a letter from his breast-pocket and unfolded it.
"What's that?" Zamanov asked suddenly, coming out of his absorption.
"A letter of Sokolov's to Panagyourishté."
"Well, well!"
"Their courier must have dropped it. I found it today right in front of Dyado Yordan's house."
"What does it say?" asked Zamanov quickly.
"It's written in code and addressed to a certain Louka Neichev. He's a simple fellow, a cobbler of Panagyourishté, who passes through town every week on his way to the market in K. But I'm sure it's intended for quite a different person, probably for the Panagyourishté committee."
"What is that paper?" the bey asked curiously, for they were talking in Bulgarian.
Stefchov explained.
"Read it, read it, let's see what's in it," said the bey, pricking up his ears.
Stefchov read the following lines:

Bai Louka,

I hope your family is in good health and that your wife is no longer ill, but she should continue to take the pills I prescribed for her. How's business? You haven't passed through our town for the last two weeks; not because of ill health, I trust. When you start on your way here, please buy me ten groats worth of belladonna from Yanko, the apothecary, as my supply is running short.
Best regards to your folks,

Sokolov.

"That letter is certainly in code," Zamanov remarked.
"Now translate it into Turkish," the bey ordered.

"If you ask me, it says nothing and everything, if you realize its hidden meaning," said Stefchov to the bey and started translating it.

"Wait a bit," said the bey interrupting him at the very beginning, "the pills must stand for bullets!"

"It may well be bullets," Zamanov remarked. The bey puffed out a cloud of smoke from his mouth, looking very proud and pleased with himself, then again was all attention. Stefchov continued.

"Wait," he said, stopping Stefchov again, "he asks how business is going! I've got it—in other words, he asks: how are preparations getting along. We're not such fools, either." And the bey winked significantly at Zamanov, as if he meant to say: "Hyussni-Bey may be old, but he's a sly fox all right; he's not easily duped!"

Stefchov went on reading. When he got to the place: "Not because of ill health, I trust," the bey interrupted Stefchov and turned inquiringly to Zamanov. "Hristaki-Effendi, that part where he speaks of illness and health is rather obscure. What do you make of it?"

"I think that illness must be taken to mean health, and health—illness," the spy answered with an air of importance. The bey pondered the question. He assumed the air of a man who had got the full meaning of this profound answer.

"We've got the whole thing," he said jubilantly.

When Kiriak continued once more and got to the word "belladonna," the bey interrupted him with a cry of joy, "Oh, there he's put his foot in it; he's said it outright: Dona's belly—she's in it too! Every time I meet that old buffalo passing by, something tells me that woman has the devil in her and that she bears a grudge against the Turkish state!" The bey was referring to sixty-five-year-old, fat granny Dona, who invariably passed the konak morning and evening on her way to church.

Stefchov and Zamanov smiled. They explained to the bey that the letter referred to a medicinal herb.

"Go on reading," said the bey, feeling he had been put to shame. Stefchov did as he was told.

" 'Best regards to your folks.' That's all."

The bey cried, " 'Best regards to your folks.' We've got it! In other words, this letter smacks of revolution from the first word to the last."

"But there's nothing serious to be gotten out of it," Stefchov remarked with dissatisfaction.

"Yes, it's obscure, a bit obscure," Zamanov added.

"That's true enough," the bey agreed, "but we'll make the doctor himself explain the passages we couldn't get."

"No, it would be of great interest to us to know its meaning now," said Zamanov peering at the letter. "Give it to me. I'll find out the secret. I have a key to revolutionary letters." Whereupon he put the letter in his waistcoat pocket.

"Good for you, Hristaki-Effendi!"

Stefchov, who was about to leave, made his salaam. "So it's settled, isn't it?" he said.

"It'll be all over by tonight," the bey said. "Go and rest in peace! My regards to Chorbadji Yordan."

Stefchov beamed with joy as he left the bey. As he reached the konak gate Zamanov caught up with him. "You'll be around tonight, won't you? You'll direct the arrest of these gentlemen," Stefchov said to him.

"Naturally, I've taken the job on," the spy answered. "Kiriak, I need a pound; could you lend me one till tomorrow?" he added hurriedly.

Stefchov's face immediately changed. He frowned and fumbled around in his vest pocket. "Take these two roubles, that's all I have."

Zamanov took the money, then added in a low voice, "Come on, give me some more, for if I breathe a word to Strandjov and tell him what you're up to, you'll get a knife between your ribs!" He laughed to show that the threat was only a joke.

Stefchov cast him an anxious look. "Zamanov, if I am informed by tomorrow that Sokolov and his companions have been jailed, I'll give you ten pounds as sure as my name is Kiriak," he said solemnly.

"All right. Let me have a few groats small change, enough to get something to eat, so that I don't need to change the roubles this evening. . . . Thank you, good-bye!" Hristaki then turned into another street and made his way to the inn where he was staying.

As he was going past Hadji-Tsacho's house he met Father Stavri and stopped him. "Give me your blessing, Father!" he said, kissing his hand. "What's your news? How are you? Are you making good money now? Are there more births or more deaths at the moment?"

"There are more weddings than anything else just now," the priest answered with a forced smile as he made ready to move on, for the spy's penetrating look disconcerted him.

Zamanov retained him, looking at him with eyes that seemed to pierce through him.

"And now's the time for weddings, for one of these days the Day of Judgment may be upon us." He winked significantly at the priest, then suddenly changed the subject: "Father, could you lend me fifty groats till tomorrow?"

The priest's face contracted. "You won't find money on a priest; but you are welcome to blessings!" And with this jocular reply the priest again made a move to leave him.

Zamanov looked at him severely and said in a low voice, "Give me those fifty groats; don't forget your son Gancho is the secretary of the committee. If I breathe a word about it, it'll be all up with you." The priest grew pale. He took a gold coin out of his pocket and slipped it into the other's hand as they shook hands before parting.

"Good-bye, Father, remember me in your prayers."

"Anathema!" the priest muttered, going his way.

It was still drizzling. "Bring me some embers and put them in the brazier, boy," said Zamanov to the servant as he entered his room.

The boy looked at him in surprise, as much as to say: "You must be a queer fellow to want to warm yourself at this time of year!"

"Bring me some embers, I tell you," the spy repeated in an imperative voice, taking off his wet jacket. The servant brought a few pieces of live coal and shoveled them into the brazier he pulled out from under the bed.

"Now go about your business!" and he closed the door upon the boy.

He then drew the letter he had taken from Stefchov out of an inside pocket, unfolded it, held the white side over the fire and waited patiently. When the sheet of paper was warm he held it up and examined it. Whereupon his face expressed a mixture of curiosity and pleasure; the paper, clean and white a minute ago, was now covered with rows of closely written dark yellow script. It is well known that the committees wrote their correspondence in sympathetic ink, the letters themselves becoming visible only when warmed. The other side usually contained various innocent and insignificant sentences, enough to deceive the authorities should the letter fall into their hands. Unfortunately, as usual, a secret cannot be kept if more than two people know it, and the provident Zamanov had also heard it.

The letter, signed by Sokolov, the president, related the activities and plans of the committee in Byala Cherkva. After he had read the dangerous letter carefully, a faint smile played upon Zamanov's ugly face. He took a pencil and wrote something in the empty space under the president's signature. Then he hurriedly left the inn and set out towards the konak.

chapter 6

a woman's soul

Stefchov had scarcely left his father-in-law's house that day on his way to the bey's when his wife went out too. The rain, which had started to fall in the afternoon, showed no sign of stopping, though it had turned into a drizzle, and it would probably go on till evening, for the sky was overcast with thick, heavy clouds.

Under the cover of her umbrella, Lalka hurried along the streets. She was in such a state of anxiety that she did not return any of the greetings addressed to her, nor did she feel the rain, which, lashed by the wind, was falling slantwise, soaking her right side up to the shoulder. Soon she reached the square where stood the men's church, whose yard had to be crossed to reach the convent.

Only then did she stop under the eaves of a house, wondering why she had come there—she had been walking in the very opposite direction from Stefchov's house. She remembered that she had gone out to save Sokolov from imminent danger. She hadn't realized how she loved him—and it came as a surprise to her! She had resolved on this step without stopping to think, she couldn't really tell how, as if driven by an invisible force. It was only now that she collected herself somewhat and began to consider how she might help him. She realized how difficult it was. She knew that Stefchov was now at the bey's, telling him to arrest Sokolov; she knew that Sokolov was at the committee meeting at Bai Micho's house. How was she to warn them of the danger? To run to Micho's herself, as if on a visit to his wife, and tell her how matters stood, was most inconvenient, unseemly, almost madness. To call on Aunt Michovitsa in this pouring rain, considering how far off they lived and how little intercourse there was between them, and that Bai Micho had quarreled with her father over some lawsuit or other, was most humiliating and unbecoming. Then how could she face telling Aunt Michovitsa that she, Stefchov's wife, was so very much concerned about the fate of an amiable but flighty young man like Sokolov, that she had thrown discretion and convention to the winds with the sole purpose of helping him? Moreover would she not unwillingly be compromising her husband, making him out to be a traitor and bringing shame upon him? For even if she were to conceal his name, everyone would guess that Stefchov had betrayed the victim she was trying to save. It would be noticed anyway that he had gone to the konak that day! O Lord, why was he such a bad man? . . . All these thoughts flashed through her mind. No, it was an ugly thing to do, quite out of the question. . . . It was beginning to pour again, and there she stood under the eaves as if besieged, helpless, weak and beside herself. If only some acquaintance would appear whom she might send to warn them! But no one was around just then. The rain was falling in torrents. Spouts of water seemed to be simply crashing down from the sky, and the streets, as well as the square she was in, were all deserted. She groaned in desperation. She saw how ridiculous and unfortunate she was, how hard it was to be the hand of Providence. She felt now how terrible her situation was, as she stood there in the street, leaning against the wall of a stranger's house when only some twenty odd paces would take her to the convent, where her aunt lived. But no, she had no business there; she would find no help there; it was certainly not there that she should direct her steps! . . . She couldn't stay a minute at the nun's and listen to her prattle, when her heart was overflowing with bitterness and when she was almost crazy with anxiety about Sokolov. There was only one consoling thought in these hard circumstances: the pouring rain which kept her prisoner there was probably detaining the police at the konak; she was sure that Sokolov had not yet been seized, so a ray of hope, however small, still remained.

Suddenly a happy thought struck her. "I could go to Auntie Nedkovich's," she said to herself. "I might send word by their Tasho." True enough, Lalka could tell her whole story to such a close friend and might entrust the boy with the delicate mission without any fear.

Whereupon she left her shelter under the eaves and stepped forth boldly into the rain and sleet. She waded through the muddy water which had suddenly come up very high and was nearly knee-deep and continued on her way beyond the square, the strong wind and the rain lashing her face.

She appeared at her aunt's soaked to the skin. Her aunt was amazed to see her arrive in such weather. "Goodness, goodness, you're wet through! Where are you going in this rain? Take off your skirt; you're sopping!" cried her aunt, greeting her in the corridor.

"Auntie, is Tasho in?"

"He's not been back since morning. He's hardly ever in, the scatterbrain. What do you want him for?"

"Goodbye, auntie," said Lalka, picking up her umbrella again. She seemed quite befuddled.

"Where are you off to?" her aunt cried in amazement. In a minute Lalka was in the street again. Fortunately the rain had stopped. The sun had pierced the clouds and was again shining merrily.

A fine almost invisible drizzle still fell from the calm air and sparkled in the sunlight like threads of a giant spider's web. A beautiful rainbow appeared in the sky, dipping one of its brightly colored ends in the dark gorge of the mountain. The leafy tree tops in the yards looked greener than ever and beautifully fresh; the clouds were taking flight and the clear shining blue of the sky spread everywhere in triumph. People appeared in the streets. Lalka felt better and her spirits rose. The rainbow which gladdened the sky filled her soul with hope. She anxiously peered at the people she met in the hope of seeing someone to confide in.

Suddenly she thought of Kolcho the blind man, whose selfless aid had saved Ognyanov from similar danger. "Oh, Lord! If only I could meet Kolcho now!" she said with a sigh, casting a troubled look upon the indifferent faces of the strangers she met.

Chance, which so often plays tricks on people and gives their fate the queerest, unexpected turns, was at its old game again, for some fifty paces off she caught sight of Kolcho, who was groping his way with a cane in one hand and a still open umbrella in the other.

Overjoyed and excited, she turned aside and quickened her steps to catch up with the blind man. He was in the very street which led to Beizadé's house; probably he was on his way there, for Lalka knew from Rada that Kolcho had free access to the committee meetings and never missed one. She hurried more and more and all but broke into a run. Her eyes were fixed on the blind man's black cloth overcoat, much too long for a man of his size, and on the large umbrella above his head. She no longer saw any of the people she passed: neither Burzobegounek, who greeted her with his left hand, nor Hadji Smion, who called out something to her from the opposite side of the street; had she met Stefchov himself she would not have recognized him.

In two or three minutes Lalka had nearly caught up with the blind man. As she came up to him, she looked about her; there was no troublesome witness. She said softly, "Kolcho, Kolcho!" But her voice was choked with emotion and she could not hear it herself.

Kolcho entered the shop of Ivan Doodi, the cobbler. His disappearance was so sudden and unexpected that Lalka thought some invisible force had carried him off through the open door of the shop.

Lalka was once more alone, alone in this busy street which now seemed to her like a desert. The only thing she caught a glimpse of in this desert was something black: it was a zaptieh carrying a gun, but to her he looked like five, ten, twenty, like a whole crowd of zaptiehs. . . . She felt dizzy; her thoughts became confused; she could no longer tell whether she was awake or asleep, but she continued to walk ahead unconsciously.

What street she had taken she could not remember, nor how or when she got home, for she was burning with fever. Her head was buzzing and all her joints seemed falling to pieces. She felt very ill and weak and barely managed to get to her room, where she collapsed on the window seat.

Lalka was seized by a fever which was soon to carry her off to her grave.

chapter 7

the committee

Today, because of the rain, the meeting was not held under the musky apple and tall box trees but in Bai Micho's room. Stefchov's man had been right.

The members, about ten in all, were sitting on the low window seats, several acquaintances of ours among them. First of all, the host, then Sokolov the president, Father Dimo, Frangov, Popov, Nikolai Nedkovich, Kandov, who had been elected a member that day amid general applause, also Mr. Fratyu, who had returned from Wallachia for Easter and been accepted after many entreaties and much repentance. He had fled to Wallachia immediately after St. Andrew's Day, promising himself never again to have anything to do with politics. He had arrived safely in Bucharest where, upon finding himself out of danger, he again became a zealous patriot and republican and presented himself to the emigrants as a victim who had barely escaped the gallows. He then wrote an unsigned article, in which he recommended the republican form of government for Bulgaria. But Karavelov,* taken up by his dream of a Balkan federation under Prince Milan, tore this remarkable work to pieces. Fratyu then presented it to Botev** for *The Banner,* where it met the same fate—Botev was at that time raving about world socialism. Whereupon Fratyu went and had his picture taken in the uniform of a revolutionary, bristling with weapons like a hedgehog. Later on, however, he thought it unwise to disseminate such disturbing pictures and put them away, along with the republican articles.

The remaining members were: Ilyo Strandjov, a bootmaker, a former exile and terrible cutthroat, Hristo Vragov, a merchant, Dimo Kapassuz, alias Bezportev or the Editor, a lame shoemaker and life-long conspirator. One member was absent, and that was Pencho Diamandiev. He had gone to K. to buy guns with the hundred pounds, instead of giving them to Tossoun-Bey as he had been told.

---

* Well-known writer and patriot.

** Bulgaria's best-known poet, killed in action in 1876.

It was already getting dark. Though it had begun about noon, the meeting was still in progress and to all appearances would go on till well into the night. Moreover Kableshkov's eloquent and fiery words held all the members spellbound, and they had been listening to him in silence and rapt attention for the last two hours.

Kableshkov, one of the most attractive and original personalities among the swarm of apostles who were organizing the April Uprising of 1876, was a young man of twenty-six, of medium height, very much on the thin side, with swarthy skin and a pale face. He was just beginning to sprout a mustache, and had coal-black hair which he was constantly pushing aside with his fingers and which kept falling in unruly locks over his broad intelligent forehead. It was his lively, fiery and piercing eyes, burning now with the ardor of a prophet, now with the inspiration of a poet, that lit up and ennobled that countenance, which looked pinched and drawn from the fever that was consuming him because of overwork and lack of sleep. No one could withstand the force of his eyes which reflected, as in a mirror, a powerful, impetuous and hardy spirit, incredible in such a frail and slender frame.

He was dressed in a blue topcoat, black trousers and a waistcoat, worn threadbare by constant traveling and riding on horseback. Now he was pacing the room, continuing the flow of his fiery speech, which was frequently cut short by violent fits of coughing.

"Yes, we must count above all on ourselves for help. We are strong enough to tackle the decaying Turkish empire ourselves. Turkey is weak, and financially ruined; the Turkish people are impoverished and will stand aside. They are under the yoke themselves. The army is demoralized and is not worth bothering about. Take the Herzegovina uprising for instance—thousands of troops were sent there, and the uprising is still at its height. And who organized it at that? A handful of people! And what will this ramshackle, frightened state do when we revolt? . . . A hundred thousand of us will rise up in arms in one day! Let them send troops then. . . . Whom should they tackle first? Moreover, are we the only ones to rise? To the west of Turkey is Serbia and the Montenegrin falcons, ready to swarm down on them; Greece is in her rear, and will not stand gaping. Herzegovina and Bosnia will flare up from one end to the other; Crete will follow suit. . . . Add to this the revolution in Constantinople which is only waiting for troubled times like these to overthrow Sultan Azis. Chaos everywhere! Our uprising will be the death knell of the Turkish Empire!" His eyes shone like live coals in the dim light.

"You've forgotten one thing," put in Micho Beizadé, "Russia.

Dyado Ivan will hurl himself upon Constantinople and they'll be done for! The prophecy will come true word for word." He meant the prophecy of the notorious Martin Zadek, in whom he had complete faith.

"Which places will be ready for the uprising?" asked Frangov.

"The whole of Bulgaria!" Kableshkov answered. "Plovdiv and Pazardjik county are making ready; the Rhodope villages along with Batak are arming secretly; Turnovo, Gabrovo, Shoumen will set Eastern Bulgaria on fire; there are no Turkish troops in Western Bulgaria. . . . The men of Koprivshtitsa, Panagyourishté and Strelcha will guard the passes of the Sredna Gora; you and your neighbors on both sides of the range will seize the Balkan mountains, and they are a fortress an army a million strong cannot take! Bulgaria will rise like one man! Our uprising will be a wonder in the history of Europe! Europe will open her eyes! I assure you that the Porte will not even attempt to crush the revolt by force of arms. It will want to come to terms with us. It has no other hope of salvation. . . ."

Kableshkov spoke with enthusiasm. He was a very clever man and must have had a clear picture of the situation which he was now presenting in a false light. But he was carried away by the force of his cause, and all means seemed to him permissible for its realization. Only this lofty faith in the sacredness of the cause he was serving could explain the assertions, tendentious or sincere, of this honest soul. And indeed he so convincing in his eloquence as to provoke no remonstrances. Everyone was already convinced of what Kableshkov was trying to convince them of. It was obvious that everything would happen in just that way.

"What conditions can we present the Porte if it tries negotiations?" asked Popov.

"If? What dirt can it eat so as not to?" remarked Father Dimcho.

"They'll be roasting eggs on its arse," said Bezportev.

"That's the least of our worries," Kableshkov replied. "So far the idea is this: Bulgaria from the Danube to the Arda, and from the Black Sea to the Aegean—a principality, independent of the Sultan, with an autonomous government. The Exarchate remains intact; tribute to be paid to Turkey; the army Bulgarian, half the officers Turks, at first. . . ."

"What about a Prince?" asked Hristo Vragov.

"Yes, what about him?" asked Bezportev.

"A European Prince!"

"Phew!"

"But you didn't say anything about Russia. Will she help us as Bai Micho says?" asked the priest.

"Father, don't be childish!" Micho scolded him with a frown. "How could it be otherwise? There are Russian generals waiting in Bucharest already!" Whereupon he looked at Kableshkov questioningly.

All eyes were turned on Kableshkov for confirmation. Realizing this, he put on a mysterious air and said in a low and confidential tone. "The first shot has only to be fired and the doubleheaded eagle will spread its wings above us!" Then he looked about him solemnly. Every face glowed with satisfaction.

"It seems to me," Mr. Fratyu began, "that a republic would be best. It could be called the Balkan Republic."

"It could also be a kingdom," remarked Frangov.

"Oh, it'll stick in our gullets," said Father Dimcho. "Is that the only dish you can stomach?"

"Come, the form of government doesn't matter; the main thing is for us to get free."

"I'm for a republic too," someone else spoke up.

"That's another matter, as we have said. What our form of government will be, who the prince will be, et cetera, et cetera. . . . We can leave all that to Gorchakov. Let the diplomats rack their brains about that," said Micho Beizadé.

"Come on, gentlemen," Sokolov cried, "to the point; you've played the giddy diplomats long enough. Time's precious. The first shots will be fired in the mountains and we'll be still debating whether it's to be a republic or a comedy. We have work to do now. . . . To hell with your republics! You're not yet astride the donkey and there you go swinging your legs. I have only one proposal to make: no more diplomacy at our meetings; leave that for Kanko's cafe."

"True enough," said Kableshkov, "This is no time for talking, gentlemen, but for acting. I have reviewed the situation for you; now let's see what you are doing. We mustn't waste time."

"That's true; it's a weakness of ours, playing the diplomat. Boicho, God rest his soul, was always criticizing us for that! It's a way we have in Byala Cherkva," said Bai Micho.

"Ah, gentlemen, that was a sad loss, Ognyanov's death, for you and for Bulgaria too," Kableshkov said with emotion, and sighed deeply.

A grave look appeared on every face at the mention of Ognyanov's name. His loss had left an empty space, a very chasm in their midst. They looked at one another, every one of them deep in his own thoughts. The tragic image of Ognyanov appeared before them, bloodstained and terrible, yet intangible. They were all sick at heart. They seemed to feel guilty for being alive while the hero had died.

chapter 8

Kolcho rejoices

Quick steps sounded along the passageway and attracted everyone's attention. Some of them went over to the window to see who it was. But the footsteps were already approaching the very door.

"That was Kolcho!" said Nedkovich.

"You must be wrong," remarked Micho: "how could a blind man hurry so?"

"I don't like this," remarked Father Dimcho. The committee members grew uneasy. Somebody banged, or rather crashed through the door.

Kolcho rushed in like a whirlwind. He was quite out of breath. They all sat there in eager expectation and dread.

"No strangers here?" he asked gasping for breath.

"No, only friends. What is it, Kolcho?" Bai Micho asked.

"Viva! Long may he live! Joy and glory! Rejoice, brothers! Go mad, I'm going mad too!" cried Kolcho as though he had taken leave of his senses, throwing his fez up in the air, clapping his hands, leaping a yard high, and, accidentally catching hold of Bai Micho, he started kissing him on the cheeks, the ears, the shoulders, and choking him. Bai Micho drew back speechless with surprise. They were all amazed by this unnatural paroxysm of hysterical joy. They all thought the poor blind man was out of his mind.

"What's the matter with you, Kolcho?" asked the doctor sympathetically, searching his face for symptoms of raving madness.

"Why, haven't you guessed it? He's alive!" Kolcho cried, throwing himself upon the doctor now. "Viva! My Count is alive!"

"What! Boicho?" The question burst from ten pairs of lips at once.

"I tell you, he's alive!"

"Kolcho, are you making a fool of yourself or has someone been fooling you?" asked Bai Micho severely.

"I tell you, he's alive, alive, Bai Micho! I shook his hand, I stroked his cheeks, I heard his voice, I all but saw him! Don't you believe me yet?" Everything about Kolcho was most convincing. They looked at one another in amazement.

"Where is he?"

"Waiting by the outside gate; he sent me to tell you. He got hold of me as I was opening it. I recognized him by his hands at once. . . ."

At that moment they saw the outside gate open and a peasant entered. He had a shabby cap on and was wrapped in a wide peasant cape with a pair of chickens in one hand. One of his eyes must have been causing trouble, for it was bandaged. At no other time would it have occurred to anyone that this peasant was Ognyanov. Now they all recognized him at once—with the spirit rather than with the eyes.

Micho made a dash for the door and called to him with a pretense of calm, "Bai Petko, come along in and tell us how things are with you!" But the vice-president's voice choked and sounded as hollow as if someone were gripping him by the throat.

Ognyanov slowly crossed the yard, which was muddy with the rain, went up the steps with a heavy tread and said in a deep voice, "I'll make a nice mess of your room with my sandals, Bai Micho, but you'll have to forgive me." And Ognyanov entered the room.

Everyone rushed to embrace the man who had risen from the grave. Inquiries, exclamations, transports, indescrible joy. Ognyanov remained the calmest of them all, outwardly.

When things had calmed down, Bai Micho said with tears in his eyes, "Take your place as President. The meeting is not over!"

"I accept, but only for today," said Boicho with a smile, and sat down in the corner. And now they noticed that Boicho's eyes were full of tears too. He was moved to the very depths of his soul by the boundless and warm-hearted concern of his comrades to whom he was bound by ties of friendship and by common ideals.

Bai Micho pointed to Kandov and said, "There, you see Kandov's become our brother too, today."

Ognyanov's and Kandov's eyes met. "Mr. Kandov, Bulgaria deserves to have us work for her."

"Even to give our lives for her," was Kandov's answer.

Bai Micho could not take his eyes off Ognyanov, and his joy knew no bounds. "This time we won't let you go so easily, Boicho," he said going out into the corridor. "Velizar!" he cried, "Fetch twenty logs from the cellar and arrange them here!" His son brought twenty rifles from the hiding-place and set them up behind the door.

"Now padlock the gate, will you?"

chapter 9

Ognyanov presides

The meeting continued with Ognyanov in the chair. Kableshkov had left, for his fever had come on again.

Many important questions were discussed, among them that of the defense of the town, for the inhabitants were on edge all the time, the rumor of a Turkish attack putting the fear of death into them. Gancho Popov was entrusted with the task of organizing a secret watch which was to guard the outskirts of the town at night. Various other measures were decided upon to lull the police into a sense of security. The letter from the Panagyourishté Committee was read. It was a long letter, containing a great many instructions and orders to the committee whose actions had to accord with the general plan for the organization of the uprising. It was signed by Benkovski.* Strandjov presented the account for the bullets and gunpowder he had received and distributed, as well as for storing the guns that had not yet been paid for and were consequently still detained in K.

"So we don't need to worry about arms," remarked Ognyanov.

"We can repulse a whole horde with our rifles and hold out for twenty days in the entrenchments," said Father Dimo. Of course there were no entrenchments whatever: it was the priest's name for the low fences of the market gardens in the outskirts of the town.

"And what if they bombard us with cannons?" asked Nedkovich.

"Then we're done for!" replied Father Dimo anxiously.

"We can set up some cannons too," remarked Mr. Fratyu. "I'd give my wooden churn most willingly. It'll roar like a proper Krupp. If other people do the same, we'll have a regular artillery," and he looked about him with a proud air.

"Your churn's no use whatever. It's ridiculous even to speak of collecting cracked churns from the old women," rejoined Ognyanov. "As for cannons, we most certainly need some. Their roar alone has a terrible effect on the enemy. Cannons can be made of cherry-tree trunks, well hollowed-out and bound firmly with iron hoops. Such

* Leader of April Uprising.

cannons were used in the Polish uprising." Ognyanov's suggestion was approved of and unanimously carried.

"Bookché will make them," said Micho.

"Bookché? Why, I know him!" cried Ognyanov.

"You know him, do you? The cooper! He's a fine fellow!" said the doctor.

"And how shall we get cherry-tree trunks? Who'll let their cherry trees be chopped down?" asked Vragov.

"That's a minor detail," said Nedkovich. "I'll see to that!"

"All right. Nedkovich is given the task of organizing the artillery," said Ognyanov smiling. "Now, next question. What else is there on the agenda, Gancho?"

"The most important question of all—the money. Nikolcho sent word from K. that we must pay what we still owe on the rifles tomorrow at the latest and pick them up immediately and bring them here; he's afraid of keeping them in his storehouse any longer. He thinks the Turks have got wind of it."

"That's important," said Ognyanov, "no time must be lost. He may get into terrible trouble if the arms are found, he and others as well."

"The worst of it is that the hundred pounds we've already sent will be wasted," remarked Sokolov.

"We must hurry and get those guns and hide them here at night. How much more money do we need?" said Ognyanov.

"Nearly two hundred pounds."

"Have you got it?" asked Ognyanov.

The committee set about tackling the problem most volubly. Some suggested that the sum be collected by voluntary contributions. This was rejected as impracticable. Micho Beizadé proposed taking the school funds and letting the future government repay the town council, but his proposal was also rejected. Then it was suggested that the money be borrowed from Kourka, all committee members signing the documents by way of security. But that proposal was quashed unanimously as the least acceptable of all. The money question eclipsed all else, yet there seemed to be no way of solving it.

All these matters which now provoke a smile were discussed and carried out in those days by people who were otherwise serious-minded enough. But their powers of reasoning seemed to be befogged by the fascinating glamor and novelty of their undertaking, which they saw in the light of their imagination. Only a fanatical faith in something can so blind reason.

Ognyanov frowned as he listened to the conversation. "I shall find the money!" he said suddenly. They all looked at him in surprise.

"Where will you get it from?" asked Vragov, the question slipping out in spite of himself.

"That's my business," returned Ognyanov. This answer cut short any further questions.

Gancho Popov asked leave to speak. "Gentlemen, it's late enough, so let's attend to another matter before the meeting is over. There are some new members who have not yet signed the pact of the conspiracy. Will they please come forward and put their names to it?" And he placed the inkhorn before them.

The new members were Vraga, Mr. Fratyu and Kandov. The last two signed without any hesitation, the former, however, not without an inner struggle. "Brothers," he said in great confusion, "and what if this paper is taken? It'll be the end of me. . . ."

"What do you mean? Aren't you a fellow-conspirator and a revolutionary?" asked Frangov.

"I am, brothers, but I have a house. . . ."

"So have we! Come on, put your name there in black and white!" said Father Dimcho angrily.

"Vragov, shame on you!" cried Ognyanov sternly.

Vraga signed with the air of a man who was quite crushed. But instead of signing "Hristo Vragov," as he did in his business letters, he wrote "Risto Vraga," as his name was generally pronounced. He resorted to this trick just in case. . . .

chapter 10

a spy in 1876

It was quite dark outside. "Mr. President," said Kandov who had kept silent so far, "I have something to say."

"I was going to speak too," put in Mr. Fratyu, "to propose that the meeting be adjourned." A few others spoke up, seconding his proposal.

"I demand to be heard! I shall make another proposal—regarding Stefchov!" the student said tersely.

"Lucky you reminded me," Frangov interrupted him. "Today Stefchov was at the konak to see the bey together with Zamanov. And his man Rachko the Stinkard was seen hovering around and looking about when we came in through the garden gate."

"Rachko?" said Ognyanov starting. "I know that idiot from the Karnari inn."

"Do you mean it's true that you tied him to a post?"

"He kept telling some such tale, but no one would believe him! We thought you were dead! He's not all there, you know."

"What he told you is true," said Ognyanov who had omitted this small incident in the brief summary of his adventures he had given the committee earlier that day. "But that's beside the point. So Stefchov is still at his spying, as before! Oh, the swine!" exclaimed Ognyanov, bursting with indignation.

"I demand the floor!" cried Kandov.

"Go ahead, Kandov!" said Ognyanov.

"I know for certain that Stefchov betrayed Ognyanov and that he is to blame for all our misfortunes!" said the student. His eyes were like two live embers which he now turned questioningly on Ognyanov.

"It wasn't Stefchov, it was Mooncho," all of them remonstrated.

"You are greatly mistaken, gentlemen!" said the student and jumping to his feet, he revealed in a voice trembling with emotion the discovery he had accidentally made. He backed his words with irrefutable proof. Violent indignation burst out on all sides. Angry cries and curses were heard. Stefchov was unmasked.

Ognyanov leaned forward frowning heavily.

"Benkovski was right when he said we were a lot of grandmothers."

"You see, he spied on us this evening as well!"

"Goodness knows what trouble we're in for!"

"We act so openly and have become so careless that I begin to feel afraid," said Frangov.

"Ognyanov, what do you think?" asked Sokolov, turning to him.

Ognyanov, who was deep in thought at the moment, started and said, "I think we were fools not to prevent Stefchov from playing the traitor at the time."

"How could we have done that?" asked Father Dimcho.

"By killing him."

"That's the punishment in the revolutionary statutes," remarked Popov.

There followed a moment of complete silence. "Gentlemen! I offer my services to kill Stefchov one of these days!" cried the student. Everyone stared at Kandov in surprise.

"Kandov! You're too hasty! Stefchov is mine, no one else has the right to kill him!" cried the doctor, whose eyes were burning with fierce hatred.

"What do you mean?" cried Kandov in a despairing voice.

"Stefchov is my affair and I will not let anyone have him," muttered Sokolov sullenly. Kandov protested.

"Cast lots! Cast lots!" several members cried. But neither Kandov nor Sokolov would agree to casting lots. Each was afraid of drawing a blank—as though it were a question not of killing a man, but of winning a throne.

Then Ognyanov said authoritatively, "If there's any question of who has the greater right to kill the traitor, I deny it to both of you. I have suffered by him; I have priority over you. But I have one objection: this murder may harm our cause. I don't think this is the time for it. What I suggest is this: Stefchov shall receive his punishment on the first day of the revolution; he shall be the first victim." This wise proposal was accepted.

Kandov was most disgruntled. Triumphant self-satisfaction could be read on Sokolov's face; for several minutes he was deep in thought, detached from the conversation around him, his eyes fixed in space. Finally he brightened up quite extraordinarily, two deep wrinkles furrowed his brow and a demonic smile hovered about his lips. He jumped up and went out to send word to Necho Pavlov not to set Cleopatra free that night; he needed her for Stefchov. For such was the terrible death he had thought of for the traitor!

When he returned a moment later he found them talking about Zamanov. "I met him the day before yesterday; he has come from Plovdiv," Gancho Popov was saying. "He suddenly came up to me and started without any beating about the bush. 'How is your business going?' he asked, winking at me to show what business he meant. And he began asking endless questions to try and get a word out of me. I tell you, the sweat just rolled down me while we were talking. . . . I imagine the swine has got wind of us."

"The devil take the son of a bitch!" said Micho angrily, "He's a relative of mine, but he turns my stomach like carrion."

"How many mothers have wept tears of blood because of that scum," said Father Dimcho. "Whoever polishes him off will seem as pure as an angel to God, though he's up to the neck in sin. . . ." Whereupon Father Dimcho piously raised to his lips a flask of rakiya which he took from a breast-pocket and then handed to Strandjov.

Just then a loud knocking was heard at the gate. They all looked alarmed. A suspicion of treachery was obvious in all of them.

Sokolov seized his revolver and dashed to the door. "Who is it?" he asked.

A soft voice answered, "Open the door!"

"It's Zamanov," Aunt Michovitsa whispered. Although the words were said in whispers, yet the ominous name reached the ears of the committee members. Shivers went down their backs.

The doctor shut the door again, went up to the icon and unfolded a letter which he read by the float-light.* A minute later he turned towards the group, his face entirely altered. His cheeks were quite sunken with fear. Everyone's heart was in his mouth.

"Betrayal?" all eyes seemed to ask.

"What is this letter?" Ognyanov asked.

"A letter of ours which we sent to the Panagyourishté Committee the day before yesterday; it is now returned to us. See for yourselves by whom," he said, handing the letter to Ognyanov.

"Read these lines!" he added pointing to a place to the left of the signature.

Ognyanov read the following:

* Float-lights, which were placed in front of icons and on graves, consisted of a wick inserted in a piece of cork which was floated in a glass of olive or other oil.

Mr. President:

You are ill advised to strew your correspondence along the street for Mr. Stefchov to find. Today I took this letter from his hands at the bey's, to whom he translated into Turkish the first page about the belladonna; while this page I later read myself in my room over a brazier, so you needn't worry. Another storm was about to burst over your heads tonight, but it has passed. You have me to thank for this! Meet elsewhere and in greater secrecy. Good luck and victory!

The Bulgarian traitor and spy,

H. Zamanov.

Now everyone was dumbfounded.

"How did this letter fall into Stefchov's hands?" Ognyanov asked indignantly, after recovering from the first shock of surprise.

"Pencho took it to give to our courier and must have dropped it," the doctor explained. (The letter had actually fallen into the street that very day when Chorbadji Yordan's maid was shaking Pencho's jacket out of the window. Pencho had not yet discovered that it was missing from his breast-pocket.)

"To think that Stefchov should find it! How can one deny the existence of fate now!" said Kandov.

"And of Providence!" added Nedkovich.

"Providence in the person of a spy! Who would have dreamt there was so much honesty in Zamanov!" said Frangov.

"It seems we're indebted to him for more than we realize," remarked Gancho Popov. "He speaks of a storm—I wonder if we weren't going to be pounced on and arrested here? You heard that Stefchov was at the konak and that one of his fellows was spying on us as we came here!"

"So there's some nobility in the man!" said Ognyanov greatly surprised.

"And great patriotism, as you see. In saving us he exposes himself to danger by signing the letter," said Nedkovich.

"Gentlemen!" cried Ognyanov in a solemn voice. "This is a sign of the times! When even the official Turkish spies turn patriots and become our allies, it can only mean we are working at a great moment, that the spirit of the people is prepared and that they are ripe for a glorious struggle!"

"I consider Zamanov a saint now," remarked Bai Micho deeply moved. And every face, which until a minute ago betrayed only fear and distress, now expressed peace and cheerfulness.

It should be mentioned that so far the wretched Zamanov had never committed a single act of political treachery. In spite of what was rumored about him, he had taken up a spy's career with the sole aim of extorting money from Turks and Bulgarians alike. He went as far as threatening the latter, to make his influence felt, but he went no further. He had no pride left in him, but his conscience was still alive. Clearly the hapless man had not been intended for a spy, but fatal circumstances had thrust him down that muddy road. Let us add that before returning the letter to the committee he had cunningly persuaded the bey to postpone the attack.

He died in exile in Asia just when the general pardon was signed at San Stefano.

chapter 11

Vikenti

Ognyanov said good night to his friends and started off along the street that led to the outskirts of the town. He soon reached the open country and set out along the road to the monastery. Everything around him was fast asleep. The walnut trees and bushes on either side of the road, dimly melting into each other, rustled sleepily; the dull thunder of the distant waterfalls came through the stillness like the accompaniment of a celestial chant, never heard before. The vastness of Stara Planina, brought nearer by the darkness of night, rose in silence to the stars.

Ognyanov stopped at the great gate of the monastery and knocked. In a little while a servant asked who was there and opened it to him. He said he was the deacon's uncle. Two of the big monastery watchdogs hurled themselves at the nocturnal visitor, but wagged their tails when they recognized him. He passed quietly through the second gate and knocked softly at the deacon's cell. It was opened.

"Who are you?" the deacon asked, not recognizing Ognyanov through his disguise; then suddenly he threw himself on his neck.

"Boicho, Boicho, is it really you?" And poor Vikenti wept with joy. He fired question after question at him.

Ognyanov gave him a brief account of everything, then went on, "But I've come to you on another matter, not to tell you my adventures."

Vikenti looked at him perplexed. "Yes, what does bring you here at this late hour?"

"Don't worry, I'm not asking you for shelter like last year, but for another service, not for me—for the cause. I'm going to set you a hard task."

"Let's hear it," said Vikenti anxiously.

"What is Father Yerotei doing?"

"He's gone to church for prayers, as he always does," replied Vikenti, surprised at the question. Ognyanov thought awhile.

"Does he stay there long?"

"Until half-past three, usually; that's his custom. It's two o'clock now. Why do you ask?"

"You know where he keeps his gold pieces, don't you?"
"I do. Why?"
"Sit down and I'll tell you something." The deacon sat down and stared at his guest.
"We've got to pay two hundred liras for the guns tomorrow. They're an absolute necessity for the organization. If we don't remove them from K. tomorrow there'll be danger. We've got to find the money. And I've promised the committee to supply it."
"Well, what are you thinking of doing?" asked the deacon.
"We've got to take the money from Father Yerotei!"
"What, are you going to ask him for it?"
"I didn't say that. He won't give it to us of his own accord."
"Well?"
"I told you, we've got to take it."
"You mean steal it?" cried the deacon.
"Yes! He doesn't need the money, and it's an absolute necessity for the people's cause. We'll have to take it, or steal it, put it as you please."
"What, steal, Ognyanov?"
"Yes, steal, in a sacred cause."
The deacon looked at Ognyanov in horror. This proposal which went so blatantly against his principles, simply astounded him. It would have aroused his supreme indignation if it had come from anyone else. "A theft in a sacred cause!" It was the first time in his life he heard such a thing said and by the most upright of men at that! Ognyanov had become a more enigmatic figure than ever to him, a man who fascinated him and subjected him to his own will. He was still captive to the terrible fascination of the man.
"Well, what do you say, Father Vikenti?" Ognyanov asked sternly.
"You're asking me to do what's impossible. I can't make up my mind to rob my protector like a thief. That's most dishonorable, Mr. Ognyanov."
"Is the liberation of Bulgaria a dishonorable cause?" asked Ognyanov, flashing an indignant look at him.
"No, an honorable one."
"Then all the means which serve it are honorable."
The deacon felt he was facing a powerful opponent, but he wanted to put up a stubborn fight. "But think of it, to rob my benefactor who loves me like a son; to rob a noble old man who loves his country—the thought revolts me. Put yourself in my place, and you'll realize what an impious theft it would be."
"It's a sacred one!"

The deacon looked in bewilderment at the man who spoke to him so calmly of so repulsive a deed. "We'd much better ask him; he might give us the sum."

"Father Yerotei is a monk and doesn't part with his money easily."

"Let's ask him. Who knows? He may take it out and give it to us," Vikenti insisted in an imploring voice.

"If we ask him, we have to tell him all about it, and he's very intimate with Yordan Diamandiev. Whenever he goes to town he goes straight there. Besides, I know he'll give us nothing; we'll only lose precious time. Hurry up, Vikenti."

"But this is dreadful! How can I look him in the face tomorrow? And when he finds the money's gone, as he most certainly will, he'll suspect me; he knows I'm the only one in on his secret."

"You won't wait for him to suspect you, nor have to look him in the face like a condemned man," replied Ognyanov.

The deacon stared at him wide-eyed. "What? You mean I should flee afterwards?"

"On the contrary. You'll have to kneel before him tomorrow and confess your sin. If he is a noble old man who loves his country, as you say, he'll forgive you. And I imagine he'll be reconciled to the loss of his money more easily after it's gone than now when it rattles in his money-chest."

Vikenti sank into profound thought. He was entirely under the impression Ognyanov's words had made on him. He saw clearly that he could never get the best of it in this uneven contest.

"Well, will you do it, Father Vikenti?"

"But it's a hard thing, brother," said the deacon almost tearfully.

"Once you make up your mind it's easy."

"But I've never stolen!"

"Nor had I ever killed. But when it was necessary I killed two men as if they were a couple of mice. And observe, I had two armed brutes against me."

"That's just why it was easier for you; you had two brutes in front of you, and I have a benefactor, a defenseless old man who trusts me as he does himself."

"You won't lay a finger on him. Make up your mind while there's time. 'Time comes, time flies, the centuries are winged,' Rakovski* says. There, take Rakovski as an example: he robbed the Cyprian monastery, where he was a guest, to organize the Legion. Be brave, Vikenti! Ognyanov would never suggest anything base."

---

* Writer and ardent revolutionary.

"Oh, let me collect myself!" cried Vikenti, putting his head on his arms. Ognyanov watched him in silence.

It was a long struggle for Vikenti. Finally he raised his head and said: "I'll do it!" Then he sighed deeply.

"How will you get in?"

"By the door, of course."

"What, does Father Yerotei leave it unlocked?"

"No, but my key fits his door. I found that out by accident; I opened it for him when he had lost his."

"And how will you open his chest?"

"He keeps the key in the pocket of his purple quilted coat, which is hanging on the wall at the moment. If it's not there I'll break open the chest. He never leaves the church before half-past three. I've still got an hour. Oh, Boicho, how could you. . . ."

"Listen, take your knife with you."

"What for?"

"You never know—you may need it."

"What, would you have me kill?" cried the deacon indignantly.

"Arms give one courage. Let me come with you."

"I don't want you, you man of blood!" said the deacon almost spitefully.

Ognyanov himself was now amazed at the young man's gloomy resoluteness, after seeing him so timid and sensitive a moment ago. "Are you no longer afraid of the sin?" Ognyanov asked, smiling.

"If there's a sacred theft, there must also be a righteous sin," the deacon answered jokingly.

"That's the catechism of the new Christian teaching," Ognyanov answered in the same spirit. "And it's a better one."

"We'll find that out in hell." And the deacon opened the door. "Wait for me here and don't make a noise."

"Good luck, and good pickings!" Vikenti went out in his slippers.

The court was dark and silent. The vines above him made the darkness denser and more mysterious. The galleries all around lay silent. Their windows were like eyes which looked out on the night. The deacon peeped in at the church on his way and saw Father Yerotei reading prayers at the lectern. He went on quickly. The monotonous murmur of the fountain deadened his light footsteps, so that he passed the easily awakened geese without arousing them. When he reached the door of the cell, he felt his knees give way beneath him, as if he had been walking for hours. His heart was beating painfully. The deacon felt his strength oozing away with his resolution. The task he had so light-heartedly undertaken now seemed hard and terrible, and quite beyond him. The inner man in him awoke, rebelling within him, condemning him and nailing him to the spot. Accidentally he touched his dagger. How had he happened to take it? He frightened himself! How did he come to be here at all, at Father Yerotei's door? He had come to steal! From his benefactor too! And it had all happened so quickly! Could he be dreaming? What force had thrust him there? Tomorrow Deacon Vikenti would awaken a thief, a pickpocket, perhaps a criminal! He was staking his whole life on that dark night! But no! There was no going back!

Vikenti went resolutely up to the door. The windows of the cell were dark. All around reigned the silence of the grave. He listened intently for a moment or two, then thrust the key into the hole, turned it softly and gave the door a push. It opened and he went in. The float-light flickered, throwing its dying light on the iconostasis. Vikenti felt for the quilted coat and found it hanging on the wall; he thrust a hand into the pocket and drew out the key, then he ran to the open closet. There he lighted a wax candle, went up to the two chests, and stuck the candle on the lid of one of them. The deacon bent down before the other one, but his knees were shaking so that he had to squat down Turkish fashion. Then he opened the chest which creaked softly. At the bottom lay several purses, one of them a green one, and other objects of value—an amber rosary, golden icons from Russia, silver teaspoons and plates, pearl-ornamented crosses, and a roll of prints from Mount Athos. Vikenti felt the purses; two of them, he could tell, held large coins, roubles and silver medjidiehs; there were small coins in the other, twenty centime pieces. Gold flashed from the green purse. From it he counted out exactly two hundred liras into his lap, making a shining pile of gold. Vikenti was no lover of money, but the sight of the glittering metal bewitched him. For this, he thought, the most terrible crimes are committed, and all his life man fights to obtain it! With this the whole world could be bought. And to save Bulgaria money was needed too; blood and the sacrifice of thousands of lives would not be enough by themselves. Could this be all the old man's gold? He was reputed to have thousands of liras. Vikenti was surprised. He began to stuff the coins into his pockets by handfuls.

Suddenly something moved behind him. He turned. Father Yerotei stood there.

chapter 12

the green purse

The old man's imposing figure nearly reached the ceiling. His long white beard fell majestically over his breast. His broad face, gaunt and mild, looked calm in the light of the candle, and so did his eyes.

He approached quietly. Vikenti knelt before him. "My son, am I to believe my eyes?" the old man said in a voice that quavered painfully.

"Forgive me!" and Vikenti raised his folded hands in supplication. Father Yerotei stood there a moment looking at him. Vikenti's face was unrecognizable in its pallor. Confusion had turned him to stone. As he knelt there, entirely motionless, he looked like an image in a Catholic church. Dead silence reigned in the cell, as if the two human beings were not there.

"Deacon Vikenti! Since when has Satan entered into your soul? Since when this greed for gold and plunder? Most holy Lord, Jesus Christ, forgive me, a sinner!" The old man crossed himself. "Rise, Deacon Vikenti!" he cried sternly. Vikenti stood up like an automaton. His head hung down like a broken branch.

"Tell me, why did you steal in here, even as a thief in the night?"

"Forgive me, forgive me! I have sinned, Father Yerotei," said Vikenti dully, in a hoarse voice that sounded more like sobbing.

"My son, may the Lord forgive you. You have set your feet on an evil road; you are headed for eternal damnation my son, and for the destruction of body and soul. Who taught you to commit this mortal sin?"

"Father, forgive me! I did not take the money for myself," muttered Vikenti, quite crushed.

"For whom did you yield to this temptation, Vikenti?"

"For the people's cause, Father."

The old man looked at him in surprise. "What people's cause?"

"The cause we are working for now, for the Bulgarian uprising. Money was needed and I dared to lay hands on yours."

The old man's gentle face cleared. His eyes, dimmed by age, lighted up; they were wet with tears. "Are you telling me the truth, Deacon?"

"The very truth, Father, I swear it by God's blood and by Bulgaria. I took the money for the common cause."

A new expression lighted the old man's face. "Then why did you not ask me for it, my son? Do I not love Bulgaria too? For lo, today or tomorrow the Almighty may see fit to gather my sinful soul unto Him. To whom then shall I leave all that I have? You are my heirs, all you young Bulgarians. May the Almighty help you to save the Christians from the race of the accursed heathen. We old men did not know how, nor were we able. Why do you look at me like that? Don't you believe me? Come, come here."

And taking the astounded Vikenti by the hand, he led him up to the cupboard, took out a big green ledger, opened it with his aged, trembling hands and said, "Read this here, my son. I shall no longer hide it, God forgive me."

Vikenti read the following entries written in the monk's handwriting:

1865. February 5. Sent his Reverence Monseigneur ______ in the city of Odessa 200 Ottoman Liras for five Bulgarian boys to continue their studies.

1867. September 8. Sent his Reverence Monseigneur ______ in Gabrovo 100 Ottoman Liras for five Bulgarian boys to continue their studies.

1870. August 1. Sent his Reverence Monseigneur ______ in Plovdiv 120 Ottoman Liras, for five Bulgarian boys to continue their studies.

Father Yerotei spat on his fingers and turned another page. "Read this!" Vikenti read:

"Be it known: in the small green purse there are 600 Ottoman Liras. These coins are for Deacon Vikenti, of the town of Klissoura, ordained in the holy Church of St. Savior, to go and study theology in Kiev, for the greater good of Bulgaria." This last note had the force of a will in case of the old man's sudden death.

Vikenti thought he was dreaming. He did not dare raise his eyes and meet the old man's which were burning now like two live embers. He only kissed his right hand with respectful gratitude, and tears flowed from his eyes, which shame kept lowered.

Father Yerotei understood and pitied poor Vikenti. He said encouragingly, "My son, be comforted. God has forgiveness for the repentant. Your desire was a good one, and praiseworthy. The omniscient God can see. Come, tell me how much money is needed for the weapons."

"Two hundred liras. Father Yerotei, you are a saint! Your name should be immortal!" cried Vikenti touched to enthusiasm.

"Do not blaspheme, my son!" the old man answered sternly. "Take the money you need and use it as the Lord shall teach you for the salvation of Bulgaria. I give you my blessing. If you need more, ask for it. As for your money. . . ."

"Father Yerotei! I thank you from my heart for your generosity and for your help. But I no longer have the right to use it. I don't want to leave Bulgaria. I will fight and die for her freedom. I have seen an example of love of country in you."

"Deacon Vikenti! . . . Very well, my son," the old man continued, "Serve Bulgaria when the time comes. And the money set aside for you will find its way back into the purse, have no fear. But I shall place it in a safe spot; all thieves are not innocent angels like you. And when I die, pray for me. . . ."

Staggering like a drunkard, Vikenti left Father Yerotei's cell; he crossed the court at a run and rushed into his room, weak with emotion.

Ognyanov looked at him dumbfounded. "What's up? You were very slow about it. Why are you so pale?" he asked quickly. "Why don't you speak, Vikenti? Did you find the money?"

Vikenti shook out his pockets and said, "There it is!" The gold coins scattered over the floor.

"How much did you take?"

"He gave the whole sum."

"What do you mean, gave? Father Yerotei? So you begged him for it? You went to find him?"

"No, he caught me stealing it."

"Well!"

"Oh, Ognyanov! What have we done, brother? How little we knew Father Yerotei! It doesn't matter about you. . . . But I who have lived here for three years under his kindness! I can't forgive myself for this. Fire fell before me tonight to open my eyes and destroy me. Yes, I would give twenty years of my life not to have such an hour in it. I, a young man, supposed to be a patriot, an ardent Bulgarian, I was crushed by the gentle moral greatness and the modest patriotism of this shadow, sinking into the grave, unknown to any one. Just think, brother, he found me in front of the chest, my robe full of gold." And the deacon told him everything in detail.

"What, he came out earlier this time?"

"At exactly the same hour, but I lost time hesitating in the court, without noticing it. Imagine my situation!"

Ognyanov sat there with folded arms, quite astounded. "Why, the man's a saint!" he cried.

"I told you we should ask, brother, didn't I?"

"I had a poor opinion of a monk's patriotism."

"Will you never rid yourself of that opinion? You're like Karavelov. You've got it into your head that the monk is an antediluvian animal who does nothing but eat and sleep, wrapped in a thick layer of fat, who spends his life in talking to the monastery tomcats! Yes, you smile and forget all the monks who have worked for the people; begin with Païssi, who was the first to write a history of Bulgaria one hundred years ago, and go on to Deacon Levski, who died for the country! The monks have never stood aside from the Bulgarian movement. Why, one of them swore in the members of our committee here the day before yesterday. And here you have another example this evening. Doesn't that convince you?"

Outside the first cocks crowed. "Good night," Ognyanov said, lying down on the window seat to sleep.

"Good night, if it can be a good one for haidouks," answered the deacon, and put out the candle. But for a long time the majestic figure of Father Yerotei rose before their eyes.

Father Yerotei was one of those fine personalities who emerged from the monastery cells and to whom Bulgaria owed so much for her Renaissance. He was even a close friend of Neophyte Bozveli. If circumstances did nothing to let him assist in the mental awakening of Bulgaria with his moral capacities, they did allow him to contribute to it by sending some ten boys to get an education in different schools. Though only a simple monk, remote from the interests of the world, his heart grieved for Bulgaria. And because he had no family or relations, it was his country that held all his affection and love. He considered himself fortunate in being of the slightest use to his people; the good he did was in the nature of a sacrament for him and only God was its witness. This profoundly religious and simple soul took care not to fall into the sin of pride over the good that he did; he feared the tempting glory of the world, for which only the vain Pharisee longs; he did good at the Savior's behest, letting not his right hand know what his left hand was doing. He had left money in the hands of various honest people to help young men in their studies, but on condition that they would never breathe their benefactor's name. Thus he found satisfaction in the manner in which he was ending his life and awaited his death in peace.

Soon after this noble act, which was his last, Father Yerotei passed away quietly. When they opened his chest, they found only a bag of small coins for the poor and for his funeral.

Vikenti was not present there. The day after the scene described, he had left the monastery and fled to Klissoura in shame.

chapter 13

a happy meeting

The day before, as soon as Kolcho left Bai Micho's house, to the great surprise of all passers-by, he set out at a run along the street to go to Rada's and claim his reward for the good news he was bringing.

This time he decided to be more restrained. His panther-like gambols, which had so thoroughly amazed the men, might well frighten out of her wits a girl who was already worried to death. But such self-restraint was beyond him. He felt this traitorous joy would choke him if he tried to rein it in for one moment.

When he approached Rada's gate he felt his heart begin to beat. To drown the sound he forced himself to sing his famous litany. The door was opened at once.

"Welcome, Kolcho," cried Rada amiably.

"Are there any strange ears hereabouts, Radka?" asked Kolcho.

"I'm alone, Bai Kolcho, as I always am."

Kolcho was literally panting with emotion. "Sit down and rest, Kolcho!" Rada said kindly, taking his emotion for fatigue.

"Be joyful, Radka, but very joyful, you hear? As joyful as your name, eh?"

Kolcho began jumping about like a child and singing, to restrain himself:

> Gospozha Seraphima
> And mild Cherubima,
> The beautiful Enocha
> The convent's shining light. . . .

Radka couldn't say a word. She guessed, but could only whisper, "Kolcho, don't frighten me!"

"I'm not frightening you, I'm just telling you to be joyful. . . . He's alive!"

Kolcho was unable to keep the resolution he had made in the street, to break the joyful news gently to Radka. That would have been easier for a man who had his sight, and whose feelings of joy could have been blunted by a thousand impressions. But the blind man lived in an ocean of darkness, now lighted by one ray of light only, inhabited by only one joy. If he did not let the news out in words, he would have to express it in leaps and bounds. . . . No matter how, he had to pour it out without delay.

At Kolcho's words, which her heart had already guessed, the girl leaned against the wall or she would have dropped. There are great joys, and great sorrows too, which frail human nature seems unable to bear. Yet they are all borne. The soul's resilience grows with the strain put upon it, when the soul is strong. Perhaps the heart's secret instinct prepares it beforehand.

Almost mad with joy, she cried, "Alive! Dear Lord! Where is he? Who told you, Kolcho? Alive! Boicho's alive! Oh, I'll die with joy! What am I to do now?" Kolcho, who was calmer now, told her all about his unexpected meeting with Ognyanov at Micho Beizadé's gate, and what had followed.

"When is he coming?"

"Tonight, at dusk; for they have lots to do now."

"Oh, dear, oh dear!" Radka clasped her hands, laughing through her tears. She was wonderfully beautiful at that moment.

"Thank you, Kolcho, thank you!" she cried in transports of joy. His heart at rest, Kolcho went out happy. That gentle devoted creature was made happy by another's joy. Nature, who had taken everything from him, had left him this gift as a consolation.

Rada could not think what to do now. How should she pass the time until her beloved visitor came? How could she hide his coming? Should she tell the people of the house or not? If she went to them, she would go mad in her impatience; if she stayed in her room her heart would burst! To kill time until his coming she set to work in her room and tidied it up. Then she made herself neat and fixed her hair before the mirror, at which she smiled, sticking the tip of her tongue out at her own reflection when she saw how pretty she looked. Then she spun around on one foot, like a five-year old, and began to sing, she knew not what, nor did she realize what she was singing. Her every sense was at the door, and the slightest sound from that direction set her quivering. She was so happy!

It was not until the following evening, after dark, that Boicho was able to leave the monastery to visit Rada. She lived at Granny Lilovitsa's in a room by herself at the end of the long courtyard whose fruit trees were in full leaf. There was a little bench outside on which Rada used to sit reading or sewing in the shade.

Her eyes had nearly dropped out of her head from watching these two days past. Those long hours full of the strain of waiting, with their burning emotion and restlessness, seemed a perfect age to her. In her impatience she came out into the yard.

It was growing late. Big stars twinkled in the sky. The warm scent of flowers came to her from the neighboring gardens in the clear night air. Strongest of all was the scent of acacia. The leaves of the trees in the yard rustled sleepily in the night breeze. The stillness was wonderful and mysterious in the starry night. Under the eaves above the bench two swallows stirred at the sound of Rada's footsteps, peeped sleepily down, and nestled closer together again. There was enchantment in the air, for love and joy dwelt there, and all this—the deep blue sky with its brilliant stars, the air, the trees, the swallows in their warm, downy nest, and the fragrant flowers too—brought calm to the spirit, speaking to it of peace, love and poetry, of fond embraces in the stillness of the night.

Rada sat dreaming. When at last Ognyanov knocked at the gate she felt faint, but ran to open it. The lovers embraced, their lips met in a long, passionate kiss.

Time was short; their joy could only be expressed in a few kisses, in a few broken words. After the first transports the two lovers, absorbed in their happiness, grew calmer. Their joy knew no bounds. Rada was exquisite in the radiance of her love. Boicho appeared to her handsomer than ever in his peasant clothes, which seemed to bring out the intelligence, expressiveness and manliness of his features.

"What have you been doing, my darling?" he said to her. "My poor child, you have become a perfect martyr! I have killed you; I have sacrificed you, Rada. Yet you have no reproaches for me; you are always the same loving spirit, the same tender heart, born only to weep, to lament and to be cherished. Forgive me, forgive me, Radka!" And Ognyanov pressed her hands in his, losing himself in the depths of her big shining eyes.

"Forgive you? I'll never forgive you!" She cried pretending to be angry. "What do you mean by all this? You can die and I'm not supposed to grieve! If you had only sent me one little word! Oh, Boicho, Boicho, please don't die any more! I won't let you—I want to be with you always to guard you like the apple of my eye, to love you so much, so much, and to rejoice in you. You have suffered so, Boicho, haven't you? Oh, how silly I am! I haven't even asked you how you've been, through all these months; all these terrible ages, they seemed to me."

"I've been through a great deal, through many dangers, Rada. But there was a providence for us, and it has brought us together again."

"No, no, tell me, tell me everything in detail. I want to know. Such stories were told about you, such rumors, each more spiteful than the last. How can people be so heartless, and think up such things! Tell me. Boicho! You are alive and with me now, and I can hear all you've suffered with courage, no matter how terrible it was!" And she looked at him pleadingly, with inexpressible love and sympathy.

Boicho could not refuse. It was her right. Besides, he himself longed to pour out his soul to someone he loved, to a responsive heart; the memories of past sufferings, of misfortunes endured, have a special savor when they are poured out in moments of happiness. Briefly and simply Boicho recounted his adventures since leaving Byala Cherkva, as he had done to the committee the night before, and to Vikenti afterwards. Her emotions were reflected in Rada's clear, childlike eyes, as she heard him; in them he read first fear, then pity, then triumph and joy. She hung on his lips; she lived through everything, and never took her eyes off him, with a loving look which went to his head.

"Oh, Boicho! Someone betrayed you!" she cried in dismay when the story got to the Turk's attack on Ognyanov at the Altunovo inn.

"I don't know; I can't accuse a Bulgarian. Perhaps I gave myself away in the Turkish cafe by a careless gesture."

"And then?" she asked, impatient and excited.

"In my room I heard the footsteps of the Turks and realized that they were coming for me. I was desperate. I saw there was no hope; I was lost. I drew my pistol and took my stand behind the door. I had six bullets: I would make a present of the five to them; the sixth I was going to keep for myself."

"Dear Lord! What terrible moments, and I knew nothing! I may even have been laughing here!"

"You must have been praying, Rada, for God was merciful to me again, and saved me from deadly peril!"

"That was a miracle, Boicho!"

"Yes, a miracle, if you like. He blinded the Turks. Instead of coming into my room, they went into the first one, that looked out onto the courtyard! As I heard afterwards a certain tax-farmer from Plovdiv, a Greek, had just arrived, and he was my neighbor. He must have looked very much like me, and that misled the zaptieh who had seen me the day before." Rada heaved a sigh of relief.

"I heard the noise, realized that there was some mistake, and that they would be with me in a minute or two. One minute only divided me from them, from my death. I don't remember now how I tore out one of the bars from the window, how I jumped down onto the road. Only it wasn't the road, but the river, which had frozen. The ice broke and I found myself in the cold water up to my knees. While I was trying to get up onto dry land a terrible noise deafened me: five or six guns were fired over my head from the window. They missed me. Then I broke into a run. I ran wildly. How long I ran in the dark, where I went, I don't know."

"They pursued you!"

"Yes. For a time I felt that, then there was nothing. I had reached the forest. Night had fallen. There was an icy wind. My trousers had frozen like boards. I went on to the west for two hours, always over the foothills, and arrived half-dead in the village of Ovcheri. Kind people took me in there and warmed me. Only, one of my toes was frost-bitten—but thank God! I stayed there two weeks, but grew afraid of getting those people into trouble—trouble always dogged my footsteps—so I went over to Pirdop, where Mouratliiski's brother is a teacher. I lay ill at his place for three months, a rather serious illness."

"Poor Boicho, you must have caught a chill spending the whole winter in the fields and mountains. You're a real martyr," said Rada sympathetically.

"That's a splendid fellow, Mouratliiski's brother. He nursed me like a mother."

"What a noble Bulgarian!" said Rada with feeling.

"And a patriotic one too. He repaid me two or three times over for the service I did his brother."

"And then? What happened then?"

"When I got well, he supplied me with money, gave me these new peasant clothes and sent me off with tears in his eyes. I set out for here."

"And no one recognized you? Boicho, be careful here!"

Ognyanov had slipped off his heavy cape and the bandage. He stood up in front of the mirror, pulled his fur cap well down over his ears, pulled his hair about, did something to his face and turned around, a different man. "Do you know me, now?"

"I'd know you even if you wore a mask! Just see how he's looking at me! How funny you look, Boicho!" she laughed gaily.

"You know me because you love me, but how would strangers guess who I am?"

"Hate makes sharp eyes too, take care!"

"For anyone of that sort I have this," said Ognyanov raising one end of his short jacket to show the handles of two pistols and a dagger which were stuck into his waistband.

"You cutthroat!" laughed Rada. "Gospozha Hadji Rovoahma was right."

"If I'm a cutthroat, you're just the opposite, you're a seraph!" He sat down again.

"Well, go on! Tell me how you got here. Who are these Mouratliiskis?" asked Rada who had heard the name twice.

"Burzobegounek's brother."

"That German here? The photographer?"

"Yes, Rada, it's a false name. His real one is Dobri Mouratliiski. He's as much a German as he is a photographer. He's a fugitive from the Stara Zagora insurrection. I took him in here and hid him under that name. He's an old comrade of mine and a very devoted fellow. You can turn to him without fear when you need anything."

Rada looked at him, startled. "Why should I turn to strangers? I don't need anything. You know that I'm living on what I saved out of my salary as a teacher."

"I meant that you weren't to consider him a stranger."

"And where will you be?"

"I'm leaving, Rada."

"Leaving again? When? Leaving me?"

"This very night, in another two hours," said Ognyanov, looking at his watch and putting it back in his pocket.

Rada went white. "So soon? I haven't seen you yet!"

"I have to be in K. at dawn. I'm on a mission, and besides I can't stay in Byala Cherkva any longer. What a pity! I haven't even managed to thank Bai Marko for his goodness to you. And to me too, how very kind he's been. Ah, there are noble souls among us, Radka, and that makes me love Bulgaria all the more. I love her so deeply too, because she brings forth such wonderful creatures as you!"

"Boicho, why are you leaving? Oh, dear. . . . No, no, take me with you. You must go; you have given yourself to Bulgaria, but take me away from this dreadful town, put me in a village where I can see you oftener, or if you like, give me something to do for the people. I'm a Bulgarian too, and your ideal is mine as well, Boicho, and if you die for Bulgaria, I'll die with you, but don't let us part; don't let me hear nothing but bad news about you. Oh, dear, it's so wonderful now!" And she put her hands on his shoulders.

"Radka, your life here is very difficult; I can see that," said Ognyanov, full of concern. "I sense what you don't tell me: my enemies here persecute you, don't they? The people's malice spares you nothing, I know. You're made the victim of prejudices and beastliness, poor Radka! There's more than one Hadji Rovoahma here, I know. And you bear it all in silence. Your sufferings make you a heroine in my eyes. My poor angel! The great cause has absorbed me entirely and doesn't leave me a moment to think of your position. I'm a hardened egoist; forgive me, darling!"

"Oh, Boicho, Boicho, if you leave me again, I'm afraid I shall lose you forever, I'll never see you again," said Rada, and her eyes grew wet. Then she added quickly, but pleadingly, "Don't leave me here, Boicho. Whether you live or whether you die, I want to be with you. I won't be in your way; I'll be a help to you. I'll do everything. Only let me see you more often!"

"No, you can't do anything. The revolution takes a man's strength; you have to be bloodthirsty and merciless, and you're a very angel. You've already done your duty, the flag with the lion you made with your hands will inspire us. That's enough for a Bulgarian girl."

Then after a moment's thought he added, "Listen, Rada, would you like to come to Klissoura to be Mrs. Mouratliiska's guest? She's living there now. I'll arrange that. There's danger there too, but at least you'll get away from all the gossip here."

"I'd go anywhere I can see you."

"I'm rousing the people in that region now and I'm better sheltered there. I'll only come to Byala Cherkva again to raise the rebellion. Until then we can see each other, Rada; after that only God knows who will come out of that struggle alive. It will be a great and bloody one. If only God blesses our arms, if only our country, this martyred country of ours, can emerge from the struggle bloodstained but free, I shall joyfully die for it. I'll have only one regret for the world, that death will part me from you. Because my love for you is boundless, dear child, because you are the mistress of my heart, it is yours, but my life belongs to Bulgaria. And I'll know that there is at least one heart on earth to grieve for me and shed tears on my unknown grave." Boicho's look darkened.

Rada caught his hands with emotion. "Boicho, you'll come through all right. God will preserve heroes like you for Bulgaria, and you will be famous, Boicho, and I'll be so happy then!"

Boicho shook his head doubtfully. "Well, my angel," he said and interrupted himself. Then taking her by the hands he went on,

"Radka, come what may, I want my conscience to be clear. I may perish, I am almost certain I shall."

"Hush, Boicho!"

"Listen, I may perish, Rada, for I go out to meet death, but I want to be at rest about you. You've joined your fate to mine, to me, a man who is doomed, outlawed; you have made me the happiest of men with your love, you have sacrificed something dearer than life for me—your honor; and you've suffered cruelly at the hands of the world for it. You forgot everything for me! If I die, I want to know that at least I leave you an honest woman in the eyes of God and the world, if I don't leave you a happy one. I want you to bear my name, the name Ognyanov; it is not shameful or stained in any way, that name, Rada. When you come to Klissoura I'll send for the priest to marry us and bless us, and there I'll consider how best to ensure your safety. My father is a rich man and loves me. He will fulfill the last wish of his only son. I would have done this here and now, but it's not possible; there is only one other thing we can do. I don't have a ring to give you, Rada, not a gold one nor an iron one. The iron that I have is for the enemy. But we don't need one. God is above us, the just and mighty God of Bulgaria, of the oppressed, of the broken-hearted, the God of suffering humanity; he sees and hears."

And taking her hand he knelt.

"Let us make our vows before him, Rada. He will bless our honest union." She knelt beside him. And they uttered broken words, heard only by their Maker.

chapter 14

around a tree-trunk

The next morning the sun shone again; the sky was blue and alive with light and joy. The gardens were fragrant and the dewy rose-bushes already showed their pink buds; the fruit trees, in full leaf and covered with snowy blossom, gave all the courtyards of Byala Cherkva a festive air; the nightingales sang, the swallows flashed through the air, filling it with their twitter, and drinking in the intoxication of air, sunshine and freedom. Nature was brimming over with life and youth. The sky and the air were nothing but a joyous harmony of life, of light, color, song, fragrance, love and happiness.

At that moment, at the end of a quiet blind alley near the outskirts of the town, Marko Ivanov stopped at a gate and knocked loudly. A brawny young man in baggy peasant trousers, bareheaded and in his shirt-sleeves, opened the door to him.

"Have they brought the trunk here?" asked Marko in a low voice.

"Yes, they have, Bai Marko, come in!" And the young man went ahead and showed him a door. "They're there—go in!"

The door was opened at once and the first thing Marko saw inside was a tree-trunk. It was the trunk of a cherry tree. Mounted on a pile of logs, our old friend Kalcho the cooper was turning a huge auger at the raised end of the cherry trunk, which was well propped up underneath. The sweat was pouring down from the tired cooper's brow.

"Good luck to you, Kalcho!" said Marko smiling and examining the work in progress curiously. "Things are going on well, aren't they?"

"There's a knack to everything," said a voice. Marko turned to the left and looked round. Micho was squatting there against the wall.

"Oh, Kir Micho," said Marko amiably, offering the vice-president of the committee his hand.

"We're having a meeting today, so I thought I'd better see how things were going as I came by."

"Where's your meeting then, out in the country?" asked Marko as he sat down without taking his eyes off the cherry tree.

"This time we're having it at the Green Dell." This was the name of a hollow in the bare hill to the north of town, the first spur of Stara Planina, so to speak. After the memorable evening on which Zamanov had brought back the letter, the committee never met at the same place twice running. Today, the meeting place was the Green Dell.

Red in the face and sweating profusely, Kalcho went on turning the huge auger with his sinewy hands. He often took his instrument out to remove the shavings and look into the hole, then he went on again. It was already approaching the necessary point, that is two hands' widths from the butt of the cannon. Kalcho shook the shavings out of the tube, looked into it with one eye, then looked around at his guests with self-satisfaction. They got up and squinted down the cannon too.

"It'll hold the weight of a big steelyard," remarked Bai Micho, "but we'll fill it with small shot. That'll bring down more of those heathen. Your cherry tree's going to work wonders."

Marko's face beamed with triumph. For in fact the cherry tree was from his garden. A considerable change had recently taken place in Marko's convictions and ideas. The revolutionary goings-on in Byala Cherkva did not leave him unmoved and apathetic for long. They aroused his interest, astonished and startled him. He said to himself: "If it's like that everywhere, as they say it is, won't all Turkey be set ablaze? Perhaps the end of the Empire is really coming, since even the children are getting armed! Who knows?" These ruminations calmed his fears and strengthened his faith in destiny. A person of a positive turn of mind and sound common sense, without a streak of imagination, he was carried away by the general enthusiasm and began to have faith. The epidemic had laid hold of his sober and honest Bulgarian heart too.

But this psychological process had not taken place all at once. Strong convictions are born under the impact of a whole series of weighty facts. First of all—last autumn—because of the rising tide of atrocities and cruelties perpetrated by the Turkish population, he had whispered to himself, "What kind of life is this?" That was the first time indignation welled up in him so strongly, the first step.

Then that spring, after Kableshkov had made his appearance, when he saw the enthusiasm of the young men who were so resolutely engaged in preparing a reckless, yet noble enterprise, he said to his wife one day, "Who knows? If anyone does anything it'll be these foolhardy youngsters."

Finally, around Easter, when discussion in the cafe focussed on the terrible obstacles that stood in the way of such a movement and the still more terrible consequences that might ensue, Marko said sharply to Alafranga, "Mihalaki, if you count your pennies for pipe and tabor, there'll ne'er be a wedding!"

Only six months earlier he had been speaking of "the bowels of hell."

And Father Stavri capped this with, "There's no catching fish if you're afraid of a wetting."

But we should say that Marko was in favor of the preparations, not of the revolt itself. His enthusiasm did not go so far as supporting it like Bai Micho, nor was his faith in the success of the contest so steadfast and blind as to make him stake everything as Ognyanov was doing. Byala Cherkva had to be prepared to withstand the attack of the bashi-bazouks* that the numerous Turkish villages of the Strema Valley would spew forth upon her. She was surrounded by them on all sides and already tempted them. If a revolt broke out all over the country, that was another matter. But who could assure him that it would be so?

At any rate Byala Cherkva had to be prepared. And he insisted on her being armed. "After that, time will show us what to do," he used to say.

Three days ago Nikolai Nedkovich had been to see him and had complained bitterly of his unsuccessful search for cherry trees. "Cut down mine," said Marko.

However, whether prompted by a very human self-interest, or by a father's love—a quite natural feeling under the circumstances—he did not allow his sons to meddle in the business. He wanted them to resist the current by which he himself had been carried away. He wanted something that was impossible. "If I'm in it, that's enough from my house," he thought. The change in him was not complete; hence the hesitations, hence the contradictions. In short, Marko represented the moderates in the people's party, an element capable of coping with any other situation but not with revolutions, which seek to achieve their aims by violence and extremes. It often plays the part of a brake on the wheels of revolution, but perhaps in this case it was not so.

Kalcho set about boring the match-hole in the cherry tree to make it a real cannon. He began working with a thin auger on a knot in

---

* *bashi-bazouks:* mercenaries, Turkish irregulars, known for their savage brutality.

the wood at the beam end. He soon finished this job too, blew into the hole, and sawdust flew out of the cannon's mouth. "Well, that job's done, you may say! There'll be a fine flash-crash-bang for the Turks," said Kalcho triumphantly.

"Bravo, Bookché, you'll be the gunner! Now Bai Lilo the blacksmith must get the iron bands on and the other ironwork, and there's a Krupp for you," said Micho.

"Sakes alive! That'll make a terrible roar," remarked Bai Marko.

"We'll place it high up at the Green Dell, and from there we can rake the whole valley. Wherever they show themselves, fire and don't spare them! The position's splendid!"

Steps sounded outside. "That's one of our men," said Micho, for the brawny young man had been ordered to let no one else in. It was Popov, the secretary of the committee. He greeted Micho and Marko. "What have you come for, Gancho?" the president asked him.

"I'm off to the Green Dell, so as I was coming by, I thought I'd drop in to see our artillery."

"That's right; we must all be there today to decide whom to send to Panagyourishté. They want a representative of our committee. I say Sokolov."

"What representative do they want?" asked Marko.

"Someone to be present at the big meeting."

"What is it going to be about, that big meeting?"

"Why, that's where the date of the uprising's to be decided. It'll probably be the first of May," declared Gancho. Marko's face darkened.

"Pooh, it'll be later. At least, let's get the blossoms in from the rose-fields first," remarked Micho.

"What, are we going to rise?" asked Marko.

"It'll break out everywhere at once."

"Don't do such a mad thing!"

"Mad or not, it's got to be done," said Micho shortly.

"We haven't been getting ready all this time just for the fun of it, have we?" added Gancho.

"Flash, crash, bang! We'll make mincemeat of 'em, Bai Marko!" cried Kalcho, excitedly.

"I thought we were just preparing to defend ourselves from the bashi-bazouks, until we find out what's going on all around us. I'm afraid we'll be the only ones to pay the piper," said Marko.

"Shame and dishonor on Byala Cherkva if she delays one moment! The whole people will rise in one day and Turkey will be done for!" cried Micho flaring up too.

Marko grew thoughtful. "Are you quite sure it'll be like that?" he asked.

"Of course we are! We're not babies! That's why I asked you to join the committee, so that you could read the letters with your own eyes, and hear Kableshkov and Boicho."

"It's one thing to have people tell you; it's another to know yourself that it's so. Think once, think twice and then three times more, but don't let's repeat the Stara Zagora business."

Micho grew angry. "It's quite different now, Marko; don't be childish. I tell you the uprising will break out everywhere. Everything is organized. Let them but name the day."

"Well, if it breaks out everywhere I'll shoulder my gun too. But suppose it only breaks out here, what then? That's what I want to get clear."

"It will!"

"Who knows?"

"It will, Marko! Shall I swear it?"

"I don't want that."

"Why, you're a doubting Thomas!"

"I want to feel things with my own fingers, just like him. We're risking our heads here."

"You must believe that we'll win through!"

"Why?"

"Because Turkey must fall now."

"What do you mean, must fall?"

"Just that. She must fall, because it's written that she will!"

Marko realized that Micho was referring to Martin Zadek's prophecy. "I don't believe in modern prophecies. The almanac foretold rain and storm, and we're having heavenly weather. Stuff and nonsense!"

"Zadek is another thing altogether, Marko. Learned men acknowledge him too!" said Micho heatedly.

"Amen, I say! You're always talking of Zadek! You leave that Zadek alone!"

Micho blazed up. "If you don't want Zadek, I'll show you another prophecy, much clearer and more profound."

"Whose is it?"

"It comes from divine Providence. Only the Holy Ghost could inspire it. No human brain could think it up." And Micho began a systematic search of his pockets. Marko stared at him in amazement.

"Oh, I must have left it in my notebook at home," said Micho annoyed. "But, wait a minute, perhaps I'll remember it. If you say you don't believe it after that, I leave you to your stupidity. There's none so deaf as those who won't hear!" And Micho pulled out his inkhorn, dipped his pen in it and began another search of his pockets.

"Have you a bit of white paper on you?"

"No, I haven't," said Marko after a hasty search of his.

"Wait a bit, I'll write it here!" And Micho rested his arms on the cannon and began to write on its smooth surface. Marko watched him curiously. Soon several rows of Church-Slavonic letters and Arab figures stood there, alternating as follows:

Т (300) **Ѵ** (400) **Р** (100) **Ц** (900) **І** (10) **А** (1)
К (20) **Є** (5)
П (80) **А** (1) **Д** (4) **И** (50) **Є** (5)

Read as letters these signs said "Turkey will fall"; added up as numbers they came to the fateful year 1876.*

Who had contrived this odd combination and discovered the coincidence? What mind had caught this glowworm in the gloom, this inexplicable trick of chance? No one knew. Modern men call such occurrences the play of chance, old people call them fate. That is how superstition explains things when reason abandons the field.

Micho Beizadé explained the double meaning of this conundrum. Marko checked it himself. He was simply speechless with amazement and answered nothing.

Micho looked about him triumphantly. Self-satisfaction and pride flashed from his black eyes, while the delicate ironic smile that played upon his lips as he looked at the bewildered Marko expressed pity for his cowardly lack of faith, and triumph, and bliss and enthusiasm all at once. It was as if that look and that smile said to Marko, "Come, speak now; come, let's hear your opinion: Martin Zadek's no use, but what do you say to this? Now do you realize who Beizadé is?"

While this conversation between the two worthies was in progress, several members of the committee had arrived unnoticed. They too had stopped off on their way, to see the gun-foundry of Byala Cherkva's Krupp. Others soon followed them, all happening to pass that way, so that all the members were present except Dimo Bezportev.

---

* In the old Cyrillic alphabet, as in Greek, the letters stood for numbers as well as sounds.

"Bezportev's nowhere to be found today," reported Iliya Strandjov. "He must have gotten drunk in one of the taverns."

"It's a bad thing to drink if you don't know when to stop," remarked Father Dimcho, raising the flask to his lips.

The members of the committee could not take their eyes off the cannon and found no words to express their admiration. It stood before them like a huge monster, without a head and without legs, with a small eye on its back and a terrible deep maw at its tail, which would belch fire and lava. On its smooth, yellow body the cabalistic phrase Bai Micho had written stood out in black letters, the terrible *Mene, tekel, upharsin* of the Ottoman empire: "Turkey will fall, 1876."

"Boys," said the vice-president, "did we say we'd meet at the Green Dell?"

"Yes, we did, let's be off."

"Well, as we're here anyway, can't we have our meeting here? If you ask me, this is the place for it now, beside this bear!" They all approved this happy thought of the vice-president's.

"Then take your seats!"

"And where will you sit?"

"Here's my throne," said Bai Micho, as he sat down on the back of the cannon. So the meeting began.

chapter 15

Marko's new prayer

Marko went out very thoughtful and much impressed by what he had seen and heard in Kalcho's munition works. "Who knows," he whispered to himself as he set off across the market gardens which began thereabouts.

He walked on to the east of Byala Cherkva as far as the river, which drops down from the mountain in numerous cascades. There he took a look at his own garden, and at the stump in it which was all that was left of the cherry tree, smiled slyly, then set out again, past gardens and meadows, to reach the highway leading to K., and the main street of the town.

After passing the Gipsy huts, set down in a dusty field at the end of the town, he came upon a big horo.* A poor man's wedding was in progress and all his neighbors of the outskirts seemed to have come to it, for the horo was endlessly long. "That's how the world wags," he thought. "They're making cannons in one place, and here people are marrying with no thought of the morrow."

But he was soon convinced at once that the revolutionary mood was not lacking here either. Bezportev was leading the dance, and he was a wonderful dancer in spite of a slight lameness. He was waving a white handkerchief over his head, dancing in a wild eccentric manner, and leading the endless living chain that followed him in the most capricious twirls and figures: at times the horo resembled an irreproachably perfect semicircle; at times it coiled around itself like a sleeping snake, to uncoil again and turn into a straight line or take any other fantastic shape. The seat of his full-bottomed trousers fluttered triumphantly at every forward dash.

Little by little Bai Marko approached the horo, which was at its height, and he saw that Bezportev was very drunk and that he dashed forwards and leapt up with such energy, with the whole horo after him, as if he were leading it out to storm a fortress. Bezportev's enthusiasm had communicated itself to the last link at the end of the chain, which was made up of five-year olds. At his orders the band

---

* *horo:* round dance.

had stopped playing and the dancers were singing as they danced, moving to one side or the other to the beat of the tune:

> Are you hoping, Kalina,
> That brother Kolyo'll come today?
> Your brother Kolyo, Kalina,
> Bringing costly gifts for you?
> A chain for your neck so white,
> A belt about your waist so slim,
> A kerchief for your fair hair too,
> And slippers for your tiny feet!

And the dance went on more madly than ever.

Marko stopped beneath the eaves of the smithy to rest a while and watch the delightful scene. Bezportev spotted him at once. He left the dance and ran up to him, still waving the spotted handkerchief and keeping step with the song. There was an expression of savage joy on his long, bony face with its red moustache and laughing blue eyes, and the animal-like enthusiasm too which comes from drunkenness, the drunkenness caused by some irrational and destructive excitement of the soul.

"Long may you live, Bai Marko, and long may Bulgaria live and her glorious sons too! Bai Marko, stand me a glass of wine! Thank you. Long life to the man that pours the wine! Forgive me, Bai Marko, I'm as drunk as a lord, but I know what I'm doing! It's I that drink the wine; it doesn't drink me. Yes, a Bulgarian who feels things. . . . For the people suffer and I cry, 'Enough of slavery and drunkenness!' Better to die than live such a shameful life. Let them say I'm as drunk as a Russian cobbler if they like. . . . Whoever says so is a traitor. My heart aches for Bulgaria, that poor Turkish slave. We want rights, human rights! We don't ask for riches; we don't ask for wives. . . . But, you'll say, people get married; how long will they go on? And I'll answer you, that's the people. . . . And tomorrow, when you give the word, they'll set fire to the houses, and be off to the mountains. A man who fears birds will never sow millet. A nod's as good as a wink to you. Long live such patriots. I kiss their hands and their feet too! But Yordan Chorbadji! We'll flay him alive with a flint stone. As to Stefchov! But let sleeping dogs lie. . . . Never mind that, what I mean is, I'm drunk, as drunk as . . . as. . . . It's love of the people makes me drunk. The hour is at hand. I'm here today and gone tomorrow, a spirit, I say. A stupid world, in a word. And whoever dies for the people will live forever. Long live Bulgaria! And what am I? An ass that fears clear water."

Suddenly the editor stopped for he saw a Turk passing by on horseback, a sight that had become rare of late. Pointing at him he began to sing:

> The battle's beginning, how our hearts beat.
> Hark to the tramp of the enemies' feet!
> Courage, brave comrades, united and free,
> No longer submissive rayah will we be!

"Forward, forward!" cried Bezportev, as if he were leading an invisible company, and dashed at the Turk. The man turned, saw Bezportev running towards him and stopped.

In a few strides the editor caught up with him and cried, "Where are you going, infidel? How dare you tread this sacred soil? This land is Bulgarian; yours is in the deserts of Asia. Go and rot there! Down, you swine, to kiss this sacred ground! If you don't the devil will take your Sultan, his men and his harems!"

The Turk did not understand Bezportev's words, but saw that he was very drunk. He grew alarmed and spurred his horse on. Bezportev dashed forward and seized the horse's bridle.

"What do you want of me, chorbadji?" asked the astonished Turk.

"Down, or I'll drink your blood!" roared Bezportev fiercely, drawing his shiny dagger.

The Turk had some kind of a weapon in his belt, but forgot it, began to tremble and dismounted submissively. "What do you want, chorbadji?" he asked, frightened by the editor's fierce looks.

"Where are you off to, you Turkish pot-walloper?"

"I'm going to K."

"And when are you going to Mecca?"

The Turk lost his wits completely; his voice sank to a whisper and he barely murmured, "Leave me in peace, chorbadji."

"Let's journey to Mecca together," cried Bezportev, "Wait, let me get on your back! You've ridden the Bulgarians for a thousand years!" And Bezportev nimbly sprang up onto him, winding his arms round the Turk's neck. "March on to Mecca!" he shouted.

Before the whole gathering, amid shouts and laughter, the Turk set off with Bezportev on his back. Sadly his horse followed its master.

"Who knows, who knows!" said Marko to himself, as he walked on home, not yet recovered from his amazement at the scene he had just witnessed. He had lived fifty years in this world; he remembered the days when a Bulgarian was forbidden to wear green* and had to get down from his horse whenever he met a Turk; he himself who had witnessed, experienced and swallowed so many humiliations as one of the rayah could hardly believe his own eyes. He saw that in the middle of the whole gathering, in the presence of a thousand spectators, a Turk had dismounted at the command of a lame and drunken Bulgarian, that that Turk had forgotten his caste and his faith, and had bent over like a beast of burden to let Bezportev mount him, and had carried him upon his back before them all! And it had all happened so simply, so unexpectedly. Yes, so terribly unexpectedly. It was no mere accident, the result of drunkenness—it could not have happened yesterday or the day before; it happened today, and all the people had laughed and applauded as if it were the most natural thing in the world. What sort of times were these? How had the rayah become so bold, and the master so frightened? Or had the hour truly struck for this empire, and was Beizade right, and the young men too? "Who knows, who knows?"

In his absorption he stumbled upon the children who were coming back from school. They were Merdevendjiev's pupils and formed a long column, marching two by two. They marched in step, like soldiers, under the command of the company commanders who marched beside them, and of the general who marched at their head. . . . Marko's Assen held high a stick to which was nailed a red handkerchief—that was the flag.

Marko stood there astounded. "They've all gone mad, from the old men down to the sucklings," he thought. "We're in for it!"

He seized Assen by the ear and asked smiling, "What are you carrying, little mule?"

Then he thought thankfully that his elder sons had not caught the infection, that he had not noticed among them that spirit of rebellion which had caught them all, even himself. "May they at least stand aside and have no finger in this mess which I've got into. My life's over; it's they who must live."

Then a bitter thought came into his mind and he went on, frowning. "Have those rascals no blood in their veins? Have I begotten nothing but peddlers? No, better have them stay out of it. One from a house is enough."

It was about noon. He reached home perturbed and irritated, went into his room, examined the pistols that hung on the wall in their holsters, then opened a closet that was hidden behind the door, with

* Christians were forbidden to wear green, a sacred color to the Moslems.

the intention of putting new flints to a pair of old pistols that had belonged to his great-grandfather and had long lain in the dust. He groped about in the dark, then got a candle to see better. When he took it into the closet what was his amazement at the sight that met his eyes! Instead of the two old pistols, he saw a whole arsenal of guns, pistols and revolvers. It was a proper armory! But also a kind of general store: in one corner kit-bags, sandals and leggings had been hung up, along with queer European clothes ornamented with braiding, and other things, strange and suspicious.

He shouted for Granny Ivanitsa, who appeared. "Mother, mother, who's been opening the hiding place? Who's brought all this junk in here?"

Granny Ivanitsa looked at him in amazement. "Who can have opened it? Certainly not I. All of them, Vassil, Dimiter, Kiro, they fool around here every hour of the day, and brush away the cobwebs. Who knows what they're looking for in the dark!"

Marko grew angry. "The devil take them for haidouks," he said scratching his head.

He held the candle at the door of the closet for a while, gazing in with a strange expression on his face. "The madcaps, the madcaps—God bless them!" And he shut the door again.

Then he went over to the iconostasis and bowed low before the image of God. He murmured a prayer which was not to be found in his prayerbook. He was praying for Bulgaria.

chapter 16

a nation intoxicated

And indeed, with the approach of spring, the revolutionary ferment spread with giant strides. All Western Thrace, its chief center, was like a volcano that spring, emitting dull rumblings that announced the coming eruption. A swarm of apostles and preachers journeyed over hill and dale, organizing the struggle. They were warmly welcomed everywhere, arms were stretched out to embrace them, hearts were opened to their words—the people thirsted for the message of freedom, and were impatient to bear their cross to Calvary. A long line of forerunners had labored in Bulgaria's spiritual field and sown the seed of national consciousness. That glorious line which began with Païssi, the monk, and ended with Levski, the deacon, both of them saints, had already tilled and fertilized the field; the first had blessed it from the heights of Mount Athos, while the second blessed it from the gallows.

Some twenty years ago Rakovski, when he had merely hinted at revolution in a village, had barely escaped from the fury of the peasants by disguising himself as a woman. Today, when the people heard that an apostle was coming, they sent deputations instead of posses to meet him. And they heard the life-giving words, they drank them thirstily, as a parched throat swallows a clear flow of water. When they were told, "Be ready, you must die!" the church gave its priest, the school its master, the field its ploughman, the mother her son. The idea spread everywhere with irresistible force; it laid hold of everything—mountain and plain, the cottar's hut and the monk's cell. Even the chorbadjis, that infamous class, the obstacle in the way of the people's progress, were fascinated by the idea which had fired the minds of the people about them. It is true that their share in the patriotic movement was relatively small, but they did nothing to stop it, for they did not betray it. Betrayal and baseness, from all sides and from all persons, came after the catastrophe, for they are its spawn everywhere. It is in vain that certain prejudiced people try, to the detriment of historic truth, to suggest that only those of the people who wore sandals had a monopoly on patriotic zeal. Entirely in vain. The revolutionary spirit, that fiery angel, touched with its wing peasant and student, those who wore hooded capes and those who wore fezes, those who wore priest's hats and those who wore chimney-pots. As in all struggles for progress in Bulgaria, science and the cross, that is the spirit, were in the vanguard. The book of Bulgarian martyrs is a clear proof of this. It is true that it was the mass of the people which supplied the main contingent, both earlier and today, but it gave what was its strength—numbers. The intellectuals had to contribute life and soul.

In short, enthusiasm grew and overflowed everything. Every day it took on larger proportions and new strength, and with it the preparations advanced apace; old and young were at work. The peasants left their ploughing unfinished to cast bullets, and the townspeople neglected their trade. Secret messengers went back and forth day and night between the different committees and the central committee in Panagyourishté; secret police observed the movements of the regular constabulary; young men went out to drill and target-practice under the command of officers and corporals; women wove leggings, braided laces for them, and packed cartridges, and old women baked rusks. The shoemakers were busy making nothing but sandals, cartridge belts and bags for the rebels; the village officials themselves—tax-collectors, mayors and others—zealously took part in the preparations. The piles of arms, bullets and gunpowder grew in each village; the Turks themselves supplied the gunpowder; cherry logs, hollowed-out, shaped and bound with iron hoops, provided the artillery! The silk flags, with lions rampant embroidered on them in gold, the fantastic uniforms of the revolutionaries, the clergy's shining vestments and crosses, the church banners—all formed a backdrop to the approaching struggle.

This general madness was evident even in the children's games. They left their marbles, their balls and their tops, to play soldier in the streets, making guns out of shinbones and swords out of sticks. The older people, dumbfounded, said, "This is an omen from heaven." But there were no omens from heaven to foretell the coming storm. No, nothing but the extraordinary prophecy, "Turkey will fall, 1876," which circulated everywhere, stirring up even the most skeptical. On the contrary, spring was early that year and had turned all Thrace into a Garden of Eden. The rose-gardens were in bloom, more luxuriantly and wonderfully than ever before. Fields and meadows promised a rich harvest, but there would be no one to bring it in. . . .

And in a few days, in secret and softly,
The growth of the nation o'erleaped several ages.

As for the indifference of the Turkish Government in the face of such open and impudent agitation, such noisy arming and preparing for an uprising, it can be explained by the growing strength of the rayah. "That's nothing but the stirring of a rabbit-warren," said the good-natured effendis. "Those are the hurrahers," said the proud rulers, and smiled disdainfully. There are words which mark a whole epoch. The "hurrahers" were an embodiment of the national consciousness which had emerged triumphant from the thirty years' struggle for an independent church. But the "hurrahers" who toasted the Bulgarian Exarchate in 1870 had turned into the rebels of 1876, who cast bullets and made cannon to welcome Bulgarian freedom.

The Turks had not yet grasped the metamorphosis. They could not move with the times, nor see the foothold which new ideas were gaining. It was, moreover, already too late for them to see it: they had neither a prison big enough, nor a chain long enough, to bind a titanic idea, an invisible Krali Marko,* that was moving mountains.

Future generations will stand dumbfounded . . . what am I saying? We ourselves, the contemporaries of this indescribable period, now sobered by a whole series of historic examples, gape and wonder at this intoxication, this sublime unreason of the people, to prepare for a struggle against a terrible empire whose military power was still great. To prepare, moreover, with the hope of overthrowing it by a force of arms was ludicrously inadequate. To challenge its supremacy in the very heart of this empire, in the "bowels of hell" as Marko Ivanov had once said, without having assured themselves of other allies than enthusiasm, a weed that blazes up and burns itself out, and illusion, a ghost that vanishes. History seldom gives us an example of such rashness, bordering on madness. The national spirit of Bulgaria has never been raised to such heights, nor is it likely so to rise again.

We have particularly stressed this prelude to the struggle because it is astounding in itself, and as a measure of the power of a great idea sown in favorable soil. The struggle itself which followed is not worthy of the name. Nor have we any intention of describing it. Of necessity, our narrative has stumbled on an episode of this struggle, which follows, and which illustrates the revolution, that appalling collapse of the brightest hopes.

* Legendary hero of Bulgarian folk-songs.

chapter 17

a smack in the face

The day after that on which we followed Marko Ivanov from Kalcho's cannon foundry to the family arsenal, Ganko's café was full of smoke and rang to gleeful laughter. It had been caused by Ivancho Yota, because Frangov had stumbled at the phrase *Drang nach Osten* in reading an article on Austrian policy in the East in the *Pravo;* Ivancho Yota had explained that it meant "dragi nash osten" (our dear goad). Deafening guffaws filled the cafe.

Only Kandov, who always sat silent in a corner, did not laugh. He did not appear to hear or see what was going on around him. His thoughts were elsewhere. A greater melancholy than ever lay on his pale, haggard, thoughtful face, something painful, inexpressibly painful, and it formed a complete contrast to the carefree faces around him, wreathed in smiles.

The laughter died down, for church was just over and everyone turned to stare out the windows at the passers-by, all decked out in their best. Among the last was Rada.

She was dressed modestly in black. Her cheeks were flushed like peonies with inner happiness. She drew all eyes, but many of the looks cast on her were hostile; some were even contemptuous, because a most unpleasant rumor about Rada had gone around town in the last few days. Hadji Rovoahma had made it known that Rada received disguised lovers at dead of night. And she swore that she had seen this with her own eyes.

The truth was that someone had caught sight of Ognyanov as he was leaving Rada's but had not recognized him. As soon as the rumor reached the nun's ears she had done her best to spread it all over the convent. From the convent the rumor spread to town. The gossips took it up eagerly, and Rada's name was bandied from mouth to mouth by the scandalmongers and by Boicho's enemies, who revenged themselves on his memory through her.

Rada herself knew nothing of this. She was absorbed in her happiness, nor could she read the cruel slander of which she was the victim, either in the eyes of her neighbors or in the sly grins of other people.

Kandov was terribly indignant.

As Rada passed the café, Stefchov bent over and whispered something to Merdevendjiev with an evil smile on his lips. The cantor turned, looked after the girl, and winked slyly. The whisper was passed on and called forth malicious grins. But Stefchov's sense of triumph was not complete with this; he ironically quoted the well-known verse of the revolutionary song, "Where art thou now, O people's love, so faithful?" and coughed rudely.

Many grasped what he was driving at and looked at each other significantly. Stefchov had cleverly hinted at a topic for conversation. Sneering jokes and sarcastic remarks now rained down on the unfortunate girl.

Kandov, who had listened patiently so far, could no longer restrain himself. "Who are you aiming all these witticisms at? Is it Rada Gospozhina?" he asked Stefchov. Silence fell in the cafe.

"What's that to you? Suppose they are meant for Rada Gospozhina, what then?" answered Stefchov stubbornly.

"If you're speaking of her, then I say you are a slanderer and a cad!" cried the student rising to his feet, choking with rage.

"Whether I'm a cad or you are is for the public to say. As to slandering Rada Gospozhina, you must excuse me. Even dogs will tell you. . . . Take my advice and don't trouble yourself to defend a girl who has disgraced herself. Don't be so ridiculously chivalrous."

Kandov flared up. He strode to the middle of the cafe and said, as he stood there pale and trembling, "You have rudely attacked a defenseless girl! Take back your words!"

"Prove to me that your girl didn't receive a visitor in secret a week ago. A girl who. . . ." Stefchov was unable to finish his sentence.

"That secret visitor was Boicho Ognyanov, her fiancé, you coward!" shouted Kandov and hit him in the face.

The sound of the blow rang through the café! Dazed by the blow Stefchov reeled back at first, then made a lunge at the student, who raised his cane. But the others intervened and separated them. The café buzzed with excitement. Inquisitive people crowded around the windows outside.

Stefchov rushed out of the café with flaming cheeks and foaming with rage, to go straight to the konak, firmly resolved this time to revenge himself on Kandov and on Rada. He would make the bey question them both about Ognyanov. Even if the student managed to clear himself with denials, the girl would be totally disgraced; it was she who was the cause of the fight that day.

But in the street his servant met him and told him that the doctor from Plovdiv had arrived; he had been summoned for Lalka, who was seriously ill. So Stefchov set out for his home.

chapter 18

Kandov

The words which accompanied Kandov's blow astounded everybody, Stefchov most of all. To him they were a bolt from the blue. But the hot-headed student's imprudence had no evil consequences for him.

Moreover, the shrewder men present realized that Kandov's outburst went deeper than mere chivalry. That unrestrained and passionate fury which had carried him away—for the sake of a complete stranger at that—was unnatural unless it had other, more personal grounds. Because of his outburst and other symptoms, always perceptible to an attentive observer, it was clear to them that Kandov himself was not insensible towards Rada. Nor were they wrong. Kandov was in love with Rada.

How had it all come about? Quite simply. The young student was one of those passionate people who only find a purpose in life if they have an ideal to worship. People like him can only find fulfillment through passionate attachments.

A young and hot-headed idealist, Kandov had returned to Bulgaria entirely carried away by those extreme theories and principles which are high-minded in an honest soul, and hideous in a corrupt creature. His first contact with life shook the profound convictions of his faith. He saw the ground was totally alien to it here, and he could no longer worship an idol with feet of clay. So he sought for a new one—it was ready to hand—in the person of Bulgaria. But another divinity had found a place in his heart before he saw Bulgaria: he had seen Rada.

This had occurred soon after Ognyanov's flight from Byala Cherkva last year. The feeling, slight at first, quickly took root and grew in his heart; it absorbed him entirely; it became a passion. Little by little Kandov became estranged from his family and friends and their interests; he avoided company and fell into a dreamy apathy which left him only when he saw Rada. This had gone on until spring, when he had started out of his torpor one day and grown indignant at himself. His passion seemed vile to him—treacherous to Ognyanov, his friend; criminal with regard to Bulgaria, to whom he was duty-bound to consecrate himself.

He grew frightened at himself and hastened to suppress the demonic emotion within him and purge it before it was too late. He felt that only another emotion, more terrible, more demonic still could save him and make a man of him. So he decided to throw himself heart and soul into the struggle that was in preparation, into its perils and uncertainties, to hurl himself into its storm-tossed, deafening waters, to absorb the heated atmosphere of mad fervor and revolutionary turmoil and get drunk on it. He wanted to cast out Lucifer by Beelzebub.

It was at this point that we saw him make his unexpected appearance at Sokolov's, with the request to be accepted as a member of the committee, and the proposal to kill Stefchov. And it was the murder of the traitor, the murder itself—something new for him and accompanied by terrible conflicts, but a noble act in this case—that attracted him the most. He depended on that murder; it was the purgatory through which his soul would pass to emerge renewed and refreshed. The blow that brought death to the traitor would bring it to another terrible tormentor in his own soul, to the enchanting image of Rada. Yes, the murder first, the baptism in blood and the revolution—a terrible but decisive step towards salvation.

From the moment this idea was born in his troubled soul, before speaking to the president about it, he played with it for several nights, with all the passion of a mother fondling her adored child. In his endless sleepless nights he planned Stefchov's destruction and he was entirely absorbed in his ardent plans, which so gripped his spirit that they allowed of no other feeling, no other interest. Kandov thought of Raskolnikov: Dostoievsky's hero had also premeditated the murder of the old woman, the usurer, for the good of humanity, and yet he was so attractive, so touching! They were both in the same boat. This coincidence encouraged and enchanted Kandov. Raskolnikov now appeared to him as a radiant and encouraging example, as an ideal. He even adopted the method Raskolnikov had used to murder the old woman: he would sew a piece of string to the lining of his coat below the armhole, so that he could hang an axe there by its head. And no one would know that he was carrying a murderous weapon.

Fortunately or unfortunately, this was postponed and Kandov's plan came tumbling down like a house of cards. He was in despair. But the revolution lay before him, ominous and fiery like an apocalyptic beast, and that somewhat consoled him for his misfortune. Yet the conflict in his soul continued and grew fiercer. In spite of all the passion with which he had devoted himself to the cause of the revolution, the thought of Rada never left him. Her image rose up treacherously before him, behind that of his country; it lay deeper within him, it was sure of itself and looked with pity upon the passing guest that had entered the home it reigned over.

If only his mind could nourish and house both these attachments, the one imposed upon him by his mind and will, the other by nature! If only he could balance them, bring them into agreement and weaken one by means of the other! He wondered how Ognyanov could love both Bulgaria and Rada with equal passion, be so divided, yet so good and strong, feel so calm and even happy! What a nature was his, large-hearted and generous, breathing so easily under the burden of two great passions that harmonized and gave him added manliness!

How he envied Merdevendjiev's comic little passion, which the mere roar of a bear had cured.

Today, when he had struck Stefchov, Kandov had felt that his was an oddly embarrassing position. He had devoted himself to Bulgaria, and had fallen in love with Rada. And by the very nature of things he had found a rival in Ognyanov, who thought as he did on the revolution. The cause united them; passion separated them.

In his gallant wrath, while punishing the insult to Rada's honor, he was revenging Ognyanov too! A terrible contradiction! But the struggle, though cruel, was not a long one. Victory went to the heart! In other words nature triumphed over the world of the spirit. Kandov gave himself over entirely to his new love.

Having suddenly stepped from the university lecture room into the sea of life, he was like one who has fallen from heaven. A guileless soul, whose heart had not been touched by the trials of life, he found himself unprepared to meet them. The first one his evil fate sent him was this love. He gave himself up to it as wholly as he had formerly devoted himself to the ideals of Socialism. The only difference was that there the mind was in action, while here it was the stubborn heart, to whose aid neither reason, nor experience, nor the wisdom of all the philosophers can come.

Whether this passion would be answered or not was quite another matter; that is, would Kandov find a happiness as great as his passion, or would the bitterest disappointment, the fiercest sufferings poison his soul? No lover has ever asked himself that question. Had he done so, he would have been no lover. There are no question marks in the grammar of love. Furthermore, Rada's heart was not free, and he knew it. But he could not see it and was still consumed by his love. Love is blind. And the Greeks knew what they were about when they so often depicted its winged god blindfolded.

As long as Rada believed Ognyanov dead she had been so crushed by her woe that it had not occurred to her to think anything of the student's visits, which in any case, were infrequent at that time. Little by little they grew more frequent, as did his apparently chance meetings with her. Time passed and things went on. Finally her woman's instinct noticed that the student was not unattracted to her. Each time she saw him the symptoms of his newborn feeling became more obvious as it grew.

At first Rada was astonished and disturbed; then she pretended not to notice anything—who knows, it may even have flattered her self-conceit. At last she was startled by the growing strength of his warm attachment. Yet, shy as she was, she did not have the courage to check it abruptly or to close the door to her admirer, who was as tactful as he was sincere. This disarmed her entirely. Only people like Stefchov could arouse enough courage in her to strike them. Rada did not know what to do.

So she went on being amiable to Kandov as a friend of Boicho's and as a man of noble mind. Poor child, she thought that she would ease his longing, the strength of which she never suspected, by welcoming him affably, and she tried to cure him with the fire of her black eyes. A bad doctor. Neither she nor Kandov knew that the only saving cure for his kind of disease lay in separation. "Out of sight, out of mind," says the proverb.

chapter 19

a morning visit

After his altercation with Stefchov on the previous day, Kandov went home very much disturbed. He shut himself up in his room and spent the rest of the day reading the same book. He only stopped reading to mark certain places in pencil, then went on reading again.

He was completely absorbed in this occupation and did not even go down to lunch. When his mother called him, he answered that he had a headache. He ate nothing that evening either. He lay for hours on the window seat, deep in thought, his eyes fixed on the ceiling. When the stillness of night reigned over the town, he got up, sat down at his table and began to write a letter. This took him until midnight. Then he threw himself down on the window seat again, not to sleep but to dream. His candle burned until daylight. The first rays of the sun came into the room and fell on the dozing student's face. He started and opened his eyes, tired and sunken from his restless night. He went over to the table, re-read the letter, folded it, looked for an envelope, found none, and laid it down on the table.

"Now, or later?" he whispered, and stood a moment in thought.

"No, later let it be later. . . . When I see her." And he began feverishly to get ready to go out.

When he was out on the street he saw that it was still much too early. The sun still hung low over the horizon; the house in which Rada lived still cast its shadow on the house opposite. He knew from experience that when the shadow withdrew to the middle of the street, as far as the gutter, the young girl was in the habit of watering the garden. She was dressed at that time and it was not an improper hour for a visit. Kandov went up and down the street several times, looking first at the Lilov's wall—Rada lived there, in the room at the end of the garden—then at the shadow. It was dreadfully slow in retreating from the opposite wall, and the space up to the gutter was still in shade. So he would have to wait an hour or more before the sun fell on the middle of the street.

Kandov, his hands behind his back, went on with his walk; he turned into other streets, so as not to draw the attention of the passers-by, who were more frequent now. The sun was already pouring its bright light over the whole of Stara Planina, the hills above town, the tiled roofs of the houses, their white chimneys, and the windows that were turned to the east. The early-rising café-keepers had opened their cafes; the grocers in their aprons were sweeping the cobbles before their shops. The braid-makers were busy beating the braid on the stones near the fountains; people passed to and fro in the streets. There was animation and life, and the town hummed with its usual mixture of noises.

But Kandov noticed nothing of all this, neither the sun nor the noise, nor the passers-by, nor the town that had come to life around him. He saw, thought, awaited, one thing only—the shadow. It was approaching the boundary line, the channel which marked the limit of his tormenting and passionate emotions, of these minutes that seemed centuries to him. The shadow retreated to the gutter leaving the other half of the street in blazing sunlight. It seemed to Kandov that the sun had just risen. He set off towards Granny Lilovitsa's gate at a quick pace. He gazed intently at the old, cracked oak door, low and studded with nails whose big, flattened, rusty heads looked like stains on the wood. He knew just how many they were, and how many lines and cracks there were on the gate, and how it creaked, like an irritated dog, when it was opened. That gate was like a living creature, with eyes, ears and a voice. How painfully, how fearfully, yet how sweetly it spoke to his heart each time he went in! What a cold, disagreeable and sinister sound it emitted, like the klepalo's call to service for the dead, when it slammed behind him as he left.

Suddenly the gate opened. A simple Bulgarian peasant came out in baggy trousers and a hat. Kandov wanted to go up to him and ask about Rada, but he felt ashamed. He looked at this simple man with emotion, and even with a measure of envy. Then he resumed his pacing backwards and forwards. A short length of time went by. The gate opened again, and this time Kandov's heart began to beat.

Granny Lilovitsa and Rada came out together. They quickly set out up the street. It was only now that he heard the klepalo. "It's probably some kind of saint's day," he thought, "and they're both going to church." He stopped as if rooted to the spot, his eyes glued to the girl who was disappearing up the street. She had not seen him, for both as she emerged from the gate and as she walked quickly away, her eyes were fixed on the ground. He noticed involuntarily that she had put on her new black dress. The grey cotton apron with its design of white circles and leaves which she usually wore had been left behind. But how rosy her face was, somehow stern yet so enchanting!

For a long time the student awaited her return. An hour went by, and then another. He heard with annoyance that the klepalo was being struck from time to time, and its dry, resonant, impertinent sound irritated his nerves beyond endurance and made him quite desperate.

"What saint's day can it possibly be?" He kept asking himself angrily. "Where can she have gone with that dreadful old woman? What's this stupid klepalo for? What are these perpetual saint's days? People are too worried for saint's days. What do I need this saint's day for, this idolator's day?" Such were the exclamations wrung from his lips from time to time as he kept watch on the street. But Rada did not appear.

The sun had long since crossed the channel, taken over the second half of the street, and now shone full on the wall of Granny Lilovitsa's house. Passers-by came and went constantly in the street, but neither Rada nor the old woman was among them. Yet the klepalo went on with its beating.

"What can this confounded saint's day be?" the student swore angrily again.

But he didn't even want to find out. The first man he asked could have told him. What would be the point? He had long since lost count of the days, never noticed the time. Spring was at the height of its splendor, but he never noticed the spring. What use indeed did he have for that spring, so abominably lovely, so treacherously delightful, when his mind was such a sea of suffering! Nature's appearance even seemed outrageous to him, as if she were making fun of him. And he spat indignantly at something. Probably at nature.

But his impatient exclamations were soon to be answered.

chapter 20

Kandov's bewilderment grows

From the street opposite came the shrill monotonous chanting of a children's choir. These voices sang the bass to another, higher, older voice which was quavering out a long-drawn church chant. This strange concert was approaching sounding increasingly loud. Almost immediately a file of children appeared, carrying lanterns and banners and long white candles with black bows on them; after them came a crowd of more children with Merdevendjiev, the cantor, followed by priests in their vestments. The scent of incense hung in the air. Lalka's funeral procession was approaching. The poor sufferer had died the night before.

Almost the whole town was following her bier. The death of this woman, cut down in her youth, had filled all hearts with grief. All hastened to bid her farewell and to honor with their presence her last journey—to the grave. Neither dislike of her father, nor hatred of her husband, stopped people. Lalka had been very lovable, gentle and kindhearted, and her memory drove all other harsh worldly feelings from people's minds. Her brokenhearted father spared no expense to make her funeral magnificent and solemn and the immense crowd made it still more solemn and moving. But what had done most to draw the world was the rumor about the cause of her illness and death, which her sister had been unable to keep to herself, for before her death Lalka had confided everything to Aunt Ghinka. The poor girl's fate drew tears to the eyes of all the women, and even men who were total strangers to her family wept. All the young men had come, and foremost were the members of the committee, deeply moved and sorrowful. They walked behind the bier.

When the procession reached the square where Kandov was standing like a post, the bier was laid down for prayers to be read, and it was then he saw the dead woman. He suddenly recognized Lalka.

She lay there calm and still, her long lashes resting on her cheeks as if she were asleep. Her face, now marble white, was barely distinguishable from the down pillow on which it lay; her small figure was lost under the piles of wreaths and spring nosegays, the farewell gifts of the brides and young married women. There was a bunch of rare white roses at each shoulder, and some had been put in her hair. She had planted these roses with her own hands. Now those hands, white and exquisite like those of a marble statue, lay crossed on her silk wedding-dress, and an icon representing the Assumption of the Virgin had been placed upon her sunken breast. The heavy scent of flowers mingled with that of the Smyrna incense, filling the air and bemusing the feelings.

As soon as the bier was set down the mother threw herself upon her daughter with a heart-rendering cry, clasped her in her arms and buried her face in the flowers like one beside herself. The words of a mother's passionate, unreasoning love and despair burst forth. those words that pierce the heart with icy horror and cause one's hair to stand on end. Each word is a piece torn from the heart, each cry a sea of bitter, never-ending pain. Weeping and sobbing arose on all sides; family and strangers, their faces wet with tears, pressed handkerchiefs to their mouths to keep from crying out loud. But Aunt Ghinka, lovely in her mourning, wept unrestrainedly; her father, supported on either side, shook his white head, heart-broken. Stefchov stood with bared head beside the bier, his handkerchief pressed to his eyes. But there were no tears in them, though instead of its usual ruddy hue, his face was pale. He looked about him in bewilderment, like one who sees nothing.

Not far away Sokolov's fair head rose above the shoulders of the crowd. His eyes were fixed on Lalka's dead face: he seemed to be absorbing the vision of the victim whom he had loved so passionately, and who had loved him. Alas, they could have been so happy! But fate had decreed otherwise! Suddenly he saw Stefchov near him. Their eyes met. With a baleful look Sokolov said to him aloud, "It was your loathsome treachery that killed her, sir! You shall answer for her death first to me, then to God!"

The prayer came to an end. The mother's voice rose in the air again. The bier was lifted and the procession moved on. Kandov joined the crowd almost mechanically. His face retained its usual calm. The moving scene he had just witnessed had not touched him in the least. On the contrary a fierce kind of joy lit up his face; he realized that as Lalka's friend Rada would be here, and he would see her. That was the only thought which the endless gloomy funeral procession aroused in him. He looked around here and there among the crowd of women, but he did not see Rada; he gazed searchingly at each black dress, each lovely head. But he did not recognize Rada in any of them. He stood aside to let the rest of the women pass by, but his eagle eye searched vainly through the moving crowd which flowed past him like a stream.

Suddenly he caught sight of Granny Lilovitsa and looked for Rada beside her. But Rada wasn't there! His heart missed a beat. What! Rada absent from the funeral of Lalka, her friend? Impossible, quite impossible! And he went stumbling through the crowd searching for her, but found her nowhere. What! Rada wasn't there! Where was she then? She had gone out with Granny Lilovitsa; where had the old woman left her all this time, alone at such a time? What did Rada have to do that was more important than following her best friend to the grave? Or was she here, although he could not see her, because his eyes were blinded? Yet he did see the old woman! Should he go and ask her? That was madness, it would be improper! The poor student never realized that his own behavior, his search among the sad procession, was in itself improper and had attracted attention.

As the procession turned into one of the narrow streets, it was met by the shrill notes of a clarinet and the beating of a drum; a merry dance was in progress here. The gaiety seemed suddenly ugly and sacrilegious in the face of such sorrow. Irritation and wrath appeared on many faces in the procession. But the music immediately stopped, and the dancers scattered and disappeared as if by magic. Silence reigned once more, and only the funeral chanting of Merdevendjiev and the children could be heard in the street.

Kandov, who was walking at the end of the procession, turned at the sound of noisy steps. He saw the editor and several others who had left the dance to join the procession. The editor was drunk, his fez was set at a jaunty angle and he looked agitated. He and his friends were hurrying to catch up with the last of the procession.

Kandov heard Bezportev's hoarse voice saying as he hurried, "Come on, don't be asses, come and kiss her hand and say 'Go with God, sister! The heavenly Kingdom be yours!' For whosoever dies for the people lives forever! You see, you geese? If you're drunk, know yourselves. And when I tell you to bow your noodles, do it. This was a saintly soul. Tell me, how many such are there on earth? But the traitors are not to be numbered; they are as the sands of the sea. But you've never seen the sea, so don't be asses, and do as you're told."

Just as he was finishing this tirade, the editor caught sight of Rachko, who passed them at a trot, carrying something to the church. He cried to the man in an imperative voice:

"Hey, there, just wait a moment! I want to ask you something. There, that's Stefchov's spy! Death to such heathen!" he added to his friends. Rachko saw the editor's angry face and went off at a run down a side street.

"Hold on to him! Let's ask him what right he has to foul the street with his stinking name!" cried Bezportev, and they all dashed after the unfortunate Rachko who, small and lithe as he was, flew along like a feather and had a good lead on his drunken pursuers. He and they soon disappeared down another turning.

Kandov saw all this absently and impassively. He bowed his head and followed the procession unconsciously. Soon he entered the church with it.

chapter 21

the funeral

The crowd which had grown like a stream in the streets literally filled the church. The bier, set down on the square marble slab with a two headed eagle carved on it, opposite the bishop's throne, was the center around which the people swarmed with lighted candles in their hands.

The service began with solemn prayers; clouds of blue smoke from the incense rose to the dome. The big candelabra at the altar were bright with candles, the chandeliers were lighted too; the church was ablaze with light. This brilliance did something to console Lalka's sorrowing family.

For the same purpose schoolmaster Kliment had been asked to give an oration. As a seminarian he had the gift of eloquence, and quotations from the Bible at his fingertips. But as he felt unwell he had declined. So Frangov was asked to speak in his stead. After a slight hesitation he accepted and took his stand on the second step of the bishop's throne. The priests interrupted their chanting and the church grew still.

Deeply moved, his eyes fixed on the dead woman, he began in a ringing, though trembling voice: "Brothers and sisters!"

But he was forced to interrupt his speech at once. Something untoward was happening at the doors. The crowd there began to murmur and stir apprehensively, bewildered whispers were heard, then frightened voices. Apprehension spread like wildfire and soon reached the front rows around the dead woman's bier. Panic and chaos took over.

"They're coming!" cried some.

"Oh, dear Lord, they're coming!" shrieked voices of women from their part of the church.

"Who's coming?" asked the men in the nave.

"The Turks! The Turks!"

The panic spread; shrieking and wailing and a confusion of voices filled the temple of God. The people scattered like a frightened flock without knowing where to hide. A big group formed round Chorbadji Yordan and Stefchov. As they were influential with the Turks everyone hoped to find protection near them, and to be spared along with them. But the greater part of the people ran hither and thither in the church, shrieking in mad fear. The young women screamed and fainted, and no one helped them; several old women dropped down on the altar steps and were trampled on. Wild fear was visible on all faces; many were even whiter and more deathly than Lalka's.

Kandov alone stood there quite unmoved by all that was going on around him. With clasped hands he stood motionless beside the bier, looking sadly at the dead woman.

Just then Sokolov's voice rose above the din. "Don't be afraid, there's nothing to be afraid of!" When the panic began he had gone up to the gallery to look out the window and see what was happening in the square outside. But he saw nothing disturbing there. There were no Turks—on the contrary, he saw the Editor and his friends coming in at the gate. He had grown hoarse with shouting to the people to quiet them, but his voice could not be heard above the tumult.

Other voices were heard too. "Keep quiet, you people; there's nothing to be afraid of!"

"Who frightened us?" cried another. "Who's been deceiving people?"

Just then the Editor and his friends came in quite breathless, and began to cross themselves. They never even suspected that they had caused the panic. For in his fear of them Rachko had dashed into the church, and when some of the old women asked him why he was running he had answered, "They're coming!"

"Who are coming?"

"The Kapassuz* and the others, lots and lots of them!" That was quite enough for the population which had been living in fear of Turkish massacres for months. And panic followed.

* The Turkish word Kapassuz, of which Bezportev (doorless) is a literal translation, is another name for Turks when used in the plural.

chapter 22

philosophy and two sparrows

Kandov did not wait for the end of the funeral service, but went out into the street again. Strange! He felt somewhat better.

The sight of death inevitably calms any emotion connected with earthly interests; the sight of mortal remains weakens the soul's dependence on this world. The cares, the ardent affections, the passions, the aspirations of life pale and grow spectral and comical when faced with eternity.

"There now, this Lalka is dead; today she's a corpse, tomorrow she'll be dust. How very white she was! Quite dreadful. She is dead, dead! And Rada wasn't there! Well, what of Rada? Strange how that girl has blinded me. Whoever sees me will say I'm mad. How do I know I'm not? What about? About her. What is she, anyway, and why these endless torments of mine, this sleeplessness? Yes, and why all this? For a woman, for another Lalka, who will die as she has done, to become a corpse and dust. I wonder if I would still love her if I saw her on such a bier being taken to the graveyard to feed the worms there. What folly! How ignoble! Or is it? Anyhow, what is this Rada, this thing, this nothing, a nothing which fills all my being and all the world, and heaven, and hell? What is she? A skeleton clothed in foul, raw flesh. An interminable heap of bones, flesh, blood, sinews, fibers, nerves, vessels, glands, tissues, cartilage, and stench, which is called Rada, and which will rot tomorrow and turn to pus and dust. Ugh! And I'm in love with all that! Destroying myself for it! My all-powerful spirit, my divine reason, my boundless thoughts have attached themselves to this foolish piece of mortality, and cling to this cobweb! Terrible, mad! How was it I didn't come to my senses before, didn't say to myself: Kandov, your vocation is another and a greater one than to sigh for a foolish petticoat? Such wide horizons lie open before me; two worlds, both of them wonderful and tremendous, open their arms to me—science and my country. And what life there is there, what exploits, glory and striving, and wonders too! Yet I don't see them. I see nothing but this pitiful creature, whose existence on earth I would never have suspected, if I had not seen her, any more than she herself realizes why she exits. Shame, shame, shame! I had to see this Lalka to realize what a nonentity has chained up my spirit. Now it awakes like an eagle, flaps its wings and spreads them to take flight and soar up freely into boundless space. Oh, how happy I am!"

And Kandov went on walking, deep in these refreshing thoughts. He felt that a weight had been lifted from his shoulders. He smiled triumphantly now, smiled and wondered how pitifully, how foolishly, this struggle in his spirit had come to an end. He had cast Rada out, as one throws a useless piece of broken crockery out the window. Rada's image lay so far, far away, in misty eternity, pale, lifeless and cloudy, like a dream shattered by sudden awakening.

He felt refreshed and renewed! The veil had fallen from his eyes, and he saw clearly, realized everything, was interested in all that surrounded him and took part in the petty affairs of life. He bowed amiably as never before, to all who met him, talked to Pavlaki Nedev about his rose-field, asked what last year's pick had been, and how many flasks of attar of roses he thought he would have this year. He bought a pound of cherries from a grocer and went home gaily—as gay as if he had been to a wedding, not a funeral.

As he was passing by a garden wall, pearly blossoms rained down on his head. He raised his eyes and saw that they came from the plum tree whose branches stretched out over the street. The blossoms were falling from a branch on which a couple of sparrows were billing and playing.

Kandov stood there as if turned to stone. At the sight of this love scene, all his eloquence vanished like a puff of smoke.

He dropped his handkerchief with the cherries and clapping a hand to his brow stood there bemused. "You're ill, you're ill, my boy!" he whispered to himself hopelessly. "You're ill, brother, seek a remedy for your head, brother Werther." And he set off again, unconscious of what he was doing.

"Yes, a remedy, a radical remedy!" he kept repeating. "But what? If it were a disease of the body. . . . But this is a wound of the spirit. Not to be cauterized with a red hot iron. What? Should I consult the doctor from Plovdiv? Doctors do not just treat bodily ills, they treat the spirit too. That's obvious, as plain as day. A pity there are no nerve specialists here. For I'm crazy, yes, crazy. It's all one, let's try him. I might get some advice, who knows? It might be useful. Yes, I'd better take advantage of his presence. I won't lose anything. But there's another problem. I'll have to confess my trouble to the doctor. I'll be ridiculous. No, that's impossible. I must find another way." And he set out for the house at which the doctor from Plovdiv was staying.

chapter 23

the remedy

When he stopped at the doctor's door, Kandov wiped the sweat from his face and knocked. *"Entrez!"* someone cried from within.

He went in. Before him stood the doctor, a man of about forty, tall, but slightly built, with a pale and sunken face, sparse whiskers and a slyly ironic expression in his eyes. He was in his shirtsleeves, and was packing his things in a bag, obviously getting ready to leave. He had closed Lalka's eyes and had nothing more to do here. Kandov introduced himself.

"Sit down, sir," said the doctor politely. "This room is rather untidy, but you'll forgive me."

The polite welcome encouraged the student. "Excuse me for disturbing you, doctor, but I've only come for a few minutes."

"Pooh, when a doctor receives patients, he's never disturbed; a doctor without patients cannot be cheerful, anymore than a sick man without health." And with this sinister joke he cast a questioning look at the thin, melancholy face of his visitor. "How do you feel?"

"Quite well, thank you," answered the student with a forced smile. "I only came to ask your advice about someone else."

"Does he live here?

"Yes, he does, but. . . ."

"Then why don't you bring him here? There's not much time, you know."

Kandov felt embarrassed. "How am I to put it, doctor? I came to consult you on a literary matter, rather." The doctor looked at him in astonishment.

"You can enlighten me on a matter of psychology which is causing me great difficulty. It's within the province of medicine." The doctor waited expectantly.

"I'm writing a novel," said Kandov stressing every word.

"So, you're a writer?"

"No, I'm trying. . . . I've begun a novel. . . . The hero is very much in love, violently, madly, hopelessly in love, with a person who loves someone else, and this passion is driving him to suicide. . . ."

"There's a German novel I read in Vienna once," remarked the doctor, scratching his head to stimulate his memory. "It told of a similar love."

"Goethe's *Werther?*" asked the student eagerly.

"Yes, a novel by Goethe," the doctor conceded. "He committed suicide, didn't he?"

"Yes, but I want you to save my hero."

"Better kill him off and put an end to his misery. Do as we doctors do with our patients, it's best." The doctor accompanied his words with another smile, as sinister as before, which betrayed the heartlessness typical of doctors, who are accustomed to looking unmoved upon the sufferings and death of their patients.

Kandov went white. "No, that would be a bad example for the readers. Suicide is infectious too."

"Of what nationality is your hero?"

"He's a Bulgarian."

"A Bulgarian? Why, the Bulgarians don't suffer from *amour désespéré*. Their hearts are wrapped up in a buffalo's hide. You know what *amour désespéré* is, don't you? Desperate love."

"Yes, desperate love," remarked the student dully.

"But I don't know of any Bulgarian's having died of a great love. A young man hanged himself some time ago, but that was because the Jew went bankrupt, and he lost his money."

"But my hero, as I told you, doctor. . . ."

"Yes, he's an exception, I understand," the doctor interrupted him, "but as he's a Bulgarian we can't let him commit suicide, it wouldn't be true to life. He must suffer." And the doctor smiled again, an unpleasant smile, looking at his watch.

Kandov noticed his impatience. He said quickly, "That's just why I came to you for advice, doctor. The development of the plot requires my hero to live, in order to do other things. But to do them I want to cure him of this terrible passion first, which paralyzes and destroys him. How can that be done in the most natural, the most probable way?"

The doctor was staring curiously and attentively at Kandov; it was the first time in his experience he had had such a consultation. He was trying to read the eyes and face of his visitor, as if to discover another meaning in his words. The look confused the student, and he blushed slowly and painfully. His confusion grew as he saw an ironical grin playing on the doctor's thin and bloodless lips. "I see. I see. You're looking for a cure for one of the most persistent of psychological diseases."

"Yes."

"They do exist, but unfortunately their action is not as certain as that of quinine against fever, Mr. Kandov." And the doctor again fixed his gaze on Kandov.

"Tell me the most certain, doctor."

"First of all I would recommend an old wives' cure: find the herb which the old women call the hated herb—I've forgotten its Latin name. Boil it on a Friday night, but in a pot that's never been heated before, and pour it over your hero when he's asleep. He'll take a dislike to his lady-love from that very hour." The doctor laughed.

Kandov frowned. "Are you telling me this in earnest, doctor?"

"Won't that do?" the doctor went on laughing. "Then I would advise you to have him drink of the waters of Lethe, and he will forget. You know the river Lethe?" Kandov's face flushed at the joke and the question, both equally impertinent and out of place.

"Unfortunately Lethe has long since run dry," added the doctor. Kandov got up to go.

The doctor waved a hand to restrain him and assumed a serious air. "Very well, then listen, if your man wants to fall out of love with his beloved, have him fall in love with another, just as blindly and madly."

Kandov shook his head. "That would be out of the frying pan into the fire."

"True, true," said the doctor grinning. "There is another cure: make him lead a dissolute life. Let him drown his soul and feelings in the intoxications of lust. Let him brutalize himself and forget."

Kandov frowned in disgust. "I need him to do great things afterwards. Furthermore my hero is of a noble nature, incapable of making a beast of himself."

"Then that's another matter. There's only one cure left, since your man is a delicate gentleman. But it's a palliative—you know what a palliative is, don't you?" The student frowned again, but nodded.

"Send him away from his beloved; send him on a journey for a year or two, somewhere far away, very far away. Let him go to Brazil, for instance, or let him travel in the Arctic Ocean and stay ice-bound for nine months and eat nothing but whale blubber. Or if you think he might catch cold there, or get scurvy, send him to the Sahara and make him king of a black tribe, which he will subject to his will. . . ."

And having sketched all these plans, peppering them well with jokes and nonsense, the doctor rose to his feet. So did Kandov. "Thank you, doctor. I shall make use of your advice," and he put out his hand to take leave.

"Good-bye. I'm glad you will, I wish your sick gentleman good health and long life, and yourself too."

But when Kandov reached the door he said to him seriously, "Pay for the advice, sir. That's what we doctors live by."

Kandov looked at him, startled. But he put his hand in his waistcoat pocket at once, drew out a rouble and put it down on the table. Then he went out quickly.

"That young fool," said the doctor to himself, carefully slipping the rouble into his purse, "thinks he's outfoxed me. I realized from his very first words that he wanted a cure for himself. I'm ready to bet that he's up to his ears in love, and dreams of suicide. The *Dummstein!*" And he went on with his packing.

"That clown," thought Kandov as he went out onto the street, "did say one bright thing among all his nonsense. He's right; it's only separation, only distance that will save me. I must go to a quite different place, a different zone, another part of the earth, where there is nothing, nothing to remind me of her. Yes, I remember now; they do recommend distance in such cases. Flight! And that's what will take me to the banks of the river that Viennese babbler spoke of. Run, Kandov, run! To Moscow, to Moscow!"

Inspired by this thought and delighted at the prospect of salvation, Kandov began to hum the refrain of a popular Russian song:

> Ah, Moscow, Moscow, Moscow!
> Head of Gold!
> Ah, Moscow, Moscow, Moscow!
> Head of Gold,
> White of stone. . . .

He went home quickly, told his family that he was leaving for Moscow next day to continue his studies, and began to get his things together with feverish haste. He packed his bag the same evening, made up a small bundle, and that night he slept deeply and soundly, for the first time in many days.

In the morning he awoke refreshed and cheerful. To prevent himself from thinking of Rada, he concentrated on his journey, the new life that he was going to live in the city of white stone. So he hummed enthusiastically:

Away from you I am unhappy,
Moscow, Moscow, my native town.
Where flames amid the forest of belfries
The greatness of the Rusian land.

The horse that was to take him across the Balkan range was brought out. "To Moscow! To Moscow!" he said to himself, putting some forgotten books into his bag. As he bent over by the window he mechanically looked out onto the street, and saw Granny Lilovitsa with another old woman. He flinched, but listened in spite of himself to what they were saying.

"So you're alone again, Granny Lilovitsa, are you?"

"Eh, what's to be done? I saw Rada off to Klissoura yesterday. My heart fairly broke when I saw her set out so sorrowful. Eh, God have mercy on her!" Kandov stood there thunderstruck.

An hour later he set out. He set out . . . for Klissoura.

That same day Nikolai Nedkovich and Frangov, surprised at the extraordinary change they had noticed in the student, went to his house to see him, but learned that he had left for Klissoura, "to look up some relations of his."

Disorder still reigned in his room; the open bag lay on the ground; things were strewn about. On the table lay a pile of Russian books. The visitors saw by their titles that they were socialist and anarchist publications, printed in London and Geneva. But the one on top was a novel, *Crime and Punishment* by Dostoievsky. Another novel lay open on the table, *The Sufferings of Young Werther*. In it there were lines and whole pages marked with red pencil.

These works indicated the resting-places which Kandov's mind had found in the mournful desert of psychological aberration. Yes, and there was a half-open letter for Rada. Then everything became clear to the visitors. Nedkovich was a tactful man, so he put the letter in his wallet, so that it would not fall into other, less delicate hands.

chapter 24

a storm before the storm

Rada had set out for Klissoura unexpectedly and suddenly. The morning when Kandov was walking about in front of her gate, a trusted man from Klissoura who was returning from K. in his cart, had come to tell her that Boicho had asked him to fetch her on his way and drive her over to Klissoura. As soon as she received this news, for which she had been hoping, she hastened to take her tearful farewell of her friend Lalka, who had died in the night.

She had long been barred access to Lalka and to Yordan's family. But her appearance at the deathbed surprised no one, nor did it arouse indignation. She was Lalka's friend and that was enough. Moreover no one had the right to deprive the dead of a farewell. Where death has entered the key falls from the door; old and young, friends and enemies, are equally welcome on the threshold of eternity. The family were touched, and moved aside to make way for her. As Rada knelt before Lalka, put her arms around her, and kissed her forehead, bathing it in tears and crying, "Oh, little sister, Oh, Lalka, what have you done?" the whole family burst into desperate wailing, and Rada herself was carried out in a dead faint.

Rada went to stay with Mrs. Mouratliiska who had come to Klissoura not long ago and who had gladly acceded to Ognyanov's request to give the homeless girl her hospitality.

The windows of the house faced north, looking out over the whole of Klissoura, its valley, and Stara Planina. The giant peak of Ribaritsa (known as Vezhen in these parts), still wearing its winter crown, sloped abruptly down, and at its foot lay the little town, here and there on its green flanks the flocks of the Wallachian nomads were scattered, and the red roofs of their huts could be seen from afar. To the east the town was surrounded by tall, hollowed-out banks and crumbling screes, bare in some places, elsewhere covered with vineyards and rose-fields. A winding path climbed the hill and led into the gully beyond; this was Zli Dol, where the road to the Strema Valley runs. Hills closed Klissoura in on the other sides too; it lay nestling in a deep valley, sunk in greenery and orchards and rose-fields which filled the air with their scent. Sad and shut-in in the winter, without any view, it was now a lovely spot, full of shade, freshness and fragrance.

Kandov had arrived in Klissoura the day before, that is the day after Rada, and had gone to stay in the home of a relative of his, a plausible pretext to be near Rada. He went to see her the very same day and found her in tears and grieving over Lalka's death. He realized that his visit was inconsiderate under such circumstances, but it afforded him relief. He even felt happy at having seen her.

Today Kandov had gone to see her again, rather early. He found her still more crushed and depressed by her grief for Lalka on the one hand, and by the rumor that an insurrection was about to break out in Koprivshtitsa on the other, as well as by her total ignorance of what Boicho was doing and where he was.

"Tell me, Mr. Kandov, what is happening?" she asked eagerly.

"There's talk of an insurrection," Kandov answered drily.

"What are they going to do now, goodness me? And Boicho's not here, not a trace of him." Kandov was looking absent-mindedly out of the window at a point somewhere on Ribaritsa.

"What do you think about it, Mr. Kandov?" asked Rada impatiently.

"I?"

"Yes."

"About the insurrection?"

"About the insurrection."

He replied unconcernedly, without turning round, "An insurrection's an insurrection! They'll fight, they'll shoot, they'll cut each other's throats—to free Bulgaria."

"What about Klissoura?"

"Perhaps Klissoura too. . . . Anyway, it's all the same."

"What do you mean, all the same? What about you?"

"It's all the same about me too." Kandov answered absently, as if he were being asked about the customs of New Zealand. But beneath that absent air, beneath that cold indifference to the events which were to decide Bulgaria's fate, black despair lay hidden. However, neither he nor Rada realized this.

"What are you thinking of doing, now that there are going to be insurrections everywhere?" asked Rada.

"Whatever has to be done."

"What do you mean by whatever has to be done? Aren't you going to fight?"

"What can I do, Rada? Only one thing, die!" answered Kandov gloomily. Three soft taps sounded on the door.

Ognyanov came in, dressed as a peasant, tired and dusty. He was returning from Panagyourishté where he had attended the general assembly at Mechka, at which the date of the insurrection had been decided—the first of May. Now he was hurrying to Byala Cherkva to take the last steps in the preparations, in the short time that was left him, and to raise the banner in Byala Cherkva on the appointed day. He passed through Klissoura to bid Rada farewell. But he had barely reached the house on the outskirts, where he usually stayed, that he found a letter from Byala Cherkva and set out hurriedly to see Rada without stopping to look up anyone.

He stood still and cast a cold and contemptuous glance at Kandov, who remained standing calmly at the window. Rada babbled a few words to express her joy, but when she saw the alteration in Ognyanov's face she stood there confounded.

"Excuse me for interrupting your conversation so early," said Ognyanov, with a bitter smile on his pale face. It was only then that he looked at Rada.

"What's the matter, Boicho?" she asked in a breathless voice and moved towards him.

"No more pretenses!" said Ognyanov coldly. She ran forward to embrace him. He drew back.

"To cut it short, spare me your tenderness . . ." and turning to Kandov he said angrily, "Mr. Kandov, I don't know how to thank you for coming all the distance from Byala Cherkva in answer to the invitation. . . ." His words were choked back by spite. Kandov turned from the window.

"What invitation?" he asked drily.

"What's all this about, Boicho?" asked Rada in amazement. "Mr. Kandov has come to see his relative. . . . He. . . ." She stopped and burst into tears.

It was the first time she had been forced to tell a lie, a fatal lie, and much against her will. At her short interview with Boicho in Byala Cherkva she had not had the time, nor had she thought of telling him about the strange courtship of Kandov, whom she had not ventured to send about his business. And now Ognyanov had found him with her, at this early hour too. Probably some talk about his visits had reached Boicho's ears, and now this dreadful chance had come to confirm his suspicions before she had had time to dispel them.

Rada hoped that Kandov himself would explain things and extricate her from the difficult situation, but he was silent.

"Kandov, suppose you tell me a likely story too; it'll amuse me," said Ognyanov acidly, casting a look of disdain at his rival.

"I have nothing to tell you; I am waiting to see what you have to say," answered the student coolly.

"That's dastardly!" shouted Ognyanov, looking at both of them.

Kandov went whiter still. His wounded pride tore him out of his gloomy apathy. "Ognyanov!" he cried.

"Shout loud, frighten me!" returned Boicho in the same tone. He was trembling with rage.

Rada rushed towards him, fearing that he would do harm. She knew the unrestrained wildness of his nature. "O God, Boicho! What are you doing! Let me explain!" she cried through her tears.

Ognyanov shot a scathing glance at her. "There's no need, Rada, don't humiliate yourself by shedding tears. And I, fool that I was, believed that I had found innocence itself. . . . The love I've lavished! I threw my heart into the street. . . . How blind I was!"

"Boicho!" cried Rada, sobbing in despair.

"Stop! Everything is over between us. The veil has fallen from my eyes. It was infatuation. . . . To suppose you loved me, a vagabond with nothing to look forward to but the stake and the gallows, while there are such chivalrous windbags about, such sage and promising cowards. . . . My God, what baseness there is in the world!" And he turned to go.

"Ognyanov! Take that back" cried Kandov following him.

Ognyanov stopped. "I repeat it: baseness and dastardliness! It was a loathsome misuse of a friend's trust. . . . Can you deny what is self-evident?" cried Ognyanov, looking furiously at the student.

"Either take your words back, or die!" roared Kandov, foaming with rage.

"Death? It can only frighten revolutionaries who want to save Bulgaria at a woman's apron-strings." Kandov hurled himself at Ognyanov, trying to hit him on the head. All the suffering and pain of many a long day turned into fury against the man indirectly responsible for them.

Ognyanov was strong. He threw Kandov back against the wall, and drew two revolvers out of his belt. "Not like porters; take this revolver." And he handed the student the weapon.

Almost crazed with fear and despair, Rada opened the window onto the street and cried out loudly to draw the attention of the passers-by. Just then the sound of bells burst out in a thunderous peal. Their echoing ring pierced the air. Ognyanov stood there motionless, still holding the revolver out to his rival. At the same time quick steps were heard outside, and the door was thrown open with a bang.

Several townspeople dashed in, all of them armed. "The insurrection's begun! Long live Bulgaria!" they cried.

"Where are the people gathering?" asked Boicho sharply.

"On the outskirts, at Zli-Dol, at Presveta. . . . Don't lose time!" And the rebels ran out, shouting, "Long live Bulgaria!" and singing, "The battle's beginning. . . ."

The bells continued ringing wildly. Ognyanov turned to Kandov. "I have things to see to now. . . . If I survive I'll give you satisfaction. For the time being keep the young lady company, so that she doesn't get frightened." And he went out quickly.

Crushed by this new misfortune, Rada fainted on the window seat. Mrs. Mouratliiska, who had heard her cry out, came hurrying in and tried to revive her.

Kandov listened to the bells like one in a trance. Then he bent down and picked up a crumpled letter that had fallen from Ognyanov's hand. He read the following lines:

"Little Count! It's no bad thing for a man to have friends: you couldn't buy little Kandov for a bag of gold. You should know that as long as he was here he never let Rada Gospozhina be lonely for a single hour, that true little dove and innocent angel of yours. Today little Kandov is setting out for Klissoura, for he received a little note from the little dove—its heart was breaking for you, so it sent for him to comfort it. . . . Much good may Rada do you, and your friend too. Lucky fellow! And you'd best know that what I'm telling you is 'a dead secret'; besides all the world and his wife, you're the only man who knows about it. . . . Go on, then, free Bulgaria, we'll make Rada Gospozhina our queen."

The letter had arrived the day before; no one knew how. It bore no signature. Kandov tore up the piece of filth, spat on it and went out.

chapter 25

the insurrection

For five days Klissoura had been in the throes of revolution. All work had stopped; every other interest was forgotten; an extraordinary excitement could be read on every face. The town was enthusiastic, restless, all agog; there was a heady atmosphere in the streets. In those five days the people of Klissoura had lived several lives; five centuries of fears, hopes, enthusiasm and despair. All that they saw and did, which before had seemed so very, very far away, now appeared like a wonderful dream, and had gone to their heads entirely.

On the 20th of April the Klissoura representative at the general assembly in Mechka arrived from Koprivshtitsa, which had risen that day, and embracing his family he told them that the hour of the insurrection had struck. The chief conspirators soon gathered at the school, and after they had all sung, "The battle's beginning, how our hearts beat," Karadjov made a fiery speech, and with enthusiastic shouts, amid the ringing of bells, the insurrection was proclaimed in Klissoura. Letters were immediately sent to the committees in the other towns of the Balkan range to support the movement in Klissoura and Koprivshtitsa by following their example. Corporals and officers of the watch were appointed; everyone hurrried home and armed himself; shots were fired; the zaptiehs were chased with bullets, but they escaped into the mountains.

All the men were led outside to the heights. Guards of from fifteen to twenty men were placed at all the strategic points to defend the city, and trenches were dug to give them cover. Almost the entire male population of the town from eighteen to fifty years of age was scattered over these points. No one was allowed to return to the town; their families were ordered to bring them food and anything else they might need. The insurgents were armed with whatever they had been able to get together.

The next day, while everyone in the church—the priests and the women because all the men were in the trenches—knelt in prayer for the deliverance of Bulgaria from bondage, the notables of the town, who had joyfully adhered to the movement, elected a council of war and a commander-in-chief of the insurgents. At noon the flag with the lion was carried with great solemnity to the heights of Zli-Dol and handed over to the defenders. The rest of the day was spent in appointing commanders of the more important fortifications on the heights, in preparing shot and everything else for the fighters, and in various other measures for the defense of the town. But the news which arrived from outside was not reassuring; besides Sredna Gora, no new regions had risen. Night found the insurgents greatly depressed.

On the 22nd of April the insurgents killed two Turkish travelers. The insurrection was now stained with blood, and the die was finally cast. But in vain did they look down from the heights hoping to see the fires in some of the Turkish villages of the Strema Valley, the signal that Kableshkov had raised the Bulgarian villages there. Then they sought shelter and hiding-places for their families in the mountains, and sent to Koprivshtitsa for help.

At dawn the insurgents arose gloomy and dispirited. St. George's Day brought joy to none, and the church bell which called the faithful to church emitted a doleful sound, as if it were tolling for a funeral. But suddenly the chimes rang out more lively and triumphant, and faces grew radiant with joy; Volov* was bringing reinforcements from Koprivshtitsa, some fifty rebels, most of them peasants from the Sredna Gora villages. He marched straight to the church where a Te Deum was held. The bells pealed still more festively.

When it was over Volov and his detachment set out for the heights with the priests and their banners. There he passed sentence of death on several Gipsies and Turks who had been caught spying. He himself cut down one of them with his sword. After these executions Volov returned to Koprivshtitsa alone. The rest of the time was spent in finishing the trenches.

During the next days depression reigned again. In vain did the watch gaze for hours on end to catch sight of the eagerly-awaited beacons in the valley. Kableshkov's expedition had returned to Koprivshtitsa, unsuccessful. The few travelers who penetrated here in the first days of the insurrection reported that all was quiet in the valley and that there was no sign of an approaching uprising. Since the day before no travelers had arrived. In their place several Turkish horsemen appeared far down the road, fired a few shots and returned whence they had come. Despondency increased. Neither the encouragement of the braver spirits, whose numbers diminished with every

* Leader in April Uprising.

passing hour, nor pretended successes, nor stern warnings helped in any way.

This deplorable frame of mind in the ranks of the defenders grew still worse on the 25th of April. They realized that they had been left in the lurch, in other words, to irrevocable doom. It was obvious. The handful of defenders which the town had been able to muster, about two hundred and fifty men all told, scattered about the place, were not enough to repel the terrible hordes of bashi-bazouks who would inevitably bear down on them from east and west. Nor could they hope for new reinforcements from Koprivshtitsa, which itself needed assistance. Discipline was relaxed, regrets, complaints, reproaches—the vanguard of demoralization—replaced the enthusiasm of the first days of the insurrection. They had not even seen the enemy yet, but felt him close at hand, inevitable and terrible.

The rebels were already like an army that has suffered defeat, though no battle had been fought, like a trembling herd of deer, cornered in a place without escape, that have heard the roar of wild beasts. Few kept their presence of mind, still fewer had even a spark of hope left as to the final outcome. Physical suffering was added to their mental torment: an icy wind blew down from the mountains at night, numbing the defenders in the damp trenches where they were forced to spend the night without even a fire. These poor tailors, who had spent their lives in peaceful labor, needle in hand, transformed now into rebels, bristling with arms, deserved nothing but pity. Dull groans and sighs were to be heard at night in the trenches where no one slept a wink for cold and worry.

"Congratulations on your kingdom, sister!" the old grannies had greeted each other in the streets on the first day of the insurrection.

"It's all up with us, brother, we're done for," even the most enthusiastic conspirators of yesterday whispered to each other now.

Despair grew. It was clearly stamped on the sunken faces. Yet no word of retreat, of flight, had fallen from any mouth. But the thought lay in all hearts. Such was the state of mind on all the heights that day. It was the same, or almost the same, at Zli-Dol, the keystone of the defense.

chapter 26

the battery at Zli-Dol

The heights of Zli-Dol, to the northeast of the town, were well situated strategically. They commanded the surrounding country and held the key to the road connecting Klissoura with the Strema Valley. From here the eye looked far down over the bare undulating meadows to the east, where the farsighted watchmen who constituted the "lines" of Klissoura's army were stationed. The detachment at Zli-Dol was the most numerous. It had been reinforced by Volov's men from Sredna Gora, the remnants of defeated detachments, and was preparing to greet the enemy's first attack with its bullets.

Particular animation reigned there that day. The light of energy shone in all eyes. But they were not turned in the direction from which the enemy was expected, but towards the valley in which Klissoura lay. All were gazing intently at the path which wound its way up the gully. There one of the rebels, a man of gigantic stature, was coming up, carrying something white, long and cylindrical across his shoulder. He was followed by a woman, tall and plump, a peasant, judging by her dress, almost bent double under an obviously very heavy load.

It was on these two that all eyes were fixed, and for a very good reason: they were carrying the artillery up to Zli-Dol. It comprised one cherry-wood cannon, all told, which lay across the giant's shoulder. The shot consisted of pieces of iron, bullets, Gipsy nails, horseshoes and so on, in a bag slung across the peasant woman's back. The eyes of the insurgents flashed with pleasure; enthusiasm reigned once more on Zli-Dol.

At last the giant carried the cannon up to the top, bathed in sweat that dripped like rain from his eyebrows and neck. "I'll be damned!" he gasped as he threw the death-dealing weapon to the ground.

The men crowded round to examine the cannon curiously. There were about twenty more like it, intended for the other fortifications, but they had not yet been carried up. This one had been brought out to be tested for its range and its shot. It was dragged up to a still higher point, from which it commanded the road and the bare ridges; it was filled with shot, fixed firmly to the ground with stakes and a big hole was dug behind it to serve as cover for the gunners.

The insurgents were burning with impatience to hear the voice of the first Bulgarian cannon. They were all as joyful and enthusiastic as children. Some even wept.

"Just listen, boys, and hear the Balkan lion roar. His voice will shake the Sultan's throne and tell the whole world that Stara Planina is free!" cried the chief of the Zli-Dol detachment.

"The sound'll arouse all our brothers in the Strema Valley and remind them of their duty. They'll fly to arms and fall upon our common foe!" cried another.

"From here we command the whole valley, just let the tyrants show themselves—we'll beat them to a jelly!"

"We won't leave a mother's son of them, I'll be damned!" roared Ivan Borimechka as he wiped his wet, scarlet face with his cap. For the giant who had carried up the cannon was our old friend Borimechka; his wife had carried up the ammunition. They had moved to Klissoura a month ago on business and had been carried away by the wave of revolutionary enthusiasm.

The gunner was setting to work. "Wait a minute, Delcho, we mustn't frighten the women and children, we must let them know first, said Nyagol the tailor.

"You're right," said another, "we'd better send the crier to cry the news in the town, for some of the women are pregnant."

"We can't possibly send anyone to town and lose all that time. Somebody's better shout the news from here, somebody with a good strong voice, that all can hear."

"Borimechka, Borimechka!" several cried, knowing the terrific power of his lungs.

Borimechka gladly accepted this new mission. He asked what he was to say, memorized it well, and climbed up to the height opposite, which was nearer the town. Then he stood up to the full height of his gigantic stature, threw out his chest, raised his head, opened his mouth wide, and gave a long cry, "You people there! We're going to fire the little cannon, I'll be damned! So the womenfolk and the brats mustn't be afraid, they're to keep calm. There are no heathen whatever here as yet. No heathen to he seen at all, I'll be damned!"

He repeated this message several times, every one or two minutes. The echoes of Stara Planina responded to his strong voice. It penetrated into every house in the town. After the families had been warned, the work was completed. Belcho struck fire, lit a big piece of tinder, stuck it on a long stick and placed it near the breech. The tinder caught fire and small clouds of blue smoke rose in the air.

In feverish expectation of the report the insurgents ran off quite a distance. Others lay down in the trenches, so as not to see anything; some even stopped up their ears with their fingers and closed their eyes. Several minutes passed. The strain was terrible, it beggared description. The blue smoke still rose above the fuse without managing to set fire to it. Hearts beat as though they would burst. The suspense was becoming unbearable. Finally a white flame ran along the fuse, which began to smoke too, and at once the cannon emitted a helpless, angry, rasping sound, as if a dry board was being split, something like a sharp cough, and vanished behind a thick cloud of smoke.

But the cough had torn the cannon open, and the charge was spat out only a few feet away. Many of the rebels who had taken cover did not even hear the explosion. Somebody said, in joke or in earnest, that he had supposed the sound to have escaped from an unmentionable part of Borimechka's anatomy.

This unfortunate result showed up the shortcomings of the artillery. The remaining cannon were hastily improved, and strongly and closely bound with iron hoops and ropes; some were even lined with tin. That same day, they brought up two cannon to each fortified point, filled them well with shot, fixed them firmly to stakes and dug holes behind them for the gunners. Every cannon was meant to be fired only once, and in a fixed direction.

Let us add that they forgot to send word to the town that the gun had already been fired. So that the poor women and old grannies waited till evening with cotton wool in their ears, in expectation of the shot that was to make the air echo and the windows tremble.

chapter 27

cross-questioning

Ognyanov was in charge of one of the eastern fortifications that had been made on a height between Zli-Dol and the Old River. This spot was strategically just as important as Zli-Dol, and it had the advantage that part of the Strema Valley was visible from it, lying in its fresh green mantle far to the east in the depths behind the bare hills. The defenders of this fortification, about thirty in all, were walking up and down in their shirtsleeves because of the heat, their faces careworn and dirty. Depression reigned here too, just as in the other fortifications.

Ognyanov, dressed in his revolutionary uniform with the inevitable two revolvers in his belt, had climbed up onto the earthworks and was looking down into the Strema Valley with his field-glasses. He was carefully examining a trail of blue smoke which some had taken for the expected beacon.

He came down into the trench and muttered gloomingly, "No, it's not a beacon, they're burning charcoal in Sredna Gora."

Just then he noticed Borimechka coming that way, driving a man before him who did not belong to the fortifications. He was a small man, a Bulgarian with a stupid, frightened face, dressed in the baggy breeches and short jacket of the day, both equally shabby, and he had a brightly colored bag slung over his shoulder.

"A spy!" said Borimechka. "We caught him in the valley. We asked him all the questions we could think of, but he wouldn't say a word. What are your orders? What's to be done with him?" An involuntary smile played about Ognyanov's lips. He had recognized Rachko the Stinkard.

Rachko had left Byala Cherkva the day before and had set out for Rahmanlari to do odd jobs of mending for the Turks, a free trade at which a number of poor people in Byala Cherkva made a scanty living. Because of his simple-mindedness he had not yet grasped either what was being prepared in Byala Cherkva or what was happening here, so he had been extremely surprised when, instead of orders for patching clothes in Rahmanlari, he had received a few blows on the back from the infuriated Turks, and been driven out with the roughest oaths. As he did not want to return empty-handed, he had decided to go on to Klissoura nearby. But the appearance of a Turkish mounted force had frightened him and he had taken to the valley of the Old River, to reach Klissoura from that side. Thus he had fallen into the hands of the outposts.

Rachko, who had virtually lost his reason at the sight of so many armed men—whom he had taken for haidouks—now more or less came to his senses. Although he had unpleasant memories of Ognyanov, the latter now appeared to him as a friend among all these strangers. Rachko's tongue was loosened, and he gave a more or less clear account of his odyssey.

Boicho heard with pleasure that he had left Byala Cherkva the day before. "What's up in Byala Cherkva?"

"Nothing, nothing, thank God, nothing."

This 'nothing' pierced Ognyanov's heart like an arrow. "Don't lie, tell me the truth!"

"There's nothing at all, you needn't worry, there's nothing up."

"What, isn't anything doing there at all?"

"So help me, there isn't. Do you want me to swear it?"

"This fool knows nothing," thought Boicho irritated. "Or can he be hiding anything? Has he been sent by the Turks? How did he manage to get through, and no one else?"

And he pierced him through and through with his penetrating gaze. "Listen, tell me the truth or I'll have them crush your head with a stone!" cried Boicho, his face suddenly scarlet with anger.

"No, you leave him to me, schoolmaster," Borimechka intervened. "I need his head. I'll pick it off with one hand and we'll stick it into our cannon to send it right into Rahmanlari, so it can tell the Turks what it's seen." And the giant fixed eyes as greedy as a hawk's on little Rachko.

"I-I'll tell you everything, everything . . ." stuttered Rachko in terror.

"Remember what I told you!" said Ognyanov sternly.

"I remember, I tell you I remember. . . ."

"Did you really leave Byala Cherkva yesterday?"

"Yesterday, that's it. The sun was right over there."

"What was going on there?"

"Nothing at all, don't worry."

"Why did you leave Stefchov?"

"He drove me out, the Lord smite him. May my name not be Rachko the Stinkard. . . . A man lives for his honor in this world. . . ." Ognyanov cut him off with a gesture.

"Whom did you see in Byala Cherkva yesterday before setting out? Did you see Sokolov?"

"I saw him, not yesterday, the day before; he was going into his house with the German."

"Hasn't there been any disturbance?"

"None at all."

"Or any Turks arriving?"

"Not a cur."

"Hasn't the bey locked anybody up?"

"I haven't heard anything of the kind."

"So everything's quite quiet?"

"Just as I told you, take my word for it."

"What are people saying there?"

"Nothing, they talk very comfortable-like."

"How 'comfortable-like'?"

"Everybody looks after his job—take me for instance—I'm a body with a house and family to look after, so I hang my bag over my shoulder and off I go to work in the villages. . . . But you'll say that's shameful—it isn't, Count; Rachko the Stinkard's the same man ever, always on his honor. What does a man live for, I ask you? For his good name in the world."

Boicho clenched his hands furiously. He had so longed to get something out of this simpleton, any tiny shred of information as to an approaching movement in Byala Cherkva. But after another useless effort he realized that he could not find anything out, for the simple reason that Rachko himself had grasped nothing, and that there really was nothing afoot in the place.

"What are you doing, Ivan?" asked Ognyanov when he saw Borimechka rummaging around in the prisoner's bag.

"We need these scissors, don't we, or am I an ass?" said Ivan drawing out a large pair of scissors and a smaller pair, besides a folded yardstick of iron.

"What are you going to do with them, cut his ears off?"

"For the cannon, I'll be damned! We need shot, don't we?" And Borimechka gave the big scissors a twist, and divided them in two. Then he bent each part over his knee; the iron gave a ringing crack and half of each half was left in his hands. He broke the yardstick as if he were breaking twigs. Then turning to the prisoner he said, "Mind, if it turns out you aren't honest, I'll wring your neck and tear your head off, and we'll cram it into the cannon too!" and he cast a terrible look at the hapless man's small head, which really would have gone into the cannon.

"Ivan, you go back to Zli-Dol and leave this fellow here. He's not a spy, he's only a big fool."

When he heard that the terrible Borimechka was being sent off, Rachko breathed more freely. "I tell you, Count, begging your pardon, I can do a job of mending for these rascals. If it's a matter of work, there's nothing shameful in work, and when a man's square with his honor. . . ."

"Which rascals?" asked Ognyanov sternly.

Rachko lowered his voice confidentially. "These haidouks, the Lord preserve us from them; they nearly did me in!" And he looked at the men in the trenches.

"Set this fellow to work on the trench!" Ognyanov called out to them and passed on.

chapter 28

discouragement in the fort

One of the corporals approached Ognyanov.

"What's up, Marchev?"

"Things are going badly," whispered the man. "The men in the trenches are getting demoralized."

Ognyanov's face darkened. "Any man who discourages the others will be instantly punished with death!" he cried angrily. "Whom have you noticed doing it, Marchev?" The man named four persons.

"Bring them here!" The accused appeared. They were elderly men, merchants and tailors.

Ognyanov shot them an angry look and asked, "Gentlemen, is it you who are corrupting the men?"

"We're not corrupting anybody," one of them answered angrily.

"Do you know how such conduct at such a critical moment is punished?" They said not a word. But their silence expressed stubbornness rather than consciousness of their guilt.

Sudden anger darkened Ognyanov's face, but he controlled himself and said quietly, "Go to your places. We have proclaimed a revolution and it is too late to go back. We shall meet the enemy here, and it's no use looking toward Klissoura. You won't save your houses and your families by going back to the town, but by staying outside it! Please don't make things hard for me."

But the rebels did not move. Ognyanov looked at them in surprise. This was obviously a protest. "What else have you to say?"

The rebels looked at each other, then one of them spoke up. "We were not in favor of all this!"

"I've never handled a gun in my life." added another.

"Who ever has?" asked a third.

"We can't shed blood."

"You're afraid, eh?" asked Ognyanov, thinking to shame them with this question.

"It's no sin if we are."

"Yes, we're afraid!" said the first man heatedly. "We have children to think of."

"We didn't find our lives by the roadside," added one of the bolder ones quite angrily.

"Your lives and your children and your houses are nothing compared to the liberation of Bulgaria!" cried Ognyanov in a voice that shook with anger. "And above all—to her honor! I ask you again not to show the white feather and force me into taking extreme measures against you."

"We weren't meant for guns and rebellions. Let us go!"

Ognyanov saw that he could not get the better of their stubbornness with fair words. He was boiling with rage, but did his best to keep his temper. He realized bitterly that it was only deep despair and terror of the struggle that had given these fainthearts the daring and resolution to admit themselves cowards out loud before their commander himself, without blushing with shame. From this admission it was only a step to panic-stricken flight. He decided to take merciless action. The infection must not be allowed to spread to the rest of the men to this extreme degree. Discipline came first.

"Will you submit to your duty, my men, or not?" he asked resolutely. And with a gloomy look and beating heart he waited for their answer.

Just then unexpected cries broke out behind him. He turned and saw Borimechka chasing a Gipsy in the meadow not far away. The other rebels crowded around to watch and loudly shouted encouragement to Borimechka, who in spite of his gigantic strides could not manage to reach the light and barefooted Gipsy. Some even aimed their rifles at him, but Ognyanov stopped them.

Obviously the fugitive had been hiding in Klissoura so far and had tried to escape and take refuge in a Turkish village. The Gipsies who had managed to escape in the first days had been the first to carry the news of the insurrection in Klissoura to the Turks, as well as details as to the disposal of the defenders. By nature and interest they were loyal allies to the Turks both here and elsewhere in similar cases. Borimechka dashed madly after the Gipsy, who took several huge leaps and skimmed over the ground like the wind. He was gaining ground, and the two were getting further and further away from the fortifications. It would have been hard to get the Gipsy now, even with a bullet. Suddenly he stopped, startled; two rebel lookouts appeared before him and he found himself between two fires. At the same moment Borimechka caught up with him, seized him as he ran and fell to the ground with him.

Gleeful shouts came from the fortifications. Then people gestured, "Here, here!"

Borimechka, infuriated, drove the Gipsy forward, raining curses on him that could be clearly heard at the fortifications; he was like a volcano in full eruption. Soon the fugitive was brought up.

The rebels surrounded him. Fierce feelings animated their weary faces. They all knew the Gipsy. He had already twice attempted to escape from Klissoura, the first time on a secret mission to the men of Rahmanlari with which the Turk at the konak had entrusted him. This Turk was being held a prisoner. The Gipsy had only been punished for his attempted escape by being kept still more closely imprisoned. There was no question of mercy now.

The commander of the fort turned to his corporal and they held a consultation in low tones for some time. "Yes, yes", concluded Ognyanov, "any gentleness and mercy would be harmful now. If they see death it may accustom the weaklings to look upon it more boldly. But the sentence must come from the council of war. Marchev, go over to Zli-Dol as quickly as you can and report the matter. My opinion and request is that they be sentenced to death. Make haste." The corporal set out.

Ognyanov turned sternly to an elderly rebel. "Uncle Marin, put a guard on the Gipsy!"

Then he turned to two younger men. "Boys, take these lily-livered rascals to the other end, take their rifles away and put a guard on them, and wait for further orders!" The four demoralized rebels blanched but submitted and set out for the place they had been sent to.

chapter 29

baptism by fire

Ognyanov paced back and forth along the trenches, deeply disturbed. His sunken face was furrowed with care.

As he stepped over towards a group of rebels who were zealously digging a new trench, he glanced at them mechanically without noticing Rachko's friendly grin, and climbed up again onto the earthworks to scan the east with his field-glasses; then with features still more frozen he came down and returned to his place. "What a people, what a people!" he muttered.

Marchev returned. "The death sentence," he panted.

"Has the council of war pronounced it?"

"Yes, death, and no delay!" added Marchev aloud, then whispered something low. Ognyanov nodded in satisfaction.

The words "death and no delay" could be heard further away. They were taken up by the whispers of the insurgents and reached the corner where the prisoners had been placed.

If they had been pale before, they now became as white as sheets. They realized that there was no joking here. Quite suddenly the council of war had taken on the shape of something very terrible and ugly, as merciless as fate. In this spot only God was greater.

One of the insurgents approached Ognyanov. "The prisoners have repented and beg for mercy."

Ognyanov answered drily, "Sentence has been passed. It's too late now." Then he added imperatively, "Braikov, take Nyagol, Blagoi and Iskrov, and march the four men down into that gully to undergo their penalty. The sentence pronounced by the council of war must be carried out exactly."

Rather shaken by all this, Braikov went off to carry out the orders given by the commander of the fortification. Not another voice was raised in defense of the condemned men. Nobody wished it thought that he agreed with them. Each felt that his life now depended on the will of the council of war, the only court, and one of no appeal.

Escorted by the four others, the condemned rebels passed through the fortification and went down the scree into the valley. "Take the Gipsy there too!" shouted Ognyanov. Then in a low voice he gave certain orders to his corporal who followed the others down into the valley.

The place of execution was a moist green dell through which babbled a tiny brook. All around there was almost nothing but rocks and cliffs. Ognyanov's fortification was on the western crest, where the insurgents had crowded to watch the execution.

To the left of the small brook stood an oak, half blasted by lightning. The two insurgents first took the Gipsy to this tree, unwound his waist-band and tied him to the trunk. Horror had struck dumb the unfortunate creature. His cracked lips were bleeding.

Not far from the bank stood the four other condemned men awaiting their turn. Sheer animal terror had distorted their features.

Marchev called out: "Bring them here too!" The condemned men moved forward. The knees of three of them gave way, and they had to be supported by the guards to the spot indicated by the corporal.

Marchev lined them up about ten feet from the bound Gipsy, presumably to be nearer the terrible spectacle which they too would shortly present to their comrades in rebellion, who now crowded the top of the cliff. They were left unbound. But horror had paralyzed them so that the idea of flight never even entered heir heads. Nor was flight possible.

There was a minute's deathly silence. Then Marchev cried out loudly and solemnly: "The Gipsy Mehmed of Klissoura, for three times attempting to escape from prison with the loathsome purpose of serving Bulgaria's foes, has been condemned to death by the Supreme Council, to serve as an example to similar traitors!"

Then he turned to the condemned rebels. "Gentlemen, line up to face Mehmed." They obeyed like automatons.

"Give them each a rifle." The insurgents, much excited, handed over their rifles. The condemned men took them, foolish amazement on their faces.

"Now, shoot this man when I give the command: one, two, three. . . ." The cliffs re-echoed to the shots and clouds of smoke enveloped the four.

The Gipsy stood there upright, just as he was, tied up to the tree. Not a bullet had hit him. The men had probably not aimed at him. But he looked like a dead man.

"For shame, gentlemen!" cried Marchev angrily. "Fire again!" And he repeated his command. Shots rang out a second time. The

Gipsy's body drooped, and his arms hung down. Applause resounded from the heights.

"Your punishment, for this time, was this baptism of fire. You owe it to Ognyanov's magnanimity and the clemency of the council of war."

As they realized that they had been spared, the four looked about them timidly and like people waking from a nightmare. A smile of joy barely pierced through the frozen yellow masks which fear had fixed on their faces. From the fortifications a renewed and joyous volley of applause rang out.

chapter 30

the Strema Valley ablaze

"Strange, strange! . . . Inexplicable! . . . Terrible! And still there's nothing. What can they be doing? What is Byala Cherkva doing? They're as silent as the grave. Silent! This terrible silence! Fearful! . . . I can't think they're simply folding their arms there and being wise. Is that idiot really speaking the truth? But Sokolov's there, Popov's there, the Editor's there. . . . My falcons are there, tried youngsters, hotheads all of them. What are they waiting for? Or are they waiting for me? But if I don't appear, or if I die, won't they do anything? Or are they deaf and blind and see nothing? Klissoura has risen, Koprivshtitsa has risen, Panagyourishté has risen. Sredna Gora is ablaze! Only the Strema Valley lies sleeping. Has there been an accident? Or an unforeseen obstacle? But that's impossible! If Byala Cherkva can't rise, it can at least send a detachment, even if it's only ten people. It would encourage the others. But it stands by, idle. All the news confirms this. Yet what ardor there was there! Preparations were so serious. . . . Is it the same in the other towns? Catastrophe, the curse of God hangs over Bulgaria if that's so!" With these gloomy thoughts weighing him down, Ognyanov, disguised as a Turk, was making his way cautiously along the Old River into the Strema Valley.

As we know, on the 20th of April he had been passing through Klissoura on his way to Byala Cherkva with the intention of raising the standard of rebellion there when the hour of the general insurrection should strike. But for Klissoura the hour had struck that very day. The insurrection had caught him in a moment of terrible anguish, and he had thrown himself into it blindly, to deaden his pain in the tornado of the struggle, and to find death among the fighters for his country's freedom. But the enemy did not appear. All communications between Klissoura and the valley were cut off. Ognyanov had spent five days and nights at the fortifications in feverish activity, organizing the defense, tortured by impatience to hear the news that Byala Cherkva had risen.

His heart bleeding, Ognyanov cursed the hour that had brought him to Klissoura. He saw how terribly that sinister silence influenced the spirits of the rebels, how it was wrecking the whole movement. In vain did he strive to encourage his comrades and swear to them that Byala Cherkva was expected to rise any minute, and the other towns after it. Finally he too began to lose hope and foresaw with horror collapse of Klissoura and with it the revolution. Then he decided upon a bold and almost foolhardy course of action: to make his way to Byala Cherkva through the infuriated Turkish villages and to get the town to rise.

He was exposing himself to terrible risks. But if Byala Cherkva rose it would fling the spark of revolution into the other places ready for rebellion all along Stara Planina. Then the Turkish forces would be split, Klissoura saved, the fire of rebellion would spread, and, who knows? The revolution might triumph! Many great changes in history have been due to very trifling circumstances. Anyhow the game was worth the candle. And the deed had found its man.

It was already noon when he found himself in the valley itself, which was now in full bloom, plunged in shade and greenery. The crystal-clear brooks babbled in the grass and the leafy oak forests. The air was redolent of roses, like the boudoir of a royal favorite. Here particularly, under the blue sky and the cheerful rays of the sun, the valley was as smiling and wonderful as an earthly paradise. But it did not draw the attention of the traveler; he saw nothing of all this. He would have preferred to see it in flames.

His route took him through the Turkish village of Rahmanlari, the nearest to Klissoura. He approached it fearlessly. As he was passing by the rose-fields at the end of the village, several armed Turks stopped him; they were the sentries. "Where do you come from, brother?"

"From Altunovo."

"Where are you going?"

"To Ahievo. Is all quiet there?" Ahievo was the Turkish village nearest to Byala Cherkva.

"Thank God, all is quiet there." Ognyanov's heart shrank with pain.

"You'd better stay in the village. We'll be attacking Klissoura tomorrow.

"I'll see about that. Good-bye." And Ognyanov entered the village.

He found the streets buzzing with excitement. Turks by the score were moving hither and thither, all armed to the teeth. The cafés were crowded too, so were the grocers', and the inn was quite full. Clearly there were several hundred Turks there, gathered from the neighboring villages to attack Klissoura. Rahmanlari was their meeting-place. Seized by terrible forebodings as to the fate of Klissoura, Ognyanov nevertheless wanted to obtain positive information about Byala Cherkva; he still believed that the town might have risen at the eleventh hour. To this end he thought of entering the inn, which was kept by a man from Byala Cherkva. But he was afraid of treachery and did not go in.

He set out again, keeping his eyes open to choose a group of Turks whom he might join. Passing the mosque, he saw that it too was full. The faithful were crowding around the doors, and more and more of them kept arriving in groups. Something unusual was afoot there. Ognyanov realized that the Hodja* was going to preach, to further inflame the fanaticism of these fierce crowds. Irresistible curiosity seized him, and he slipped in among the congregation. He was not wrong; at that very moment the preacher was mounting the wooden bench which serves as a pulpit in the Turkish places of worship. In the light that fell on him, Ognyanov made out that he was not an ordinary village hodja, but a softa** who had probably come from K. for just this.

Silence fell at once. The softa began solemnly. "Oh, ye faithful! Once, in the glorious reign of our great Sultans, the world trembled at the very name of Osmanli. East and West bowed down before him, the seas sent him gifts, kings and queens prostrated themselves and licked the sacred dust before the throne of the Caliph. Great was Allah then, and his Holy Prophet Mohammed. But as can be seen, we have sinned grievously against God, we have drunk and fornicated, we have fraternized with the unbelievers and accepted their laws. And lo, God has allowed us to be cursed by the accursed, and trodden on by the downtrodden. Eh, Allah, Allah! Send us the sword of the angel Asrael to pour the blood of they enemies over the East and over the West! To stain the seas and glorify the skies. . . . Here is my word, Oh ye faithful! Whet your knives, prepare your arms with prayer, and be ready, for the hour has struck to wash away our shame with the blood of the Giaours before the face of the one great God of Islam!" In this spirit and in this heroic strain the orator began his speech. He went on with it for a long time, with the rapt attention of his congregation, whose eyes flashed ominously.

"So that's what they're up to here!" said Ognyanov to himself without waiting to hear the end, and he went out onto the street.

* *hodja:* Turkish priest.

** *softa:* Moslem theological student.

"The rumors about these preachers were true after all. We preached rebellion against the Turkish government; their apostles preach the destruction of the Bulgarian people! So we have a fierce struggle, the struggle of a people against a people; it's no use deceiving ourselves any longer. Bulgaria is not large enough to contain the two side by side. So be it! There is no retreat! Bulgaria's die is cast! Yet how has our sacred, longed-for revolution begun? Oh, God! Protect Bulgaria!"

And he began pacing up and down the square again. The service was over and the congregation poured out into the street. Small groups were formed who discussed animatedly their impressions of the sermon. Ognyanov went up to one of them and listened in on the talk. He realized what the situation was now. At first the revolt of Klissoura had frightened the Turkish population of the surrounding villages, because it was thought that Russian troops had come to the town. Goaded by this fear they had prepared to take their families and seek safety in flight. Soon, however, the fact that some Turks had escaped from the town, and the awkward way the rebels themselves had handled matters, made it clear they were dealing with simple rayah, mostly tailors and a few teachers; they recovered all their boldness and self-confidence. They decided to deal with Klissoura themselves without waiting for military aid. Ognyanov also realized that the men of Rahmanlari had reconnoitred the situation very skillfully, and that the enemy knew approximately the disposition and strength of each post. Tossoun-Bey was expected the next day from K. with new detachments of bashi-bazouks, and they were immediately going to attack the rebellious towns.

These discoveries alarmed Ognyanov. He now realized more than ever the need to bring on the insurrection in the other Bulgarian towns. They had to steal a march on Tossoun-Bey. He continued his eastward journey.

He safely passed through the Turkish village of Tekiya. At its western end stood guards, a sign that there was no danger to the east. Here too he noted a great excitement. Here too they were awaiting the appearance of Tossoun-Bey in order to join his hordes.

"To Byala Cherkva, to Byala Cherkva! Faster! Tossoun-Bey must first come up against the iron breast of my Byala Cherkva! And that will be, oh that will be, as soon as I get there. With the editor alone I can proclaim the insurrection, and in half an hour I shall have five hundred men under the banner! The town will take fire—either it goes up in revolt or in flames! Forward, forward! O God, give me wings!" And Ognyanov sped on towards Byala Cherkva.

He felt that in another two or three hours' march he would see in the distance the white chimneys of the town and the tall pediment of the church, and his heart beat wildly with joy.

Not far beyond the village his road dropped into a shady valley which cut across the plain. From the bottom of this valley he caught the confused sounds of pipes and drums. Probably it was a wedding in some Turkish village, but a most untimely one, it would seem. However, soon all grew quiet again and he forgot about it. But as he came up on the opposite side of the dip, the music struck up once more, quite close in front of him. Surprised, he climbed a hillock and then a sight lay before him that made his blood run cold.

The plain ahead of him was black with Turks advancing to this barbarous music. Red flags were waving in the air. The rabble was moving ahead noisily and in disorder. Over their shoulders rifles, scythes, axes and spears flashed in the sunlight, and so did the scimitars of the bashi-bazouks. Most of them were in waistcoats and shirtsleeves because of the noonday heat. This wave had emptied the Turkish villages through which it passed. No discipline held the disorderly ranks together, but one goal, fierce and savage, bound them all and drove them forward, inspiring them all: blood and loot. Guns and swords, to shed the blood, and for the loot, a long file of carts to carry it away. To the sound of the pipes and drums the horde advanced, drunk with fanaticism, approaching slowly but irresistibly like a swarm of locusts.

A single horseman, tall, lean, black, with a white turban on his head, rode ahead—their leader. He moved to the Gipsies to stop.

"Hey, Mussulman, come hither!" he cried to Ognyanov. Ognyanov approached, with a low salaam.

"Where do you come from?"

"From Tekiya."

"What is the news there?"

"There is none; all is well, praise God!"

"What do they say, are those men in Klissoura numerous?"

"Why, quite a number, it seems, Allah protect the kingdom."

"Who are they?"

"Muscovites they say. . . ."

"Silence, you pimp! There are only mangy rayah there!"

"Forgive me, Bey-Effendi."

"Where are you going?"

"To K."

"Back you go with us!"

In spite of himself Ognyanov turned pale. "Bey-Effendi, please let me. . . ."

"Back!" roared Tossun-Bey and, spurring his horse, he set off.

The horde moved on. The pipes and drums struck up again. The stream carried Ognyanov back with it. It was senseless to think of resisting, or of making his way through the mob which poured over the whole place.

The unfortunate man let himself be borne on by the crowd. He was in despair, prostrate with grief and helpless. His last hope was vanishing. He walked mechanically on as in a dream, pushed and stepped on by the tumultuous crowd, which swelled and grew more ferociously merry hour by hour. And this wave of human beings carried him back, always back, towards the bare hills behind which Klissoura lay hidden.

chapter 31

one more attempt

Tossoun-Bey's horde arrived in Rahmanlari by evening, more numerous still, and more fanatical. It found another horde of Turks there who had come from the villages nearby to join them. For Tossoun-Bey was to attack Klissoura the next day with a force of about two thousand men. The village was crammed with people. It could scarcely hold the new arrivals. As it was a clear night most of them lay down to sleep in the street.

Willy-nilly Ognyanov did the same. He lay alone, on a dung-heap just opposite the inn, which was kept by a man from Byala Cherkva. Although it was late the lights still shone through the windows of the inn. It was still full.

Ognyanov had decided not to sleep, nor could he have done so. He would somehow have to slip away from this horde of Turks in which he was trapped, that very night, while there was still a chance; tomorrow it would be impossible.

He kept his eyes fixed on the lighted windows, his thoughts racing. He was racking his brains as to how to slip through the close guard that had been set on the outskirts. Thanks to his Turkish clothing and his fluent knowledge of the language, he hoped this would not be too hard. But alas—what was the use of his getting away, of returning to his trench safe and sound? Byala Cherkva would remain quiet and Klissoura's fate would be sealed.

To try to set out for Byala Cherkva that night was all but impossible; the guard had strict orders to let no one through, so as to prevent casual desertions. To leave things till tomorrow was still less possible—and even if it were, he could no longer have set out for Byala Cherkva. He felt he could not be absent from Klissoura in such a terrible hour. His absence would be construed as flight, as cowardice. No, that was impossible. Yet how could he get word through to Byala Cherkva? Couldn't he make one more attempt? And Ognyanov cudgelled his brains again.

Finally an idea came into his head. He decided to try and persuade the innkeeper to send one of his sons to Byala Cherkva the next day; the boy might find a chance Turkish traveler with whom to go for greater safety, as it would be market day in K.

The plan seemed attractive. Although it would be difficult to carry out, the importance of his mission was worth the effort and the risks it involved. Yes, great risks: first he would have to reveal himself, he would have to place his fate in the hands of a none too trustworthy innkeeper. Fortunately he knew him and his family, as the eldest son had been his pupil, and that reassured him somewhat.

He got up from the dung-heap, passed unhindered through the gate into the yard, crossed it and approached the small window of the little room at the end of the yard, built on to the stable; here he began to pace up and down by the shed, hoping to see one of the family. He did not dare tap on the window or the door for fear of causing alarm.

For a long time he walked up and down, but no one came either in or out. The innkeeper and his sons were busy indoors, serving the Turks. Probably only his wife was in the room with the small children. Having come to this conclusion he finally summoned up courage to knock on the door.

Chance came to his aid however. The door opened and a woman's figure appeared. Ognyanov recognized the innkeeper's wife. She was coming out with a measure of barley under her arm for the stable. Ognyanov went up to her and spoke clearly in Bulgarian. "Good evening, Aunt Avramitsa." She turned around in surprise, or rather in fear.

"Don't you recognize me?" he added in an ingratiating voice, to calm her, then hastened to identify himself. "I'm your Nanko's schoolmaster, Ognyanov."

"Who, the Count?" she asked in surprise, moving the barley to her other arm. "Why are you dressed like that?"

Then she remembered. "Come in, come in. Just let me pour the barley into the horse's nosebag and we'll go to our room."

Half a minute later Avramitsa and Ognyanov went through the little corridor into a small dark room. The innkeeper's wife struck a match and lit a tin lamp which dimly lighted up the room and her visitor. "You can get out into the kitchen garden through that little door there, and then over the thorn-fence and into the street. You'd better know that in case of need," Avramitsa whispered, showing Ognyanov a small, very low door, so low that a man would have to bend almost double to get through it.

"What are you doing here?" she asked.

"I was going to Byala Cherkva from Klissoura. I ran into Tossoun-

Bey beyond Tekiya and he made me turn back." In response to such hospitality Ognyanov felt bound to reply with complete frankness. Besides, he was forced to depend on her.

Avramitsa looked at him compassionately. "Oh, dearie me, those poor people in Klissoura, what is to become of them? That pack is after them!"

"Klissoura's done for, Aunt Avramitsa, it'll be put to the sword. I was trying to save it, but unfortunately I couldn't get through to Byala Cherkva."

"Why; what could you have done there?"

"I was going to raise Byala Cherkva too, and then the villages around would have risen also, and Tossoun-Bey would have had to withdraw."

"A pox on him, the black Gipsy! Well, what are you going to do now?" Avramitsa asked again, not knowing what Ognyanov wanted of her.

"Where's your Nanko, is he here?"

"Yes, he is."

"And Kouzman?"

"He's here too."

"Where are they?"

"In the shop with their father, serving those brutes and keeping an eye on them, so they won't carry anything off."

Ognyanov thought awhile. "Could we send somebody, Nanko or Kouzman, to Byala Cherkva tomorrow?" The mother looked at him in amazement. Her face grew worried.

"He might set off with one of the Turks from this place, whom he knows. Tomorrow's market day in K., and Rahmanlari men trade there."

"But it's not safe at all, schoolmaster."

"If he's with a Turk, it'll be safe enough. It's quite peaceful there. Nobody'll touch him."

"Why do you want to send him there?"

"To take a letter to one of my men and come back at once. By noon tomorrow he'll be back."

Avramitsa now recalled Boicho's first words and realized what kind of a message he wanted to send to Byala Cherkva by her son. Her face was anxious. "Well, schoolmaster, we'll have to ask his father about that."

"Aunt Avramitsa, I beg you not to tell Bai Avram anything about this. Can't you send for Nanko quietly, have him come and see me?"

Ognyanov knew his former pupil adored him and would do anything he asked him to.

The woman's face grew stern. "No, no, we mustn't do anything behind Avram's back."

"But Bai Avram won't let him go!"

Clearly the woman's former benevolence had cooled. In a flash all the danger to which her child would be exposed, should he set out for Byala Cherkva, had crossed her mind. She felt fearful in front of this strange and terrible man. She was sorry she had not sent him away at once, and looked about her in fear and trembling. But her kind heart would not let a cruel thought enter her mind.

Ognyanov noticed her great embarrassment. He realized that such a weighty matter should not be discussed with a weak, irresolute woman. Time was passing and he had to think of getting away. He decided to press matters and find out where he stood. "Aunt Avramitsa, ask Bai Avram to come here a minute. I want to talk to him."

Avramitsa was obviously much relieved. "I'll go and whisper in his ear, you stay here. And remember that little door. If you hear anything bad outside. . . ." And out she went.

chapter 32

Avram

Ognyanov remained alone. He decided to be frank with Avram, to show this man full confidence and surrender himself to his honesty or dishonesty. The task was worth a hundred lives like his own, if only it could be carried through. In any case he would have to trust to Avram's feelings as a Bulgarian: he might refuse any service, but he would not betray him.

He heard soft footsteps in the passage outside, the footsteps of a man, and guessing that Avram was coming, he stood up to face the door. It opened and the innkeeper entered. His fat ruddy face was wreathed in smiles. He shut the door. "You're welcome, Count, heartily welcome! And how's your health? It's a good thing you've come to see us and have a chat. I'm that pleased, so I am. We're all pleased, the wife's pleased, and so are the boys. Nanko hasn't seen you for half a year. You're his teacher and guardian. Welcome, most heartily welcome! . . . Well, well, well." There was no end to the innkeeper's enthusiastic exclamations.

Ognyanov was delighted. He was encouraged to explain the situation to Avram in a few words, repeating the request he had made to his wife a little earlier. "Of course, of course, why not! What need to ask? Who wouldn't help the people's cause?"

"Thank you, Bai Avram," said Ognyanov touched. "In this great hour every Bulgarian must make sacrifices or do something to help his country."

"Who wouldn't lend a hand, is there any Bulgarian who wouldn't? Anybody who spares himself in such a great cause deserves God's curse. Very good, very good. Which boy do you want?"

"Let's send Nanko. He's got his wits more about him as he's the older."

"Of course, of course. Your pupil. He'd give his life for you. Won't he be glad when I tell him? Have you written the note?" and Avram's voice trembled with joyful emotion.

"I'll write it at once," and Ognyanov looked through his pockets. "Haven't you got a piece of paper?"

The innkeeper took a soiled piece of paper out of his pocket, placed his inkhorn in front of Ognyanov and said, "You write the note and I'll go back to the shop. You know these curs, they're regular thieves."

"Come back soon, Bai Avram, with my Nanko, for I shan't be waiting long, as I told you."

It only took Ognyanov a moment to write the note. It contained the following few lines:

"The insurrection has broken out and is at its height. Don't delay a moment, proclaim the insurrection at once. Have one detachment attack Tossoun-Bey in the rear, and the other go to rouse the villages. Courage and faith! I shall be with you soon to die for Bulgaria. Long live the revolution!

Ognyanov."

He congratulated himself on his success; he had never supposed he would find such readiness and patriotism in Avram. He listened impatiently to catch the footsteps of father and son. The noise from the street and the barking of dogs could only faintly be heard. The little lamp flickered sadly, sending up a column of evil-smelling smoke to the ceiling.

Suddenly a shrill, heart-rending cry, a woman's weeping, in the next room, broke the stillness. Ognyanov started. He realized that it was Avramitsa who had screamed. Why such despair? In spite of himself he felt frightened.

He listened intently again in the dimly lighted room, and heard something like muffled steps in the shed retreating in the distance. Then he went up to the small door and tugged at the handle. The door did not open. He gave it another strong pull. But the door never moved an inch. His hair stood on end in horror. "They've betrayed me!" he groaned.

At the same moment there was a slight noise outside. It seemed as if a key was thrust into the lock. Sudderly the door opened, and the evening breeze blew in through the opening. Ognyanov fixed his eyes upon the dark hole that opened towards the garden. Then a head appeared in it. It was Avramitsa.

"Come out quickly!" she whispered softly. Although her face was only faintly lighted by the little lamp, Ognyanov saw tears glistening on it. He squeezed through and found himself in the garden.

"This way," said Avramitsa softly, pointing to a plum tree near the fence. Then she disappeared in the darkness.

Ognyanov climbed over the thorns and found himself in a back street. It was deserted. He set out along it at a run. But the street brought him out at the inn again.

There he came up against a crowd of armed Turks. They were pouring through the gate and disappeared into the yard. Ognyanov vanished into the darkness too.

chapter 33

the night

Long after midnight, after a rather perilous journey, Ognyanov arrived back at the fortification.

Its defenders were still awake, lying there in the darkness on straw mats and rugs brought from their homes. They were talking quietly under their hooded capes, their eyes turned up to the starry moonless sky. Ognyanov slipped noiselessly among them and threw himself down, exhausted physically, and morally spent. He tried to concentrate his scattered thoughts, or at least to get the sleep he needed so badly to greet the day refreshed. But his thoughts winged their way through space, scattering like a swarm of frightened bees, and sleep fled his eyes. It is not easy to go to sleep on the eve of battle, or rather of a catastrophe.

A conversation was in progress rather quietly, to one side of him, among a little group of rebels who lay close by. Their talk drew his attention. "Turn it any way you like, it's all up with us," said one.

"We've been had, brother, no doubt of that," sighed another.

"We must have been out of our senses to follow those rascals. We've set our own houses on fire," said a third.

"What did we need an insurrection for?"

"It's too late to think of that."

"Well then?"

"We must find a way out."

"There's only one way, to take to our heels," said a voice that Ognyanov knew.

"That's it; no tears will be shed for those that get away."

"Only for those that stay," added another.

"Let's make off tomorrow across Vurlishnitsa."

"Better do it now."

"We can't, the guard'll stop us."

"Tomorrow, tomorrow."

"Yes, in the confusion."

"They'll all be taking to their heels then, the others'll get ahead of us."

"The only cur's Ognyanov. Take care he doesn't see us."

"Pooh, Ognyanov made off yesterday."

"Is that so?"

"We're the only fools here."

Ognyanov raised himself up and cried out, "You lie, you scoundrels. I'm here!" When this terrible voice rang out through the darkness all fell silent.

Ognyanov had listened to the talk with indignation and horror. There was no doubt that it expressed the general mood of the rebels in this fortification as well as in the others. The voice of one of the talkers seemed very familiar to him, he had heard it long ago. But he could not remember whose it was.

"My God, my God!" he thought as he drew his cape well over his chest to keep out the biting wind. "What a combination of events! What disappointment! What treachery! Care for this cursed life after this if you can, keep on wanting to live! We'll be going into battle tomorrow, and I know already how it'll end! There's panic in every heart. Their hands are weakened and their minds darkened by the fear of death—after they came here to seek it themselves. These people were enthusiastic, they were full of hope, they believed like children—and now they tremble like children. The cowardice of one carries the rest with it. Byala Cherkva and the rest have deluded our hopes and demoralized the town. It's baseness, it's a treacherous betrayal of the common cause. That's all that nest of intriguers can do, hatch treachery, and breed traitors. It knows how to breed men like Kandov and Avram, it knows how to raise girls like Rada! Ah, that Rada, she's poisoned the last hours of my life! And now I'm looking for death, leaving the world now with curses on my lips. . . . How happy I could have died, dear God, loved and warmed by the rays of love, certain that at least one pure tear would be shed over my unknown grave! . . . To have to die when all is dead for you in this world, when you see your idols fallen in the mud, your ideals buried! Love! Revolution! How hard and hopeless such a death is. But how longed for, how necessary it is for wretches like me!"

The mountain wind howled sadly over the sleeping plain. The leaves of the forests around them rustled with a dull and sinister sound which the darkness made still more dreadful. All the peaks, the valleys and mountains around, all nature seemed to be groaning. The stars twinkled restlessly in the heavens. From time to time a night-bird croaked in the wilderness, then dead silence reigned once more. . . . The wind from the mountains soughed over the heads of the rebels who lay in the trenches like someone wailing in the distance. These wails found a painful echo in their hearts and made them start and peer tensely into the darkness. Then they fell again into a restless doze, full of pale ghosts of horror, interspersed with shivers of cold and the wind's icy kisses.

At last the shrill choir of the cocks in Klissoura broke through the night air and filled the lonely mountain with their lively greeting, the forerunner of dawn, of the golden sun, of life and of the renewal brought by spring.

chapter 34

the morning

Despite his troubled state of mind Ognyanov finally fell asleep and slept soundly for two hours. They say that condemned men sleep soundly on the eve of their execution. Towards morning he started up and looked around. Nature was waking up. It was growing lighter everywhere. The sky, a pale, watery blue, had lost its last twinkling star. To the east it grew paler and paler. A fiery band of red lay over the mountain peaks there, like the glow of a distant fire. Transparent mists still hung in the folds of the ravines on Ribaritsa, while its snowy crest was already flushing in the reflected dawn to the east. Only Bogdan was still wrapped in mist, cold and dreary. But little by little the mists melted away, the light grew whiter and stronger, and the green mountain forests and hills all around smiled and gazed joyfully on this spring morning under the clear blue sky. Somewhere in the forests early nightingales began to sing.

Ognyanov got up, glanced down at the rebels who lay there shivering under their rugs and capes, and set off towards Zli-Dol. He was going to discuss the situation with the Council of War. He soon disappeared into the valley that lay across his road. It had grown quite light by now; the sun had risen.

In the trenches the rebels had all gotten up and set to work finishing the new trenches, supervised by their corporal; these trenches had become necessary because their numbers had been increased by a small detachment which had been sent there the night before.

The men were less discouraged now. Marchev had told them that Ognyanov had reconnoitred the country beyond Tekiya and that he knew for certain that Byala Cherkva was going to rise that very day. This news restored their courage somewhat. The boys perked up, their faces looked more cheerful, they even began to joke, and some hummed comic songs. Humor, so characteristic of Bulgarians, was not long in making its appearance. Pointed jokes were made at the expense of the four from Klissoura who had been sentenced to shoot the Gipsy.

"To miss Mehmed at five feet and have to shoot a second time!

Poor devil! That minute of life you gave him is as good as a hundred years of torture. He's paid for all his sins!" said one.

"Devil take you!" said another. "You've made a martyr of him. So now he's in paradise with Mohammed."

"That's a lie," said a third, "Dicho and Stamen the Crow threw him into the pond there, and now he's with the frogs." Laughter greeted this sally.

"Well, of all the shots! To be so near and not have one bullet hit him!" cried another. "I couldn't have missed him at that distance if I'd spat at him."

"I'll bet my head you never aimed at him!"

"That's right, even my grandmother couldn't have missed him at that distance."

"We aimed all right," one of their butts defended himself.

"Yes, with your eyes shut."

"Well, I did shut my eyes, but only when I pulled the trigger." Laughter broke out again.

Others teased Rachko about his name. "Well, Stinkard, who stuck such a famous name on you, eh?" one man asked him.

"Rachko, that can't be your name, you're just fibbing," another teased.

Rachko was offended. "Who's fibbing? Ask the Count!"

"No, no, you're lying, prove the truth of your name!" And the joker told him exactly what proof he required.

"Did you men know that he took us for haidouks yesterday?"

"He's right," remarked one. "Borimechka fleeced him. He took his scissors and yardstick from his bag."

"That he did, he took them all right, he took them right out of my bag, that one, the bad lot," Rachko asserted.

"What did he want them for?"

"He broke them up to make shot for the cannon."

"Then we'll be taking Sebastopol for sure."

"If our battery does as well as Zli-Dol's not a Turk'll be left alive."

"And the kingdom of Klissoura will be untouched forever," laughed another.

"What are they waving for there?" asked one of the men, turning to the east. They all turned in the same direction.

The lookouts were giving the pre-arranged signal to the fortifications that they had sighted an enemy. At the same time two of them ran to Zli-Dol to give the Council of War all the details.

The runners had barely arrived when two mounted detachments of twenty Turks each appeared from the direction of Rahmanlari. One advanced along the road, the other across country. With bated breath the rebels watched to see if any other forces would appear after the horsemen. But no others came into sight.

Two groups on foot, stronger than the Turks in number, immediately left the fortifications to meet them. The bigger group came from Zli-Dol.

"Who's at its head?" asked the rebels, gazing at the leader.

"Why, don't you see, it's Ognyanov!" several cried.

"It's the Count, it's the Count, I'm ready to swear it. . . . No matter what he's wearing, I know him. At the Karnari inn, you may call it a lie, but it's the truth. . . ." But nobody listened to Rachko.

The Turks stopped when they saw the Bulgarian detachments and retreated. "That's singed their whiskers, the curs," some of the men remarked joyfully.

"No fighting today either."

"Byala Cherkva must have given them something to do," others reasoned. And the trenches hummed with cheerful talk and busy stir.

chapter 35

battle

Noon came and went. The sun stood high in the heavens.

In Ognyanov's trenches the rebels were finishing their lunch and hastily cramming the leftovers into their bags. Their dusty, careworn faces, unwashed since Sunday, had a restless look. Their disquiet was clearly apparent. The slight success had raised their drooping spirits, but only for a moment. They knew that if that day were not decisive, the following one would most certainly be so. They felt the storm approaching rapidly. From time to time they cast worried glances to the east across the bare meadows where the scattered lokouts could be seen.

The sun beat down. To the right of the battery, brought up and placed in position the night before, Ognyanov, who had just returned from Zli-Dol, was very busy with several others; they were in a hurry to finish the new trench. As we have already mentioned, the Council of War had sent them a reinforcement of ten men the night before, and the existing trenches were insufficient.

"Schoolmaster," cried a peasant of fifty. Ognyanov turned.

"What is it, Uncle Marin?"

The peasant from Verigovo handed him a paper, simply folded in four. "They've brought a letter for you."

"Who brought it?" asked Boicho before unfolding it.

"Ivan Borimechka. He was looking for you here last night but couldn't find you, so he gave it to me, and asked me to hand it over when you got back."

"Did he tell you who it was from?"

"From the schoolmistress."

Ognyanov's heart was seared with pain as if a snake had bitten it. He crushed the paper convulsively, intending to throw it away, but remembered that this might be noticed and instinctively thrust it into his coat pocket. Then he quickly and feverishly set about his work again, to deaden the sense of pain that oppressed him.

"What does Rada want of me now? Is this a time for it? Why is she writing and what does she want of me? When will I see fighting at last, to meet my death and put an end to everything!"

Just then there was an unusual stir among the rebels. They all crowded together along the top of the trench and stood there gazing to the east.

Ognyanov raised his head and fixed his eyes on the bare ridges. The lookouts there were signaling the alarm. Several guns were fired at once, the signal that a strong enemy force had been sighted. They were soon beating a hasty retreat shouting, "Turks! Lots and lots of them!"

Panic seized the trenches. Their defenders moved to and fro, their faces quite pale. "To your posts! I command you!" roared Ognyanov now seizing his Martini rifle from a pile on which he had laid it with the others.

This shout of Ognyanov's brought the insurgents to their senses and they returned to their posts in the trenches. At critical moments the courage and presence of mind of a single man has a magical effect on the masses and subdues them. At such times whoever wants to take command can do so.

Several of the lookouts now came up panting. Ognyanov met them. "What did you see?"

"Turks! A terrible horde, coming this way . . . there must be a thousand of them. . . . The road is black with bashi-bazouks!" Ognyanov motioned them to hold their tongues.

"Stay where you are!" he called to the trenches seeing that several men had left their posts, unable to hold out.

"Crowds and crowds of them," said several men who were looking over the top of the trench.

"To your posts! Every man at his gun!" Boicho's command rang out sharply. The men went back to the trenches.

"You can see them now."

And indeed, far off on the main road, where it comes out around the shoulder of the hill, the head of a dense column made its appearance; it crept nearer every moment, growing longer and longer, moving forward like an endless caterpillar. It was Tossoun-Bey's horde. The nearer it approached the clearer were its denseness and its numbers. The Turks marched four abreast, twenty small banners and three big standards—white, red, green and other colors—waving over the column. Soon it had filled the whole road from Koula to Byala-Voda, a distance of two miles.

Confusion reigned again in the ranks of the rebels. Not a man could stay at his post, each one of them stood up and looked around him timidly. It was only Ognyanov's fierce looks that restrained them somewhat. The black column continued its march along the road until it reached the little well at about a bullet's range from the trenches. Then the guard at Zli-Dol emptied several long-distance guns; our trenches fired too, at Ognyanov's command. The cannon roared also. Thick smoke covered the fortifications, and the shots rent the air, echoing in the mountains. Several men in the front ranks fell.

Just then Ognyanov noticed the heads of three men making off down the road towards the Old River. These rebels were fleeing from the trenches under cover of the first confusion and smoke. In this group of fugitives Ognyanov instinctively recognized his neighbors of last night who had discussed their plan of flight.

In a couple of strides he had reached the ridge of the hill under which lay the scree and the valley. The fugitives had taken a narrow path, hollowed out by the torrents, and were walking in single file.

"Back! Return or I'll shoot you down!" he cried, taking aim.

The fugitives turned and stood stock still, as if they had been turned to stone. They had left their guns in the trench. Ognyanov recognized one of them as Deacon Vikenti, shaved and in uniform. The poor boy was scarlet with shame. Mechanically they turned back.

"Uncle Marin, bring these cowards back and stick them into the trenches. If any of them try to get away I give you leave to bash in their heads." And Ognyanov quickly strode back to his post.

"Couldn't you have fired your rifles once at least, you sons of bitches, for the honor of the cause, before you ran away?" Uncle Marin scolded them as he drove them towards the trenches with his gun at their backs.

This firm conduct of their commander quelled the other rebels. They refrained from showing their fear as best they could, but only for a few minutes. The lips of most of them were cracked and bleeding.

The Turks had not fired a single shot as yet. The fall of their fellows, brought down by the first volley from the trenches, caused a momentary confusion in their ranks. They carried the wounded to the fences of the rose fields and retreated in a body. This initial success encouraged the rebels and they kept up an energetic fire against the enemy. The whole mountains and the hills seemed to shake at the incessant firing. Small white clouds, perched along the different heights, indicated the trenches. They went on firing even when the Turks had retreated so far that they were out of range.

A long way off, behind the horde, a group of horsemen could be seen. They were Tossoun-Bey's general staff. The horde had drawn back and was crowding about them. It stayed there in a dense throng for a considerable time. Apparently, a consultation was being held and the plan of attack was being changed.

At last a stir could be noticed, and the horde split up into several groups that drew apart from each other. Then, as at a signal, all these groups dashed forward in open file with wild cries, and came at the trenches at a rush. Some ran up the steep slopes to the mountains, others towards the gully of Zli-Dol, others again towards Sredna Gora and the valley through which the Old River flows, opening a pass towards Klissoura; a fourth group dashed towards the vineyards, making for our trenches. The rebels greeted them with volleys from a distance, but the Turks only began to shoot when they got within range.

His face blackened with gunpowder, furrowed by the sweat as it ran down his cheeks, drunk with the smell of blood, dazed by the whistling of the bullets which flew over his head. Ognyanov stood up one moment to empty his Martini which spat white smoke, and stooped down under cover the next. From time to time he shouted without looking around into the smoke that surrounded him, "Shoot! Fire! Courage, brothers!"

Suddenly he heard Uncle Marin's voice next him saying to someone, "Down, my boy, get down. . . . They'll hit you!"

Involuntarily Ognyanov turned to his right and through the remnants of smoke that the breeze was blowing away he caught sight of an insurgent standing there without stooping to take cover, shooting at the enemy, entirely exposed to their bullets. Such boldness was simple madness. To his amazement Ognyanov recognized Kandov.

In his astonishment he went up to him almost mechanically and put out his hand through the smoke, saying, "Give me your hand, brother!"

The student turned, gave Ognyanov a silent, icy look, but squeezed his hand hard. It was a sign of reconciliation between the two rivals before their bleeding country, perhaps also a last farewell.

A little trickle of blood ran over Ognyanov's hand as it held Kandov's. That blood flowed from the student's arm. Ognyanov noticed it without surprise or astonishment, nor did he realize the significance of this warm little trickle of blood. He was much more surprised at seeing Kandov there.

Indeed, on leaving Rada's room, soon after Ognyanov, the student had gone to the place where arms were being distributed and from there to the trenches near the Old River. From there he had been sent to this place the night before with the reinforcements, and had not yet been noticed by Ognyanov, who was entirely absorbed by the cares of his office.

Ognyanov drew back and stood looking around. It was only then he noticed that the trenches were nearly empty. The rebels had disappeared. Only five or six men, of whom Kandov was one, still remained and kept up the fire, which was growing weaker and weaker. Shots came few and far between from the other trenches as well, for they too had been deserted by their defenders. Enemy bullets, on the other hand rained down and made the least movement above the trenches dangerous.

In despair, maddened with rage, Ognyanov kept up the unequal fight with a handful of brave friends, firmly resolved to die at his post. By now, of all the earthworks on the eastern slopes, it was his alone that offered resistance.

"Oh, my God!" somebody cried out in pain near by.

Ognyanov started at the cry and glanced to the left, where it had come from. Vikenti had fallen on his back in the trench. A stream of blood spouted from his breast just below his throat, staining the loose earth beside him. The wound was mortal; he had washed away his disgrace in blood.

Uncle Marin carried him over to a shelter to be carried back to the town. But there was nobody there. The heights were deserted.

A dreadful silence hung over the empty trenches. Only a few shots from the heights to the north and west of the town, which had so far been unmolested by the Turks, mingled, quite uselessly, with the fire from Ognyanov's trenches, which now drew the enemy bullets as a magnet draws iron.

The Turks continued to advance in swarms, shooting incessantly. They crept cautiously through the vineyards and rose-fields which still separated them from the fortifications, bending low to take any cover that offered itself, instinctively throwing themselves down whenever they noticed that they were going to be fired on from one of the heights.

One by one they captured the trenches which the general panic had emptied. Instead of the rebels or their dead bodies they found nothing but weapons, bags, clothes and other loot. They found the cherry-tree cannons too, that had been brought up the day before, two or three to each position. With the exception of two, they were still loaded, for no one had thought of firing them, nor had any spirit been left in the men to do so.

The Turks appeared on the height of Shaikovets above the town itself. Guns were fired against them from the streets, bringing down the standard bearer and another man. But the fate of the battle and of the town, which was already burning in several places, had already been decided in favor of Tossoun-Bey's hordes. In black swarms, with savage cries, they came rushing down the ridges towards hapless Klissoura, like a flock of black crows on a fresh carcass.

chapter 36

Rada

As soon as the first shots on the heights announced to Klissoura that the fateful battle had begun, the people were seized by a fearful panic and fled towards Koprivshtitsa through Vurlishnitsa, a narrow gorge of Sredna Gora, through which a river of the same name runs to join the Old River at the southwestern end of the town.

Mrs. Mouratliiska, with whom Rada was staying, quickly collected her more valuable possessions and her children to leave the house and flee with the others. She stopped at Rada's room to call her. But in spite of all her entreaties Rada refused to come, for she was resolved to remain in the house. Kind Mrs. Mouratliiska begged her on her knees and with tears in her eyes to set out at once; she could not leave her to such a terrible fate. The Turks had already appeared on the heights above the town, every second was precious.

"You go, Aunt Anitsa, take the children, but I beg you to leave me," Rada cried as she pushed her to the door.

Mrs. Mouratliiska looked at her in terror and wrung her hands. Through the windows she saw the Turks bearing down on the town. She could not make up her mind what to do.

Obviously only despair could have roused such unreasoning stubbornness in Rada. She had indeed fallen prey to terrible despair.

Ever since that dreadful quarrel between Ognyanov and the student she had been prostrate, crushed by her lover's contempt. In her bewilderment she had been unable to defend herself, and she had not seen him again. Indeed Ognyanov still labored under the dreadful delusion of her infidelity, and was filled with a boundless abhorrence and loathing of her. If he died in battle he would die with curses on his lips and in cruel, unendurable torment. This thought was terrible for her. It never gave her a moment's rest. Her conscience accused her, for she might have reassured him and shown him his error, but she had not done so. This noble man would go to a terrible death in despair, for he had gone out to seek his death, he did not fear it; and it was her duty to make it at least an easier one for him, to let him die at peace, consoled by the thought that he died beloved and worshipped. Perhaps she might even have snatched him from the jaws of death—perhaps then he would not have sought it purposely—and have saved him for herself and the country. But he had not come down into the town a single time. In vain had she tried more than once to go to the trenches on one pretext or another to see him at least one moment, even if she should draw down on herself the anger of his fiery look; but she was persistently denied access to the fortifications. Her only consolation was to speak with Staika, Borimechka's wife, who was her neighbor, Borimechka had come into the town three times on various errands and, stopping to see his wife on the way, had given her news of Ognyanov. Through Staika Rada had heard that Ognyanov was still alive and well, that he was extremely busy, but that was all. In those six days, which seemed like as many centuries, her love for Boicho, so unfortunate and yet so brave, increased with her suffering. Her passion became almost a religion. She imagined him as a knight, more handsome still in the beauty of his manliness and surrounded by a radiant halo of glory, meeting death with a bitter smile, up on those heights, without turning once in her direction to cast her a look, to whisper a farewell to her, who could not live without him and whom he had crushed with his contempt. The night before she had seen Borimechka for the first time, and had let herself go and wept bitterly before him. Kind Ivan had consoled her as best he could and promised that Boicho should have the note she had at once scribbled hastily in pencil. (As we know, it was handed to Ognyanov just as the battle began.) But not a line did she get in reply, even by word of mouth, and her grief and despair knew no bounds. She felt that she could not live if Boicho carried his scorn to the grave into which she had thrust him; the fountainhead of love and happiness had dried up forever in her life and it was loathsome to her. What was left to her after this? Helpless suffering, bitter regrets, the world's contempt, and despair, eternal despair. What use did she have for this life? Who needed it? On whom could she depend without humiliation? Byala Cherkva now seemed as dark and ugly to her as the grave. Should she go to Hadji Rovoahma again and submit to her? Or to Marko? Should she turn to him for protection? How would she dare? She would die of shame before that kindly soul. Probably he was aware of the filthy slanders about her, and regretted all his goodness to her. For Rada had heard the ugly rumor that besmirched her name in Byala Cherkva the very day she left the town. No, no, only Boicho himself could console and save her! But what if he died? Mouratliiska was right in wanting to live. She had someone and something to live for, there was someone to mourn for her, because she had someone to love her. But what of herself? She could not bear the burden of her unhappiness, she was too weak. There was nothing for her to do in this sad world to which no ties bound her any longer. But suppose Boicho lived? How terribly he would despise her, because she could not clear herself; circumstances were against her. His wounded pride could not forgive her. The blow his heart had sustained was far too heavy. And Boicho would never, never see her again. He was implacable where honor was concerned, she knew that. No, no, she had to die. It was easy to find death now, even a glorious death, under the ruins of this heroic town. Let Mrs. Mouratliiska go, she herself would stay, would die! Yes, as Boicho had not told her to live, had not deigned to send her even one little word, she would die! And if death passed him by, let him know that Rada had been an honest girl, that Bulgarian women did not fear death, and that she had offered herself in sacrifice to her love for him.

Such were the thoughts, born of despair, that moved this tender, sentimental girl, broken by misfortune. They moved like dark storm-clouds in Rada's mind when Mrs. Mouratliiska, weeping bitterly, tried to drag her away, entreating her to come with her. But Rada would not stir.

Just then they heard Bulgarians shouting in the street. Mrs. Mouratliiska looked out of the window; she saw some of the insurgents passing and called out, "Bai Hristo, what's happened up there? Where is Ognyanov? Why are you running away?"

The man answered breathlessly, "A mess, a terrible mess, Anichka! Ognyanov, poor devil, he's still up there. So many have fallen. Run for all you're worth, run to Vurlishnitsa!" And the rebels hurried on. Obviously Bai Hristo had come from Ognyanov's trenches. Rada screamed like a madwoman. It was only then, after fruitless efforts to drag her away, that Mrs. Mouratliiska left her house.

It was certainly high time to do so, for, not long after, Rada heard women shrieking desperately at the north end of the town, which the Turks had already entered. As she stood there, distracted and overwhelmed with grief, she saw a crowd of bashi-bazouks through the window; they were running down a street with bare swords, and cut down a couple of men they caught up with. She could see quite plainly something red gush forth from the fallen men; she had looked on death, terrible death, in its grimmest form, and a mad fear of it seized her.

The desire for life awoke with tremendous force in the young girl, and it stifled all other feelings in her, paralyzing all her resolution to die, with which her despair had filled her till now. She hastened to escape, to save herself from death, or the life which the lustful, bloodthirsty villains might leave her. She opened the door to run down the stairs, but heard the gate burst open with a crash and at the same moment, through the branches of the fruit trees in the garden, she caught sight of an armed man, followed by another figure, quickly coming towards the staircase where she had stopped, as if turned to stone.

She came to her senses, turned back into her room, slamming the door quickly shut and locking it, then, half-dead with fright, she hid in the opposite corner. She had scarecely done so when knocks and kicks began to rain down on the door and a terrible voice like the roar of an animal resounded outside. As the door remained closed, the man outside began to break it down as though with a club, the door creaked, one side of it gave and the barrel of a gun was placed in the opening to serve as a lever. Rada heard the dry boards splintering as they gave under the onslaught of the steel, she saw a huge foot coming through—the enemy was coming in.

Then unutterable horror laid hold of her and blotted out all her thoughts. Death appeared a thousand times preferable to the terrible moments that were approaching. She dashed towards the iconostasis, lit a candle at the flickering float-light before it, and ran quickly back to her corner. There on the table was a bag of gunpowder, forgotten by the rebels. With the candle still in her right hand, Rada began to fumble at the opening of the bag with her left hand to make a hole big enough for the flame. Just as she was doing this the door fell to the ground with a loud crash and Borimechka's giant figure appeared on the threshold. Staika followed close behind him.

But Rada did not see them and approached the candle to the gunpowder.

chapter 37

two rivers

At that very moment Ognyanov was far away in the mountains. He was the last to retreat from the trenches when the Turks were already coming up the earthworks, while others took aim at him from the trenches they had already captured nearby. Blood-stained, blackened with gunpowder, his coat pierced by bullets in two places, he escaped by a miracle. He had sought death, but the instinct of self-preservation, stronger than any power of volition at the moment, saved him.

Now he was on the height above Vurlishnitsa on the left-hand ridge, at the foot of which ran the little river. Tears trickled down his cheeks, furrowing the blood, the sweat and the dust on his face, which the powder had blackened. For Ognyanov was crying.

He had halted and was looking down on the terrible picture presented by the wreck of his revolution. He was bareheaded. Down in the valley a frightened mob of rebels, women and children were running into the mountains in mad panic. The shouts and screams of these unfortunates came clearly up to him. Opposite him lay Klissoura in flames.

Suddenly his eye fell on his blood-covered right hand. He remembered that this was Kandov's blood. And in a flash his thoughts leapt from Kandov to Rada. His hair stood on end, he thrust a hand into his breast-pocket and drew out Rada's crumpled note, which he now opened.

He read the following lines written in pencil in a weak and trembling hand:

"Boicho!

You left me in scorn. I cannot live without you. Please send me just one word. If you command it, I shall remain alive. I am innocent. Answer me, Boicho. I live in torment. If you don't, farewell, farewell, beloved, I shall bury myself under the ruins of Klissoura.

Rada."

Bitter pain twisted Ognyanov's face. He turned his eyes to the town where the fires were growing more numerous. At various points, new flames kept shooting up from the roofs, licking the air with their pale red tongues. Clouds of black smoke rolled over the town; merging with the clouds in the sky which hung low over it, they brought an early dusk to the burning town. The fires spread rapidly on all sides. Their blood-red flames lighted up the screes and gullies of Ribaritsa, and were mirrored in the waters of the Old River. Ognyanov looked for the two-storied house in which Mrs. Mouratliiska lived. He soon found it and recognized Rada's two windows with a pang of emotion. The house was not on fire as yet, but the buildings around were already burning, bringing the peril close.

"Poor girl, she must be there! Oh, this is terrible, terrible!" And he dashed down the gully into the valley. He hurried, or rather slid down the screes and scrub, and turned back towards the mouth of the river, heading for Klissoura.

The narrow valley of the Vurlishnitsa was packed with fugitives of both sexes, of all ages and conditions. This terrified mob of people stretching all along the river, was like another river flowing in the opposite diection. The panic had emptied Klissoura in an hour and crowded this mountain valley. They were all running, all fleeing, panting and breathless with fear, like people whose pursuers were at their heels. Some had come out with nothing but the clothes on their backs, others were laden with blankets, household goods and other odds and ends, often even with the most unnecessary objects, picked up in their haste. The choice was sometimes positively comical. One wealthy householder who had left hearth and home had taken nothing but a pendulum clock with him, which he most certainly did not need at the moment. Further on a woman was carrying a sieve, and it impeded her considerably in her flight. One met old women and young girls fleeing barefoot over the stones, carrying their shoes in their hands, so as not to wear them out. Ognyanov collided with these frightened people at every step, or stumbled over women who had fallen or fainted by the wayside. Many of them screamed desperately, but no one stopped to help them up. He saw all these horrors, bewildered and dazed, but hurried feverishly on to the town, with thought only in his mind, to save Rada. His eyes sought her instinctively among the terror-stricken faces of the women and girls he met with, then he ran on once more. These people were strangers to him, they were ghosts, they did not exist for him. He could not even understand why these people were fleeing, he had no thought for them, just as they had none for him, nor did any one wonder or ask why he was going back when all were pressing forwards. There was no reason, there was only a path. At every step the scenes of horror grew more terrible and more frequent. At a turn in the valley he came upon a little girl who had fallen into the river, exhausted with her flight, wild with fear, bleeding and shrieking for help. A little further on lay a baby, blue in the face with screaming for its mother, who had probably abandoned it as too heavy a burden. Old grannies, men and women passed the poor infant by without hearing or seeing it. Each thought only of himself. Fear hardens hearts, it is the supreme, the most loathsome form of egoism. Disgrace itself does not stamp such an ignoble seal on a face as fear does. Ognyanov bent down mechanically, picked up the baby and moved on. Under a bush, to one side of the path, a woman had miscarried; her face contorted with pain, she stretched out her arms to the passers-by. Wailing, hoarse cries, the screams of chldren, filled the air. To crown all these misfortunes, it began to rain in torrents, beating down upon the tired fugitives and filling the wild mountain gully with its patter. From minute to minute the storm grew in violence, muddy streams tore down the slopes into the river, pouring over the unfortunate fugitives' feet, while the rain dashed against their faces, wetting them to the skin and freezing them to death. Children screamed heartrendingly, as their mothers dragged them along by force through the streams, slipping and falling among the stones. The weeping and the cries rose higher and higher.

The gullies in the pass repeated the wild echo of suffering and storm, which blended with the roar of the river. Suddenly through the rain Ognyanov recognized a woman in the crowd opposite, the first person he had recognized in that crowd. It was Mrs. Mouratliiska, a baby in her arms, followed by her three older children. He waded across the muddy stream to meet the tired mother.

"Where's Rada?" he asked. She opened her mouth, but was unable to speak. She could only point towards the town.

"At your house?"

"Yes, yes, hurry," was all she managed to gasp. Weak as she was Mrs. Mouratliiska could hardly cope with the hard going. Her eyes were popping out of her head with the effort of covering the hard road. But instead of muscles she had energy, an energy inspired by the love of her beautiful children.

"Where are you carrying that baby?" she asked in a feeble voice, hardly audible above the noise of the rain.

Ognyanov looked down. It was only now that he noticed the child he had picked up somewhere and was carrying without realizing it. And for the first time he felt the small thing's weight and heard its wailing. He looked at Mrs. Mouratliiska bewildered.

"Give it to me, give it to me." And she took it from Ognyanov, clasped it to her soaking bosom with her left arm, clasped her own child with her right, and went her way. It was quite dark when Ognyanov reached the mouth of the Vurlishnitsa. From that spot you could see the whole of Klissoura. The rain had extinguished the fires; only here and there under the roofs the flames still flickered, sending red streaks of light through the windows into the dark streets. The crash of houses caving in came from afar. Flames leapt up again and passed on to other houses. Suddenly Ognyanov noticed a big new fire had broken out in the southern part of the town. Great flames leapt up with loud cracklings and flashes and millions of sparks sprang into the air. Ognyanov realized that they came from the place where Mrs. Mouratliiska's house stood. Yes, it was on fire. At the same moment the upper floor of the house fell in, amidst a sea of flames and yellow smoke. Rada's room was on that floor.

He hurled himself like a madman into the burning streets filled with infuriated Turks and vanished among them.

PART THREE

chapter 1

the awakening

Within a few days the insurrection was crushed everywhere. The struggle was a complete failure; it collapsed in panic fear. Revolution — and surrender.

History offers examples of rebellions as sacred and as doomed, but of none so tragically inglorious as this. The April uprising was a stillborn child, conceived in the infatuation of a most ardent love and choked by its mother in the throes of childbirth. It died before it had lived.

It was an uprising without a history. It was too brief. Golden hopes, deep faith, titanic strength and fervor — the accumulations of several centuries of martyrdom — all went overboard in an instant. It was a terrible awakening!

And how many martyrs it produced! How many victims! How many deaths and downfalls! Yes, and a little heroism! But what heroism! Peroushtitsa was another Saragossa. Yet Peroushtitsa is unknown in the history of the world.

And then Batak! That name alone winged its way beyond the struggle, beyond the fires and the smoke, encircled the world and fixed itself in the memory of the nations!

Batak! The name, in both its senses, describes our whole revolution.* Fate sometimes enjoys such puns. But in this case fate played Providence for us: if she gave us Batak, she also gave us Alexander II.**

If this movement with its unfortunate consequences had not brought about the War of Liberation it would have deserved nothing but inexorable condemnation; common sense would then term it madness, the nations would have called it shameful, and history — a crime. For alas, history too, that old trollop, bows to success.

* The town of Batak suffered more than any other in the Turkish atrocities that followed the uprising, almost the whole of the population being wiped out. But the word "Batak" in Turkish also means "slough" and hence "failure," "impasse."

** The Russian Tsar under whom war was declared on Turkey almost exactly one year later, which led to the liberation of Bulgaria in 1878.

Poetry alone would have forgiven it and crowned it with a hero's laurels, for the sake of the rapture which sent those meek Anatolian tailors onto the heights of Sredna Gora — those sublime heights — with cherry tree cannon! It was a poetic madness. For young nations, like the young, are poets.

For three days and three nights Ognyanov had been wandering about Stara Planina. He was heading eastwards, so as to come out above Byala Cherkva, for he did not know what was happening there. For a peaceful citizen it is a six hours' march from Klissoura; sixty wouldn't suffice for a revolutionary escaping from the posses.

In the daytime Ognyanov stole into the forests and thickets to sleep like beast in some hollow tree, and to evade the posses, and by night he journeyed on through the blackness and the wilds, despite the dark and the rain, shivering with the cold which blew from the snow-covered heights of the Balkan mountains, wandering at random, often backwards instead of forwards. He lived on grass, in other words he starved like a wolf. He did not dare beg for hospitality in the hovels he came across occasionally: the doors of most of them were guarded either by the sentinel of betrayal or by that Cerberus with an ominous bark — fear.

Often at dusk when he chanced to be on some peak he saw the sky glowing red to the south. At first he had taken this phenomenon in the heavens for some queer refraction of the rays of a sun already set. But at night the dim haze of color grew brighter, extending along the whole horizon. It seemed like an aurora borealis glowing in the south. It was the glare of the flames which were reducing so many flourishing villages to ashes. A terrible and majestic sight.

Tonight the pass over the range opened up to a still wider view to the south. And Ognyanov was horrified by the sight of flames along Sredna Gora. It looked like a volcano, belching fire from about twenty craters, and causing the whole vault of heaven to glow in a radiant mist.

Ognyanov tore his hair. "Bulgaria is done for, done for!" he kept saying desperately as he watched the flames. "This is what our sacred struggle has brought us to. Here are all our proud hopes — drowned in blood and flames! O God, O God! And there," he added, pointing in the direction of Klissoura, "there my heart received its death-blow too. The two ideals I believed in, the two idols I worshipped, crumbled into dust together, the one destroyed in the panic, the other in the ignominy of faithlessness and in the grave. Now I am a ghost without a soul, lost and unable to find its grave!" He may not have looked like a ghost, but he certainly looked like a skeleton.

All the nomad sheepfolds and the Bulgarian huts in the mountain had been warned to afford no hospitality to any suspicious-looking wanderer. The Bulgarians themselves went further; they pursued such people and denounced them to the posses; their cruelty even went so far as to finish off some wounded or half-famished revolutionary with a bullet. Only two weeks ago these same mountain folk had welcomed the apostles as their dearest guests. Stara Planina was no longer the kind mother of heroes sung of in legends, but rather a wicked stepmother. The terror and cowardice of the towns and villages had spread to the most deserted recesses of the mountain, had invaded the beech woods and moorlands, the haunts of haidouks.

chapter 2

the shepherd's loaf

Dawn that day had overtaken Ognyanov in a small beech wood, covering the northern flank of a hill above one of the headwaters of the Ossum, to the east of the bare peak of Ambaritsa. He was exhausted and starving, and his stomach was trying to digest some bitter herbs.

At about a hundred paces from where he stood was a sheepfold belonging to nomads, full of bread, cheese, milk and curds. He was like Tantalus dying of thrist beside a cool stream, unable to drink from it.

A wolf will never starve to death with a flock of sheep near by. The teeth of the watchdogs do not tear so cruelly as those of hunger. Ognyanov decided to follow the wolf's example. He çame out of the copse, crossed the little river and climbed resolutely up towards the hut.

Inside were two women, a grandmother and a young bride, busy mending, and two boys braiding something. The sheep dogs were probably with the flock, not far off. Catching sight of the stranger, bareheaded, with deep sunken eyes, and dressed in outlandish clothes, the women cried out in fear.

"Vat you vant?" somebody called from outside. Whereupon a tall, white-haired old nomad appeared with a cocked rifle. Ognyanov recognized Kir Yani,* who often came down to Byala Cherkva to sell his butter. And he knew Boicho too.

"Good day, Kir Yani, give me a hunk of bread, for God's sake," Boicho hastened to say by way of making his peaceful intentions quite clear.

Kir Yani eyed him from head to foot. Whether he recognized him or not, he was not favorably impressed by his inspection. With a frown he went into the hut, and broke off half a loaf, saying something to one of the boys.

"Now, go avay, me not vant get into trouble. Somebody see you, Christian man," he said severely, handing the bread to Ognyanov.

---

* *kir:* Mr. (Greek).

Ognyanov thanked him and quickly headed down the gully towards his hiding place in the copse. "God!" he said to himself with bitterness, "a Greek, a half-savage, took pity on me: and only yesterday the Bulgarians set the dogs on me and drove me away with curses."

He began to tear the bread with his teeth, quickly, ravenously, his eyes shining with greed. Hunger had blended the noble fire of his glance with a dull animal glare. At that moment Ognyanov would not have spared his own father, had he tried to take the bread from him. Count Ugolino ate his own children to save himself from starvation. For hunger is a counselor more terrible than despair itself.

In the gully Boicho drank some water at the rivulet and started up the steep slope to reach the copse. He immediately felt the beneficial effect of the food; he had regained some of his strength.

As he neared the copse, he heard distant voices which made him turn around. A group of Circassians were running down the hill on which the sheepfold stood, waving to him to stop. Several hounds dashed ahead of them (it is well-known that in those tragic days the posses, which consisted for the most part of Circassians, were accompanied by hounds especially trained to track people down like game and to attack them). Kir Yani in his white cape stood on the top of the hill, looking on with interest at the manhunt he had arranged. For along with the hunk of bread he had given the fugitive, Kir Yani had sent his boy to denounce him to the posse which was concealed not far off.

Hospitality and betrayal! To this wild nomad's hardened heart these two things were not incompatible. He was quite sincere in both: he had fed the hungry in the person of his acquaintance, to perform a duty of humanity, yet denounced the revolutionary to keep out of trouble. He was now calmly watching the hunt.

Ognyanov saw his doom approaching. However with that presence of mind which deserts most people in times of danger, but with him had become second nature, he immediately weighed his chances of escape. Across the stream behind him was a rise of ground which would screen him for a minute or two from the view of the posse as it dropped down into the hollow. In that brief space of time he could get into the beech wood, but that would not help; they would overtake him. It was impossible to escape from the bullets and the hounds by running. In the gully by the river there were some low bushes, between the two water-worn banks. But these bushes could not hide him either, for if he misled his pursuers, the hounds were sure to find him. There, as everywhere else — death!

But Boicho had no time for hesitation: he had to take some decision or other. He instinctively decided on the gully and rushed down the steep slope with the speed of an arrow. The slope helped his flight. In a moment he was making his way through the thickets at the bottom of the gully with its rocky banks. At the foot of the rock gaped elongated cavities, as though it had been undercut. Ognyanov crept into one of these holes that looked like wild beasts' lairs. There he waited to sell his life as dearly as he could.

For several minutes Ognyanov strained his ears, revolver in hand. These seconds seemed ages to him. The barking drew nearer, then became fainter again, and finally died away. He waited. What could it mean? The posse had probably been misled, but not for long. Ognyanov guessed that they must be looking for him in the copse, and, not finding him there, they would naturally think of the gully, to which the hounds would lead them in any case. An animal's instinct is not deceived twice. How long the agony of this tense waiting lasted he could not tell. His eyes were glued to the gully and the dead leaves which trembled by the rivulet. Every minute he expected to see the muzzle of the hound — that animal seemed to be fateful for him — peering into the cave, or to hear it barking.

A sudden bark rang out. Ognyanov's eyes glared, large and terrible, and he bristled like a hedgehog. With a convulsive movement he aimed his revolver in readiness.

chapter 3

northwards!

The bark which sounded to Ognyanov's right, close at hand, was not repeated. Instead, he heard another noise, that of footsteps. Yes, men's footsteps were approaching, they were coming down the steep sides of the gully, for the banks crumbled and little lumps of soil rolled to the very edge of the fugitive's hiding-place. Soon two feet, shod in sandals, appeared at the opening and passed by; another pair of feet followed, and also passed on; a third man passed, as silently and noiselessly as the others, and he too disappeared. Then a fourth arrived: he did not pass by, however.

He stopped and bent down. Then Ognyanov saw in profile a long dishevelled head, the head of a gorilla. Its owner began to tie up the lace of his leggings which was dragging on the ground. Motionless as a statue Ognyanov crouched there, his revolver cocked.

The head looked into the hole. Then it was raised, and a sharp hissing sound pierced the silence. It was the signal for the others to turn back. And again the head bent down and peered into the hole. Ognyanov decided to shoot.

"And who are you?" inquired a booming voice.

"Bai Ivan!" cried Ognyanov. It was indeed Ivan Borimechka.

"The schoolmaster, I declare!" cried the others, bending down. Without waiting for an invitation Borimechka crept into the lair and started shaking Ognyanov's hands with tears in his eyes. The other three followed. They were from Klissoura.

Boicho's first question was: "What dog was that barking?"

"There wasn't any dog, that was Borimechka," replied the others. Ognyanov smiled, for he remembered that trick of the young giant's. Then he showered them with questions.

"We made a fine mess of it! I'll be damned," said Borimechka sighing thunderously.

"Courage, Bai Ivan! God won't forsake Bulgaria."

"But Klissoura's done for," one of the others spoke up gloomily.

"It's a heap of ashes; it's still burning," the second one added. The third only groaned.

"Brothers, there's no point in regrets! We meant well — we failed.

Courage and patience! The sacrifice won't have been in vain. . . . Have you eaten?"

"Not a crumb since we set out," answered the men from Klissoura miserably. They need not have spoken. Ognyanov could see their emaciated faces. He broke up the remains of the loaf and gave it to his guests.

They threw themselves on it ravenously. But Borimechka refused. "You keep the bread for yourself, you look as lean as a man of God. . . . I've got some lunch." So saying Borimechka took out of his bag a skinned hare, covered with dark clots of blood. He cut off a piece, dipped it in salt, and started tearing it with his sharp teeth.

"Why, that's raw!"

"Raw or not, a hungry man's not so particular. You'll see no fire where revolutionaries are fleeing," Ivan answered munching the tough meat. "These Christians here are keeping Lent, and a nice fat bit turns their stomachs; they've been eating weeds like tortoises," he added licking the hare's blood from his lips.

"And how did you kill that hare? Did you shoot?" asked Boicho curiously.

"I took the hare because there wasn't a boar: I'd have caught that too and strangled it with my bare hands." Borimechka had indeed cornered the hare himself in a thicket without firing a shot.

"And what are you up to in this hole?" asked the giant, examining the cave.

"A posse of Circassians was after me, and it's a wonder they didn't get me; they had hounds with them."

"Is that why you asked where the bark came from? I see. The hounds must have spotted other game, mark my words, and gone chasing after it. That must be it — Bai Ivan knows his business."

"That must have been those infidels we spotted over there, on the opposite slope," one of them said.

"A curse on them! Posses at every step! The mountain's fairly swarming with Turks and Circassians. . . . My blessings upon you for the bread, Ognyanov, I was just about reeling with hunger."

Only now did Ognyanov begin to feel reassured. He realized he had been saved by a miracle, such as he had had to thank his stars for more than once in his life. "Where are you going now?"

"We're making for Wallachia. And you?"

"I've been on my way to Byala Cherkva for three days, and you see how far I've got. . . ."

One of the men from Klissoura spoke up. "Those chaps from Byala Cherkva turned out pretty cagy; they just lay low."

There was resentment in these words. Not so much anger that Byala Cherkva had not revolted, as spite because it had not suffered like the rest. Alas, such is human nature. Misfortune is easier to bear when we know that others share it, even though they be our friends or kinfolk. It is that cruel feeling, so highly developed in all our hearts, that provides the impulse to heroic deeds in the soldier and sends him headlong into battle, heedless of death, while all around him are mowed down. Let that hero face danger alone, and he will flee in panic. One of our proverbs says, "What the whole world shares is a wedding feast."

"What have you heard about Byala Cherkva? asked Ognyanov.

"I told you — they're a sly lot. It's only we who were fools enough to set about freeing the Kingdom of Bulgaria!"

"And still I can't make it out; people seemed so keen in Byala Cherkva!" Ognyanov said to himself thoughtfully.

"Oh, drop it, it's as well they kept a whole skin. A fat lot of good if they'd gone up in smoke too!"

"There's a lot of villages burnt to ashes," another one remarked. "Did you see how the sky glowed last night?"

"I did," answered Ognyanov gloomily.

"The bottom's dropped out of everything. Call that an uprising! It was a shameful mess. And we, old donkeys that we are, were taken in. The folk who fooled the people will have to answer for it before God. If things weren't ready, why didn't we sit tight?"

Ognyanov listened in silence to their hints and curses. They grieved him, but did not make him angry. Their words, though not entirely just, were natural enough in the mouths of these men whose lives were ruined. He himself had more than once blamed the people in his mind, as they blamed their leaders. Those are the regrettable but inevitable consequences of failure.

"What's all this slobbering and moaning, as if goodness knows what had happened? The Lord and the Holy Virgin willed it so. Why, if Klissoura is razed to the ground, it's not the end of Bulgaria, is it?" said Borimechka, by way of consolation.

"Bai Ivan, how's your bride? What did you do with her?" asked Boicho.

"Staika? I'll be damned, she got through all right. I took her to Altunovo and from there to . . . Why, I forgot to tell you what happened with the schoolmistress!"

Ognyanov shivered at these words. He had a foreboding of what had happened to Rada, but dreaded to hear the terrible truth spoken. He had seen the house where Rada lived collapse that night, had seen the flaming ruins under which the young girl was buried, if she hadn't put an end to her life first. It was too late when he wanted to save her. And the thought weighed upon him heavily. And even another feeling, which he did not wish to acknowledge, stirred his soul and caused him not a little anguish.

"The pretty dear, she had a narrow escape."

"You mean she's alive?" cried Boicho.

"Yes, she's alive, she's alive, schoolmaster. But if it hadn't been for Borimechka. . . ."

"Where is she now?" asked Boicho astounded, searching Ivan's large, goodnatured, rough face in an effort to learn everything instantly.

"Don't worry, she's in good hands, she's well taken care of where I sent her," said Borimechka reassuringly.

At that Boicho felt the blissful sensation of a great weight being lifted from his heart. His face was radiant as he turned with deep emotion to the young giant. "Thank you, Bai Ivan! You've saved me from terrible anguish!"

"Well," continued Ivan, "it's lucky my Staika let me know in time. For when Anichka, you know, the landlady, was running for dear life, she met our Staika and said to her, 'Staika, dear, tell Ivan—that's me, you know—that Rada refuses to run away; I begged and begged her, but it was no use; so don't leave the schoolmistress, but take her with you by force.' When I heard that, I'll be damned, I wasn't the man to leave her, was I? I rushed to the house—she'd gone and locked the door. I knocked and banged on it, I called to her—no answer. So I broke down the door and went in, and what should I find but Rada standing there by the table, candle in hand, and a bag on the table."

"The bag with the gunpowder!" Ognyanov cried horrified, as he realized how Rada had determined to kill herself.

"A bag of gunpowder sure enough, so she'd be blown skyhigh in a thousand pieces! Think of that, the silly girl. But at the time I'd no idea it was gunpowder," Borimechka continued, "so I went right in and straight up to her. And then, as if God had willed it so, a gust of wind came and put the candle out. . . . 'What are you doing here, schoolmistress?' says I. 'Everyone's making off, what are you doing here?' So I grabbed hold of her and off and away to the mountain, and our Staika trotting along behind. Staika kept trying to comfort her, and she crying and moaning all the time. . . . If you only knew, schoolmaster, how many tears she shed over you! I was sure you were dead, but I kept stringing her along—one's got to use cunning, you know—and I say, 'Schoolmaster's safe and sound, don't you worry, schoolmistress!' But with all that it had got pretty late, so at Vurlishnitsa it was all packed with Turks—no getting through that way—a tight corner, I can tell you! What was to be done? So we took to the forest and got home to the village at midnight. I landed schoolmistress and Staika over to Vulko, my brother-in-law, you know, and took to the mountains again! So you're alive after all, eh? . . . Well, I'll be damned!" Ognyanov silently pressed Borimechka's hands.

"I let them in Altunovo, but they must be in Byala Cherkva now, for Vulko was to take them there next morning with veiled faces, Turkish fashion. Altunovo's the devil and all with the Turks. But in Byala Cherkva it's all quiet they say. So when you get there, schoolmaster, look up Staika, my wife—you know—and give her my greetings and tell her you've seen me here safe and sound. And tell her I eat nothing but fried hares and cheese pie, and not to worry about me."

"I don't think I'll go to Byala Cherkva now, Bai Ivan."

Borimechka looked at him in surprise. "I thought that was where you were headed for!" he said.

"No, I don't want to now!"

"Where do you want to go then?"

"I'll see."

"Come along with us to Wallachia."

"No, you go along alone and separate; it's unwise for too many people to go around together."

Dusk descended over the gully and filled the cave. The brook babbled plaintively. It was nearly dark. The fugitives could hardly see one another. Ivan Borimechka and the men from Klissoura prepared to leave.

"Let's embrace three times, schoolmaster. God knows how many of us will come through alive," said Borimechka. They took leave of each other, and parted.

Ognyanov was alone. He lay down on his face and wept like a woman. The suffering and misfortune that had welled up in him burst out in a hot stream of tears. It was the first time that this young man of steel had ever cried aloud. His inner fortitude was broken. Grief, bitter disappointment, a bad conscience, misery over the countless victims who had fallen in vain; and also the death of his love, irredeemably destroyed, resentment, hopelessness, loneliness, a sense of the aimlessness of life, a host of memories, both bright and gloomy—and equally poisonous—all went into those tears.

He had given encouragement to these poor people, victims of the fire he and his comrades had fanned, but he himself was crushed. He had silently borne this terrible punishment in front of them. He had tried hard to keep his self-control before the men from Klissoura, while his heart was bleeding and writhing in his breast like a crushed snake. And then there was Rada, whom he could not forget! Who had wept for him! He railed at himself that his heart could feel pain other than that for his country. But try as he did he could not prevent it from aching. . . . Let it ache, all was over, there could be no question of forgiveness, of reconciliation, he would never again return to Byala Cherkva! Yet that confounded heart kept pulling him on in that direction, as if seeking its other half. No, no, he would never return there, never again go to Byala Cherkva, the cradle of his love; it was now as black as a grave. He had told her in Klissoura that he was through with her and her faithlessness. While the fire was raging in Klissoura, he had risked his life to save her, but it hadn't been out of love, it couldn't have been love, some other impulse must have prompted him. Chivalry perhaps. And he'd done it unconsciously, not realizing what he was about. Yes, he would certainly not go there now to see, even from afar, an idol he had rejected. His pride rebelled. He would set out for Wallachia, somehow or other he would get there, so many people were going. In Byala Cherkva he would have to hide like a wild beast, he might be denounced by his enemies, besides he had no business there. . . . To Wallachia, Wallachia, that hospitable land of liberty. There he might again do something for Bulgaria until her wounds healed. There one could breathe freely. To the North, to the North! And Ognyanov set out to the north.

The sky was cloudy. Dense darkness reigned over the empty waste of the mountain. All night long he trudged uphill and down, to get as far away as possible from his original course, and as he did so a new resolve seemed to add wings to the strength the food had given him.

In the morning he found himself on a peak from which there was a beautiful view of a lovely green valley! He recognized the Strema valley; Byala Cherkva lay at the foot of the mountain! His fate had to be fulfilled.

chapter 4

the banner

Like a man awakening from deep slumber, Ognyanov realized his blunder. He thought he had been making for the north, while all the time he had been going in the opposite direction! But it was too late.

He had descended the mountain just above Byala Cherkva; at daybreak he found himself on that barren slope of the Balkan mountain, far from any scrub or other suitable hiding-place; he saw it would be madness to turn back, to expose himself of his own accord to imminent death. The only thing he could do was descend into the deep valley of the Monastery river, which would provide good shelter, and go from there into Byala Cherkva. He was forced to submit to the decree of fate, and made up his mind to go to the place he had been fleeing from all night.

Like Kandov, Ognyanov was in love for the first time. He was a novice in love's struggle which is unlike any other. A wounded person generally hates the enemy who has dealt him the blow. But a wounded heart often loves its enemy the more. More than that, it excuses. Alfred de Vigny would have said it pardons. Hurt pride, which in matters of love bears the name of jealousy, either kills the hand which has dealt the blow or turns to it for help in healing the wound. The first remedy heals the wound more easily, or rather dulls its pain by causing another, stronger still; the second pours balm upon it and probes it with a red hot poker. But most people have recourse to the latter. For love, the most selfish of feelings, is inclined to compromise.

Fortunately for Ognyanov, the wound in his heart had been caused by his imagination and not by Rada's treachery. The first reasonable explanation would put an end to his suffering. Chance had to intervene. And this chance had presented itself.

But Ognyanov saw in it the malice of fate. Therefore when he reached the hollow where the Monastery river has its source and saw a small sparse pine wood growing on a stony ravine, he immediately changed his mind.

"No," he said, "I can spend the day among the fir-trees and start back tonight. I'll get clothes to disguise myself in some village up in the mountain, and then—on to Wallachia! Never, never will I go back to Rada!" So saying, he crept in between the trunks of the firs, among the piles of fallen needles, overgrown with wild herbs, which would hide him from view if he lay down. He lay there for many long hours patiently awaiting the darkness of night.

Towards evening on the opposite slope Ognyanov noticed something black, moving and waving in the air. It looked like some giant bird hovering there. He gazed at it in surprise. "A flag!" he said to himself in amazement. Indeed in the evening sunlight he made out a red banner, stuck on the rock on the top of the hill. It fluttered gently in the breeze and must have been visible from Byala Cherkva.

There was no one by the banner, Who had stuck it there? What for? Was it a signal for revolt? That was what Ognyanov took it for. There was no other reasonable explanation.

Ognyanov could no longer restrain himself. He threw precaution to the winds, jumped out of his hiding-place and quickly climbed up to the peak he had descended earlier, to have a look at Byala Cherkva. It seemed to him that he heard faint and distant reports of gunshots. Where did they come from? He peered at the town. Suddenly, thanks to the clear transparence of the air, he made out some puffs of white smoke, such as are made by firearms, at the upper end of the town.

"Revolt! Byala Cherkva has risen!" he cried out joyfully. "My true friends Sokolov, Popov, the editor, and Bai Micho didn't sit quietly by! The revolt must have broken out in other places as well. And that banner was the signal! The dying fire has flared up again. A rebellion, dear Lord! There's still hope!"

And he flew down over the slippery grass, down the steep ravine, steep enough to make one dizzy.

chapter 5

the graveyard

It was quite dark when Ognyanov came out of the gloomy, boulder-strewn valley of the Monastery river. He passed by the monastery, but did not think it worth while to look in on Father Nathaniel: he had lost enough precious time as it was. The conviction that a revolt had broken out in Byala Cherkva had galvanized him into life, and had restored all his physical and spiritual strength.

He took the road to the town, and a few minutes later was able to distinguish the black outline of the old houses, of the chimneys and fruit trees. Then he left the road and ascended the ridge which overlooks Byala Cherkva from the north and on which the school-house is perched.

From this height he looked down upon the town. It was asleep. Not a light anywhere. No unusual sound or other sign indicated that a rebellion was on. Only the normal barking of dogs could be heard. This was surprising. He considered for a moment what to do. It seemed unwise to penetrate into the town and knock at the doors of any of his friends. He decided instead to go to the boys' school; it wasn't far. There he could hear from the old wife of the caretaker what was happening in Byala Cherkva. Soon he was scrambling over the western wall of the school and into the courtyard.

Looking about him, he realized he had hit on the graveyard, which takes up a great part of the enclosure. The old church rose up from among the graves, silent and dead, looking very much like a giant grave itself. At the further end of the yard the black mass of the school building and the various buildings stood, all steeped in darkness and slumber. The deathlike stillness Ognyanov encountered everywhere, instead of the noise and tumult one would expect of a town in the throes of revolution, shook him and made him fear the worst. The awful silence and darkness of the graveyard seemed to exude a chill; the grave-stones stood there motionless in the fantastic shapes given them by the night, looking like people, or corpses half-emerged from their graves. He could not help a shrinking in his heart, and secretly wished to get away from this cold kingdom of darkness and mystery without further delay.

At such moments an involuntary tremor seizes a man's soul. We cannot come into contact with the next world without feeling a chill creep over us. The lid of the coffin, as it falls on the dead body, separates the two worlds which are ignorant of each other, and antagonistic. Mystery and darkness inspire fear. Night is an enemy, a grave is a secret! No one is brave enough to endure the atmosphere of a graveyard at night without a shudder; nor is there an atheist who would laugh at such a time—he would be scared by his own laughter. I doubt whether Hamlet would have played the fool so wittily with skulls, at night and alone in a graveyard!

Suddenly, in the darkness to which he had grown accustomed, Ognyanov perceived a dim, motionless spot of light, very much like an eye, which came from a low window of the church, a float-light no doubt, or a candle. That weak ray of light was pleasantly out of tune with the surroundings, the only living thing in the general darkness and stillness of the town. It flickered in such a friendly, pleasant fashion, almost merrily. He could not restrain his curiosity, and slowly made his way across the graves to the window from which the light came and looked in.

The candle was burning in one of the great brass candlesticks by one of the pillars. The weak flame shed its light on no more than a small round patch of floor around the candlestick. The rest of the church was in darkness. In that small, dimly lighted circle Ognyanov could just distinguish certain indistinct shapes stretched out. There was something there. What could it be? He pressed his forehead against the cold pane and peered intently. Then he realized what it was.

Three men were laid out on a mat, three corpses. Black gouts of blood gleamed dully upon them and on the mat. The little flame cast a trembling and frightened light on the scene. The contorted faces with their gaping mouths bore the imprint of a horrible death. The eyes of one of them, almost starting out of their sockets, were fixed sternly on a spot in the dome of the church. The other body was turned slightly to one side. One eye, in which the reflection of the flame flickered, looked straight at Ognyanov's window. He shuddered with the horror of it, but could not find the strength to tear himself away; the dead man's gaze held him transfixed, glaring at him with its unearthly glitter from the candle and seeming to peer like a living person who knows you and demands recognition. Suddenly Ognyanov groaned. He had recognized Kandov. A big black gash gaped in his neck. His throat had been cut.

Ognyanov left the terrible sight and hurriedly retraced his steps, stumbling now and then over the graves, which seemed to cry out angrily in the darkness.

Upon reaching the wall he tried to puzzle it all out, why and how had the wounded Kandov come to Byala Cherkva? How had he and his companions been killed? Had there been a revolt here, and had he fallen in the fight, or had he simply been seeking refuge and been discovered and killed? What did that banner on the mountain mean? What was that shooting in the town? How could one account for the present silence? Ognyanov could find no answer to these questions. In any case some great calamity had happened here. He began to consider what course to take next. To enter this lifeless town in the dead of night and knock on the gates in complete ignorance of how the land lay seemed to him dangerous and foolhardy. The terrible silence reigning in Byala Cherkva chilled him to the core; it was far worse than the most ghastly noise. It looked like a trap. He finally decided to spend the rest of the night in the Monastery valley and to decide on a course of action the next day. And he climbed back over the wall.

chapter 6

the messenger

Ognyanov spent the night in a mill by the Monastery river. Very early in the morning he climbed up the ravine above the holy well, where the great rocks lay scattered about as though tossed by some giant hand. Among these he found a hiding place, unnoticed by anyone, and from this vantage point he could see everything in the valley below.

The valley was deserted. The noise of the river echoed and soared among the granite precipices; the roar of the millwheels resounded in this mountain cranny. Above was the cheerful blue sky, bathed in the rays of the early morning sun, which already glinted on the crest of the ridge. The early swallows flashed through the air, chasing one another in marvelous, trackless zigzags, and bathing in the invisible waves. Wild saplings, which had sprung up among the rocks, swayed in the early morning breeze; the golden wave of the sun slid down the green northern slope, broke over the black patch of fir-trees, flowed down the smooth young grass and gilded the top of the ravine in which Ognyanov lay. But not a soul passed along the path in the valley.

Ognyanov was growing more and more restless in his eagerness for news; the suspense was unbearable. He scanned the valley in the hope of catching sight of someone, to find out what was happening and, if possible, to beg for some clothes, with which he might smuggle himself into the town. But no one appeared and his impatience increased. Only the noise of the river was in harmony with his restless soul.

At last his face lit up. For the door of a mill opened and a girl came out and went down to the water where she began washing her face.

"Mariika!" Ognyanov said to himself, for his eyes had recognized the orphan daughter of poor Dyado Stoyan. He now remembered that after her father's death she kept house for her uncle at the braid mills. Providence was coming to his aid.

It took him but a minute to rush down to the river, and half hidden behind a rock, he called her by name. Mariika was already wiping her face on her apron. She turned around as she heard the voice and, recognizing Boicho, ran up to him.

"Bacho Boicho,* is that you?"

"Come here, Mariika," said Boicho and beckoned her to his hiding place.

The girl stared at him with wide eyes and every sign of joyful surprise. His face was terribly emaciated, his clothes spattered with mud and blood, he was bareheaded and had the exhausted appearance of a man who for many a long day has been struggling with hardships, lack of sleep, enemies, hunger, privation, and the elements themselves, facing danger at every step. An unexpected encounter with anyone else at that time and in that deserted place would have scared the girl, but Ognyanov attracted her with a fascination that was both sweet and terrible.

"What's happening in the town, Mariika?" were his first words.

"The Turks are there, Bacho Boicho." Ognyanov pressed his forehead and thought for some time.

"What was that shooting yesterday? What happened?"

"Yesterday, Bacho Boicho? I don't know, Bacho Boicho."

"Didn't you hear the shooting?"

"I wasn't in Byala Cherkva yesterday, Bacho Boicho." Mariika could give him no answer, but Boicho already guessed the truth: there had been an attempt at a revolt which had been immediately crushed by the Turks, who held Byala Cherkva now.

So he had arrived too late. Had he been there one or two hours earlier Ognyanov might have changed the course of events. This delay was one of those fatalities which often change the fate of a whole nation. . . .

After a few minutes' thought Ognyanov asked, "Mariika, is there anyone else at the mill?"

"Uncle Mincho; he's still asleep."

"You know where Dr. Sokolov lives, don't you Mariika?"

"Yes, I do—at Granny Yakimich's."

"That's right. Do you know where Burzobegounek lives, you know, the German, with the side-whiskers?"

"The one who makes black people, is it?"

"The very one, Mariika," said Ognyanov smiling at the guileless epigram on the poor photographer.

"Could you take something to them, dearie?"

"Of course, Bacho Boicho," the girl answered joyfully.

---

* *bacho:* from *brat,* brother, form of addressing an older man.

Ognyanov searched his pocket and took out a pencil and a very crumpled piece of paper. It was Rada's letter. At the sight of it perspiration appeared on his pale forehead. He tore the empty half-sheet off with a trembling hand, put it against the stone, wrote a few words on it, and refolded it.

"Take this paper to Dr. Sokolov, Mariika; if he's not at home, take it to the German! Tuck it away carefully somewhere about you!"

"All right."

"When they ask you where I'm hiding, tell them, but only them, don't let anyone else know, do you hear? Say I am at the deserted mill beyond Hambar's." Mariika looked towards the northern end of the valley where the lonely ruins of the mill could be seen.

Ognyanov did not sign the note, nor did he mention his hiding-place for fear of its missing its destination by some mischance and falling into dangerous hands. He had full faith in Mariika's devotion, but did not dare give her a message by word of mouth alone, lest she do harm out of sheer simple-mindedness.

And in order to impress his instructions and the importance of her errand still further on Mariika he added softly, "For if you lose the letter or let yourself be tricked into telling anyone else that you've seen me or where I'm hiding, the Turks will come and cut my throat. Be careful, dear!" At these words Mariika's face grew serious and scared, and her hand involuntarily touched the spot under her armpit where she had concealed the note.

"I'll just tell my uncle that I'm going down to get some bread," said Mariika.

"All right, Mariika, only mind you don't forget what I told you."

Mariika went into the mill. Boicho hid again behind a stone and waited to see Mariika set out on her errand. He waited a whole hour in great suspense. At last he saw Mariika come out, tripping barefoot over the sharp stones that covered the path, on her way to Byala Cherkva.

chapter 7

Mariika fails

When she reached the little meadow by the monastery, Mariika stopped quite out of breath and looked about her anxiously. But having assured herself that nobody had seen her she ran on again. She did not meet a soul all the way to town. The country was deserted, and so was the street by which the young orphan was about to enter the town.

Suddenly Mariika stopped again. She saw three Turks approaching from the other end of the street. Fear gripped her, and without stopping to think she turned sideways among the vegetable and rose gardens, so as to enter the town by another street from the west. She was going very much out of her way, for the distance from there to Sokolov's house was much greater.

Mariika finally reached the west end of the town, an open field to her right, to her left the town and the narrow street between two rows of small huddled shops. The street was completely deserted; not a soul, Turk or Bulgarian, was to be seen. All the shops were closed, so were the doors, and the windows that had shutters, but this absence of life reassured the innocent girl, who ran as fast as she could along the street. She had barely covered a small distance when something made her turn around and glued her to the spot. Not far away above the fields rose a cloud of dust from which the heavy tread of footsteps, the trampling of horses and a confusion of voices came to her ears. Soon the cloud drew nearer and the source of all this clamor appeared. It was Tossoun-Bey's horde.

After three days of sack and plunder it was returning tumultuously and triumphantly from Klissoura, now reduced to ashes. Foot-soldiers and riders were jumbled together, heavily loaded with arms and booty. In a short time the throng had surged up to the street like a muddy wave, filling it and flowing along it with a wild tumult of shouts and grunts. This was only part of the horde, consisting of several hundred bashi-bazouks, all from the country to the east of Byala Cherkva. Now they advanced victoriously with their banners, their booty and their trophies, all they could carry with them. Everything else followed behind in an endless string of carts.

To lighten their loads the bashi-bazouks had put on the more valuable pieces of clothing plundered from the unfortunate people of Klissoura. And so this bloodthirsty mob had at the same time a most comical appearance, like a carnival parade in the Asiatic style. Many wore costly women's jackets of lynx and sable in spite of the hot weather. Some were even decked out in the golden vestments pillaged from the Klissoura churches and put on, no doubt, to desecrate them. Tossoun-Bey himself, the leader, was dressed up in a magnificent European dressing-gown of grey cashmere edged with crimson cloth and with long red tassels hanging from it. It later became known that Tossoun-Bey had no idea what the garment was used for and, taking it to be some noble outer robe, desired to enter Byala Cherkva in state. . . .

Only a single live trophy garnished his triumph, a prisoner with his hands bound behind him — Rachko the Stinkard. It was a revolting sight!

But Mariika hardly saw it. The very moment she caught sight of the mob, she vanished from the street and passed along others, all equally deserted and silent. At last she reached Sokolov's door. She pushed, but it wouldn't open. Then she pounded on it several times.

"Who's knocking?" asked the old woman from inside.

"Granny Yakimitsa, please open the gate," the breathless Mariika said with difficulty. "What do you want here?"

"I want to see Dr. Sokolov. . . . Oh, do open the gate!" cried the girl piteously.

The old woman muttered something angrily, but opened it. "What do you want him for? He's not here!" she said sharply.

"Where is he, Granny?"

"Tell me and I'll tell you. They took him yesterday and there's been no sign of him since. Be off with you," said the old woman shutting the gate again. Mariika stood before the closed gate, baffled.

Then she dashed on to the photographer's gate, which was not far off. Mariika pushed it.

"What do you want, girl?" a woman asked, pale, ragged and bent.

"The German. . . ."

"What do you want?"

"Let me see the German," said Mariika pushing past the woman to enter the courtyard.

"Are you crazy? Don't you know they cut his throat?" the woman returned, angrily pushing Mariika into the street.

The frightened child turned numb with fear at these words. It now flashed across her mind that they might cut her dear Boicho's throat too, that the Turks she saw were after him, that they might seize her letter, for someone must have told them she bearing a letter from her Bacho Boicho. What now? What was she to do? She looked about her and it was only then she saw that the street was empty; not a soul was passing. And fear seized her, and she burst into tears.

She was still in that desperate state when a tap on her shoulder made her look up. It was Kolcho. He was the only one walking the streets, tapping his way along the cobblestones with his stick, a dreamy and worried look on his face.

"Why are you crying, child?" asked the blind man, peering at Mariika with his vacant eyes, as if trying to recognize her. Had Mariika known Kolcho better, she would have told him Ognyanov's request, would have told him how matters stood, and Kolcho would have replaced Sokolov. But she was scared by this stranger and ran across the street, then took another turning.

"Lassie! Mariika!" cried Kolcho who, with his miraculous instinct, had that very moment recognized her for Dyado Stoyan's girl by her crying alone. He had knocked at Sokolov's gate to ask Granny Yakimitsa about him just after she had left, and had heard from the old woman that a girl had just now inquired about him too. Some premonition told him that that girl was none other than Mariika, that if she had been looking for Sokolov it was for some very important reason, that her not finding the doctor accounted for her frightened sobbing. Who could be sending her to Sokolov at such a time? Someone who was ignorant of the state of affairs here, some outsider. Could it be he? Rumor had it since last night that Boicho had not been killed, that he had escaped into the mountain and was probably wandering about there now. Might Boicho have come down into the Monastery valley where Mariika lived in her uncle's braid-mill, and sent her with a message to Sokolov? Yes, yes, Mariika was an instrument of Providence!

At that conjecture Kolcho's loving soul was choked with emotion. As he walked he started shouting, "Lassie! Mariika! Mariika! Come on, lass!" But he got no answer. Kolcho lost hope and sighed deeply.

Meanwhile he had come to the square. There it was not silent and deserted. It was full of bustle, the sound of voices, of horses clattering on the cobblestones. In other words, a crowd.

People were talking in Turkish. What was it all about? Surprised, Kolcho stopped by the cafe and pricked up his ears.

A voice was screaming from inside in Bulgarian. "There you are — you see what a disgraceful business it was. Trying to burn our town down over our heads. It was a near thing, we might have all been killed off like dogs, all of us, the place might have been razed to the ground, not a stone would have been left standing! And where are these rascals now, I ask: whom did they ask about raising a rebellion? Bring them to me now, I'd teach them a lesson! Rebel indeed! Against whom? Against the Sultan, against their father and benefactor who cares for us as if we were the apple of his eye, who sees to it that not a hair shall fall from our heads. For hundreds of years we have lived under the shade of the Sultan's throne, and have prospered, our grandfathers and our fathers, and we ourselves, and we shan't find anything better, nor our grandchildren either! We must gather our wits together, or there'll be the devil to pay. Whoever doesn't like it here had better pack up for Muscovy. We know when we're well off." Kolcho recognized the speaker — it was Chorbadji Yordan.

"Long live His Majesty the Sultan!" cried a second voice. That was Mr. Fratyu.

These two men now expressed the panic which reduces a man to a brute beast. The first was only hateful, for his words were at least sincere; he had said and believed all that even before the uprising; the second was loathsome, for his words were dictated by cowardice. Fratyu's cry met with no response, but he found it in the very silence that ensued. The times were such that the Chorbadji Yordans were right, and the Fratyus, honest. Every base, despicable act of the vanquished was permissable, for every act of violence on the part of the victor was permitted. *Vae victis!*

The April catastrophe was terrible not so much because of the massacres of Batak as because of the baseness and degradation it brought with it.

Kolcho sighed deeply and turned back, bending his steps towards Aunt Ghinka's house.

chapter 8

the meadow

About noon that day a family was sitting in a lovely meadow at the end of the town, under the shade of the green branches. At the southern end of the meadow stood the stone wall of a garden with a gate opening onto the meadow, while to the north stretched a magnificent view of Stara Planina with its bleak summits, steep ravines, cliffs and picturesque and verdant slopes. The meadow and the garden belonged to Chorbadji Yordan, whose family had gathered there.

With the exception of the present company, it was seldom that anyone showed himself in these parts. True, the town had calmed down somewhat after its surrender, and people began to move about the streets. But no one could pluck up courage to go outside into the surrounding country, whether on business or simply for an airing, to enjoy the bright beauty of nature.

Only Yordan's household dared venture so far afield. For Yordanitsa had fallen ill with grief over Lalka's death and been confined to her bed for several days. Today she had been taken out for a walk and a breath of fresh air by the doctor's orders, passing through peoples' backyards to reach this garden of Yordan's just outside the town. The walk had not failed to bring about the desired effect, and they had taken a turn or two in the meadow as well. A pair of magnificent big buffaloes, which also belonged to Yordan, were grazing there.

A zaptieh, squatting to one side, watched over them to keep the Chorbadji's womenfolk from harm. There were two strangers in the group: a plump, round-cheeked peasant woman, and Rada.

The peasant woman was Staika, Borimechka's wife whom Aunt Ghinka had taken into her service since yesterday. She had also offered her hospitality to Rada. Neither Granny Yordanitsa, nor any other member of Yordan's family had raised any objections. On the contrary, the sight of Rada, their poor Lalka's gentle friend, was a source of sweet and sad comfort, and their former contempt and hatred of her had given place to more kindly feelings for the unfortunate, homeless girl.

As we have seen, Staika and Rada had made friends already in Klissoura and had suffered equally at its fall. Thanks to Staika, Ivan had been able to save Rada in time. All the way to Byala Cherkva Staika had tried to comfort her, and when they reached it two days ago she would on no account be separated from Rada. Simple and primitive as she was, she nevertheless understood Rada's unhappy situation and shared her sorrows.

A little while ago the conversation had turned to Boicho, and Gospozha Hadji Rovoahma assured everyone he had been killed in battle. Staika compassionately observed Rada's face change color and grow very pale. And she conceived a terrible hatred of the nun who spoke so lightly of Boicho's death.

"Like as if she's seen schoolmaster killed with her own eyes! And what's she licking her chops for, the old cat?" Staika said to Rada in angry whispers.

"Hush, hush," Rada answered softly.

Staika listened to the conversation which went on, then again whispered to Rada, "That black one there's got whiskers. Why don't she shave 'em?"

Rada smiled in spite of herself but answered, "Keep quiet, sister."

It was the first time Staika had seen Gospozha Hadji Rovoahma, and she didn't know she was her mistress's aunt. By way of revenge, she had taken several amber beads of her rosary when the thread had broken and they had scattered all over the ground, and she now slyly watched the nun looking for them. Finally she giggled out loud and pulled Rada by the sleeve.

"What are you laughing at, Staika?"

"Look at Hadji Vrana* worryin' about a few grains of maize."

"Hadji Rovoahma, dear," said Rada correcting her in a low voice.

But fortunately Staika's impoliteness had passed unnoticed by the others, for at that moment all eyes were turned upon Stefchov who was approaching. Chorbadji Yordan's former son-in-law was about to start for Gyumyurdjina, but the trouble that had broken out had delayed him, and he could not enter yet upon his new duties there.

When he came up to them, they all hung upon his every word. He gave a glowing account of today's crowning victory — that of the deputation of which he was a member. The deputation headed by Yordan Diamandiev had been sent that very day to welcome Tossoun-Bey, who was coming to attack the town as a center of

---

* Vrana is Bulgarian for rook.

insurrection, and to beg for mercy. With the greatest difficulty the deputation had succeeded in saving Byala Cherkva from the fate of Klissoura, but at the price of three very hard conditions. First, the town was immediately to pay down a thousand pounds to Tossoun-Bey for him to pacify his horde which had been promised the looting of Byala Cherkva, and to disband it; second, all arms were to be handed over, to the last penknife; and third, to hand over to the authorities every suspect person. This complete surrender, which had not saved Batak from Mehmed Tumrashli, saved Byala Cherkva. Tossoun-Bey entered the town with only a part of his horde to receive the arms. Thus Chorbadji Yordan and Stefchov too, in part, were now the saviors of the town.

As he related all this with complacent pride, Stefchov from time to time cast spiteful glances at Rada, who never once turned to him. But the presence of this hateful man oppressed her terribly. The insolent tone of his voice jarred upon her nerves, and every sound he uttered found a sinister echo in her heart. She saw in him the dreadful image of the calamity which had pursued her happiness, and he filled her with a fear and hatred she could not overcome.

"My God," she thought to herself, "so many people, all the decent people, perished or are being destroyed, and this man is alive and triumphant. He's a great man now and honored everywhere—is it because he's so hateful and wicked?" But suddenly she turned towards Stefchov with an animated expression on her face, for he was speaking of Boicho, and what he said of him was, for a wonder, most heartening to her.

"So the scoundrel's alive after all!" Hadji Rovoahma said, obviously puzzled.

"He was alive when he took to the mountains," Stefchov explained. "But whether he's still alive I can't say. The eagles may be pecking his bones somewhere or other." The pain these words stirred in her made Rada press her hand to her heart.

"I tell you the Count is alive, the Count isn't one to die," put in Hadji Smion. "He's died so many times and he always turns up alive again. I don't believe it. When I was in Moldavia everyone kept saying haidouk Yanulescu had died, the newspapers said so too. . . . Well, we all said 'God rest his soul,' when one day, as I was traveling near Tourgou Nemtsou, whom should I meet but Yanulescu—curse him! 'Good morning, Domnule Yanulescu,' says I to him. And so he only takes my watch—simply because I'd wished him good morning. I mean to say he didn't kill me. My point was, a bandit doesn't die. . . ." And Hadji Smion winked amicably at Rada, which was his way of telling her, "You listen to me, the Count's alive."

"If only the rascal doesn't turn up here—he'd burn the whole place down as he did Klissoura."

"Just let him try. . . . And if only we could get hold of the bear-dancer too, and polish him off, like young Kandov and the rest," said Stefchov.

"That was a pity, but it couldn't be helped; a few people had to be sacrificed to save a thousand," someone said.

"To be sure, scoundrels, why do they come here?"

"Why do they come? They came to seek refuge," Aunt Ghinka broke in with animation.

Stefchov looked at her in surprise. "So according to you, Sister Ghinka, Dyado Yordan didn't do the right thing?"

"Oh, yes, he was grand—and you were grand too! One would think you were Jews or Turks, not Bulgarians at all! Just stop and think what those men went out to die for!" cried Aunt Ghinka, her face glowing and her eyes shining.

"You're crazy, crazy," her ailing mother said with a deep sigh.

"So, according to you," Stefchov retorted spitefully, "when these friends of yours, these patriots, do us the honor to visit us, we should have the children out from school to welcome them with songs, and offer them hospitality, treat them to baklava? Nothing to wonder at, some people made rusks for them. . . ."

"I know, I know," Aunt Ghinka interrupted him angrily, "hand them over to the Turks, cut their throats, kill them off, drink their blood, like you did with those boys yesterday. Did you see Kandov's mother drop down in the middle of the road! Oh, sister, oh! O Lalka! God, O God!" And Aunt Ghinka leaned against the trunk of the walnut tree and covering her eyes with a handkerchief, wept bitterly and loudly.

This sudden fit of grief was on behalf of the revolutionaries who had been killed yesterday, but most of the party took it to be for Lalka, whose name had been mixed up with Aunt Ghinka's lamentations. Rada ran up to her with tears in her eyes, to console her. The mention of the dead girl upset Granny Yordanitsa and she too started sobbing. All this wailing infuriated Stefchov, for he supposed they were crying for the revolutionaries.

The zaptieh, who had gathered what they were talking about, went up to Stefchov and Hadji Smion and said in a low voice, "Have you heard the news? Another comita from Klissoura has come down into the Monastery valley."

"What! Who told you that?" asked Stefchov with a start.

"Arabia, the Gipsy, saw him when she was picking herbs."

"When was that?"

"Today about noon."

"Has she told the authorities?"

"I don't know."

"They must be informed at once," muttered Stefchov snatching up his fez from the grass. "It was touch and go today, we might all have gone to the devil, and now another rapscallion turns up!"

"It must be he; that's clear," said Hadji Smion unexpectedly.

"Who?" asked Stefchov.

"The Count—I told you he was alive, didn't I?"

"All the better; there'll be one more throat to cut."

Hadji Smion was scared by his own words which had slipped out, goodness knows how, quite against his will. He grew pale. "Where are you off to, Kiriak?"

"I'm going."

"Don't meddle, let the poor fellow be," said Hadji Smion pleadingly. "There must be some little corner in all Byala Cherkva to hide him in. If it's for the Count—everybody likes him."

"You're crazy, Bai Hadji!" cried Stefchov looking at him with hatred in his eyes. "Byala Cherkva must be saved." And without so much as saying good-bye, he set out towards town, continuing his conversation in undertones with the zaptieh, who saw him off to the end of the fence.

Hadji Smion stood there dumbfounded.

chapter 9

the ally

Hardly anyone noticed Stefchov's sudden departure: they were all busy comforting the grief-stricken Granny Yordanitsa.

"Chorbadjiika, you'd better get back into the garden, for our Turks are stirring in the orchards there," said the zaptieh, as he approached and took his gun to rejoin Stefchov, who was waiting for him.

Granny Yordanitsa got up to go into the garden. Aunt Ghinka, supporting her by the arm, led the way, while the others followed. Rada and Staika were the last. Staika pressed her friend's hand firmly and said, "Rada, schoolmaster's alive, did you hear?"

But Rada made no reply, engrossed in fresh worries. For something told her that this new victim of the Klissoura disaster, who had come down from the mountain today and whom Stefchov was so bravely going to denounce, was no stranger to her, that it might be he and her heart was heavy with inexpressible anxiety.

"Look, why's that barefoot girl so fast?" asked Staika, stopping and pointing to a girl who was hurrying across the meadow towards them.

It was Mariika. The poor anxious child was returning, after trying in vain for hours on end to discover Sokolov's whereabouts. She was overjoyed now to see Radka, the only person who was close to Boicho and who might help her. Although she remembered Boicho's instructions, Mariika felt that Rada was safe, and that her Bacho Boicho had merely forgotten to send her to her Aunt Radka too, and she could tell her everything.

Rada went to meet her. "Come here, Mariika, come, how are you?"

The girl stopped in front of her, looked about her fearfully and asked, "Aunt Radka, do you know where the doctor is?"

"You mean Sokolov, Mariika? I don't know. Is anyone ill?" Mariika stammered in confusion.

"Who is sending you to the doctor, dear? Is anyone ill?" Rada repeated.

"No, Aunt Radka, Bacho Boi—". Mariika broke off in terror. But Rada understood. She felt faint and looked about her timidly.

At the same moment Stefchov came up, fixing Mariika with the eye of a hawk. He had noticed her and turned back because of her. "What are you holding in your hand, girl?" he asked.

Mariika turned pale. She drew back with a guilty air and hid her hands behind her.

"Give me that piece of paper, girl; I want to see it," said he, advancing towards her. The girl screamed wildly, and made a dash across the meadow towards the pond.

A dark suspicion formed in Stefchov's mind. He guessed that the paper the girl was running away with contained some important secret. He recognized her as Dyado Stoyan's daughter. What did she want with Rada and from whom was she bearing a letter at such a moment? Might it not be from Ognyanov? Could he be the rebel who had come down from the mountain? His face lit up with evil joy at the thought, and he dashed after Mariika.

Rada's breast was heaving with anxiety as she gazed after Mariika, who, catching sight of the cowherd beside the pond, turned about and ran in another direction. Thus she was rushing straight into the arms of Stefchov who was hurrying to meet her. Seeing the new danger she screamed again, as if begging for help against her cruel pursuer.

Staika watched the scene in bewilderment. She could not make out why Stefchov wanted the scrap of paper so badly; but she realized from Rada's face that it must not fall into the hands of that man. Once that was clear in her mind, she bounded across the meadow, as light as a deer, and overtaking Stefchov, seized him by his coat-tails, to hold him back and give the girl a chance to escape. Stefchov turned round and looked at the peasant woman. He could scarcely believe his eyes at the sight of such brazenness.

"Why are you chasing the girl, uncle?" Staika asked angrily, still holding fast.

"Let go, you pig!" Stefchov shouted contemptuously, tearing himself loose. "Damn you, you yokel, it's she who put you up to this. I know, I know. . . . Kosta, Kosta, catch her!" he shouted to Yordan's cowherd, whom Mariika's shriek had woken up.

He barred her way. The poor girl stopped as in a daze before her new pursuer, then turned back like a trapped deer and fled to the buffaloes, as though seeking help from them against her fellow creatures.

Staika, whose primitive nature was thoroughly roused, was about to hurl herself on Stefchov and the little cowherd, for they seemed to her as chickens to an eagle, but she stopped where she was, motionless. Rada was making desperate signs to her to return.

The astonished peasant woman no longer dared come to Mariika's assistance. It made her heart bleed to see the girl, half dead with fright, throw herself down on the grass beside the buffaloes and lie there motionless. Ever since that terrible night at the mill Mariika fell into hysterical fits and fainted whenever she was frightened. The buffalo which was grazing bent its tremendous head over the motionless girl, sniffed about her face gently and compassionately, and again raised his damp nose, calmly munching along with an impassive look in his large blue eyes.

Stefchov hastily undid the half-buttoned front of Mariika's dress and searched for the paper, for he had seen the girl put it there as she ran. But he found nothing. They searched under her and around her, but the note had disappeared, as if it had vanished into the earth.

Stefchov looked about him in a rage. "Could that beast have swallowed it?" he said, and looked at the buffalo severely. Golyu seemed to understand he was suspected of theft, and opened his frothy mouth wide. But only some halfchewed blades of grass clung to the sides.

Stefchov was perplexed. He could not understand what had become of the scrap of paper. "The little bitch must have dropped it somewhere in the meadow," he said, and started hunting for it with Kosta.

Mariika soon came to. Her first motion was to put her hand in her bosom. Finding the paper gone, she started crying with fright. She got up and went her way whimpering.

Stefchov and the little cowherd spent a long time looking. Finally Stefchov set off for town at a quick pace. He had probably found the note. As he passed by Rada, he said with a savage look, "We'll see his head stuck on a pole today!"

Crushed with anxiety, Rada remained there motionless. Staika was standing beside the buffaloes. She shared Rada's fears, but simply could not make out why she had not been allowed to help Mariika escape. She still looked angrily in the direction Stefchov had taken, unconsciously patting Golyu's curly forehead. Golyu sniffed the hand of this stranger who was caressing him, and stirred slightly, shifting his foreleg.

"Rada! Here's your letter!" cried the peasant woman lifting the crushed scrap of paper from the ground. In fact Golyu had trodden on it as he sniffed the unconscious Mariika.

Rada seized it, and unfolding it with a trembling hand, threw a rapid glance at the contents. "It's from Boicho!" she cried. She pressed her hands to her breast, almost choking with emotion.

The note contained only two lines: "I've come down from the mountains. Bring or send clothes and news. Hurry." It was not signed.

Rada read it again and again, and then she noticed with a pang of emotion that these words were written on the blank half of the very letter she had sent to Boicho by Borimechka in those terrible hours. The name, written in pencil, had been torn off too. Tears rolled down her cheeks.

"What does the letter say, Rada?" asked Staika.

"He's alive, sister, he's alive! Rada said, quite out of breath.

Staika laughed out loud, she was so happy.

"Schoolmaster's alive, Rada! Didn't I tell the old crow don't know a thing for all her gabble?"

"Boicho's alive, sister, alive! Tell Aunt Ghinka I didn't feel well, so I went home. Don't say a word about the note." And she moved away towards the market gardens.

chapter 10

love and heroism

Above all the young girl needed time to collect her thoughts and come to a quick decision. She hid behind a clump of trees close by, where she could not be seen, and considered the situation intently. It was critical. Boicho's life hung by a thread—and he suspected nothing. Of course it must have been Boicho whom the Gipsy saw. Yes, yes, it was he. But he must be warned as soon as possible of the impending danger, and provided with means of escape. This was no easy task for her, a lone girl; the country was deserted now, and crossed only by occasional bashi-bazouks, roving about in search of plunder. She shuddered at the thought of meeting these ferocious creatures. But she feared nothing when it was for Boicho's sake. Her love would brave all the cruelty of fate and of man. Yes, she would set out immediately. But of course, he wanted clothes too, the ordinary clothes of a peaceful citizen, so as not to rouse suspicion. Disguised, he might even enter Byala Cherkva. That was a problem. Where should she turn to for clothes, who would run the risk of giving his own? And what time was there to search for clothes when every minute was precious? Then another thought struck her, which should have occurred to her from the first: where was Ognyanov hiding? It didn't say in the note. Probably, out of precaution, he had confided the secret to Mariika, to tell Sokolov by word of mouth. And Mariika had already gone! How silly she hadn't thought of asking her where Boicho was? Thank goodness, she had heard at least from the zaptieh that he was in the Monastery valley. It was a large valley, but she would go over every inch of it and find Boicho. Alas, his enemies would not waste so much time, for they knew exactly where he was awaiting the answer to his note. But she would find him, would get there before them, long before them, for she was borne by wings. Only one thing was impossible—the clothes! And it was clothes he wanted most of all; O God, O God! And time was flying so, and she had no one to ask for advice.

All these thoughts and considerations passed through her mind with lightning speed. She decided to leave her shelter and hurry on to the Monastery valley. But first she looked carefully through the branches of the bushes, towards the garden. Before the gate stood a man in a large fez, dressed in European clothes of grey! At first she took him for Stefchov; but no, this one was shorter and looked different—she recognized Kolcho the blind man. Her heart leapt for joy, although Kolcho, being blind, could not be of much help in this matter. But she could at least exchange a few words with him. God himself had sent him.

But she was dismayed to see Kolcho about to cross the threshold and enter the garden. She called out, "Bai Kolcho, Bai Kolcho, wait!" and darted towards him.

Kolcho heard the cry and stopped. In a moment Rada was at his side. "Bai Kolcho!"

"Radka! I was looking for you," said the blind man. And drawing close to her he whispered, "They say Boicho's alive!"

"Yes, yes, indeed he is, Kolcho," said Rada breathlessly.

"They say he's in the mountain," added Kolcho.

"No, Kolcho, he's come down into the Monastery valley."

Kolcho looked startled. "Is that so, Radka!"

"Yes, yes, Bai Kolcho, he's there now. I got a note from him. He wants clothes, he needs clothes, Bai Kolcho. He's been denounced to the Turks, some Gipsies saw him. But I'll run and warn him. He'll escape. They mustn't catch him, but he'll be recognized everywhere as a revolutionary. You see, he needs clothes! O God, O God! Time is so short!"

While Radka was pouring out her fears and apprehensions in a voice broken by tears, Kolcho had already discovered a way out. "I can find him some clothes," he said.

"Really, Bai Kolcho? Where, tell me, where can we get clothes?"

"Quite close by, at a friend's house."

"Don't be long, Bai Kolcho, hurry as fast as you can!"

"Wait here a minute," he said.

And he turned quickly back. Rada waited impatiently under the cover of the gateway. Scarcely more than a minute or two passed, but they seemed to her like hours. Beside her impatience to be off, she was afraid that someone might come out of the garden and see her there alone and in such an excited state.

She sighed heavily under the strain of the suspense. At the same moment a little girl appeared with a bundle in her hand. The blind man had put in a fez, a long jacket and grey homespun trousers. They were the clothes he had just been wearing. In his kindness of heart he had thought of adding two more things which Rada in her excitement had forgotten—a loaf of bread and about a hundred groats, which he had put in one of the pockets.

But Rada didn't even stop to look at the bundle; she took it from the girl and sped away to the north through the gardens. "O God, O God!" she kept saying to herself bitterly. "He doesn't even want to see me any more! What have I done to him? I love him. . . ."

As we said, the country was deserted—the Bulgarians were afraid to set foot outside the town; only the bashi-bazouks haunted it. And for a girl and alone, the danger was even greater and more terrible. But Rada didn't even think of it. Great love has only one measure: self-sacrifice.

chapter 11

the bashi-bazouk

Hidden in the deserted mill, Ognyanov waited for some friend, or at least for Mariika to return.

This half-dilapidated mill stood by itself at the farthest end of the valley not far from the thundering waterfall, and beyond it there was no other building. Great holes gaped in the walls, where the windows and doors had formerly been, and the wind had carried off part of the roof. These gaps in the walls served Ognyanov as windows, commanding a view of the path, which followed the river up to the very waterfall, and then wound up the mountain to the right of the stony bank. He waited a long time, impatient and tense; the hours passed by, the day was nearly spent, but not a soul appeared in the part of the valley visible from that spot. Ognyanov was bewildered. The terrible uncertainty he was in increased every minute, developing into an anxiety that defied description.

He tried to imagine what could have caused the delay. The worst of his suppositions was that Mariika had been unable to find the doctor or Burzobegounek, who had perhaps been forced into hiding. Of the terrible danger that might confront him any minute he had no inkling, for he could not guess that his presence there was already known to friends and foes alike, and that his fate depended on the question of who would get there first—the enemies or the friends.

Suddenly to his alarm Ognyanov noticed a man walking along the path. It was a Turk. He was a tall, burly figure, wearing a green turban on his head, a sword belt from which a large yataghan stuck out, and baggy trousers. On his back he carried a leather bag.

He must be one of the Turks Mariika had told him about, a bashi-bazouk! What was he after? Ognyanov drew his revolver and stood on the alert. The bashi-bazouk continued walking ahead with long strides.

He drew level with the deserted mill, some fifty paces off, without turning and passed on. Ognyanov was quite at a loss. But he was condemned to complete inaction and immobility. There was only one thing he could do, and that was to wait and see.

The Turk walked on. He crossed the river, stepping from stone to stone, and started making his way through the dense tangle of weeds forming a green patch of color at the very foot of the cliff itself, then stopped.

Ognyanov grew pale with fright. This was the only path he might escape by into the mountains, in case of need. The terrible overhanging precipices were inaccessible from any other point. Ognyanov was alarmed. Was his escape route being cut off? Would this man be followed by others?

The Turk took off his turban to tuck in the end, which had become undone, and Ognyanov had a full view of his face and head. What he saw was a handsome, youthful face with a broad, white forehead, crowned with a mop of fair hair that hung over it in curls. Ognyanov uttered a cry of surprise, and, taking his stand before the window, put two fingers to his lips and whistled.

The shrill, piercing sound filled the valley and was re-echoed by the rocks. The bashi-bazouk peered at the mill from which this sound had come and seeing Ognyanov's urgent gestures, came running towards him. It was Sokolov.

The two friends embraced affectionately. "Boicho, Boicho, so you're alive, brother; what are you doing here?" cried Sokolov moved to tears.

"What about you, doctor, in that rig?"

"What are you doing here, brother? When did you come?"

"Last night. Why have you been such an age?"

"I!" asked Sokolov in bewilderment.

"Couldn't Mariika get hold of you before?"

"Which Mariika?"

"What? Didn't she find you?" asked Ognyanov greatly puzzled. "I sent you a note by her this morning."

"Nobody found me, nobody could have found me," Sokolov answered.

Ognyanov looked at him in surprise. "Then why are you here? Who are you looking for?"

"I? I'm on the run."

"On the run, doctor?"

"Yes. Can't you see my clothes?"

"And you left Byala Cherkva like that?"

"I cleared out last night and have been hiding in Hambar's mill till now."

"What, we were so close to each other without knowing it? This is most extraordinary. Whatever can have happened to Mariika?"

said Ognyanov who was beginning to feel anxious. “And where are you off to now?”

“To the mountains; I’ve been waiting for them to bring me a passport and some money. But I’m not leaving you now. We’ll face life and death together. Oh Boicho, what terrible misfortunes have befallen our country, brother! Who would have thought it possible!”

“Sit down and we’ll have a long talk.”

chapter 12

the story of a town that failed to revolt

Huddled in a corner the two of them told each other the happenings of the last nine days in Klissoura and Byala Cherkva. Sokolov's story, or rather report, shed light upon everything, and Ognyanov now had the clue to the mystery. The revolt had not broken out in Byala Cherkva when Klissoura rose. Neither in Byala Cherkva, nor in all the other villages and towns, equally well or even better prepared for it. The premature rising had ruined everything. At the news of the revolt in Klissoura the committee had been divided; some were for defending themselves only in case of attack, but against provoking it in any way, only rising in revolt if reinforcements came from outside; the others were for unfurling the banner, immediately, come what may. There was yet a third opinion on the matter, and it was the general one—to surrender. By a trick, while the committee was deciding to raise the standard, the most ardent members, that is, the doctor, Popov and the Editor, were locked up in Father Stavri's cellar; a deputation headed by Chorbadji Yordan was sent to K. to assure the authorities of the submission and loyalty of the inhabitants of Byala Cherkva and to ask for protection.

The government, which had trouble enough on its hands, was delighted to accept these assurances, and sent fifty bashi-bazouks to Byala-Cherkva to collect the arms and to remain and guard the town. Soon there was a pile of guns, pistols and daggers in the courtyard of the konak. With this surrender as a lightning-conductor, Byala Cherkva was saved. There was only one victim, Marko Ivanov. He was handcuffed and led away to Plovdiv on foot, because of the cherry tree. It was never discovered who had denounced him.

Five days later, yesterday, a flag appeared on the mountain, provoking much conjecture and a host of rumors and hopes! There was general excitement; rumor had it that several thousand insurgents were coming down from the mountain to the aid of Byala Cherkva. This military force was supposed to be led by Russian and Serbian soldiers. No one knew where this unexpected help came from, it simply came out of the blue. Kableshkov had so often talked of a mysterious army ready to fly to their aid when the time came that even the most credulous began to believe. Joyfully people kept looking at the banner, and peering at the summit of the mountain. Some even thought they saw people with guns on their shoulders on the slopes, taking the brushwood for an army. Others, whose sight was keener, could distinguish the Muscovites by their large shaggy caps.

At that point Father Stavri came, unlocked the cellar and said, "It's a shame to keep you under lock and key any longer, my children. Micho was right—come and see what's coming down from the mountain."

The three prisoners flew out of doors. Half an hour later, with a following of about twenty cobblers, they had seized the konak, including the bey, the arms and the power! Enthusiasm spread in the town. Byala Cherkva was up in arms! The standard with the lion on it, which Rada had embroidered, was raised in the middle of the square. But just then a most crushing piece of news struck terror into every heart: the cowherd came rushing down from the mountain at full speed and announced there wasn't a soul there. And Tossoun Bey was already on his way to Byala Cherkva to raze it to the ground!

Simultaneously another piece of news doubled people's anxiety. Three revolutionaries from Klissoura had descended from the mountain and taken refuge in the school at the upper end of the town. They were Kandov, wounded in the arm, and two other boys from Klissoura. The old woman who looked after the place hid them in the attic of the school, gave them bread, for they had eaten nothing but grass for two days, then following their instructions, she informed Burzobegounek, who brought them clothes, fezes and some tobacco.

They had hardly finished smoking their first cigarette when they saw through the cracks of the eaves that the school was being surrounded by Turks. Burzobegounek was also in the attic at the time. There was no hope of escape. The Turks started shooting at the building from the yard, through the attic windows. They wounded the two youths from Klissoura, who then crawled down and gave themselves up. They were cut to pieces on the spot. Burzobegounek jumped down, fired twice, wounding a man, but immediately dropped, hit by a dozen bullets. His throat was cut.

Only Kandov remained where he was. All the Turks aimed at the opening in the attic where he was expected to appear. But he did not. Suddenly the rotten floor of the attic gave way, and Kandov fell onto the gallery. He stood up, leaned against the railing, folding his arms, and cried, "I'm ready, shoot!"

The Turks took him for the leader and thought he was giving himself up, for he spoke in Bulgarian. They waited.

"Barbarians! Shoot! There will be plenty of Bulgarians left!" he cried again. This time they understood.

By way of answer thirty rifles spat at this easy target. But not a bullet hit him. He ran along the gallery, dashed down the stairs and down through the yard towards the church, the way being clear. Again they shot at him, but missed. He had just reached the threshold when two bullets struck home, and he fell over into the church. His throat was cut too. . . .

From there the Turks ran off to look for the doctor. Many citizens joined in the hunt. Dead or alive, the doctor had to be caught in order to save the town from Tossoun-Bey's terrible wrath. He must be the scapegoat.

At nightfall the frightened owner of the house he was hiding in threw him out. In the street Sokolov was sighted by the posse, which was in hot pursuit. But he managed to gain on his pursuers. Flying down the long Mihlyuz street he kept pushing at the gates, hoping to slip in somewhere, but not a single gate was unbolted and he continued to run; at the square it seemed to him that there were not one, but two posses giving chase, for about a dozen men in front of him barred his way. He then darted to the left and turned back into another street; for a moment his pursuers lost track of him, and he was able to stop and catch his breath for a few minutes.

But the danger was in no way diminished. The posse would be rushing down that street in a few minutes, and if not here, would catch up with him elsewhere and shoot him down, for it was a clear starry night. To try and come out at the end of the town was hopeless; all the exits were guarded by watchmen. One hope of salvation remained, and that was to hide with friends. Fortunately he remembered that Father Dimcho's house was not far off. He ran up to it and knocked at the gate. It was opened. He was greeted by Father Dimcho, a committee member.

"Hide me, Father," the doctor said.

"Impossible, doctor! They've seen you coming in; it'll be bad for me too," the priest whispered and gently pushed him out.

And in fact the dumbfounded Sokolov caught sight of the posse approaching from the opposite street and he dashed blindly on, running into a blind alley at the end of which lived a cousin of his. He pushed open the gate and begged for hospitality.

Bai Necho at once took in the danger of the situation. "Are you crazy, doctor, do you want to burn my house down? You know I have a wife and family!" And with these words he seized him by the arm and opened the gate for him.

The doctor wasted no time in getting out of this blind alley, and followed Petkancho's street. As luck would have it, he ran into the very people he was fleeing from. Sokolov rushed like mad before his pursuers. "Stop, or we'll shoot! Wait, doctor!" one of the Bulgarian policemen shouted to him.

Sokolov did stop, but not where the zealous policeman asked him to, but further on, in front of Sarafov's gate. Sokolov, who was his family doctor, besides being his friend, decided to try his luck and knocked almost at random.

"Who is it?" asked Sarafov. The doctor identified himself. Instead of opening the gate, the fugitive heard Sarafov bang the house door, and that was the only sign of life he gave.

chapter 13

the story continues

"My God, what a disgrace!" Ognyanov groaned in pain.

"The town's seized by panic, brother, denunciations, cowardice everywhere. Byala Cherkva is not what it was," Sokolov muttered gloomily.

Ognyanov sighed deeply. "Denunciations and cowardice, you say! They are the monsters bred of every abortive revolution. They follow in its steps like wolves and crows after a battle. But who put up the flag on the top of the ridge? It was a red scarf tied to a pole."

"I don't know."

"Who do you think could have done it?"

"The Turks." Ognyanov looked at him incredulously.

"Yes, the Turks," continued the doctor; "it didn't appear till yesterday, when Tossoun-Bey was setting out from Klissoura, determined to attack Byala Cherkva and destroy it. It was said he had threatened to even on his way to Klissoura. All he needed was a pretext. I expect the rumor about the numerous forces coming to our aid was spread with the same treacherous purpose. It was Tossoun-Bey who came instead."

"So he must be in Byala Cherkva now."

"Yes."

"And terrible things must be taking place," said Ognyanov with emotion.

"Not terrible—cowardly," the doctor replied; "the man I sent to town today told me Tossoun-Bey had spared Byala Cherkva because a deputation was sent to welcome him with all solemnity. As he passed by the konak he saw a great pile of arms, brought by the inhabitants themselves, in the courtyard. The cherry-tree cannon was there too. Poor Bai Marko, I'm sorriest for him." Ognyanov sighed.

"Yes, Bai Marko, it's terrible about him. He was a victim of filthy treachery—like Kandov," added Sokolov.

"And who denounced Kandov and his friends?" asked Ognyanov, whose forehead was furrowed.

"Oh, I forgot to tell you. It was Yordan Diamandiev. The silly old woman went and told the priest in secret, and he told Yordan. He stood in the square himself, yelling at the bashi-bazouks: 'Go on, shoot! What are you waiting for? We won't have bandits in our town, we don't want any enemies of the Sultan!' "

"Oh Lord! Poor Kandov, he fought like a hero at Klissoura, and it seems he died like a hero here. I was horrified when I saw him! And how did you escape finally?"

"I hid in a house—where do you think, Boicho?"

"With friends, of course—not with Chorbadji Yordan!"

"Friends and fellow-conspirators would have none of me, as I told you," the doctor answered bitterly. "They all banged their doors in my face."

"Then who was it? Go on with your story."

"All right," the doctor began, "the posse was gaining on me, and I was reaching the end of the town. Then I took a desperate decision —to try and pass through the sentries' bullets and make for the open country, for between two evils it was the only chance of salvation I had left. When I came to about thirty paces from Vulcho's courtyard where the sentries were lying in ambush by an old fence, a gate opened slightly. I heard the creak and stopped. I looked up and immediately realized I was before Milka Todorkina's gateway. The girl herself was standing on the threshold. I went up to her and said, 'Milka, a posse is after me, can you hide me?' 'Come right in, doctor!' she answered, and I entered. A minute later the posse rushed past the gate and went on."

"So she saved you?" cried Ognyanov.

"Yes, Boicho, Milka, a girl who's lost her reputation. Providence in the shape of Milka Todorkina! The harlot, the outcast, the scandalous Milka Todorkina! Poor thing! She has nothing to fear for, nothing to lose, nothing to grieve over!"

"Nevertheless, it was real heroism in a fallen girl, among so much prudent heartlessness and honorable meanness!" Ognyanov remarked. "My God! What a place for decency to find its only refuge!"

"Now they're probably turning Byala Cherkva topsy-turvy looking for me. Let them catch me if they can!"

"What are your plans now, doctor? Where are you off to?"

"To Wallachia, of course!"

"That's where I was going too, but the flag on the mountain made me come down."

"Just as it made me take to the mountain. . . . But where can you go with those clothes? And you're bareheaded!"

"That's why I sent Mariika to you with a note, for you to bring me what I need. It's strange she hasn't come back yet."

"It doesn't matter now," said the doctor. "When it gets dark we'll go over to Hambar's mill, and Bai Lilko will get you everything. And by luck I've got another old passport with me. It'll do for you. We have some food in the bag."

"That's fine. But I didn't come here with the intention of fleeing again. I thought I'd find a rebellion."

"And it turned out a mess . . ." answered the doctor angrily. "All we did was endanger the town."

"Have you heard any news from other places?"

"Only vague rumors. It's the same disaster everywhere. . . . The revolt didn't spread—nothing but catastrophe after catastrophe. You must know more about it?"

"Yes, I saw the fires from the mountain—twenty places at once," said Ognyanov.

"It seems the people weren't ready for such an uprising! We made an appalling mistake," said the doctor. "What frightful losses for Bulgaria, so many victims—and all in vain!"

"It was a mistake all right. But the revolution had to come and the victims had to fall. I even wish there were more of them and their fate more horrible still. We can't beat Turkey with our own forces, but we can at least gain the sympathy of the world by our terrible sufferings, by our martyrdom and the streams of blood that flow from the body of Bulgaria. It is a sign of life, after all. No one thinks of a dead man—only the living have a right to life. If the European governments don't intercede for us they don't deserve to be called Christian or civilized! Even if nothing comes of it, we have nothing to repent of. We did our duty as men; we tried to win our freedom with our blood. We failed—it's a pity, but there's nothing to be ashamed of. It would only be a disgrace and a crime, if we folded our arms, if we spit on our ideal, if we forgot the blood and the fires in which Bulgaria is plunged today."

"Ognyanov," said the doctor after a short silence, "I would guess we are the only ones to think so at the moment; all Bulgaria now is cursing us for their misfortunes. Go and listen to what people are saying—now everyone declares Stefchov was right."

chapter 14

important conversations

This was the first mention of Stefchov's name between them. Ognyanov frowned. "What! Is that loathsome creature still alive?"

"A loathsome creature?" asked the doctor turning to him. "Stefchov now is the cleverest, the most devoted, the proudest fellow in the place. I wasn't able to drink his blood. You know, I had Cleopatra ready for him. . . . He's triumphant now, along with Chorbadji Yordan. They look on him as the savior of the town! Whereas they'll shoot us down like dogs if they catch us."

"All the same, he's loathsome. Poor Lalka, she must be very unhappy."

"But don't you know? Lalka's dead."

"Dead? Is it possible!"

"She died on the 18th of April," the doctor said in a whisper.

"How many misfortunes in so short a time! He killed her, the coward!" cried Ognyanov.

"Yes, he killed her." And with tears in his eyes the doctor told Ognyanov the cause of her death.

Deeply moved, Ognyanov took his hand. "Brother, we are equally unhappy." Sokolov looked at him wonderingly.

"Lalka, your beloved, is in the grave," Boicho continued sadly. "Another one, whom I love is also in . . . the grave . . . she's lost to me."

"But your Rada's alive, she's in Byala Cherkva!" cried the doctor.

"Alive? . . . Yes, alive, but to me she's dead." Sokolov looked at him in astonishment.

"Yes, dead forever," Boicho repeated gloomily. "Poor Kandov, God rest his soul! Why did I have to survive him?"

The doctor now looked at him in real wonder. "Boicho, you didn't have a quarrel with Kandov in Klissoura, did you?"

"A deadly quarrel."

"About Rada?"

Ognyanov frowned. "Let's not talk of it now."

"You must be crazy, Boicho! To suspect Rada! That's monstrous!"

"Monstrous? I thought she was innocence itself, brother, and what did it turn out to be?" groaned Ognyanov. "I trusted her, I loved her, I can't tell you how much! My country seemed brighter then, I had more faith in myself, my courage was indomitable. And what a defeat! Imagine! It'll tell you everything when I say that after that day in Klissoura, I fought, not with the hope of beating the enemy, but of dying under his blows. . . . Don't talk to me about it," he added, his head bent in sorrow.

"You're mistaken; Rada loved you truly, and still loves you, but she's very unhappy and grossly maligned—by you to begin with!" said the doctor indignantly.

Ognyanov threw him a reproachful look. "Doctor, for the sake of poor Kandov's memory, stop talking about this sad business!"

"It's precisely his memory too I want to clear of your suspicions. . . . Don't think he acted in an underhand way. It's true he was in love with Rada. You know what a dreamer he was, and carried away like the devil. That strange passion of his made him retire from the world, and from the committee too—but it didn't have the least effect on Rada's feelings; he never insulted her by any dishonorable proposals. Her shyness prevented her from telling you, but she complained to Lalka of Kandov's platonic courtship. It's lucky I thought of it. Here, read this letter of his, written on April 19th, the very day he followed her to Klissoura. Nedkovich gave it to me," said Sokolov, taking out Kandov's letter from his wallet and handing it to Ognyanov.

Boicho glanced through it hastily, and tears shone in his eyes. For a moment his face was lit up by happiness. "Thank you, Sokolov, your explanations have lifted a terrible weight from my heart. I feel reborn."

"Poor Rada! How happy she'd be if she knew! I wasn't able to see her. I only found out she was desperately unhappy, probably on your account, for she thought you'd been killed, as we all did. Write to her, send her a few lines before we start to cheer the poor girl up."

"How can I write?"

"You must write; humanity demands it."

"No, what humanity demands is not that I should write, but that I should go to her and fall on my knees and beg her forgiveness. I was cruel, cruel to her, to the verge of cowardice."

"Yes, I would have advised that myself, but it's impossible now."

"Impossible or not, I'm going," said Ognyanov resolutely.

"What! Going to Byala Cherkva!" cried the doctor in dismay. "Its madness now. Byala Cherkva is ablaze. Yordan and Stefchov are the saviors there. You're going to sure death!"

"You know, doctor, that I don't lay great store by my life when my honor's at stake. The whole of Tossoun-Bey's horde could not stop me. I must ask that martyr, Rada, to pardon my cruelty which drove her to seek her death in the flames of Klissoura." Ognyanov told him briefly of the incident.

"In that case, brother, I can't hold you back," said the doctor deeply moved.

Ognyanov thought for some time, then he said softly, "Then there's something else—Rada is mine; I married her just before I left Byala Cherkva the last time—married her before God, and instead of rings we exchanged vows. I can't leave her—you understand? And if we arrive safely in Wallachia, I'll call her to share the poverty, the misery and sufferings, which are an emigrant's lot. Oh, she'll come gladly to share my fate, as she did here. She is a heroine in her love, doctor, and I wouldn't give up her heart in exchange for the whole world." The doctor's admiration could be read in his face.

"I'll start when it gets dark, and be back tonight. And what's more, believe me, safe and sound. I shall not, I will not die—not yet, doctor, for Rada is alive for me, and Bulgaria is not yet liberated!"

chapter 15

a meeting

The doctor was looking through the breach in the wall. "Someone's coming; it's Mariika!" he said.

Ognyanov also looked down the valley. "It's not Mariika. Mariika's smaller and she had a blue dress on."

"This one's in black and she's carrying a bundle."

"Rada!" cried Ognyanov jumping up. The doctor leaped to his feet too.

Ognyanov stood in the doorway of the mill, waving with both his hands. Rada, who had been wandering about among the boulders for some time, looking for Boicho, now saw him. She rushed towards him and was in the mill in a moment.

"Radka!"

"Boicho, Boicho!" she sobbed, scarcely able to catch her breath, and pressing his head to her cheeks. The doctor watched the scene, moved to the depths of his soul.

"But how is it you're here, Radka?" Ognyanov asked quickly, as soon he had regained his self-control.

"Mariika gave me the note you had sent the doctor. Oh Boicho, why did you torture me so?" Rada was saying, shedding tears of happiness. "You're no longer angry with me? You had no right to be angry—you know there was no cause."

"Forgive me, darling, forgive me!" said Boicho, kissing her hands. "Solokov's just made me see how wrong I was. It hurt me horribly too. I was going down to the town myself to ask you to forgive me . . . my cruelty . . . I was unworthy of the love of an angel. You'll forget it, Radka, won't you, you'll forgive me?" said Ognyanov looking adoringly at her tear-stained eyes, full of bliss and boundless love. . . .

But suddenly Rada grew as white as the wall, drew back from Boicho and cried, "Run, Boicho! I forgot to tell you. Run for dear life. You were seen here and the Turks are coming for you! Hurry, run and hide in the mountain!" Rada repeated in terror.

"How's that?" asked Sokolov, as if he couldn't believe his ears.

"A Gipsy woman saw you and told them before I had seen Mariika.

On my way here, a gang of bashi-bazouks were coming through the vineyards, then they took the road in this direction. They're coming for you, Boicho. Oh, Lord, I forgot to tell you at once. I wasted a whole hour looking for you in the valley. We'll see each other another time. Now run for all you're worth."

In spite of the presence of mind which distinguished him at critical moments, Boicho was dumbfounded by this terrible news that came to him at such a moment of supreme joy, caused by the unexpected meeting with the young girl, now dearer to him than ever, and more charming and radiant in the heroism of her love. Boicho was overwhelmed; he could not come to a swift decision. He felt unable to bear such a sudden parting now, after this meeting he had so longed for. Plunges like this shake a man to the foundations of his being; meanwhile every minute was precious.

"Yes, fly? And what about you?" asked Boicho.

"Don't worry about me. Hurry, get off at once. Here, take this—some clothes — and run, Boicho. Farewell, we'll get together again, Boicho, dear Boicho, wherever it may be. Good-bye. . . ." With these words she handed the bundle to Ognyanov, took him by the hands and drew him by force towards the door of the deserted mill.

"No," said Ognyanov firmly. "I can't leave you at such a moment. If those savages are close behind you. . . ."

"Yes, Boicho, they're coming!"

"They're coming, and if they find you alone in such a wild spot, those brutes? No, I'd rather die here, defending you. . . ." But Boicho immediately understood the unreasonableness and utter uselessness of such a desperate decision.

Suddenly he asked her, "Rada, could you come along with us?"

She greeted the unexpected proposal with delight. "Yes, yes, of course I can, Boicho, I'll walk with you to the end of the world. Let's run, let's run, Boicho!" Ognyanov's eyes brightened.

"If only we can get up to the 'Little Chair' above the waterfall, from there I can keep them back till nightfall, while you take Rada further up," said Sokolov. The "Little Chair" was the name of some jagged rocks above the waterfall. A well armed man, hidden behind those rocks, could hold the path against a whole horde, for it was the only way that wound up the cliff towards the mountain.

There was no time to lose. "To the mountain!" Boicho cried, or rather almost commanded. And he was the first to cross the threshold, casting a glance round the valley. It was already too late. Among the ravines and the sharp rocks opposite, the Turks showed like black specks. They were lying in ambush behind the stones and bushes there, for only their heads and guns were visible. Someone in white baggy trousers stood on the summit, pointing towards the mill. It was the Gipsy woman. The ravine on the near side was also bristling with Turks, crouching behind the stones.

Ognyanov and the doctor realized they were cornered, and no longer thought of escape; it was out of the question.

The Turks continued very cautiously to descend and to install themslves behind the boulders of the ravines and in various other hiding places. They were about a hundred men.

The path down the valley was clear. Boicho turned to Rada and said to her, "Rada, go, walk down the path, just walk along the river."

But a terrible thought immediately crossed his mind, clouding his face, and he said, "No, better stay her. . . ."

The same decision could be read in Rada's eyes. "I'll stay with you, Boicho, with you. . . . "she whispered, folding her arms on her breast. And so much grief, love and tragic devotion filled her shining eyes! Such readiness to die!

Ognyanov and Sokolov counted their bullets. "Eighteen in all," the doctor said.

"Enough to die honorably with," said Ognyanov softly.

Tossoun-Bey had brought his horde and commanded it in person. Before showing himself in the ravines he had closed in on the valley, thus encircling the rebels — or rather the rebel, for he was convinced only Ognyanov was there.

Before giving the command to fire, Tossoun-Bey ordered his men to shout in Turkish, "Give yourself up, Consulos Comita!" Only the echoes in the ravines returned the sound.

Rada had huddled in a corner, speechless. "Courage, Rada!" Boicho said to her sadly.

She made a sign with her hand as if to say, "In Klissoura I was frightened, for I was alone and rejected. Now I'm not afraid to die with you, since you love me. You'll see. . . ." Boicho understood the heroic meaning of her silent answer, and his eyes grew moist. The minutes were flying by.

Ognyanov and Sokolov, standing close against the walls for cover, grasped their revolvers firmly. They looked towards the two ravines from which they expected a shower of thunderbolts at any minute.

A minute passed. That must have been the time-limit set by Tossoun-Bey. Then gun-shots rang out from the ravine to the west, to the east, and also from the valley itself. The besieged listened to the bullets whizzing by through the openings of the roof, through the holes of the walls, and heard them hit against the stones to fall flattened at their feet. The mountain valley echoed with the sound.

Suddenly the shooting stopped.

In spite of its many openings, the walls had sheltered the three unfortunate people. No one had been hit. Only Rada had fallen to the ground in a faint. The poor girl's courage had failed her. Her kerchief had slipped off her head and her black hair fell in waves over her shoulders and over the dust. The second round would certainly soon follow, and Rada, lying there, was exposed to the bullets.

Ognyanov bent down, put his arms around her and moved her over to the most sheltered corner, placing the bundle under her head. He pushed her slightly, but she did not stir, she lay there unconscious, insensible of everything about her. And then at the sight of that lovely pale face with its closed eyes and pale lips, of this unfortunate girl, who had linked her life with his and from whom he had to part with the unbearable foreboding of what her fate must be when his hand could no longer defend her from these brutes, desperate, inhuman grief filled him. "Should I kill her myself?" he wondered.

Receiving no answer from the mill, the attackers grew bolder and descended to the lowest boulders, very close to the valley. The circle around the mill was drawing tighter all around, and the moment for decisive action was approaching.

"Give yourself up, Comita." No answer.

A fresh volley of bullets immediately rained upon the mill. As the noise of the shots grew louder, the Turks crept closer. Since there was no sound from the mill, they concluded that the rebel hiding there was unarmed. The bullets continued to spatter against the walls; it was a regular assault.

The Turks were much nearer now. The moment had come. Ognyanov stood by one of the windows, the doctor by the door. They exchanged glances, and each emptied his revolver into the thick mass of the enemy. This unexpected reply brought down three men, and disclosed the strength of the mill. The Turks realized that there was more than one defender. That confused them somewhat, but only for a moment. The victors of Klissoura dashed towards the dangerous wall with a fierce yell.

Some were firing from the ravines, others shooting into the breaches to prevent the defenders from appearing there and taking aim. The assault was reaching its height.

"Our time has come, doctor, farewell — forever, brother!' said Boicho.

"Farewell, brother!"

"They won't take one of us alive, doctor!"

"Of course, Boicho; I have three more bullets. I'm keeping one for myself."

"I'm keeping two," said Ognyanov, and involuntarily turned towards Rada. She was still lying there, but her face had become as white as a sheet; a thin stream of blood flowed quietly from the left side of her chest and ran into the folds of her dress in little trickles. A bullet had glanced from the wall and hit her. She was already dead. She had passed from unconsciousness into eternal sleep.

Then Boicho left his post, approached her, knelt by her, took her cold hands and pressed a long kiss on her icy lips; he covered her forehead with kisses, and her wound, where the blood was already cold. It was impossible to hear whether he said anything to her, whether a whisper accompanied his farewell kiss, whether he said, "Till our meeting beyond, Rada!" so loud was the shooting outside and the patter of the bullets in the mill. He covered her with his ground sheet. As Boicho stood up tears were streaming down his cheeks. These tears contained an ocean of suffering.

Who knows, perhaps also a fervent gratitude to providence!

chapter 16

disaster

During this last silent farewell, which lasted only half a minute, Sokolov kept up the fight with their hundred odd enemies single-handed. Suddenly he turned and saw Rada. His hair bristled, his eyes glowed like those of a tiger, and without taking any precautions he drew himself up to his full height in the doorway, as if in scorn of the bullets, and turning to the horde he cried in perfect Turkish, "You mangy dogs! You shall pay dearly for every drop of Bulgarian blood!" And he emptied his revolver into the crowd.

With renewed fury the mob attacked the inaccessible fortress that the ruined mill had become. A fierce yell, followed by a new volley of shots pierced the air.

"Oh!" groaned the doctor, dropping his revolver. A bullet had pierced his right hand. His face wore an expression of unutterable horror and despair. Ognyanov, firing into the mob and himself now covered with blood, noticed it and asked, "Are you suffering much, brother?"

"No, but I used up my last bullet, I forgot."

"I have two more in mine, take one," said Ognyanov, handing his revolver to Sokolov. "Now let them see how a Bulgarian apostle dies!" And pulling out the great yataghan from the doctor's belt he rushed out of the door and hurled himself on the mob, dealing terrible blows right and left. . . .

Half an hour later, the whole horde emerged from the valley, triumphant and savage, like demons wild with glee, bearing Ognyanov's head stuck on a pole. The doctor's skull, hacked to pieces by their knives — the first hit, from a bullet, was self-inflicted — could not serve as a trophy. Rada's head was also left behind, for reasons of policy: Tossoun-Bey proved more cunning than Tumrashli.

Behind followed the killed and the wounded, loaded on a cart.

With savage cries the mob entered the town. It was more deserted and silent than a graveyard. The trophy was set up in the square.

Only one man hovered about there like a ghost. It was Mooncho. As he recognized the head of his beloved Roussiyan, he fixed his wild, idiot's gaze upon it, and spat out, with a shower of saliva, a terrific curse against Mohammed and the Sultan.

They hanged him over the butcher's shop.

The idiot was the only man who had dared to protest.

glossary

aga, pl. *agalar* (T): master
aman: mercy, have mercy
bacho, bai (B): from *brat,* brother; form of address to an older man
bashi-bazouk: Turkish mercenary irregulars known for their savage brutality
bey (T): Turkish governor
cadi (T): judge
chelebi (T): gentleman
chibouk (T): a long pipe
chorbadji (T): one of the wealthy class of Bulgarians
comita, comitadji (T): a revolutionary, member of a revolutionary committee
doctoritsa: feminine of doctor; the doctor's wife
dyado (B): grandfather, used of old men
effendi, effendim (T): title of government officials and members of learned professions
gechmish ola (T): welcome
giaour (T): unbeliever, infidel
gospozha (B): Mrs., an honorary title
hadji (T): title given to Moslems and Christians alike who have made the pilgrimage to Mecca or Jerusalem
hadjiika: feminine of *hadji*
haidouk: outlaw, brigand, famed in folksongs as a type of Robin Hood
hodja (T): Turkish priest
horo (B): round dance
iconostasis: where the icons are placed against the wall
kaval: shepherd's flute
kehaya (Gk): head man
kir (Gk): Mr.
klepalo (B): board struck with wooden mallet, used instead of church bells which were long banned in the Turkish provinces inhabited by Christians
konak (T): the governor's residence, seat of the local Turkish government
mashallah (T): bravo
onbashi (T): police sergeant
pamid (T): a kind of grape
rakiya: the local brandy, usually distilled from plums
rayah (T): the non-Moslem subjects of the Sultan
softa (T): Moslem theological student
voivoda (B): commander, haidouk chieftain
zagariya (T): white wheat
zaptieh (T): a Turkish policeman